GLIMPSE OF SPLENDOR

A novel by

Kay Moser

Illustration and Cover Design by Anne Olwin

ISBN 1493640143

DEDICATION

To Ruth Spencer, beloved mentor
To Lillian, Alice and Chan,
true friends

Chapter 1

Mark Goodman was determined to make Rachel D'Evereau his wife and his life when he limped through the door of St. Mary's Church on Christmas Eve. He had waited fifteen tumultuous years and even fought his way back from death's door to be here at this moment.

"Thank you, God," he murmured as he paused just inside the sanctuary and stared at the beauty of the old church he had loved as a boy. The word "home" flew through his mind; tears flooded his eyes and, in spite of his desperate attempt to stifle them, overflowed down his cheeks. Embarrassed, he wiped his face with his bare hand, but the depth of his emotion had overwhelmed him, and for the first time since he had left the physical rehab center, he felt too weak to stand.

The church was already packed for the midnight service, so Mark leaned against a back wall. From that position he could see straight down the center aisle, and as the choir organized themselves into a processional, his gaze traveled down the beautiful old marble floors, past the pine-draped pews, up the poinsettia-decked steps to the altar, and finally to the ancient golden cross suspended above it. His ancestors had built this church and hung that beloved cross after carrying it over treacherous seas from France. He felt his throat tighten as the words "Forgive me" ran through his mind. He had been away too long.

Mark distracted himself by searching the front pew where he knew he would find Rachel. A spark of joy shot through him as he recognized her petite frame kneeling in prayer close to the center aisle. To her right, Lovey, the elderly housekeeper at the D'Evereau plantation, knelt. Yes, he thought, I really am home at last. I made it in spite of everything. I made it home!

He knew that it was truly a miracle that he had made it back to Louisiana. The years of his absence had been action-packed and sometimes dangerous. He had traveled around the globe to every hot spot on the map, reporting for various news agencies. In short, he had been running away. He knew that now.

Moreover, he knew that not one of those years or a single one of those miles had changed the one essential element of his life. He loved Rachel. He always had, ever since he was a boy, and for as long as he lived, he would continue to love her. There was no remedy for such a love. Distance could not dissolve it; time could not dim it. Even harsh words had not been able to kill it. Mark had finally come to understand that God was in the middle of it and that only He could bring it to fruition.

Through all the recent months of surgeries and therapies, Mark had first rebelled, then finally understood and accepted God's way of dealing with him. He had learned the hard way that his job was to lay down his pride and simply follow. This had been no easy task for an arrogant, headstrong man like Mark, but God had given him weakness, fear and dependence to teach him. Then God had raised him up from his cripple's bed and sent him home to Rachel. This time Mark planned to listen, to succeed, to make Rachel his. Tough battles loomed ahead. He had no doubt that Rachel would be a hard sell, but the hardest struggle would be putting away his pride and following the God who had brought him this far.

It was no accident that Mark had chosen Christmas Eve to return to Louisiana to claim Rachel. Exactly fifteen years earlier on Christmas Eve she had broken off their engagement when he refused to marry her before his deployment to Viet Nam. She had been furious with him, but Mark deployed shortly thereafter feeling certain she would come to understand that his decision was proof of his love for her. Instead, she married Collins Greyson, the spoiled, weak son of a wealthy Dallas family, leaving Mark stunned and enraged at the facility with which she'd set aside his love for her. Collins, true to his own character, had continued drinking until he died in a car wreck.

Mark watched as Rachel settled back in the pew. Eighteen months she's been widowed, he thought, and God forgive me, I'm glad she's free. If only I'd known sooner....if only I hadn't blown up and cut off all communication with her and set out to live my life on the edge. Thank God Lovey wrote me; otherwise, I'd never have known. And if I hadn't had the motivation of coming home to Rachel...well, I don't know what would have happened to me.

The organ suddenly filled the church with a joyous "Oh Come, All Ye Faithful," and Mark's mind was jolted back to the present. The congregation rose to their feet and began to sing as the acolytes, bearing candles and cross, preceded the pastor in their stately procession toward the altar. Mark saw Rachel's face for the first time as she turned toward the center aisle, and his heart lurched at the sight. She looked thinner, and there was an air of sadness about her, but she was so beautiful. How he longed to be at her side!

The pastor had just reached the altar and was leaning over to kiss it when Mark saw Jack D'Evereau, Rachel's father, slip into the pew behind Rachel. Of course, Mark thought; Jack never misses midnight mass In Louisiana even if he does have to turn around and drive back to Texas before dawn.

The service had begun, and Mark leaned against the wall, content simply to watch Rachel and anticipate the moment when he would come face to face with her again. An ornate, standing candelabrum decorated with Christmas greenery and five large candles cast a glow on Rachel's golden hair, and Mark's emotions soared as he enjoyed her beauty.

He soon lost touch with the service as he contemplated the moment when Rachel would look up into his eyes and know he had returned. The way Mark had it planned, he would leave the church quickly when the service ended, and he would wait for her in the parking lot. When she came to her car, expecting to go to Uncle Philippe's for his annual Christmas morning breakfast, Mark would step forward and quietly speak her name. The moon was full; she would have no trouble recognizing him. He was positive she would throw her arms around his neck, just as she had always done when they were younger. He was positive because he was absolutely certain she loved him; it had been that certainty that had brought him through the last six months of pain and effort. He had lived and learned to walk again by feverishly repeating one mantra....God loves me, Rachel loves me.

Mark's attention was jerked back to the service when he realized that the members of the congregation had risen and were reciting the Lord's Prayer together. Moments later the pastor invited the members of the congregation to offer each other a sign of peace. Rachel turned to hug Lovey and then leaned over the back of the pew to kiss her father. How Mark ached to feel Rachel's arms around him in even the briefest of formal hugs, but he comforted himself by letting his mind bounce forward to the moment of reunion that he had planned.

Not much longer now, he encouraged himself silently. The service is almost over. Patiently he watched as Rachel turned back toward the altar.

Suddenly Mark came to full attention and stared in amazement as the man standing next to Rachel leaned over and kissed her lightly on the lips. Angry questions seared through Mark's mind. Who is he? How dare he kiss Rachel like that? Furious, Mark searched Jack's face, but Rachel's father didn't seem to be the least bit perturbed by what had happened. Relax! Mark ordered himself. He's just a friend of the family. Maybe he's even a cousin or something.

No! He internally exploded again. That was no cousin's kiss. I don't like this! When is this blasted service going to end? He crossed his arms and stood upright, rigidly staring at the man he had identified as a rival. The man was well over six feet tall, broad shouldered and dark haired. Mark decided he was about forty and far too sure of himself.

The first rows of the congregation began to move toward the altar rail to take communion. Mark's attention was drawn back to Rachel. He watched her kneel, receive communion and stand. She waited a moment, then leaned over to help Lovey rise from her knees. As they solemnly began their way back to their place in the first pew, Rachel linked arms with her. When the man who had kissed Rachel caught up with them, Rachel smiled up at him, and curse words formed in Mark's mind. He struggled to cut his unholy thoughts off, but when the time came for him to walk forward to receive communion, he declined the opportunity. His mind was hardly on spiritual matters.

After what seemed like an eternity to Mark, the service finally ended.

Mark hurried toward the door, ignoring the pain that shot up his back, and positioned himself in the parking lot. He abandoned his first plan to approach Rachel immediately; instead he stood back in the shadows and watched. Soon the man he had identified as his rival appeared, escorting Rachel and Lovey to a car. Realizing his long-held dream of surprising Rachel had been postponed by this rival, Mark simply tightened his jaw, and struggling not to limp, turned and stalked away.

"What did you expect?" he demanded of himself as he slid behind the wheel of his rental car. "She's beautiful and smart and fascinating—not to mention very wealthy. Any man would want her, and every unattached man from Dallas to New Orleans must be after her. This may not be as easy as I thought, but never mind all that. I'll do whatever it takes. She belongs to me. She always has; she always will. Failure is not an option. I'm going to marry her this time."

As he drove toward his Uncle Philippe's house, he hastily made a new plan for his reunion with Rachel. The whole family will gather at Uncle Philippe's, he thought as he drove, everyone including Rachel and her father. But if I just show up, Uncle Philippe will turn the party into a loud celebration of my return, and I won't get to be alone with Rachel. I've waited so long and worked so hard for this reunion with her; the last thing I want to do is share it with a crowd of relatives.

Mark parked his car a little distance from his Uncle's house and watched as others began to arrive and enter the old mansion. At last the car he was waiting for appeared around a curve in the long drive. Mark's heartbeat accelerated when he realized that the strange man, the man who had kissed Rachel, was driving. Good, he thought. He'll have to drop them off at the door, then go park the car. This is my best chance.

Leaving his car, Mark walked to the side verandah of the house. There he could wait close to the front steps but still stay in the shadows.

When the car drove up to the front walk, Mark's rival did just as Mark had suspected he would. In the courtliest fashion he stopped the car temporarily, got out and walked around to open the doors on the passenger side. After helping Rachel out of the car, he helped Lovey. The rival escorted the women up the walk to the steps before returning to the car and driving away. Mark's heart began to beat wildly as he saw Rachel wait outside while Lovey moved forward into the house. Rachel was alone on the front verandah.

Mark's moment had come. He stepped into view and said simply, "Merry Christmas, Rachel."

At the sound of his voice she turned toward him, and just as he had envisioned, a glorious smile lit up her face.

"Mark!" She raced to him, reached up and threw her arms around his neck.

At last, Mark Goodman was able to put his arms around his beloved. In an instant, the preceding fifteen years of separation disappeared for him; he was—quite simply—truly home again.

Far too quickly she pulled back so she could look up into his face, but Mark slipped his hands down to her waist, so he could hold on to her. He was so thoroughly in the moment that all action seemed to be happening in slow motion. He lifted his right hand, stroked her golden hair, and cupped her head in his fingers as he slowly leaned down and softly brushed her lips with his. He felt sure he would burst with sheer joy.

"Where did you come from?" Rachel demanded, and by doing so broke Mark's sense of slow motion. "Why didn't you let anyone know you were coming? We would have—"

Driven by his long-denied, pent-up emotions, he stopped her questions by kissing her again on the lips, this time more forcefully. When she pulled away from him, he forced himself to release her as he silently cautioned himself, Take it easy! You've been thinking about this for months, but she is totally surprised.

Rachel's eyes filled with tears as she stared up at him. "You're really here. I can't believe it," she stammered. "After all this time. Why didn't you let anyone know you were coming?"

Mark knew the impossibility of explaining his actions in such a short time, so he settled on, "I wanted to surprise you."

"Everyone will be surprised all right!" she exclaimed nervously, then rattled on as she wiped tears off her cheeks, "but they'll all be so glad to see you and—"

"I don't care about them, Rachel," he interrupted. "I came home to see you, only you." He paused so she could weigh his words.

Silence fell between them until Rachel chose to lighten the moment. "Mark! You're taking my breath away." She did her best to laugh. "What on earth do I say to a comment like that?"

"Don't say anything right now." He reached up and stroked her hair. "Just know I love you. I always have."

He leaned over to kiss her again, but before his lips reached hers, an angry male voice with a strong French accent demanded, "Rachel, is everything all right?"

Rachel pulled away from Mark abruptly, whirled around and stammered, "Yes, Louis, everything is fine. This is Mark—"

"I know who he is!" Louis interrupted angrily.

"He's an old friend of mine," Rachel stammered. "We used to play together at Belle St. Marie, and when we were in college—"

"We were engaged." Mark finished her sentence emphatically as he locked eyes with his rival. "I've traveled a long way to see Rachel; I'm sure you understand and won't mind giving us a few moments alone."

"I'm sorry to disappoint you, but I do mind," Louis responded firmly. "I mind very much. I am Rachel's escort this evening. My father and Rachel's relatives await her in the house, and that is where she is going. Come, Rachel." He held out his hand to her. "We will join your family now."

Mark placed his hand on Rachel's arm and gently prevented her from moving. "I appreciate your position, Louis, and of course Rachel will join you in a moment, if she chooses. I've come a long way, and I have something private to say to her. I'm sure you understand."

"I'm sure I don't! I've come over from France—"

"France is next door compared to where I've come from!" Mark stubbornly stood his ground.

"Frankly, I couldn't care less where—"

"Miz Rachel, are you all right?" Lovey's voice mercifully broke into the stand-off as she walked out the front door. "Lord a mercy! Is that you, Mr. Mark?"

Rachel seized the opportunity to ease the tension between the men, "Yes, Lovey. Look who's here! It's Mark!"

"Saints be praised!" Lovey exclaimed as she threw her arms around Mark. "You're a sight for sore eyes for sure. Just wait till everybody sees you. Why, they're gonna have a fit!"

Mark's chance of having another minute alone with Rachel evaporated.

"It's far too cold for you out here, Rachel," Louis curtly announced. "You must go inside."

Rachel darted a glance at Mark, and when he nodded, she accepted Louis' arm and went into the house.

"I'm real glad you've come home now, Mr. Mark," Lovey said, "ain't a minute too soon."

The adrenalin that had driven Mark all evening evaporated, and his chest constricted. For a frightening moment he couldn't draw a full breath. As weakness overwhelmed him, he limped to the nearest white pillar and leaned against it.

"Mercy!" Lovey exclaimed. "You ain't yourself at all."

"Just give me a minute," Mark gasped as the pain he had learned to live with shot up his back.

"We've gotta get you inside," Lovey insisted as she hurried to his side.

"Not like this. Just a minute more; it'll pass."

"Things are starting to make sense to me, Mr. Mark. I've been wondering why you didn't come right away—"

"We'll talk about it all later, Lovey." Mark cut her short. "Don't say a word to Rachel. Promise me!"

"This ain't my story to tell, but you just be sure you tell—"

"Mark, my boy!" A male voice suddenly boomed from the

front door. "Where in the name of heaven have you been?" Philippe D'Evereau, Mark's uncle, barreled out the door and grabbed him. "What a surprise!" He slapped Mark on the back repeatedly, so caught up in the sound of his own enthusiastic voice that he failed to see Mark wince.

Lovey saw Mark's pain and threw herself between Mark and his uncle, declaring, "Mr. Mark's all mine, Mr. Philippe! I'm the one who found him out here, and I'm the one who's gonna show him off to the family."

"She's always loved you, boy," Philippe boomed, "loved you like a son."

"Yes sir," Mark agreed as he draped his arm over Lovey's shoulders, "and she can be as possessive as a mama bear."

"I ain't no mama bear," Lovey retorted, "but you're coming inside this minute. You've come a long way, and you're gonna just say hello to everybody and go right on up to bed. They can all visit with you later." She put her arm gently around his waist and encouraged him toward the front door.

A wave of tenderness for the loving old housekeeper inundated Mark. He smiled down at her and squeezed her shoulder gently as she surreptitiously supported him. His plan to have a quiet, meaningful reunion with Rachel had failed, but his exhausted spirit rallied as family members raced each other to greet him.

Home! He had made it home. He now knew there was a war ahead, a war for Rachel's hand, but he had, at the very least, landed on the beach.

Chapter 2

"You should've just let Mr. Andre bring me home. There's no need for you to leave the party so early. It ain't even three o'clock," Lovey fussed as she and Rachel entered the main hall of Belle St. Marie. "Besides, Mr. Andre is old like me, and he needs to go on to bed."

Rachel smiled as she remembered Andre Simone, her beloved Grandmere's gallant old friend and Louis' father. "Lovey, you know perfectly well that Andre was having the time of his life reliving decades of memories with Cousin Philippe. They'll be telling tall tales until dawn."

"Well then, you should've let Mr. Louis bring me home like he offered to."

"No, this is better." Rachel sighed. "Believe me, I was more than ready to come home myself. It's been a long day, and we have all those guests coming for Christmas Dinner in just a few hours. Besides, I think Louis was really fascinated by his father's tall tales about his love for Grandmere. "

"Those weren't tall tales, Lovey said quietly, "at least not from Mr. Andre's side. He was in love with your Grandmere. Still is, even after she's been gone all these years. Of course, she never gave him no reason to hope; she loved your Grandpere too much, but that didn't stop Mr. Andre from wishing things could be different."

Rachel said nothing, obviously lost in her own thoughts as she methodically placed her keys and purse in their usual place on the antique console. Slowly she removed her coat and put it in the closet before returning to the console to stare at herself in the ornate mirror that hung above it.

Lovey watched her a minute before saying, "You ain't told me the real reason you left that party and brought me home yourself, have you?"

Rachel shook her head, but did not turn away from the mirror.

Lovey walked up behind her, and when their eyes met in the mirror, she asked quietly, "It's Mr. Mark you've got on your mind, I'm guessing. What happened before I came outside, Miz Rachel? What's got you so upset?"

"Oh, nothing really. Louis and Mark were both getting angry, and I was stuck in the middle. It was pretty awkward, really."

"That doesn't sound like nothing for you to get this upset about. What else happened?"

"Mark kissed me."

"Well, of course he did. He ain't seen you in—"

"No, Lovey, you don't understand. He didn't just kind of kiss me; he really kissed me!"

"I see. And did you kiss him back?"

"No!" Rachel said quickly. Then she added, "I wanted to, though. I really wanted to." She turned to face the old housekeeper and demanded, "Lovey, what on earth is wrong with me? I've finally gotten control of my life again; things are going along smoothly. I'm practically engaged to Louis.... Then Mark shows up, and I'm all...all...all. Oh, I don't know what I am!"

"I think you and I need to talk. I'm gonna go into the kitchen and make us some hot chocolate. Then we can sit and—"

"No, Lovey, thank you, but I just want to go to bed. Suddenly I'm so weary I could drop right here and sleep for weeks."

"If you're sure—"

"Positive." Rachel gave Lovey a slight hug before dragging herself toward the staircase. "Leave the door open, so Andre and Louis can come in. I know I should wait up for them like a good hostess, but I just can't. I can't keep my eyes open, I'm so tired," she mumbled as she began the steep climb.

"Good night, Honey," Lovey called after her, but Rachel gave no sign she had heard. Worried, Lovey watched as Rachel disappeared upstairs. Then she turned toward the kitchen.

"She ain't just tired," Lovey mumbled to herself. "She's real upset, and I don't have to guess why. Mr. Mark finally came home. Now she's gonna have to face those feelings of hers she's been holding down so long. She ain't ever loved another man like she loved Mr. Mark, but she's scared to death of her feelings. Scared she's gonna get hurt again."

Lovey stared out a kitchen window into the darkness and began addressing the Almighty just as if He was standing next to her. "What are we gonna do, Lord? Miz Rachel has come a long way, but You and I know she's got a ways to go yet. We need a plan."

Lovey fell silent as she continued peering out into the darkness, then suddenly she scolded herself, "Listen to me! Ain't I something, telling You we need a plan? You already got a plan; I oughta know that by now. I've just got to do whatever You give me to do. Well okay, that's just what I'm gonna do, so things are gonna be just fine. I'm going to bed now, Lord, and I ain't worrying any more. Don't forget. You're in charge."

When Rachel reached her room, she was so tired she shed most of her clothes and left them on the floor where they fell. Utilizing her last ounce of energy, she climbed into the tall, canopied bed that had stood in this room and sheltered her ancestors for generations. She managed to crawl between the covers just seconds before her mind whirled down into the vacuum of the dreamless sleep she so desired.

Two hours later she awoke with a start and sat up suddenly. It was so dark she could see nothing, but she heard someone walking in the hall outside her room. For several panicky seconds her cobwebbed mind couldn't place where she was or even how old she was. As she stared in the direction of the footsteps, her heart pounding, she remembered that she was in her childhood room at Belle St. Marie and that she was a grown woman. The present came rushing back to her; it was early Christmas Day, and the footsteps outside the door undoubtedly belonged to her guests for the holidays. Andre Simone and his son, Louis, were finally returning from Cousin Philippe's party. Relieved, she sank back on the pillows, but her fear was soon replaced with suffocating sadness.

"It should be Mark out there in the hall," she whispered as tears welled up in her eyes. "He should be the one coming back from Cousin Philippe's—but not to the guest room. He should be coming here, to my room, to me, to my bed, to our bed." Her tears drenched her cheeks. "Should have been, should have been!" she whispered fiercely. "My life is full of 'should have been's.' It should have been Mark outside the door just now; it should have been Mark fifteen years ago! What an idiot I was! Why didn't I see how much I loved him? Why didn't I wait for him? Why did I let my pride ruin my life? How could I have ever married Collins when I could have had Mark?" Rachel turned her face into the pillow and sobbed.

When her tears finally quit running, she lay there exhausted, her eyelids stinging, her mind weighed down with depression. Soon the bed, empty of Mark, became a hateful place, and she left it. Wearily she pulled on a warm robe and walked through the French doors onto the second-floor verandah.

It was pitch black outside, the full moon snuffed out by a thick layer of clouds. Nevertheless, Rachel walked to the railing and peered out into the darkness, struggling to see even one of the hundreds of pine trees that surrounded the house. Her eyes could find nothing to divert or comfort her. She listened for the smallest sound of life, anything to distract her from her grief, but the land was perfectly still; even the night birds had fallen silent. In desperation she wrapped her own arms tightly around herself, hoping to comfort herself with the feel of her own hands if she couldn't feel Mark's arms around her.

I can't bear it! she shouted mentally. I can't! I gave up Mark for Collins, and look what Collins did to me. Endless affairs with other women, drinking bouts that kept him holed up somewhere for days while I worried myself closer and closer to my own grave. It still amazes me that he managed to put himself into the ground before he worried me to death. Fifteen years of my life wasted! Fifteen years that I could have spent with Mark. And the children! Where are the children Mark and I could have had? Where is my family?

Unable to bear her own thoughts, Rachel began to walk. To divert herself, she began circling the large, antebellum house by walking the length of the verandah that surrounded it on all four sides. As she walked, she dragged her hand along the top of the railing just as she had done when she was a child. Back then, walking the whole circle, dragging her hand along, had been a joyful experience. She had felt so tall and powerful as she gazed out at the plantation bathed in sunlight. How gaily she had called out to her Grandmere in the garden below, "Look at me, Grandmere! Look at me!" Now she felt helpless, beaten. There was no sunlight, and her Grandmere had long been in her grave.

When she turned the third corner and started down the eastern verandah, she detected someone standing at the railing. Rachel slowed her pace but continued advancing toward the person. Finally she was able to see Lovey standing erect, her arms relaxed at her sides, her face confidently turned toward the east. In one hand she held a book.

Rachel stopped, her heart suddenly filled with love for the

dear soul named Lovey. She has her Bible, Rachel thought, and I bet it's the Bible that Grandmere gave her when she was a child growing up in this house under Grandmere's protection. That Bible and Grandmere have always been Lovey's anchors, securing her life from outrageous waves of fortune.

Rachel stepped forward and broke the silence as gently as she could. "Lovey, are you okay? What are you doing out here at this hour?"

"I'm watching," Lovey answered quietly without taking her eyes off the invisible landscape.

"Watching what? Even the moon is covered up."

"I know, Honey."

"Lovey, are you telling me you're just standing out here watching the dark?" Rachel, bewildered and a little worried, asked.

"I ain't watching the dark, Honey. I'm watching dawn come."

"But, Lovey, that doesn't make any sense. It's still pitch dark. You could catch cold out here waiting for dawn to come."

"I ain't waiting for dawn. I'm watching it come."

"Lovey, I think maybe you need to go lie down." Rachel paused, trying to think of the most diplomatic way to handle things. She was all too aware of the fact that the doctor had cautioned her that Lovey should be taking life easy now. "I don't understand why you're out here in the dark—" She stopped speaking as she realized that her intellect was not the tool she needed to understand Lovey's behavior. Giving up the fight to understand, she said simply, "Your words make no sense to me, Lovey, but my heart is telling me to listen."

"Listen to your heart, Honey. It's a good one, full of love, and you can trust it."

A picture of Mark's face, pleading with her to listen to him fifteen years ago, swept through Rachel's mind and conquered it. Her tears began to fall again, and Lovey reached out and drew her into her arms.

"Oh, Lovey! What have I done with my life? Thrown it away on the wrong man because of my stupid pride! All those dark years, and for what?"

"Your Grandmere used to have some real dark times too, Honey. Times as dark as this night. And she spent a good many of them standing right here."

"I know what you're going to say, Lovey. Be like Grandmere. But I can't! Grandmere was a saint. She was always able to deal with her dark times; she was always able to wait for the dawn."

"No, Honey, not wait for it. She watched it come."

"How could she watch dawn come when it was pitch dark? Don't you mean she waited until some light showed on the horizon and then watched dawn come?"

"No, Baby." Lovey hugged Rachel close to her side. "When it's darkest, that's when God is doing His work in you. He is the dawn, and you don't need no light to see Him. You just gotta be willing to look at Him no matter how dark it seems to your understanding."

"I just can't seem to do that, Lovey. It's so dark! The present is dark, and the past is even darker. How can I ever believe in the future?"

"Are we talking about Mr. Mark now?" Lovey asked quietly.

"Yes. Oh Lovey! Fifteen years of darkness lie between us."

"You ain't living in those fifteen years, Miz Rachel. You're living now."

"But there's darkness now. I couldn't even respond to his kiss. I wanted to, but I just froze. Lovey, I actually felt afraid when I saw him. Why on earth was I afraid?"

"You're just afraid of your feelings, Honey. That ain't surprising, is it? You've been hurt awful bad."

"What am I going to do?"

"Just give yourself some time. Just believe that even though your eyes can't see nothing but darkness, there's plenty of light around you, and in time you'll see it and be able to follow it." Lovey paused before asking, "Do you remember your Grandmere's eyes?"

"Yes, of course I do. They were always so peaceful. Deep pools of serenity."

"Why do you think that was?"

"I always thought she must be seeing a world the rest of us couldn't see."

"She was. The light in the middle of the darkness. That's what she was seeing."

Rachel stepped away from Lovey as she shook her head. "I'm not Grandmere, Lovey. I know you want me to be, but I just can't. She was full of faith and courage. That's too tall an order for me. I'm just not up to it."

"I know you are because you're Miz Elinore's granddaughter. Even more important, you're a child of God. That's a fact, Honey, and one of these days you're gonna have to choose to trust God because He ain't ever gonna turn away from you, and He ain't gonna be satisfied with no middle ground."

"Neither is Mark. That's what scares me."

"You're right about that. Mr. Mark ain't going away this time, Honey. You better choose to look at the light in spite of all that darkness in your past with Mr. Collins because Mr. Mark ain't gonna leave again. And he ain't a man who plans to lose twice."

"I know," Rachel whispered. "I know."

"Now, let's go on inside and get some rest, because I know Mr. Mark, and he ain't gonna wait long to get himself over here."

Around ten o'clock Christmas morning Rachel dragged herself into the dining room to share breakfast with Louis and Andre. She was exhausted to the point of tears and thoroughly confused about her feelings for Mark. Hour after hour she had vacillated between longing to be with him, aching to hear his voice, and burning with fury toward him because he had thrust himself into her life again without any notice whatsoever. "How dare he think he can just waltz in here whenever he chooses and expect me to be waiting!" she had muttered to her dark bedroom. Only moments later her words bore a different meaning entirely. "Oh, if only I had waited for him! Why couldn't I see that he wasn't rejecting me? He wouldn't marry me because he loved me. He was trying to save me pain, and what did I do? I just turned my back on him and walked away."

There was a third sentiment that honesty placed on her lips after she had wrestled with her feelings for several hours. "I'm afraid to let myself love him again. I'm afraid to love anyone that deeply," she whispered. "What a coward I am, but there's the truth."

Now, as she entered the dining room, she struggled to put Mark out of her thoughts and to be a good hostess by serving her guests a late breakfast from the buffet. Seconds after she entered, Louis' face betrayed his concern for her; he came to her side immediately and took her in his arms.

"You have not rested well," he murmured. "It's easy to guess why. Come sit down."

"No." She pulled away as she spoke. "We should eat. You two must be famished." She went to the buffet and began filling two plates with Lovey's cooking. "Please, don't wait for me," she urged as she handed the plates to Louis. "Seat yourselves and eat while the food is hot. I'll just fix myself a plate and join you in a second."

"Oh no, My Dear," the elderly, gallant Andre protested. "I will certainly seat you before I even think of settling in myself." When Rachel made no reply, Andre looked at Louis for explanation. Since none was forthcoming, he adopted his usual convivial tone. "What a pleasure it is to be here once again, after so many years, in the dining room of Belle St. Marie for Christmas Day celebrations! Your Grandmere, my beloved Elinore, always made this day the best day of the year. It thrills my heart to see her granddaughter carrying on the grand traditions—"

"I couldn't agree more," Louis interrupted as he took his father by the elbow and tried to steer him to a chair, "but you go ahead and sit down, Papa. I'll seat Rachel."

"Indeed you will not!" Andre protested. "I may no longer be able to care for my beloved Elinore, but I shall certainly serve her granddaughter, and no man, not even a younger, handsomer one who happens to be my son, will take the privilege from me."

"Now, Papa," Louis said, struggling to match his father's tone, "this is surely not a dueling matter—"

"Choose your weapon, sir," Andre challenged playfully, "and do not think for a moment that my advanced age will prevent me from winning the hand of Rachel."

Rachel smiled at them, and for a moment her exhaustion lifted. "You are both incorrigible!" she said. "Still, I am fortunate indeed to have two such determined suitors. I thank you, Sirs." She curtsied elegantly. "I suppose there's only one fair solution to so grave a matter of honor—you may both seat me."

As she walked toward the table and the chair which Andre had pulled out for her, Lovey hurried in from the kitchen carrying two silver baskets. "I've brought you some hot biscuits and some of my cornbread, Mr. Andre," she announced. "You remember how Miz Elinore always bragged on my biscuits." Adroitly she placed the silver basket of fragrant biscuits in Andre's hands and gave the other basket to Louis.

"Of course I remember!" Andre exclaimed as he turned toward the table with the basket. "Elinore always said you surely had heavenly help when you made biscuits."

"Personally I think the angels themselves make Lovey's cornbread," Louis gravely commented as he made a show of turning toward the table with his silver basket.

Quickly, while the men were distracted, Lovey turned Rachel toward a window that faced the front lawn. Through the window Rachel saw Mark crossing the lawn and walking past the house.

Startled, she gasped slightly, but before the men looked up, Lovey whisked her back toward the table.

Rachel felt so light-headed from the sudden motions that she instinctively placed her hand on the table to steady herself as she set her plate down with a clatter. Andre reacted with his characteristic chivalry.

"My Dear, you are faint!" he cried. "Louis! Help Rachel to her chair. May God forgive us! Here we two men are carrying on while the lady we love is fainting from lack of nourishment."

"I'm fine," Rachel murmured as Louis assisted her into her chair.

"A cup of tea!" Andre announced. "The lady needs a cup of tea." He snatched up the silver teapot from the sideboard and rushed to her side. "Don't worry, My Dear, we'll have you fixed up in no time. Just be calm."

Rachel weakly smiled up at him, but she felt anything but calm. She knew exactly where Mark was going, and her whole being wanted to race after him. Instead, she did what she knew was expected of her. She allowed Andre to enjoy taking care of her and dutifully drank the tea he poured for her.

Lovey walked over and patted her on the shoulder as she said, "I need to talk to you in the kitchen when you've finished your breakfast and are feeling like yourself again."

Rachel knew that Lovey was giving her a chance to get away from her company and follow Mark. "Yes, yes," she murmured. "We do have some details to settle."

"Whatever needs doing, Louis and I are at your service," Andre insisted.

Louis reached over and covered Rachel's hand with his own. "Papa is right, Rachel. You have exhausted yourself. I won't let you make yourself sick on our account."

Andre beamed when he saw his son's hand on Rachel's. "You must listen to Louis, My Dear," he insisted. "He is absolutely right."

"I do have more guests coming for Christmas dinner in a few hours, Andre," Rachel reminded him.

"And you must be rested for them," Louis insisted as he continued to hold her hand. "You are the main attraction. It is you whom your guests want to enjoy. I won't allow you to tire yourself further."

"My son will handle everything, My Dear. Leave all in his capable hands, just as my dear Elinore used to depend on me."

"Drink your tea, Rachel," Louis urged as he leaned over and

kissed her on the cheek.

She did as he asked, but her thoughts were on Mark, not on the solicitous, handsome man at her side. In her mind's eye she could see Mark walking down the path to the pond, the path, which they had traveled together every summer for years. Under her feet she imagined the feel of that path, the buoyancy of it that only centuries of pine needles, layered on top of each other and slowly interwoven by time and weather, could create. As she drank her tea, she glanced out the window and saw the light fog that had so often accompanied them on that path, the gentle, embracing moisture that soothed and drew them deeper into the woods. She knew that at this moment Mark was feeling the pine needles under his feet and the fog on his cheeks as she sat in the dining room, listening to the exuberant chatter of Andre Simone. Any other time she would have been entranced by his stories about her Grandmere, but at this moment she only felt trapped. She was separated from what she needed most: time with Mark, time to unravel the tangle of her emotions.

"Rachel, Rachel." Andre's insistent voice drew her back to the table. "Do you remember Christmas Day at Belle St. Marie when you were a child of eight or nine, My Dear?"

"Yes," she answered vaguely, then realized how valuable one of Andre's stories could be to her now. If he would talk, she wouldn't have to pull her thoughts away from Mark. "But I would love to hear your recollections. After all, I was only a selfish child, my attention on all the presents, no doubt."

"You were never a selfish child, My Dear," Andre protested. "You were always the sweetest—"

"Forgive me, Papa," Louis interrupted, "but we must see that Rachel eats. Pass me the biscuits. I'm going to butter one for her."

"Oh yes, of course." Andre quickly passed the silver basket to Louis before announcing gravely, "I entrust her to your care, son."

"Please go on with your story," Rachel insisted as Louis encouraged her to eat.

"I believe I am remembering the Christmas when you were eight," Andre continued. "It actually snowed. Do you remember?"

"I do," Rachel responded as eagerly as her divided mind would allow. "I was eight, and I thought I was the luckiest girl on earth because that snow kept Daddy and me here for three days."

"Yes, and it kept me from having to return to New Orleans.

It was glorious! What a time we had!"

"Snowed? Here in Louisiana?" Louis inquired skeptically. "Papa, aren't you letting your imagination run away with you?"

"I certainly am not, although I must admit there was no more than three inches on the ground."

"I think you two are conspiring to fool me," Louis said. "I wouldn't have forgotten snow in Louisiana."

"You certainly would have if you spent your Christmases in Paris with your grandparents. You were in boarding school in France in those years," Andre explained triumphantly. "You do remember that, don't you?"

"Of course, Papa. So what happened here at Belle St. Marie?"

"Tell him, Rachel," Andre prompted. "He always thinks I am exaggerating when I speak of Belle St. Marie in the good old days."

"No, no, you tell him, Andre," Rachel encouraged, unwilling to detach her mind from the present and Mark. "You remember it better than I."

"It was bliss, sheer bliss, my boy. We all went to midnight mass and then to Philippe's, as usual. But the next morning Rachel started shouting from the upstairs verandah, calling us all to come see. We flung on our robes and joined her, and lo and behold, what did we find, Rachel?"

"A winter wonderland," Rachel responded unimaginatively. "You describe it, Andre, please." She allowed herself a quick glance out the window. Mark is probably almost to the pond, she thought. He's about to walk around the last bend right before you see the pond. We always used to stop there and grow quiet because we never knew what fantastic creature might be swimming on that pond, and we didn't want to risk startling it. Has he stopped at the bend? Is he thinking of me? Does he remember the time when we—

"Rachel." Andre dragged her back into the conversation. "Do you remember what I built for you that Christmas Day?"

Confused, caught between past and present, she couldn't possibly find her eighth year in her memory. "I'm sorry," she said.

"You must remember the makeshift sled I fashioned for you," Andre insisted.

"Yes, of course. The sled. I remember now."

"You'll never guess what we made it out of, Louis," Andre declared. "Tell him, Rachel."

"Oh, let me think." Rachel struggled to remember.

"Rachel! You can't have forgotten! Elinore was sure you were going to get killed on that sled."

"I'm sorry, Andre," Rachel murmured. "I'm just not thinking very clearly—"

"Rachel." Louis pushed back his chair abruptly. "I can't permit you to force yourself to play the good hostess with us when you so obviously need rest. Let me take you upstairs."

"Yes," Rachel agreed eagerly. "I do need to rest, but there's no need for you to see me upstairs. I'll just go lie down. I'm very sorry to abandon you." She rose from her chair as Louis reached around to help her.

"My Dear!" Andre sprang to his feet. "I'm so sorry you're feeling weak. Forgive me for carrying on in such a manner. I shall see you to your room myself."

"Really, it isn't necessary."

"Of course it is," Andre insisted. "I know what you're thinking, and you're quite right. Louis should not escort you upstairs. That is the privilege of an elderly gentleman, not a young one. Here, My Dear, give me your hand." He held out his arm for Rachel to lean on, and Rachel accepted it as the fastest way to get upstairs and be left alone so she could go find Mark.

"Louis," Andre directed as he began to lead Rachel from the dining room, "find Lovey. She will want to take care of Rachel."

"Of course," the younger man agreed as he turned toward the kitchen.

Andre escorted Rachel up the staircase and to her bedroom where he insisted she sit down at her dressing table and wait for Lovey.

As soon as she was sure he had started back down the stairs, Rachel hurried out onto the verandah and scanned the plantation as far as the fog would permit her to see. "I can't stand this any longer!" she whispered urgently. "I'm at war with myself, and talking to Mark is the only way to establish even a temporary truce. I have to get out of this house without anyone seeing me, but how?"

Chapter 3

Mark was frustrated as he walked down the path toward the pond where he and Rachel had so often played when they were children. Out in his professional world of photojournalism, he was accustomed to getting what he wanted, sometimes in spite of tremendous opposition. All he wanted on this foggy Christmas Day was Rachel's presence, and that was the one thing he could not seem to engineer.

As he crossed the front lawn of Belle St. Marie just moments earlier, determined not to limp, he had noticed that the lights in the dining room were glowing brightly. Though he stubbornly refused to look up, it took no particular imagination to guess that Rachel was serving Louis Simone and his father, Andre. A late brunch was the tradition at Belle St. Marie on Christmas Day. Since the D'Evereau family and guests always stayed up late partying at Cousin Philippe's after the midnight service, the brunch allowed everyone to sleep in, and the larger Christmas dinner was enjoyed at three in the afternoon.

Flashes of memory floated through Mark's mind, bringing happy images of Christmases past when he was a teenager and a college student. In those years, he had always been included in the group that gathered for both these meals. The mansion had, of course, been owned by Rachel's grandmother, Elinore D'Evereau, and her gracious embrace had pulled him, a distant cousin, into her family immediately after his arrival in the neighborhood. Thanks to her, Belle St. Marie had been his real home.

As Mark began to think about Miss Elinore, as he had learned to call her, his frustration disappeared into the mist. A regenerative gentleness entered his spirit, a gentleness that Miss Elinore always brought to him even now, many years after her death. He had been blessed to know her throughout his youth and college years; nevertheless, whenever he conjured up her face in his mind's eye, she always looked exactly the way she had looked the first morning he had met her. He always saw her deep blue eyes first, and somehow, in a way he could never explain, her eyes always instantly communicated her unconditional love for him. She could always make him feel that he was the one person who could make her life complete.

The boy Mark had arrived at Belle St. Marie with a tempestuous nature. He was prone to sudden, often negative mood changes, but Miss Elinore had always been able to send his anger or unhappiness flying. Now, all these years later, Mark grimaced as he admitted, "I could use her presence right now. I could use the love that shone from her eyes and the peace and hopefulness she produced in me." He stopped and looked around the woods until he spotted an ancient pine that had fallen and was now thickly covered with velvety, green moss. Leaving the path, he settled himself on the pine and grew still, allowing his memories of his first days in Louisiana to fill his mind.

What a mess I was when I first met Miss Elinore, he thought as he shifted his weight on the fallen pine. So confused and angry, and....yes....so afraid. No child should have to endure what I had to experience when I was twelve....to be in the car crash with my parents and forced to watch them die. No child should have to experience that and survive to live with those memories and that loss. I was so afraid and very angry with God. It seemed outrageous to me that I should have walked away from that car crash and only three days later stood in the cemetery as they buried my parents. It still seems outrageous to me.

And since there was no one else to raise me, I was uprooted from the high plains of Texas and sent to the lowlands of Louisiana to live with my mother's brother, Philippe. A crusty old bachelor, that's what he seemed to be to me. Of course, now I realize he wasn't really very old, and what I perceived as dislike of me was his perfectly explainable reluctance to reduce the freedom of his bachelor existence by bringing a twelve-year-old into his life. I definitely felt unwanted, but I'm sure that no matter how hard Philippe might have tried, I wasn't going to allow anyone to get close to me. At least, not until the first time I walked across the lawn at Belle St. Marie on my way to the pond to fish. I remember that day so well....

Twelve-year-old Mark felt more unwelcome than usual when his Uncle Philippe's political cronies arrived for a strategy session. His uncle had showered him with presents since his parents' death, in a futile attempt to make possessions substitute for the affection he had not learned to feel for the boy. The latest of the elaborate presents had been a sophisticated fishing rod which was accompanied by Philippe's zealous encouragement that Mark go explore a pond on the property of Belle St. Marie. Mark gladly took the hint, and after meeting his uncle's friends, jerked up the new rod and headed out to the pond.

"I'll never care about anyone again," Mark muttered to himself as he trudged down the path, barely visible in the pine woods, toward Belle St. Marie. "If I never care, I'll never be hurt again. I can take care of myself! I may just be twelve, but I'm big for my age, and pretty soon I'll be able to go out and get a job. And when I do, I won't take anything from anybody ever again. I don't want anybody, and I don't need them!" He looked disdainfully down at the fancy fishing rod. "I could have made a better fishing pole than this in five minutes, and now that I think of it, that's exactly what I'm gonna do. I'm gonna make me a real fishing pole and give this thing back to Uncle Philippe. That'll show him how I feel! The law may be able to make me live with him until I'm sixteen, but I don't have to be dependent on him for anything."

A pine bough overhanging the path slapped him in the face, and he uttered an obscenity, an obscenity he had recently heard for the first time from one of his uncle's guests. Saying the word made him feel tougher, but also a little sorry. His father had never allowed such language, and he knew that his mother would be grieved that he had uttered such a word. Yet the horrific changes in his life seemed to require a more violent language of him, a language that would somehow make him seem and feel invincible.

Confusion stopped him for a moment in his walk as he attempted to pull together the pieces of his conflicting feelings. I've got to get tough, he thought, but then he remembered the face of his mother, and he added, but I can't forget who I am, where I came from. A wave of grief and desperation overwhelmed him. "If only I could talk to Dad.... What would Dad say?" he whispered. "Dad was tough, but he was also kinda good or something. I don't know the right word." Unable to make his feelings fit into a coherent ethic, Mark gave up the effort, turned back to the path and trudged on.

After walking another five minutes, he saw the trees part and the path continue on to the wide lawn in front of Belle St. Marie. Mark stopped a moment at the sight of the imposing, pristine white mansion with its double verandahs draped around all four sides. It was a much grander house than his Uncle Philippe's. He knew little about the mansion except that it was the center of the grand D'Evereau family presence in Louisiana. He knew that it had been a place of power for well over a century, but that now it was inhabited only by an older, distant relation of his named Elinore D'Evereau.

Mark had seen her from a distance; his uncle had pointed her out at church, but he had never actually met her. Somewhat intimidated by the mansion, he boasted to himself, "Someday I'll have a house bigger than that one." Then he shrugged his shoulders and boldly walked across the lawn near the front verandah. He had almost walked past the steps up to the main entrance when he suddenly heard a sweet voice from the shadows, and the woman he recognized as Elinore D'Evereau stepped forward and walked down the steps toward him.

"Good morning, Mark." She greeted him warmly, but it was not her voice that snatched his attention. It was her eyes. They looked like dark blue crystals glittering in the sunlight, and they were so compelling he could not drag his gaze away from them. Warmth surged through Mark's whole body, and his heart seemed to want to leap toward the woman. "I have been wanting to meet you so much," she continued, never averting her gaze from him. "This morning when I woke up I just knew something special was going to happen. And here you are, the something special I was expecting. Come on up on the verandah, and let's get to know each other."

Mark stood rooted to the spot, held by a battle between the love in her eyes and the dark anger that had lived in him since the death of his parents. She waited a moment, and when he said nothing, she turned slightly toward the steps and held out her hand to direct him up onto the verandah. When she did so, she unlinked her eyes from his, and Mark's resolution to remain detached came flooding back over him. "No thanks," he replied stiffly. "I gotta go."

She turned back toward him and said quietly, "I know it feels like you have been abandoned, Mark, but you are not alone."

"You don't know anything, lady!" Mark almost shouted. Stunned by the furious tone of his own words, he fell silent. He had never spoken to a lady that way. "I mean—"

"I know what you mean, Mark." She saved him from an explanation. "You mean I'm not living in your skin. That's true, but even so, I do know something of what you are feeling. Believe me, I do."

"How could you?" he demanded, his anger blazing again. "You aren't me."

"No, I'm not you, but I am a human being who has felt the horrible pain of losing my loved ones. I do know the hurt you are feeling."

"So what's that to me?" he retorted.

"What's that to you? Quite simply, it means that you don't have to suffer alone. You can be comforted by those who have felt the same pain you now feel. And most of all, you can be comforted by our assurances that your pain will lessen, and good things will come into your life again."

"Nothing good ever happens to me! Not anymore!"

Miss Elinore stepped forward and placed her hand on his shoulder. He was so surprised he looked directly into her face, and her eyes commanded his entire attention. "That will change, Mark Goodman," she said firmly. "I promise you; that will change." She patted his shoulder, turned, and walked back up onto the verandah.

When she turned back to him, Mark refused to look at her. "I'll see you later," she murmured kindly. "You're always welcome here, Mark. Always."

Mark just nodded stiffly, turned and walked on down the path as fast as he could without running. His heart was pounding a mile a minute, but not from physical exertion, and he was petrified with fear that he was going to start crying. When he finally reached the shelter of the woods, he stopped to consider what had happened to him.

Looking back in the direction of Belle St. Marie, he felt an almost overwhelming desire to return, but at the same time he felt unexplainably afraid. He was confused about both of those feelings and a bit ashamed of himself. What's wrong with me? he demanded silently. Didn't I just decide that nobody was ever gonna hurt me again? And here I go getting all soft the minute an old lady smiles at me. Well, forget her! I'm going my own way from now on. He turned back in the direction of the pond and stalked off.

In a few minutes he stopped again; he had lost the path. It just seemed to disappear, to simply stop at the base of an enormous magnolia tree. Its large, dark green leaves looked newly polished in the clear morning light, and its gigantic white blossoms shone pristine, their cupped petals sparkling with drops of morning dew. Mark was momentarily amazed by the size of the tree, but his greater concern was his loss of the path to the pond. He walked closer to the lowest boughs of the tree, huge arcs of leaf clusters topped with flowers, arcs that swept the ground before turning up. Their clean, citrus-like fragrance was enticing, and even a twelve-year-old boy was not immune to their invitation to sniff a blossom.

Mark leaned over a bough, lowered his face toward one of the flowers and drew his breath in suddenly. The glorious scent stole his mind for a moment, and he was content to simply stand and slowly gaze upward toward the top of the tree. Then he dragged his thoughts back to his journey to the pond and began to search for the path. Finally he saw it to the left of the tree. The path, which had been walked for centuries, had obviously always brought those who walked it to an encounter with this tree, and they had always respectfully circumvented it.

Mark shifted the fishing rod in his hand, was reminded of his purpose and took the path to the left of the tree. Once he had circled the magnolia, he discovered that the woods began to thin, and for the first time he saw the pond ahead. He hurried forward and soon stood at the edge of a pond like none he had ever seen in Texas. The surface was glossy but dark, almost black, and like a black mirror it reflected an image of everything that bordered it or hung over it. Large cypress trees draped in gray moss found their doubles in the black-mirrored pond, as did the green shrubs and swatches of gently-tinted wildflowers.

Mark was fascinated; he flung his fishing rod away from him and dropped to the ground on all fours. Slowly he inched forward to the edge of the bank, lifted himself up and leaned forward over the water. There he was, a duplicate of himself staring back at him. He studied his earnest face in the water, his fair skin and dark green eyes framed by curling dark hair. Pictures of his parents' faces flashed through his mind as he remembered that his hair and his mouth were his father's, and his eyes were his mother's.

A wave of desperate grief overwhelmed him, and his throat muscles tightened as he fought back the rising tears. In spite of all his efforts, he was overwhelmed, and his tears began to flow over his lids and fall into the dark water below. His whole being ached for communion with his parents, and he began to consider how easily he could join them. This black pond could be his deliverance, his entry into whatever world his parents now inhabited. As he watched himself cry, he saw his mother's dark green eyes overflowing with tears. His mouth was pinched, his lips pressed tightly together, just as he had seen his father's when life was distressing him.

All he had to do was leave the solidness of the bank. The dark pond would do its work, and he would be free of his miserable life. Certain now of what he must do, he began to rise from his knees to dive into the deep darkness below.

Suddenly he heard a loud, sweeping sound to his left, but before he could turn his head, an enormous white swan glided in and landed on the water in front of him. The swan paddled a few seconds, turning its body in the water until it faced Mark. He sank back down on his knees as he stared at the size and startling whiteness of the swan. An involuntary "Wow!" escaped his lips.

The swan looked directly into Mark's eyes, as if it had come to communicate. All thoughts of suicide fled Mark's mind as the bird mesmerized him. Slowly the swan paddled toward him, pausing when it was no more than twenty feet away. Time stopped for Mark, and as he stared back at the bird, unexplainable peace surged through him. Indeed, a new thought flashed through his mind: life—right here, right now—was grand.

The swan, however, had more to give Mark.

In an instant it turned golden, and its stunning, glittering color was mirrored by the dark water. Mark's eyes widened, and his mouth fell open in amazement. Without thinking he rose to his feet, his eyes glued on the swan. The bird flapped its enormous wings gently, and swirls of golden, glittery particles shone in the sunlight before settling on the black water. Mark's spirits soared; he had never felt such joy!

Just when he thought he would burst with his ever-increasing happiness, the golden swan spread its magnificent wings, flapped them several times and lifted itself off the water. Mark watched as the bird soared into flight, leaving trails of golden glitter that drifted slowly down to the water. With the sunlight flashing off its golden body and its glowing wings cutting effortlessly through the air, the bird circled the pond before disappearing into the distance.

Mark sank to his knees and stared up at the sky where the swan had disappeared. In a while he settled back on his heels and looked down at the dark pond. It had lost all its negative power over him; it would never again be able to do anything but reflect light back to Mark. The boy felt profound peace for the first time since the death of his parents, and he stayed there for quite some time reveling in it.

In time Mark began to hear a high-pitched, sweet voice singing in the distance. His mind was hazy as he tried to drag it back from the glory of watching the golden swan, but still that voice seemed to be calling him in some profoundly personal way. After a few moments of hesitation, he rose and cocked his head, trying to discern the location of the source of the voice. He picked up his fishing rod and slowly ambled back down the path, listening intently for the location of the voice. As he moved nearer, he realized that he was listening to the sound of a little girl singing.

Soon he came to a secondary path that split from the main one. Pausing, he realized that he would have to leave the main path to find the source of the intriguing voice; he would have to explore something new. He hesitated a moment, then turned and made his way down the overgrown path.

As the woods grew denser, the natural light dimmed under the thick canopy of pines overhead. The voice became more distinct, and once again Mark felt hesitant. He'd already experienced a remarkable event, and that fact coupled with his natural shyness made him pause frequently and wonder if he truly wanted to continue, but the lilting voice was compelling.

Finally he ducked down behind some bushes and proceeded forward stealthily, trying to catch a glimpse of the little girl without revealing his own presence. After several moments of moving cautiously through the brush, he reached the edge of a clearing in the woods. Crouching behind the bushes, he peered out into the clearing, and there he saw a little girl whom he judged to be about nine years old. She was gleefully turning in circles as she sang childish, repetitive songs. Mark grinned at the sight of her. She had abandoned herself to the happiness of the moment—singing, turning, her arms flying around her body, her white pinafore billowing out in the breeze, her long golden hair trailing behind her. She had thrown her head back to look at the sky as she sang and pirouetted around the circle of the clearing.

Mark was amused by her childish antics and delighted by her blithe spirit. Finally the little girl made herself thoroughly dizzy. Giggling all the way, she staggered toward a fallen log and threw herself down on it. She could barely sit up straight—a fact she obviously enjoyed, for her giggles turned into laughter. Mark watched intently, perfectly content to stay hidden and enjoy the spectacle. She's a pretty little girl, he thought, but she's just a kid.

Soon the little girl, having grown bored sitting on the log, jumped up on top of it and began to pretend it was a tightrope. Cautiously, her arms held out parallel to the ground to help her keep her balance, she began to walk the length of the slippery log. She was walking away from him in the dim light, and Mark began to feel an unaccountable apprehension as she became harder and harder to see. He sternly but silently reprimanded himself, what's it to you? She doesn't mean anything to you. She's just a little girl. Still he began to hold his breath and wish fervently that she would get down off the log or at least come back out of the dark distance.

Finally she did reach the end of her "tightrope," turned cautiously and began the feat of walking back. The closer she got to Mark, the more easily his breath came and his muscles relaxed somewhat. When she finally reached the end of the log that lay close to Mark, the little girl made an elaborate curtsy to her invisible audience. Then she stood silently on the log and turned her eyes in his direction. Mark froze; she seemed to be looking directly at him.

A bright shaft of sunshine broke through the high canopy of pine trees and illuminated the spot where the little girl stood. Her long, blonde hair turned golden as it glistened in the light, and Mark was so startled by its similarity to the golden color of the swan that he gasped. For the third time that day he was infused with unexplainable warmth, and he felt genuinely happy.

The little girl continued to stare in his direction, her golden hair shining and her dark blue eyes radiant in the warm, yellow light of the sun. For Mark, those brief moments connected the little girl to the golden swan, and he longed to know who she was. The swan was gone, and he had no control over its return, but this little girl need not fly out of his life. If he could learn who she was, perhaps he could see her from time to time.

As he considered this possibility, another voice called from the woods, "Rachel! Rachel!" and he jumped at the sudden sound. Fortunately for him, the little girl had turned her eyes away and did not spot him behind the bushes.

"Where are you, Rachel?" the voice called again.

"Over here, Aimee," the little girl answered. "On the tightrope log."

Mark waited and watched as a young black girl entered the clearing.

"Where have you been, Rachel?" the black girl demanded.

"I've been looking for you everywhere."

"Right here," Rachel responded nonchalantly as she stared down at Aimee. "I'm dancing with the fairies, Aimee. I'm singing and dancing with the fairies."

"What fairies? There ain't no fairies in these woods."

"Sure there are," Rachel insisted, "there are fairies everywhere."

"I don't see no fairies."

"That's because you don't believe in them," Rachel answered in a superior tone. "They won't show themselves to people who don't believe in them."

"I ain't gonna believe in fairies. I believe in angels because Grandma says they're real."

"Fairies are kinda like angels, Aimee, only they're smaller. But they can fly around like angels and make you happy and make you sing and dance."

"God ain't gonna like it if you believe in fairies because they ain't angels, and He only favors angels," Aimee warned.

Rachel tossed her head back and retorted, "I don't care! God doesn't like me anyway, and I don't like Him."

"Rachel!" Aimee sounded scandalized and more than a little scared by Rachel's words. "Don't say things like that. You're gonna get us killed."

"I'm not afraid."

"Well, you oughta be. Come on down off that log. Grandma sent me to get you; she wants you to do something before supper."

"Oh, all right," Rachel agreed. "I'll come if Lovey wants me, but later I'm coming back to dance with the fairies again." She jumped down off the log and joined her friend.

"No you ain't either," Aimee protested.

"I will if I want to," Rachel argued as the girls walked out of the clearing together.

Mark cautiously shadowed them as they returned to Belle St. Marie. When they reached the lawn, he stayed in the woods and watched as they made their way around to the back of the mansion, climbed up the back steps and entered. Only then did he come out of the woods and head across the front lawn.

Just as he stepped on the walk that led to the verandah, a gentle voice called to him, "Mark, how was your fishing?"

He looked ruefully at his perfectly clean, dry fishing rod before glancing up to the verandah. "Not too good, ma'am," he answered sheepishly.

"Maybe tomorrow." Miss Elinore emerged from the shadows of the verandah and smiled down at him.

Her dark blue eyes captured him. He could not look away from them, and he yearned to talk to her. Much to his amazement, he wanted to tell her what had happened at the pond, to share his experience with her, but he was afraid she would think he was crazy.

"Maybe it wasn't fish you needed to catch today," she suggested as he continued to look up at her, desperately wanting to open up, but afraid. "Maybe what you needed to catch today was an enlarged perception of reality."

"Ma'am?" Mark cocked his head as he struggled to understand her sophisticated words.

"I meant, maybe you needed to see the world in a different way."

"Yes, ma'am." Mark suddenly looked at the ground and began shuffling his feet. "I mean….well, this really crazy thing….well…."

"Mark," Elinore encouraged him, "come sit down and talk to me a few minutes."

Mark hesitated, then climbed the steps, and she led him over to a wicker loveseat and beckoned for him to sit beside her.

"Tell me what happened," she said gently.

"Well…I was down by the pond, and this swan landed on the water, a real big white swan, I mean, really big." He stopped, obviously unsure about how much to reveal.

"There are many white swans in Louisiana—"

"Not like this!" Mark suddenly blurted out.

"Why not?"

"Because this one—this one turned—" Mark stopped and ducked his head, certain he was about to embarrass himself. Finally he muttered, "Golden."

"How wonderful," Miss Elinore murmured as a gentle smile passed over her face. "How like God."

Mark raised his head and studied her. "Then you don't think I'm crazy?"

"No." She smiled gently as her eyes caressed him. "Not crazy—just very blessed."

Mark sat perfectly still, remembering what he had seen, until he had worked up the courage to ask the question he needed answered. "What does it mean? The golden swan, I mean."

Miss Elinore's eyes grew misty as she pondered his question. Finally she asked, "How did it make you feel when you saw it?"

"All peaceful…you know…like things are okay."

"How did you feel before you saw it?" she asked.

"I wanted to…I was going to…I wished I was dead," he confessed.

"How do you feel now?"

"Kinda happy or something. You know, like life is.... good."

"Yes, I do know…like life is good." Miss Elinore smiled at Mark, then moved her graceful, white hand to Mark's cheek and touched it gently before adding, "Maybe that's all we need to know about the golden swan or about any of the mysterious things in life. Maybe we don't need to understand. Maybe we just need to notice that they are wonderful gifts to us, that they bring us joy and healing when we need them."

"Who would give me something like a golden swan?"

"God would."

Amazed, Mark stared at her, then asked, "Why?"

"Because He knows you, and He knows you need help. Most of all, because He loves you, Mark."

"But why a golden swan?"

"Why not? It accomplished God's purpose, didn't it?"

"Yeah, I guess so."

Miss Elinore gently stroked the back of his head, then offered, "Occasionally God shows us a glimpse of splendor, His splendor, to encourage us to press on toward our heavenly home where all is splendor because all is God."

Mark looked into her blue eyes. He was not at all sure that God even liked him, but he was sure that she did. He smiled at her. He liked this Miss Elinore a lot. A whole lot.

"Why don't we go get some dinner, Mark? I bet Lovey's got something all ready for us. I want you to meet Lovey and my granddaughter, Rachel, and Lovey's granddaughter, Aimee." He hesitated a few seconds, so she stood, held out her hand, and murmured, "Come home."

"And I went into Lovey's kitchen for the first time," the grown Mark said as he dragged his thoughts back to the present, "and there sat Rachel, and I've never been the same." He stood up and left the moss-covered, fallen log behind as he headed for the pond. "She was just a kid, a pretty kid, but still just a kid. In spite of her age, when she looked up and smiled at me, she sealed my fate for life. From that moment on there hasn't been a day in my life that I haven't thought about her."

Mark arrived at the edge of the pond, picked up a pebble

and skipped it across the dark surface. Everywhere it bounced on the water it left ripples which caught the golden light from the shafts of sunlight and reflected that light back to him. "I never saw the golden swan again," he murmured. "I guess I didn't need it anymore. I had Rachel, and with her came Miss Elinore and Lovey."

He thought of Rachel back at the plantation house, entertaining Louis and Andre, and he muttered. "But I sure don't have her now!"

Chapter 4

I've got to just slow down! Rachel counseled herself after she had reached the cover of the woods. No one in the house can see me now. She took several deep breaths before admitting to herself. I'm not at all sure I should be doing this. It seemed like a good idea when I left the house, but now I don't know. I mean, exactly what is he going to think if I just show up at the pond? I know he's there, and he'll know I knew, and he'll think I came running out to see him, which is exactly what I'm doing, but maybe I shouldn't be. . . Maybe I should just be playing it cool, keeping my distance.

Frustrated by her conflicting emotions, she ran her hands through her hair and shook her head to clear it. After all, do I really want to get seriously involved with Mark? Of course, I do! What an idiotic thing to ask....but on the other hand, my feelings for him are so strong. . . .maybe I'm just setting myself up to get hurt again. I can't do that! I won't do that.

But it's Mark, for heaven's sake! she scolded herself. And you've always loved him...you know you have. At that thought a massive balloon of longing inflated in Rachel's chest and threatened to burst.

Overwhelmed by her conflicting emotions, Rachel dropped her head in her hands as tears began to flood down her cheeks. "Oh, no!" she whispered desperately, "I can't do this. I just can't start crying. I can't let Mark see me this way. I've got to pull myself together." Through her flowing tears, she looked around, searching for a place to sit until she could take control of herself. When she spotted a flat rock nearby, she left the path, threaded her way through the underbrush and sat down gratefully.

"I am going to look a mess," she murmured as she searched her skirt pocket for a tissue. Not finding one, she gave up, pulled the hem of her skirt back and dried her cheeks and eyes with the bottom of her slip. She took several deep breaths as she repeated to herself, "Calm down, just calm down."

Once she felt fairly certain her tears had stopped, she reprimanded herself. Now Rachel, you can't allow yourself to be a wave tossed around in the sea of your emotions. You have to decide what you want before you see Mark. Now think! You're not a kid anymore, and neither is he. It's been 15 years since you were around him, so you don't really have any idea what he's like now. Time changes people. Look how much you've changed in the last 15 years. Besides, do you really want to get involved with a man again? Any man? Are you willing to open yourself to the deep hurt a man can bring into your life? Look what Collins did to you! Why risk it again?

Children. The word shot through her mind, negating all her fine reasoning. What about children? What about family? There was no escaping it; Rachel was well aware of her age and the time limit which nature inevitably imposed. No husband means no children, she thought. No children.... I can't stand that. I must marry again. I must risk it. Obsessively smoothing her skirt back over her knees, Rachel continued arguing with herself. Maybe I've just been drawn into a whirlwind of emotions by Mark's sudden appearance. But I can't let him send me into a tailspin; I've got to consider the last 18 months. It's been a long haul, but I have pulled myself out of the deepest hole of my life. Not so long ago I arrived here a totally shattered woman. I had discovered Collins' affair with Shawna, and before I could even begin to deal with all that emotional garbage, he was suddenly dead. His drunk driving finally caught up with him and my whole life, from my childhood on, caught up with me. She sighed loudly and forced herself to still her hands. But the good news is that I have faced up to the heartbreak and pains in my past and learned to perceive myself in a new way, as a worthy person. I need to stay in the secure space I have created.

"Don't rock your boat now, for heaven's sake," she whispered earnestly. "Louis is safe. He's steady and dependable. You can make a great life together, one that's not filled with drama all the time."

Unpersuaded, Rachel cut off her own thoughts. ""I better go. I've got guests waiting at the house, and Mark won't stay at the pond forever. If I'm going to do this, I just need to get on with it and keep calm." With shaky resolution, she stood up, carefully walked back through the underbrush to the path, and stopped to straighten her clothes. Once again, however, her heart sank as she thought, maybe I should just go back to the house, avoid all solitary involvement with Mark.

After another moment of temptation to play it safe, she made her decision. "No, I'm not going to blow this out of proportion. I can do this," she assured herself as she straightened her spine and lifted her chin. "I'm in charge of myself, and I can certainly have a casual conversation with Mark without coming unglued. I just have to remember what I've suffered from marriage to Collins, what a safe haven Louis can offer me, and just keep my feelings under control."

Composed and determined, Rachel continued down the path more briskly. At last she turned the final bend in the path before the pond and saw Mark.

His back was turned to her, and he was listlessly skimming pebbles across the glassy water. Rachel stopped abruptly at the sight of him as her heart lurched and began to pound in her chest. Banging her forehead with the palm of her hand, she silently demanded, get a grip on yourself! This won't do at all. It just won't do!

Mark reached down for another pebble, but as his fingers encircled the stone, he stopped, dropped the pebble, stood up straight and turned around. When her eyes met his, she dropped her hands to her sides and helplessly stared at him.

Neither one spoke for a long moment, then slowly a smile of tender joy blossomed on Mark's face. He took several steps toward Rachel.

When she saw him coming, she yearned to race toward him, to throw her arms around him, but she slammed the lid on her emotions. She flashed him a vibrant, but superficial smile and declared, "Mark! How nice to find you here. I saw you cross the lawn earlier, but I never dreamed you'd still be down here. I just had to have a breath of fresh air before—"

Mark laughed lightly. "It won't work, Rachel. You and I both know why you came down here on a cold, damp morning."

"I don't know what you mean," Rachel answered. "I just wanted to get some fresh air, but I am delighted to run into you."

"Really? And why is that?" Mark's eyes began to twinkle, and Rachel recognized that he was teasing her just as he always had.

Determined to beat him at his own game, she tossed her head nonchalantly, walked around him and moved to the edge of the pond. Casually she stooped down to pick up a pebble.

"You never could skim a pebble across the pond, Rachel, so why don't you quit pretending and just admit that you came down here because you wanted us to have a chance to be alone?"

Embarrassment followed by a burst of anger shot through Rachel, but she was determined not to lose control of herself or the situation. Slowly she turned toward him and smiled calmly in spite of her pounding heart. "Well, the truth is, I never really got to welcome you home last night. There were so many people crowding around, and I just wanted to see you again and tell you....tell you....how glad I am you're home."

"Well, that's very nice." Mark grinned, then his eyes turned serious, and he walked toward Rachel and enclosed her in his arms. "Rachel, Rachel," he murmured in her ear. "I've missed you so much."

As Mark pulled her close to him, Rachel pressed her face against his neck, and all the long-ago joy of feeling her skin bonded to his flooded through her. She desperately wanted to melt into him and never emerge again. Her emotions struggled with her reason as she fought frantically to keep her recent resolutions in mind—to remember her torturous marriage to Collins and the safety Louis could offer.

"I've missed you, too," she admitted breathlessly as she finally pulled away and regained control of herself. "How are you? What have you been up to?"

"I'm fine, and I will fill you in on the last 15 years of my life later, Rachel. Right now, I'm more concerned about you. It's not like you to be so distant. What's going on?"

"Nothing," Rachel lied. "I just don't know what you expect from me. It has been 15 years, after all, and I've heard very little from you."

"You were married, Rachel."

"Yes, of course, but I mean in the last year or so since Collins' death. I haven't heard a word from you and I....I....well, I just...."

"I couldn't come to you, Rachel."

"Well, of course not. I'm sure you were very busy and...."

Mark took her face in his hands and peered down at her. "What's wrong, Rachel? It's me. . . . Mark. I'm here now. I know everything about you, and I love you."

Tears stung Rachel's eyes once again and her throat ached as she pushed down a sob. "You don't know everything about me!" Rachel whispered fiercely. "You don't know anything about me! I've changed, Mark. It's been 15 years, and those 15 years have shredded me and made me into a different person. You don't know me!"

"I know you had a rough time with Collins. I know his death must have been a nightmare for you." Gently Mark wiped her tears away with his fingers. "But Rachel, I don't care what's happened to you. I don't care what you've done. Don't you know that nothing could keep me from loving you?"

"We're not kids anymore, Mark." Rachel abruptly turned away so she wouldn't be tempted by his face. "We're not teenagers. We're not even college students. There's been so much water under the bridge. You just don't know what I've been through and what it's done to me."

"I know that the essential part of people never changes, Rachel. I know who you are, and I love who you are. We can deal with whatever you have suffered through, and we can deal with it better together."

"It won't work. I wish it would, but it won't. We can't regain what we had." She pushed past him, took several steps, and turned back to state emphatically, "We're stuck in the present, Mark. The past is lost to us."

"That's a lie, Rachel. The past is not lost to us. We are still the people we were. We may have been battered and bruised by life, but we are still the people we were when we were kids, and it's up to us to make our present what we want it to be."

Rachel stubbornly shook her head as she struggled not to cry again, "I just want peace and stability. No more drama, Mark!"

"What about love?"

"It's too dangerous," she mumbled as she turned to leave.

Obviously frustrated, Mark exploded, "Why won't you give us a chance?" he demanded furiously. "What's the real reason, Rachel?"

Rachel recoiled at his angry tone. For a split second she felt all the fear she had felt when confronting her violent, drunk husband, Collins, and in that second she instinctively threw her hands over her face to shield herself from blows.

"Dear God," Mark exclaimed softly as his anger immediately evaporated. Slowly he held out his arms to her, "Rachel, darling, come here. It's okay," he soothed. "Surely you know I would never hurt you."

Embarrassed, Rachel dropped her hands to her sides. "I don't seem to know anything about men anymore," she muttered "I don't know why Collins acted the way he did."

"He was a fool. Any man who would hurt you, who would even risk losing you is a fool--"

"You risked it. You left me!" Rachel blurted out.

"I went to war, Rachel. Surely you've come to understand that it was my love for you that made me refuse to marry you. I couldn't risk making you a young widow—or worse still tying you to a cripple if I came home wounded."

Rachel turned away from him, and silence fell between them. Mark waited, making his most valiant effort to be patient, but the question that had to be answered would not go away. "Why did you marry Collins 6 months after I left?" he asked. "Why didn't you wait for me?"

Rachel hung her head and closed her eyes as she remembered the immature young woman she had been, as she probed her own understanding of that difficult time. When she finally spoke, her voice was dulled with sadness, "I just wanted to stop my pain, Mark. I thought he would stop my pain—"

"But he gave you a new kind of pain, didn't he?"

Searing anger shot through Rachel, and she whirled around and demanded, "How would you know? Where were you? Always off in some jungle or on some escapade in the desert, first for the army and then for some newspaper."

"Obviously I didn't know enough. Lovey wrote me. Uncle Philippe kept me informed, but nobody ever even hinted that—"

"Lovey didn't know how bad things were," Rachel said, cutting him off. "But some time during all those years she must have told you I wasn't happy."

"Yes, several times her letters mentioned that you were. . . . well....she said she was worried about you."

"Then why didn't you come back?"

"You were married." Mark fell back on a secondary reason while he struggled with his pride. Finally his love trumped his ego, "Okay, because you had dumped me! Didn't you?"

"Yes," she whispered, "I did." She bit her lip as the anger drained out of her, only to be replaced by remorse. "Oh, how could I have done that?"

"I don't know," he said quietly, "but you did, and I was hurt, and you were married."

"Yes, I was married," Rachel agreed, "back then. But, Mark, I haven't been married the last 18 months, and I haven't heard a word from you. Where have you been?"

Mark said nothing, and Rachel's anger rose again.

"Where have you been, Mark?" Rachel demanded. "Off

playing war correspondent? Is that why you didn't come? If you still loved me so much and you knew I was alone and in trouble, why didn't you come help me?"

"I would have come if I had been able to, Rachel. I swear it."

Rachel considered him coolly. "Well, that's not good enough, Mark," she replied. "It's the same story all over again. You wouldn't marry me before because of a war. You wouldn't come to me when I needed you because of your adventurous job. I don't want to live like that. I can't, I just can't."

Silence fell between them. At last Rachel looked up at Mark and quietly asked, "Do you have any idea how good all this makes Louis look to me?"

"You don't love him, Rachel!"

"No," she admitted, "not like I loved you, but he's a fine man, Mark. He's interesting and sophisticated and quite cultivated and—"

"I don't want to hear about Louis," Mark interrupted her. "I just have one question for you. Do you really think you will have an easier time creating a meaningful life with a man who hardly knows you? With a man who couldn't possibly know you enough to love you the way I do?"

"I honestly don't know, Mark. I just don't know, but I'm going to try because—because—" Rachel stood and faced Mark squarely. "All I know is that I never want to feel deeply again. If I marry Louis, perhaps I could create a pleasant life, a life without pain. I don't ever want to risk loving again as deeply as I loved you—"

"Not 'loved,' Rachel, 'love.' You still love me. For heaven's sake, think about what you're saying!" Mark raised his voice. "You're not stupid, Rachel. In fact, you're the smartest person I know. You know there's no joy in anyone's life without a little pain. You know—"

"I know that I don't want any more pain! That's what I know!"

Mark stood silently before her, his jaw clenched. Rachel quickly composed herself and changed the tone of her voice. "Mark, please, I don't want to talk about this anymore. Can't we just enjoy the fact that you're home? Look, it's Christmas. Let's just try to enjoy it. Why don't you come join us for Christmas dinner?"

"You must be crazy!" Mark retorted. "I'm not sitting around the table with you and Louis, your light-weight, undemanding suitor. I didn't come all these miles to share you with anyone, Rachel."

"What right have you to call Louis "light-weight,' and who gave you the exclusive right to me anyway?"

"Years of loving you gave me the right, and I won't come and share you with another man."

"Fine! Don't come," Rachel agreed. She turned and stalked away from him.

Mark called after her, "This isn't finished, Rachel!"

Rachel whirled around and shouted at him. "Of course not! You have always been the most stubborn man alive, and I'm sure that that part of you hasn't changed one bit!"

"Ah, so now you agree with me," Mark taunted her.

"I do not agree with you!"

"You just said my stubbornness hasn't changed a bit. I told you the essential characteristics of a person don't change. If I haven't changed, what makes you think you have, Rachel?"

"Because I know I've accomplished one thing in the last year for sure. I've learned to quit making the same mistakes I've made in the past."

"I'm not a mistake, Rachel. I'm the man you've been waiting for all your life."

"What you are is an arrogant— Oh! You are impossible, and this conversation is ended!"

Rachel hurried out of the clearing and raced down the path, across the lawn, and into the kitchen of the house. When she arrived, she threw herself into a chair at the kitchen table and beat her fists on the tabletop.

Lovey calmly watched her and waited. When Rachel stopped, Lovey said quietly, "I guess Mr. Mark be coming to dinner."

"Over my dead body!"

"I best set another place at the table." Lovey smiled knowingly and turned to walk toward the dining room.

"Don't bother, Lovey! I told you he's not coming, and it's a good thing because we would just end up killing each other if he did. How could I ever have thought I loved him?" Rachel demanded, then suddenly jumped from the chair and stomped out of the room.

Lovey looked heavenward for a few seconds before she said, "Yes, Lord," and started toward the dining room door again. "I best set another place."

Half an hour later Lovey was standing at the kitchen

window watching Mark limp across the back lawn. "Lord, have mercy," she breathed a prayer for him. "There he is in pain again. Something bad done happened to that boy, something he ain't tellin' us. No wonder he didn't answer my letter." She hurried to the door and called out, "Mr. Mark! You better not pass without coming in to see your old Lovey."

Mark straightened up and tried to stride naturally toward the kitchen door. When he entered, he gathered Lovey into a hug, "You'll never be old to me, Lovey. Have I ever missed you!"

"And I's missed you, Mr. Mark. We's all missed you."

"I'm not so sure about that." Mark said sarcastically as he released the old housekeeper.

"You and Miz Rachel must have had some fight down at the pond."

"She's impossible, Lovey!" Mark declared. "Absolutely won't listen to reason."

"Miz Rachel had a real hard time of it ever since you was kids."

"I know that, but—"

"No, you don't, Mr. Mark. You just knew Miz Rachel when she was here at Belle St. Marie. You don't know what all she suffered back in Texas through her growing-up years, and you don't know nothing about her marriage. Even I didn't know nothing about that till I found her collapsed in a heap on the front verandah before dawn one morning."

Mark's gaze turned dark with concern. "Maybe you better tell me about all this," he said as he sat down at the table. "After talking to Rachel, I see I don't know as much as I thought I did."

"Not now, there ain't time. I's just gonna get you a hot cup of coffee. Then you can warm up before you goes home to get yourself all dressed up for Christmas dinner here at Belle St. Marie."

"I'm not coming to Christmas dinner here, Lovey, and that's final."

"Yes, you is." Lovey poured him a cup of coffee as she talked. "Cause you's the smartest man I know, Mr. Mark, and you ain't about to leave Miz Rachel here all evening with a couple of wealthy suitors like Mr. Louis and Mr. Billy."

"Who's Mr. Billy? I haven't heard about that one."

"He got a lotta money, and he be crazy to have Miz Rachel."

"What do you mean he's crazy to have Rachel?" Mark demanded.

"I mean he's crazy to have her on his arm."

"You mean he doesn't love her?"

"Mr. Billy don't know what love is, but he do know how profitable a beautiful woman like Miz Rachel can be, especially if her last name be D'Evereau."

Mark stared at his coffee cup, obviously battling with himself. "Does Rachel know what he's up to?"

"Sometimes I think she do, but I ain't sure. He's mighty helpful with that school of hers." Lovey turned toward the stove to hide the smile that was growing on her face. She knew Mark would rise to the bait.

"What school?" he demanded, just as Lovey knew he would.

"You's got a heap of catching up to do 'fore you can get back into the game. Miz Rachel, she start a school for kids who ain't doing good in the regular town school. Lots of them lives on these D'Evereau acres, and they comes to Miz Rachel's school for special tutoring. That Mr. Billy, he helping her fix up the old school building that belong to the church." She broke off her explanations and continued to busy herself with her cooking to give Mark time to think about what she was saying. Then she added, "It being Christmas, I wouldn't be surprised at what that man brings Miz Rachel for a Christmas present. And seeing how mad she is at you, she just might accept it."

Mark suddenly pushed his coffee cup away and stood up. "What time is dinner?"

"Oh, you best be here by 3:00."

"Is that when this Billy guy is coming? I want to be here before he arrives."

"Oh, he ain't coming to dinner," Lovey commented casually.

"Why not? I would think he wouldn't miss it."

"He sure wouldn't, if he'd been invited."

Mark took a few steps toward Lovey and stared down into her face trying to fathom what she was hinting at. Finally he gave up and demanded, "I thought Rachel was interested in him. Why didn't she invite him?"

"Cause Mr. Louis already here. You can't mix them two mens any more than you can mix oil and water. But one thing's for sure. That Mr. Billy gonna show up anyway. I feels it in my bones. So you get on home and fix yourself up real handsome."

"What's wrong with the way I look right now?"

"I ain't gonna waste my time answering that, Mr. Mark. You already seen Mr. Louis. You knows what he look like. And while I's on the subject of Mr. Louis. He be awful sweet to Miz Rachel.

You gotta quit being so ornery."

Mark stifled his desire to defend himself, sighed heavily and gave Lovey a hug. "Thanks, Lovey. What would I do without you?"

"Lose Miz Rachel again," Lovey responded bluntly as she turned to stir a pot on the stove. "Now get on home."

"I'm going," Mark said as he turned toward the door, "but I'll be back, and I'll be as charming and handsome as humanly possible."

After she heard the door close, Lovey murmured, "Thank you, Jesus," as she continued to work. "That's good he's comin' but I ain't fooled by that smile of his. There be something that boy ain't tellin' me, Lord. I ain't never seen him limping before." She looked up at the ceiling, "I know You knows, and You gonna tell me. It just be a matter of time."

Chapter 5

When Mark reached the front door of Belle St. Marie about 3:00, he noticed a car coming slowly up the drive. Eager to see Rachel before anyone else arrived, he tapped lightly on the heavy, old door, and without waiting, walked into the large entry hall and continued into the formal parlor. Immediately, he spotted Rachel standing by the fireplace looking at the blazing fire. Louis stood at her side with his arm draped lovingly across her shoulders.

Mark's temper flared at the sight of the man's hand on Rachel's shoulder, but he managed to rein his anger in. A loud knock on the front door echoed into the room, and when Rachel turned to go to the door, she saw Mark for the first time. Obviously startled, she stopped in her tracks as Mark waited anxiously for her reaction. When her eyes flashed with joy, he released his pent-up breath.

"I'm glad you came," she said.

"Me too," he answered, then grinned at her. "Very glad."

"I believe you have already met Louis." She nodded toward the other man.

Neither man spoke or moved. Once again a knock was heard from the front door. "Excuse me," Rachel said nervously, "I must answer the door." She hurried from the room, leaving the two rivals together. When she returned, Claire and Robert Carlyle, distant D'Evereau cousins, accompanied her, as well as a woman Mark had never met.

"Marge." Rachel turned to the unfamiliar woman. "May I present Mark Goodman, a long-time friend of mine and the nephew of Philippe. Mark, this is Marge Sutton, a retired school teacher, and a tremendous supporter of a school I've started." Turning to Louis, she quickly added, "And, of course, I think you all have met Louis Simone."

Mark winced as Robert clapped him on the shoulder and exclaimed, "Marge, you should have been at Philippe's early this morning. This guy gave us all the surprise of our lives."

"The best Christmas present we could have received," Claire insisted as she stepped forward and kissed Mark on the cheek. "We've missed you, cousin."

Mark hugged her before formally shaking hands with Marge.

Louis stood at a distance and watched these greetings, but when they had finished, he walked forward and kissed each lady on both cheeks as he murmured something in French. Shaking Robert's hand, Louis welcomed him to Belle St. Marie as if he were the host of the event, then turned to usher the ladies to chairs.

Annoyed by Louis' presumption, Mark listened as Louis began the conversation by commenting, "Mark is an internationally traveled journalist, Marge. I'm sure you'll want to hear all about his adventures."

"Indeed!" Marge exclaimed as she looked over her shoulder at Mark. "Why, I've seen your work in all the news magazines. Do come and sit down." She patted a place on the sofa next to her. "I want to hear all about your latest adventure."

Outmaneuvered by Louis, Mark took the seat offered to him and reluctantly answered Marge's persistent questions while he watched Rachel nervously hover close to the door. She looked positively relieved when she heard another knock at the door and was forced to hurry from the room to welcome her guests. Moments later she returned with Philippe and his administrative assistant, Lisette, whom Mark had met at the party. Andre Simone hurried in from the hallway, exclaiming, "Merry Christmas, everyone! Lovey is busy in the kitchen, so she appointed me the official collector of coats."

Andre began collecting coats, as another knock at the door was heard and Rachel turned back to the hall.

"I'll get it, My Dear," Andre insisted. "Go sit by Louis and let him take care of you. We must remember that you've been unwell this morning."

"Unwell?" Claire asked.

"It's nothing really, just a bit tired," Rachel assured her. Andre reappeared in the parlor with Fr. Tim, the pastor of St. Mary's Church, located on Belle St. Marie property, and Rachel hurried toward him.

"Merry Christmas!" she exclaimed as she gave him a casual hug. "I'm so glad you could join us." Smiling up at him warmly, she led him over to Mark. "Mark, I don't think you have met our local pastor. Fr. Tim, this is Mark Goodman, Philippe's nephew." The two men shook hands as Rachel added, "Fr. Tim has been my strongest advocate in the school I mentioned."

"And why wouldn't I be?" Fr. Tim asked. "You are giving the children an opportunity they've never had." He turned directly to Mark and added, "I'm very proud of her."

"We all are!" Andre exclaimed. "Aren't we, Louis?"

"Of course," Louis agreed as he walked to Rachel's side and kissed her on the cheek. "Very proud."

Rachel's face flashed crimson as she looked over his shoulder at Mark and their eyes met. "Please, everyone, make yourselves at home," she stammered, "while I check with Lovey to see how dinner is coming along." Avoiding Mark's eyes, she hurried out of the parlor.

When Rachel reached the kitchen, she was delighted to find that Alice had joined Lovey to help serve dinner. "Lovey, we need to set another place," she announced. You'll never guess who showed up."

"I's already set another place, Miz Rachel."

Rachel cocked her head for a second before concluding, "Oh, you must have seen Mark coming across the lawn."

"I seen him coming, Miz Rachel, but he wasn't on no lawn."

Rachel grinned at her, "You knew he would come, didn't you?"

"I knows Mr. Mark," Lovey chuckled.

"Where did you seat Mark at the table?"

"I put him just where he need to be," Lovey said mysteriously. Rachel knew better than to argue with her, but she suddenly remembered that Mark would not have one of the elegant place cards she had made earlier that week for her guests.

"Oh dear, Mark won't have a place card."

"I's already taken care of that, Miz Rachel. Mine don't look as fancy as yours, but I figure it will do okay. Now you go on into your guests and lead them into the dining room. Alice and I's ready to serve."

"Whatever you say, Lovey," Rachel agreed good-naturedly.

"And take a big breath before you goes anywhere," Lovey added. "You looks all worked up to me."

"I expect it ain't easy for her," Alice chuckled, "having both them men that love her in the same parlor."

Rachel blushed scarlet as Lovey turned on Alice. "For your information, Miz Rachel is used to heaps of suitors. Now dish up that gravy and put it in that silver piece I showed you and don't make no more comments about the family."

"Yes ma'am!" Alice grinned at Rachel before turning away. "Wish I was used to heaps of suitors," she added slyly.

"Get on back to your guests, Honey," Lovey softly ordered Rachel, "and leave everything in the Lord's hands. He ain't messed up nothing yet."

Rachel returned to the parlor, but before entering, she stood at the door and surveyed her guests. An unexpected but welcome contentment flowed through her as she looked from face to face. The room was filled with people she loved. Some were old friends and long-loved relatives, and several, like Marge and Fr. Tim, were new friends who had helped her recover from the pains of her past life in Texas and to start a new life in Louisiana. As she looked at each one, she paused and took joy in the uniqueness of each, until finally her eyes fell on Mark's face. He was listening to some story the loquacious Andre was telling, but when Rachel looked at him, he glanced away from Andre and met her gaze. Rachel's pulse quickened. She struggled to avoid revealing her feelings, but she could not drag her eyes from his. Mark is home! sang in her head. He's home!

Louis silenced her internal song when he came to her side and took her hand. Hastily Rachel announced far too loudly, "Dinner is served. Shall we gather in the dining room?" Before anyone else could react, Louis offered Rachel his arm; flustered, but unable to reject him, she accepted him as her escort and tried not to look at Mark.

When they reached the dining room, there was a chatty bustling in the room as each person looked for his or her place, and the gentlemen seated the ladies. Rachel had intentionally seated Philippe at the head of the table since he was the oldest male member of the D'Evereau family present. At the other end of the large table Rachel had placed herself. Louis pulled back her chair and seated her; then much to her surprise he seated himself directly to her right. For a moment Rachel was confused, for she remembered that she had placed Fr. Tim at her right. Hurriedly she glanced down the table until she found Mark seating himself close to the other end. Ah, she thought, Lovey's been up to some mischief. A gentle smile of amusement danced across her face as she realized that Lovey had condemned Mark to watching Rachel share the dinner with Louis and given him absolutely no chance to talk to Rachel himself.

When Lovey and Alice entered with silver containers of

food, Rachel gently tapped her crystal goblet with a silver spoon. "Fr. Tim," she said, "will you please bless the food?"

Rising from his chair, Fr. Tim prayed, "In the name of the Father, the Son and the Holy Spirit. Lord, we thank you for this opportunity to gather together in Christian fellowship on Your birthday. We thank You for the food You have provided for us and especially for all those who have worked to prepare it for us. Most of all we thank You for choosing to be born of a virgin into this sinful world so that we might have eternal life. We ask you to assist us in living out a life of virtue and commitment to You. We pray in the name of Jesus Christ, who lives and reigns with You and the Holy Spirit, one God for ever and ever. Amen."

"Amen!" Andre seconded as Fr. Tim seated himself again. Lovey and Alice began to serve the food, which was met with enthusiastic compliments, and separate conversations began around the table. Each time Lovey or Alice reached Rachel's place, Louis made a show of serving Rachel himself. Andre beamed at the two of them from his place at the head of the table, and Mark glowered from his.

As the dinner progressed, the conversation turned from appreciation of the food to various topics of interest to the guests. Philippe asked for an update on the school Rachel had started in the old school building at the Chapel.

"We now have over 30 students," Rachel answered.

"Wonderful!" Philippe responded as he turned to Mark and explained, "Rachel offers special classes after regular school hours to the kids around here who need tutoring. She's even managed to help some of them catch up on their work and move up to their normal grade in the public school."

"Aren't there plenty of government programs providing those services?" Mark asked.

"There are some programs," Rachel answered, "but they mostly help the children in town. The children who live out here in the woods have fallen through any safety net the government thinks it has established."

"And on top of that, they're receiving very little, if any parenting," Marge added. "Most of our students are living in old trailers and tumble-down shacks back in the woods just hoping that their mothers show up eventually and bring home a little food."

"I remember kids like that when I was growing up here," Mark admitted, "but I just assumed that they had benefitted from government programs and moved on up in society."

"I always made the same assumption, and when I returned to Belle St. Marie, it was quite a shock to find children here in such need." Rachel shook her head sadly.

"But things are improving now, thanks to everyone's efforts," Fr. Tim added. "Rachel and her staff are giving the students a new appreciation of their own God-given worth and a new belief in themselves. Their day-to-day lives are clearly better as well as their hopes for the future."

"Interesting," Mark observed. "Specifically how do you see the students' new understanding of themselves changing their day-to-day lives?"

"Spoken like a journalist!" Andre exclaimed.

"And why not?" Marge demanded. "He is a journalist. You just pipe down, Mr. Simone."

"Yes ma'am!" Andre agreed as everyone broke into laughter. "I do not want a school teacher after me."

When the guests were quiet again, Fr. Tim answered Mark's question. "As Philippe said, some of them have returned to the public school, and we have hopes that a few will go on to college. Others have been able to obtain the first real jobs of their lives, and they can now improve their financial status."

"Which in some cases means quite simply that they can now eat three meals a day," Marge interjected. "And that's no small accomplishment with many of these kids because they come from abject poverty."

"It is indeed no small accomplishment," Fr. Tim agreed.

"I, for one, can assure you that this is the most meaningful teaching I've ever done," Marge said. "I've never been so certain that I was changing young people's lives as I am in this school, and I feel so grateful to spend my retirement years teaching these children."

Claire spoke up. "I have been wondering: do you think our efforts at the school are producing a reduction in drug and alcohol abuse among our students?"

"We can't prove that statistically," Fr. Tim admitted, "but I have no doubt that we are having that effect. I know for a fact that I have been called to deal with fewer drug overdoses."

"I'm out of the loop here, Rachel," Mark admitted. "Exactly how did this school get started?"

"Quite accidentally, I assure you," Rachel laughed. "I ran into two truants hiding out in the woods one day last spring."

"Sassy and Chelsey," Marge added, "quite an interesting pair. Rachel began tutoring them."

"And bribing them with food," Rachel admitted. "I also took Lovey's advice and set up a point system where they could earn a way to buy clothes and things if they spent several hours each day studying with me."

"And from that beginning you managed to form a school?" Mark asked.

"The need was there," Marge answered for Rachel. "You have no idea how many students are roaming around avoiding the public schools."

"And it doesn't hurt that we bribe them!" Claire quipped and set off a round of laughter at the table.

"Whatever it takes," Fr. Tim insisted.

"As long as it does not endanger Rachel," Louis added gravely and brought the laughter to a halt.

"What do you mean, Louis?" Mark demanded. "How could this endanger Rachel?"

Louis coolly studied Mark for a moment as the whole table became shrouded in uncomfortable silence. "Those of us who have been here in the last year know that these are rough kids, especially the teenagers in the group."

"We've only had trouble with one girl, Louis!" Marge protested. "Don't blow it out of proportion."

"That one girl is not only badly behaved herself; she seems to attract violent behavior, Marge. You can't deny what's happened so far," Louis quietly responded.

"What has happened, Rachel?" Mark demanded.

"Nothing that needs to be discussed at Christmas Dinner," Rachel answered curtly. "Let's change the subject." She turned to Philippe and abruptly asked, "How is your bid for governor coming, Philippe?"

Caught off guard, Philippe hesitated before finally commenting, "It's going to be a tough fight, but with Lisette running my campaign, I feel sure I'll win."

"You've certainly got my vote," Marge assured him, jumping into the void. "I like everything you're saying about education, and if there's anything I can do to help you, just call me."

"Make a note of that, Lisette," Philippe lightly ordered his campaign manager. "We'll give the hard cases to Marge; no one would dare refuse her."

"I know I wouldn't," Andre laughed. "Her reputation as a tough disciplinarian precedes her, and I had my share of paddlings when I was a schoolboy. I don't crave any more."

"But you need some more," Marge teased, "the way you tell

those outlandishly exaggerated stories, and I'm just the teacher to give them to you."

Andre pretended to panic and looked down the table at Rachel. "Help, Rachel," he cried. "You know I'm innocent of all wrongdoing. Defend me!"

"Don't look to Rachel for help, Andre," Marge warned. "You know very well your tendency to stretch the truth is legendary, and that kind of prevarication will get you into big trouble with me."

"Prevarication! What a ridiculous accusation!" Andre turned to Fr. Tim. "I ask you, Fr. Tim, have you ever heard me stretch the truth even the tiniest bit?" When Fr. Tim declined to answer, Andre turned to the whole table and asked, "Has anyone here at this table ever heard me stretch the truth?"

All the guests at the table, except Mark and Louis, erupted in laughter. "In all the years I've known you, I've never heard you tell any story truthfully," Philippe answered for them all.

"And I'm sure none of us wants you to change a bit," Rachel said. "I'm also sure we're all too full for dessert right now, so why don't we adjourn to the music room and sing some Christmas carols and perhaps, just perhaps, we can talk Andre into spinning a few yarns."

"I might be persuaded...." Andre agreed as everyone slowly began to rise from the table, chatting with each other and making the usual comments about the excellence of the food. Louis was especially solicitous in helping Rachel rise from her chair, and as she moved toward the door to lead her guests across the hall into the music room, he placed his arm protectively around her waist and walked with her. His actions were noted by all the guests, many of whom gave each other sly nods and winks.

Philippe, however, was watching Mark, and when he saw Mark's dark expression, he slowed his pace to wait for him. For a few minutes they were left alone in the dining room, and Philippe hurriedly said, "Don't give up, my boy. He's a tough adversary, but Rachel has always loved you."

"I've only given up once in my life, Uncle, and I lost her. I've no plans to make that mistake a second time."

"Good! But you've got quite a fight on your hands, my boy. It's going to take some patience, and it's more complicated than you know."

"I presume you are referring to Billy what's-his-name," Mark muttered.

"Billy Ray Snyder. Well...let's just say that he's part of it."

"At least Rachel didn't invite him to Christmas dinner," Mark observed.

"How could she? Louis is here, and believe me, when you meet Billy Ray Snyder, you'll know that no one in her right mind would try to mix Billy Ray Snyder and Louis Simone. Billy Ray was born behind the barn, and Louis—well, you know his pedigree."

"And what about me, Uncle? What's my pedigree?"

"The best, my boy. Your saint of a mother, my sister, was a D'Evereau. Need I say more?"

When Mark and Philippe joined the others in the music room, they discovered that Andre had seated himself at the piano and was playing Christmas carols as he encouraged the others to gather around and sing. All the ladies began to move toward the piano, but when Rachel turned to join them, Louis gently took her arm and kept her close by his side. Mark's temper flared as he watched Louis holding Rachel close to him, peering down into her face and obviously speaking quite earnestly to her. Once again she tried to move away, but Louis did not release her. Mark fought his impulse to charge across the room to free Rachel from Louis and was relieved to hear a loud knock from the front door echo down the hall. Rachel left the room to answer the door.

When she returned to the music room, Rachel was accompanied by a man Mark had never met. Various members of the crowd greeted the newcomer enthusiastically, and Mark quickly understood that this was Billy Ray Snyder. He sized up his adversary. Handsome, no doubt about it. Perfectly dressed and groomed. Smooth, very smooth with the ladies, especially with Rachel. But there was something of the used car salesman in him. Having made his own assessment, Mark glanced at the faces of the various guests, making notes of their reactions to this newcomer to the group. Louis stared coldly at Billy, a fact that did not surprise Mark. The rest of the guests seemed happy enough at Billy's arrival except for one noticeable exception. Lisette looked even angrier than Louis, and when Billy Ray tried to shake hands with her, the room seemed to suddenly fill with acidic air. Lisette even went so far as to turn her back on Billy Ray and stalk away from him. The rest of the guests began to talk nervously, making an obvious attempt to cover over whatever problem existed between the two.

For the next hour Rachel's guests chatted amiably as they circulated around the room and out into the hall visiting with each other. Mark's trained reporter's eyes paid close attention.

He had no problem understanding Louis' resentment of Billy Ray; obviously they were competing for Rachel's favor. But why did Lisette so obviously hate Billy Ray? Mark noticed that every time Lisette and Billy Ray accidentally ended up in the same conversational group, a dramatic potential for explosion seemed to develop from nowhere, and either Rachel or Philippe hurriedly intervened to keep things calm.

Andre stopped playing, stood and pleaded with Rachel, "My Dear, you must come play for us. I am no more than the poorest substitute for my beloved Elinore, but you are just like your saintly Grandmere. Only your graceful touch on these ancient ivory keys can complete this Christmas Day in the true Belle St. Marie tradition. Please, My Dear, give this old man a bit of ethereal joy. "

Rachel, in spite of her exhaustion and the sudden longing for her Grandmere which his words brought, could not refuse such a request from the gallant old man.

Reluctantly she moved toward the piano, and Andre rose from the stool and graciously seated her before the ivory keys. When she began to play, her guests eagerly seated themselves and grew quiet to listen to her remarkable talent.

Rachel reverently played her Grandmere's favorite Christmas hymn, "Let All Mortal Flesh Keep Silent" and then with tears rolling down her cheeks, she played "Ave Maria" and "Panis Angelicus," just as her Grandmere had always played them on Christmas Day. Overwhelmed by her memories, she rose from the piano stool, and her eyes met Mark's. There she found tears that told her that he, too, was remembering her Grandmere, his beloved Miss Elinore, as he had always called her. Andre quickly stepped forward to embrace her, his own eyes also full. "Oh, My Dear, I remember too. Your Grandmere, my beloved Elinore, how she would have loved this day here at Belle St. Marie!"

"Yes, she would have loved it." Rachel desperately struggled to regain her composure as she wiped the streaming tears from her cheeks.

Mark stepped forward and took Rachel's face in his hands and tilted it up toward his. "She's here," he insisted. "She's here."

"Of course she is," Andre agreed as he handed Rachel an elegantly monogrammed linen handkerchief. "Now, we must take control of ourselves. No more tears. Tears are the last thing Elinore would want today. It is Christ's birthday, and you know how your grandmother felt about her Jesus."

"Indeed I do," Rachel murmured as a new flood of tears overwhelmed her at the thought of her Grandmere's faith. "I'm so sorry," Rachel addressed her guests between quiet sobs. "Please forgive me."

"Hush now, Rachel." Claire rose from the loveseat and came to Rachel's side to gather her into her arms. "We all understand; really we do."

"Of course we do," Lisette chimed in mechanically.

"What we need to do, Rachel, is to celebrate your grandmother's life," Billy Ray said, "and I have just the way to do it." He walked to Rachel's side and handed her a roll of large sheets of paper. "Merry Christmas, Rachel."

"What is this?" Rachel asked as she automatically accepted the roll of paper.

"Open it and see," Billy Ray urged excitedly. "Over here," he beckoned to the piano as he walked toward it and closed the lid. "Spread out the papers here, Rachel, and the rest of you gather around."

Curious, most of the other guests formed a semi-circle and peered over Rachel's shoulders as she opened the roll of papers and Billy Ray weighted down the corners with various decorative objects at hand.

Suddenly Rachel understood what the papers were. "These are plans for the renovation of the school building!" she exclaimed. "You said they wouldn't be finished until February."

"For you, Rachel, I will move mountains. They are finished, and here is the check to cover the costs," Billy Ray announced grandly as he handed Rachel a check.

"But, Billy Ray, we have to bid out the project," Rachel protested without looking at the check. "We don't know what it will cost, but it will definitely cost too much for one person to fund it."

"Look at the next page, Rachel, and you'll see that I've already bid out the project. I negotiated the best deal possible for us. I know exactly what it's going to cost, and my check will cover it."

"Oh, Billy Ray, this is far too expensive a project for you to pay for!" Rachel objected. "We must gather a group of contributors. Really, I insist. No one person can afford to fund this project."

"I can, and I have," Billy Ray replied firmly, "and furthermore, Rachel, you can't argue with me because this is your Christmas present—a Christmas present you can't refuse."

"It's simply too expensive, Billy Ray," Rachel protested.

"It's a small token of what you're worth to me, Rachel, and it's for the school. It's for the kids that need help. You can't refuse it." Obviously very pleased with himself, he leaned over and kissed Rachel lightly on the lips. He had managed to give Rachel an expensive Christmas present, and he had done it in the presence of both Louis and Mark.

Rachel struggled with herself for a moment; she did not want to be obligated to Billy Ray Snyder, but she really needed the old school building to be renovated. All the while many of her guests were encouraging her to accept it, but both Mark and Louis remained as silent as stones.

Finally Rachel closed her fingers tightly around the check. "For the children, Billy Ray," she said. "Thank you." She stood up on her tiptoes and lightly kissed him on the cheek. Many of the guests applauded and complimented Billy Ray's generosity. Eventually even Louis swallowed hard and managed to say, "Very generous, Snyder," and Mark added, "A great help to Rachel, I'm sure."

Rachel waited until everyone had settled down before asking, "Does anyone have a pen?"

"I do, My Dear," Andre spoke up as he reached into his coat pocket and produced a fountain pen for her.

"Thank you, Andre." Rachel smiled up at him as she accepted it. Then, much to everyone's surprise, especially Billy Ray's, she placed the check on the top of the piano, flipped it over and endorsed it. When she had finished, she turned to Fr. Tim and handed the check to him. "This money belongs to the school, I believe. And you are the logical overseer of the funds. I have endorsed the check to be deposited in the school fund."

Billy Ray's face fell as he heard her words, but all the guests broke into applause, and he quickly covered his disappointment. Mark grinned and laughed quietly.

Several hours later, after returning to the dining room and enjoying Lovey's famous pecan and chess pies for dessert, Rachel's guests began to leave, and Mark took the opportunity to slip back to the kitchen to ask a favor of Lovey. "After I've gone, will you place this small package on Rachel's pillow for me? It's her Christmas present. Of course, it's nothing to compare with what Billy Ray gave her—"

"I's sure she gonna love it just 'cause it come from you," Lovey encouraged him.

"I hope so," Mark answered solemnly.

"It been quite a day, ain't it? Lovey observed.

"Frankly, I didn't expect it to be so emotional. When Rachel began to play the piano, my determination to marry her and make a life together—well, it just doubled. I can't live without her, Lovey."

"I knows that, Mr. Mark. I knows."

"I guess I just took too much for granted thinking Rachel loves me the way I love her. It's not going to be nearly as easy to win Rachel's hand as I thought it would be. I've definitely got plenty of competition."

Lovey fell silent and her eyes glazed over as she thought deeply about Rachel.

Finally she spoke quietly, "It ain't gonna be Mr. Louis and Mr. Billy Ray that stand between you and Miz Rachel, Honey. It gonna be something else entirely, something much harder to defeat."

"Yeah, I sense that, but the truth is, I'm not sure I even know what I'm fighting here. Sometimes I catch Rachel looking at me with her eyes full of love, but then she shuts it off just like you shut off a faucet." He sighed heavily, "Boy, I really do miss Miss Elinore. When I came here as a boy after losing my mother and father, Miss Elinore became both mother and grandmother to me. I really need her counsel now."

"I misses her every day, but especially on days like today. It just don't seem right to have Christmas without Miz Elinore."

"You know, for just a moment, while Rachel was playing the piano, I felt like Miss Elinore was actually in the room with us."

"I knows what you mean. Sometimes I feels her presence so clearly that I just knows if I turns around, I's gonna see her, but when I does, she ain't there."

Both of them stood silently for a moment until Mark gathered Lovey into a big hug. "I'm so glad you're here," he said, and as he released her, he handed her a small box. "This is for you. Merry Christmas, Lovey."

"Oh, Mr. Mark, you shouldn't have gotten me nothing," Lovey protested as a big smile broke across her face, "but I sure is glad you did."

"Open it, Lovey," Mark insisted.

Lovey wiped her hands on a clean cloth and excitedly took the box to the table and sat down. "I ain't got no idea at all what this could be." Carefully she unwrapped the package, "I's sure going to keep this pretty paper. I's going to put it in my memory book."

Mark stood next to the table and watched happily as Lovey opened the box.

"Oh, Mr. Mark, it's the prettiest thing I ever seen!" Lovey exclaimed as she drew a silk scarf from the box. "And it's gonna match the new suit Miz Rachel give me for church just perfect." She stood up from the table and hugged him. "Oh, thank you, Mr. Mark. I loves it."

"And I love you, Lovey," he said as he hugged her back. "Now I better go out to the parlor before someone steals Rachel, but I'll see you tomorow, I'm sure, and we'll have a long visit. Don't forget about Rachel's gift, please," he reminded her as he started for the door.

"Don't you be worrying yourself about that now. I's gonna take care of everything," she assured him.

When Rachel finally went up to bed that evening, she left Andre and Louis sitting in front of a dying fire in the parlor. It was a good day, she thought as she opened her bedroom door. It wasn't perfect—how could it be without Grandmere and Justin here? She went over to the dressing table and picked up a picture of her Grandmother and her brother, Justin, taken when he was a teenager. Smiling down at them, she ran her finger across their faces, wishing fervently that she could touch them again. "I miss you," she whispered, "but I think somehow you know that." She sighed, put the picture down and walked over to the French doors, where she stood for a moment looking out at the dark pine forest. "And, of course, I wish Daddy could have stayed over for today, and I wish that Mother—oh, there's no reason to even think about that. Things are the way they are. Still it's been a good Christmas. I've come so far since Collins died, and now—now Mark is back. I still can hardly believe it." She sighed tiredly, then ordered herself, "To bed, Rachel, to bed. Stop thinking."

With those words she turned abruptly toward the closet and pulled out her robe and slippers, then went to the bureau for a nightgown. Quickly she slipped out the bedroom door into the hall and headed for the bathroom and a soak in the tub.

When she returned to her room, she still had not heard the men come upstairs. It feels good to have this space to myself, she thought, as she turned off the lamp on the bureau. I've enjoyed their company, but I'm glad that Andre is leaving in the morning for a few days and that Louis leaves the next day. Rachel moved to the side of the canopied bed and reaching for the coverlet, turned it back. It was then that she saw the small, simply wrapped gift.

"What's this?" she asked quietly as she picked it up. "How did it get here?"

She put it on the table next to the bed, pulled back the sheets, plumped up several pillows against the mahogany headboard and climbed into the bed to settle against the comfort of the down pillows. "Oh, this feels good," she sighed. She turned her head and looked at the gift for a few minutes. Mark—his name drifted through her mind, and she smiled. "It's from Mark, I know it is."

Still, she didn't reach for it. Instead she thought of the three men who were now in her life, and she laughed softly. Who would have thought I would ever have three men interested in me again? That's the sort of thing that belongs to my college days. Still, here they are, at least for the moment. But am I interested? I swore I would never marry again after living through the nightmares with Collins. I had no confidence left, certainly not the kind of confidence to build a successful marriage on. Rachel pulled a soft blanket up to her shoulders and snuggled down as her thoughts continued more positively. I am feeling different about myself now. I don't feel like I have to scramble all the time to achieve something so I'll like myself or so someone else will love me. That's good. Yes, that's very good. It took a long time and many hard knocks before I figured out that I'm okay, that God made me okay when He made me. But I wonder if I could hold on to that feeling if I married again. When you try to live with someone....well, you can't possibly please them all the time, so you start feeling so....so worthless. And they don't seem to mind helping you feel worthless either!

Oh! I don't want to think about all that now. It's Christmas, for heaven's sake. I don't need to sort out life right now; I just need to enjoy it. Rachel nodded vigorously at her conclusion, then suddenly giggled out loud. "Three men!" she whispered. "It's ridiculous, but then Billy Ray isn't really even in the running. He's just not interesting to me. But Louis is. We do have a lot in common. That beautiful first edition of Byron's poetry he gave me for Christmas last evening—that gift really sums up a great deal about the man who gave it. He's cultured and conservative, always analytical and balanced. Life with him would be comfortable, not just materialistically speaking, but emotionally speaking. With Louis, there's no drama. I don't need any more drama in my life! Still, could I ever really love him? I mean, really passionately love him? Could I ever love him the way a woman needs to love a man to marry him? I don't know. But then I don't know if I even want to love that way. It makes me too vulnerable.

"Maybe I don't want a man at all," Rachel whispered. "It's just too risky to love."

She glanced at the small gift on the table as her thoughts continued. Now Mark's back in my life. Bolting in just like he always did—so sure of himself, so determined to have what he wants, so stubborn, so passionate about everything, so— Rachel struggled for words to describe this man, Mark, whom she had known since she was nine. Finally she gave up.

She reached for the gift and slowly unwrapped it. Mark had obviously wrapped it himself. She untied the clumsy bow, and the paper fell away from a small, navy-blue hinged box. He hadn't bothered with tape, just covered the box with paper and tied a piece of ribbon around it. She smiled. "That's Mark," she whispered. Slowly she opened the clasp of the box and lifted the lid and quickly drew in her breath when she saw the contents. The box was lined with navy silk, and on the lustrous fabric sat an incredibly life-like, golden swan.

"How exquisite!" she exclaimed as she held it closer to the lamp. "Where on earth did he find such a thing? Who could make something this beautiful?" She stroked the head of the swan with her forefinger, then ran her finger down the swan's neck to its intricately carved and gilded feathers.

Slowly she removed it from the box and held it in her hand, watching the lamplight bounce off the perfectly etched feathers. It was surprisingly heavy, yet it appeared gracefully light enough to fly off her palm. She turned it in the light, mesmerized by the beams that reflected from its surface. After several moments it occurred to her to turn it over and search for the name of the artist. When she did, she found an inscription: "Always, totally yours. Mark"

Rachel settled back on the pillows as she held the golden swan next to her heart. "He knows," she whispered. "He knows what I need—totally reliable love, but does he have it to give to me?" She thought back, all the way back to their childhood. She saw him at twelve, at fifteen, at eighteen. She saw him in college and leaving for Viet Nam after he had refused to marry her. She saw him as the grown man he was now. He had never changed; he never would. He had been right that morning at the pond when he had said that people don't change. He was the same Mark he had always been. She knew him, really knew him, and he really knew her. He knew every one of her strengths, but they had never threatened him or driven him away. He knew every one of her failings, every one of her faults. But he loved her anyway.

Suddenly she felt frightened. Such a love from him required her to open herself totally to him, and she had never trusted any human being enough to do that. Her whole life had taught her that people liked her and then, with no apparent reason, disliked her. People came and held her close, but then they disappeared and left her alone. There was no constancy, no consistency in human love—that had been her experience. Yet, if she allowed herself to love Mark, she would have to believe the constancy she needed could, and, in fact, did exist. She would have to trust him.

Carefully she replaced the swan in the navy silk. It was hard to turn it loose, to let it leave her fingers. It was almost impossible to close the lid of the box. After she had forced herself to do so, she reached for the lamp switch and turned off the light. Seconds later she snatched the box back to herself and curled herself around it.

"How will I ever learn to love that way?" she asked the darkened room. "And do I want to?"

Chapter 6

Filled with a confusing blend of longing and anger, Mark wandered aimlessly through the woods on the property of Belle St. Marie the afternoon after Christmas Day. He wanted desperately to be with Rachel, but the fact of Louis and Andre's presence with her forced him to wait.

Demanding of himself as always, he was giving himself a thorough scolding about the way he had planned and conducted his return. Worse still, for the first time in all those months of surgeries and therapies, he was questioning his ability to win Rachel's hand. He chastised himself quietly.

"What a fool I am! Why did I think that all I had to do was show up in Louisiana and Rachel would fall into my arms?" He fell silent again as he walked further down the barely visible path in the woods, kicking pine cones out of his way. "But I know she loves me!" he insisted, then admitted under his breath, "I just don't know how much. Will her love be strong enough to conquer her fear? Does she love me enough to risk being hurt again?" His thoughts took the form of an argument with himself. I'm an idiot, part of his mind claimed. My love for her is so strong that I'm projecting it onto her.

But another part of his mind protested, I know she loves me!

Mark stopped short as a truly threatening thought emerged. She loved me in college too, but she married Collins Greyson rather than wait for me. I was right not to marry her, wasn't I? Why can't she see that I was protecting—not rejecting her? The truth is so obvious—I loved her too much to tie her to me and then march off to war. Why was that so hard for her to understand?

He tried for the hundredth time to put himself into the mind of Rachel at age nineteen, but once again his pride seemed to stop his reasoning. She dumped me, he thought bitterly, but why did she choose a lightweight like Collins? His money? His social position? She could have waited for me! Why didn't she just wait? Mark picked up a sizeable stick and threw it into the underbrush as hard as he could.

When he calmed down a bit, he argued with himself again. What difference does the past make anyway? Rachel isn't nineteen now. She's not a little girl or a teenager anymore. She's a grown, mature woman who has been through way too much pain. The real question that's bothering you, Mark Goodman, is: would she actually marry Louis to avoid a real relationship?

Mark winced at the thought, then stared up into the pine trees. "You don't know enough," he whispered. "There's something much deeper going on with Rachel. There always has been." He searched his mind, struggling to find a defining moment in his past relationship with Rachel that would explain her current behavior. There was some memory, something he needed to bring to the front of his mind, but for some reason he did not want to face it.

"What has really been going on all these years with Rachel?" he asked quietly, then grew silent as his thoughts continued. What's the deal with her? She didn't really marry Collins Greyson for his money or his social position or to get even with me. I knew that then, and I know it now. So why did she marry him? I have to understand her true motivation, because Louis Simone is just another Collins Greyson. What is it that makes her choose such men? It's not money; she's always had money. It can't be social prestige; she's always had that."

Quite suddenly Mark felt very uncomfortable as a nagging thought, a moment of truth, forced itself into his mind. "I know what it is," he whispered, "because I've had the same problem in my relationships. It's a fear; in fact, it's the very same fear that made me stop fighting for Rachel fifteen years ago. That made me choose to move out into the world and engage in superficial relationships. Sure, I had to go to Viet Nam, but I could have relentlessly stayed in touch with her. Instead, I gave up because she rejected me. She hurt me, and I quit. It's as simple as that."

The only difference between Rachel and me is that she stayed in Texas and engaged in one superficial relationship, her marriage to Collins Greyson. While I....well, there were quite a few women. Let's just leave it at that. The point is how can I expect Rachel to change something I couldn't change until I faced death?"

Mark suddenly felt so uncomfortable that he began to walk quickly through the woods, pushing his thoughts aside. However, some minutes later a physical obstruction stopped him from running from his feelings. That obstruction was the ornate, iron gate that marked the entrance into the D'Evereau family cemetery. Without intending to, Mark had brought himself to the burial site of his ancestors, including his own parents.

He sighed heavily as he opened the gate into the cemetery. I guess it's as good a time as any to visit my parents' graves, he thought, but he did not walk in the direction of their graves. Instead, his disturbing thoughts led him toward the grave of Miss Elinore. When he reached it, a great sadness washed through him as he stood next to her crypt and simply stared at her name engraved in the mossy marble.

Elinore DuBois D'Evereau. He certainly had not consciously set out on his walk with the intention of visiting the grave of Miss Elinore, but somehow his subconscious had brought him to the very spot where he needed to be.

He had always been able to speak openly about his feelings to this woman who had loved him like the mother he had lost and the grandmother he had never known. Their talks had enabled him to dig deeply into his psyche, to uproot any rank weed that threatened to spoil the crop of his life, to bring it to the surface, to the light of truth that Miss Elinore always projected. With her help he had always been able to sort things out. She never judged him. She never blamed him. He never felt any guilt or shame in her presence. Even as a teenage boy he had been able to tell her his thoughts and to feel the kind of receptive love that made it possible for him to know and like himself. And he was here now because once again he needed that love, as desperately as he had needed it as a boy, and he knew it.

He began to talk very softly. "I'm afraid, Miss Elinore. When I lay in that tent with that bullet lodged next to my spine, I was absolutely fearless in my ability to love, in my ability to expose myself. But now I'm here at Belle St. Marie, and it's finally possible to actually act on my feelings, and I find myself afraid again. I know that I lost my parents and I know that Rachel always had problems with hers, and I know that those experiences have shut us down emotionally in the past. But....but are we just helpless captives of our past?"

"That be up to you," a familiar voice answered.

Mark did not whirl around in surprise; instead he ducked his head and smiled. I should have expected this, he thought. It was inevitable. He raised his head, looked at the name "Elinore" engraved in the marble and smiled again before turning to look into the eyes of Lovey. "I should have known that Miss Elinore would bring you here to speak for her," he said quietly.

"I don't knows if I can speak for Miz Elinore, but I's got an idea of what she want to say to you. She want to say that whatever you's wrestling with, you don't got to wrestle alone. You's got God to help you. You's gonna have to make some daring choices, but you don't have to make them alone. Miz Elinore, she'd say it in more fancy words, but that be what she'd say."

"Yes, Lovey, I am sure she would mention God first, followed quickly by the word 'choice.' I just don't know how to translate her advice into the actions I need to take."

"You's skipping over the God part," Lovey observed. "Goin' straight to the action part."

Mark stared at the ground and said nothing.

"I brought these here flowers from the dining room table for Miz Elinore," Lovey suddenly changed the subject. "I missed her so much yesterday, and I felt so bad about not getting down here to visit her, but I's just getting old now and Christmas Day just be too much for me to handle." Slowly she walked to the head of the grave and placed a vase of evergreens and red roses next to the inscription. "She couldn't be with us for Christmas dinner," Lovey said sadly, "and I missed her."

"We all missed her," Mark agreed.

"No, not everyone. There was people there yesterday who never even knew Miz Elinore."

Mark felt a flash of anger. "I'm not sure she would have invited some of them," he snapped.

"Oh, she most likely would have invited them if they had no other place to go." Lovey smiled up at him. "But they sure wouldn't have left Belle St. Marie the same people they were when they come. Miz Elinore always seem to be able to change people into their best selves."

"Yes, she did have a way of transforming people," Mark agreed. "I guess they're all still at the house. All Rachel's guests, I mean."

"You means Mr. Andre and Mr. Louis, and yes, they still be up there, but Mr. Andre, he going to leave in the morning to go visit some friends. That would've left just Mr. Louis, but Mr. Billy Ray, he call and say he coming over in the morning to go down to the school building with Miz Rachel. Something about the bids he gotta check with her. If you wants to know what I think, I think he don't want to leave Miz Rachel alone with Mr. Louis."

"Sounds like him."

The kindly housekeeper turned to him. "They's all gonna be gone day after tomorrow," she encouraged, "and Miz Rachel, she gonna be by herself."

"They're leaving so early?"

"Oh, just for a few days. They be back for New Year's Eve." When Mark made no response, Lovey added, "I figure a couple of days be long enough for anything to happen, wouldn't you say, Mr. Mark?"

Mark grinned at her. "I hope so, Lovey." Then he grew serious. "I've been thinking about Rachel a lot, and the thing is, I've been gone a long time, and I don't even know all the things she has lived through."

"Do you know you love her?"

"Absolutely. During all these years my feelings have not changed one bit, and I know they never will, but maybe Rachel and I are doomed to always be separated by circumstances."

"Circumstances don't control the world, Honey. God controls the world. But he ain't gonna drop Miz Rachel in your lap. He gonna expect you to do your part, and if you really wants her—"

"I've always wanted her," Mark interrupted. "No matter how many miles I've traveled or how many experiences I've had, Rachel has never been off my mind. I've known some other women, but it was never like what I feel for Rachel."

"Then you got your work cut out for you, ain't you? And that work begins on your knees. Ain't no other way."

"I know, but I've got to be smarter about it this time, and that means I need more information about Rachel."

"You need more information about yourself and Miz Rachel," Lovey concluded as she turned and walked toward a stone bench.

Mark stumbled slightly as he turned to follow her. Lovey looked back at him with a question in her eyes, but she said nothing. As they both settled on the bench, Mark asked hurriedly, "Will you tell me more about Rachel since she came back here? What was she like right after her husband was killed in the car wreck?"

"Well, it seem like everything that ever gone wrong in Miz Rachel's life came to the surface. All the bad things that ever happened to her had to come out, or she wasn't gonna be able to go on living."

"What bad things, Lovey? I know her husband was a drunk, a wealthy drunk, but still a drunk."

"Yes sir, he sure was, but I think Miz Rachel's troubles started long before Mr. Collins come into her life. You remember how upset she used to be every time she come here at the beginning of the summer?"

"Yes, I do. I couldn't understand her at all; she was mad at everybody for no reason I could see."

"That pretty well says it," Lovey agreed. "And I figure she had a right to be. Back in Texas her daddy and her mama, they was always fighting over everything, acting like they hate each other and hate Miz Rachel, too."

"That marriage must have been the mistake of the century."

"Well, it sure didn't help Miz Rachel any 'cause she always get blamed for her mama being upset. Then there was that Mammy Cassie person." Lovey shook her head in disgust.

"Yes, I vaguely remember Rachel talking about her. She really hated that woman."

"She had good reason, Mr. Mark. That be the meanest woman that ever lived. I can't even think about her without my blood boiling."

"As I remember it, she was pretty much in charge of taking care of Rachel, wasn't she?"

"Yes sir, Miz Rachel's mama just let Mammy Cassie raise her—if you can call what she did raising a child."

"Did you ever meet Mammy Cassie?"

"No, I ain't ever met her, but there was plenty of times when I threatened to go over to Texas and give that woman what for, but Miz Elinore she say I ain't gonna help Miz Rachel by stirring that pot. She say the best thing we can do for Miz Rachel is to love her while she's here, so that's what we done. We spent three months trying to make her feel like she's worth something after they spent nine months telling her she's not."

Mark sat silently for a few moments and let his mind wander back to the summers when Rachel arrived from Texas. "What I remember most about the first week or so of Rachel's visits was that there was one expression she used constantly. No matter what anyone said to her, she answered 'I don't care!' She was totally belligerent about everything."

"Oh, she cared; she cared a lot. But she been through so many months of hurts and she buried them hurts so deep 'cause there wasn't anything else she could do with them. If she complained or fought back, her mama got sick, had one of them headaches of hers. Then her father got mad at Rachel, and Mammy Cassie tell her one more time that she be a devil chile." Lovey fell silent for a moment, then suddenly blurted out, "I tell you I could strangle that woman! She still alive, and I ain't too old to do it yet."

Mark put his arm around Lovey's shoulders and gave her a small hug. "Okay, Lovey, okay. You better calm down now. I've got the picture."

"I ain't in any mood to calm down, Mr. Mark. I gets fighting mad when I think about it. It always take Miz Elinore a couple of weeks to get that baby girl to accept the love that was here for her. And I tell you it just about broke Miz Elinore's heart and mine to send her back to Texas at the end of the summer. We knows what she got to go through before she's here again."

"And that went on for years," Mark reflected. "I remember when she came to college as a freshman. She was really wild; in fact, she was self-destructive."

"It be a good thing that you was there and was older than her 'cause at least she listen to you. Miz Elinore and you be the only two people Miz Rachel ever listened to."

"She always listened to you, Lovey, and I know she listens to you now."

"Well, I know she been listening to me in the last year 'cause I seen her doing some changing. Course, truth is, she just been listening to her Grandmere. I's just been saying what Miz Elinore would say if she be here."

"What has happened to Rachel since she came back? Did you even know she was coming back?"

"Mercy no! All I knowed was that the house been all closed up for years, but one night something woke me up and told me to go round to the front verandah. When I did, there was Miz Rachel leaning against one of the pillars, all slumped over like. She looked terrible, and I didn't have no idea what was wrong with her. I just got her in the house, and I got her to bed, and believe you me, as soon as I could get myself to the telephone, I got her daddy on the line. I figured if anybody know what Miz Rachel been through, it got to be Mr. Jack."

"I'm surprised that Jack knew anything. I thought Rachel had quit talking to him after her brother was killed in Vietnam. Didn't she blame Jack for his death?"

"She sure did, and I can't say as I blame her. And you's

right; as soon as Mr. Justin was laid in the ground in the cemetery here, she turned her back and walked away from her family. Of course, Miz Elinore been gone home to the Lord about a year or so at that time, so Miz Rachel couldn't turn to her. "

"So why did you call Jack after you found Rachel here?"

"I called Miz Rachel's house in Dallas, but there weren't nobody there. Then I called Mr. Jack 'cause there weren't anybody else to call. That's when I found out about Mr. Collins being dead and Miz Rachel being hurt."

"Rachel was hurt?" Mark's heart began to race. "You never wrote me anything about Rachel being hurt. Was she in the car with Collins when he had the accident?"

Lovey fell silent, and tears welled up in her eyes.

"Lovey," Mark prodded her to go on, "how did Rachel get hurt?"

"That Mr. Collins, he hit Miz Rachel and knock her down, and she hit her head on something and split it open. When she woke up in the hospital, she found out that Mr. Collins was dead."

Mark lowered his head into his hands, gritted his teeth and said nothing.

"The hospital people, somehow they find out about Mr. Jack and call him. He come to Dallas and help Miz Rachel bury Mr. Collins. Then he took Miz Rachel home to East Texas."

"I knew Collins was a drunk, but I never knew it was as bad as that," Mark muttered.

"Didn't nobody know what Miz Rachel was putting up with all them years, but after she got here, she just couldn't keep it inside any longer. For the first couple of months, all she done was talk and talk about the past. Then she sleep some and wake up and talk some more. I tell you, Mr. Mark, the things I heard about that Mr. Collins! If he wasn't already dead, I would've gone to Dallas and killed him myself. He didn't have no right to treat Miz Rachel that way. All them women he was involved with, and all that drinking. He didn't have no right!"

"No, Lovey, he didn't." Mark's chest tightened with anger. "I just wish....well, I wish I'd stayed in touch with her. How did she get back here?"

"Well, her Daddy, he took her home to East Texas, but she just run into the same mess she grew up in, but this time she be a grown woman, so she just get up in the middle of the night and drive herself over here. The Lord, He brought her over here. I's sure of it, Mr. Mark."

"I'm sure you're right, Lovey. She must have found some answers here at Belle St. Marie, because she seems so much happier now."

"She did, she surely did. She found out where her worth come from, and that be the one thing Miz Rachel need to know more than anything else. She need to find out that none of the bad things that been said to her or done to her have anything to do with who she is or what she worth. Miz Elinore, she tried to teach Miz Rachel that every summer, but it seem like Miz Rachel, she got to be half dead before she can begin to learn the truth about herself."

Mark squirmed on the bench, then folded his arms tightly across his chest. "Half dead," he choked the words out. "Yes....sometimes that's what it takes."

Lovey peered up at him intently and waited for him to go on, but he cleared his throat, changed directions and asked a question. "So she changed her view of herself, is that what you're saying?"

"Yes, sir."

"How did she do that?"

"Miz Rachel, she always had plenty of courage. You know that. The trouble was, she just always used that courage to fight off the world. But when she come here, she be desperate enough to learn and to make new choices, no matter how hard they be."

Mark thought about Lovey's words, but they weren't enough of an explanation for him to believe in. "There has to be more to it, Lovey. You must have played a bigger part than you're giving yourself credit for. What did you say to her?"

"I just told her that her worth come from God, that she was worthy the minute He thought of her."

"But that's exactly what her grandmother told her all of her life," Mark protested, "and her words seemed to just bounce off Rachel."

"I think that be true 'cause Miz Rachel weren't down low enough in her life to hear it. She weren't ready to give up her anger."

"You mean at her mother and Mammy Cassie?"

"Oh, she was plenty mad at them, but I think she was mostly mad at her daddy."

"Why Jack? What had he done?"

"I think it was more what he hadn't done." Lovey paused to think about her own words, then nodded. "Yes, I think that's what it was. Anyway, she wouldn't let him come over here, but he finally showed up anyway, and they had a big fight. It was something to hear, I tell you, but it seemed to clear the air between them. Then Rachel start seeing that he was just another human being who made a lot of mistakes that he was sorry for, and she start forgiving him. Once she was on that road, she just kept going, and she forgave Mr. Collins for what he done."

"But exactly how did she do that?" Mark asked earnestly. "I need to know."

Lovey studied his face for a minute before commenting, "I think you does need to know, Mr. Mark, 'cause you needs to do some forgiving too. But you's gonna have to ask Miz Rachel about a lot of this 'cause it happened inside of her, and I only know about it from her talking. She be the only one who can tell you what was really going on inside her. I can tell you one thing, Mr. Mark, you be sure and ask Miz Rachel about them diaries she found in the attic."

"Diaries? What diaries?"

"She found diaries dating back before the War Between the States, and they spoke powerful to Miz Rachel. You be sure and ask her about those diaries, and you ask her about them black girls she run into in the woods; you know, the ones they was talking about at the table yesterday."

"Before Louis shut down the conversation."

"He don't like Miz Rachel working with them kids at the school. He don't seem to know how good it is for her."

"Or maybe he doesn't care," Mark commented bitterly.

"All I knows is he be the kinda man gonna make everything about himself. He ain't good for Miz Rachel."

"Lovey, something else came up at the table yesterday, something I need to know about. Louis said Rachel's students are dangerous. What's the story there?"

"You remember Garth Gunner?"

"The man who ran down Miss Elinore. Of course, I do. He was lucky the Sheriff caught him before I did."

"Well, they let him out of prison, and he come right back here and done all kinds of meanness. Mr. Jack come over from Texas, and he got a search party up, but Gunner already gone to South Carolina, so they thought things was okay. But soon as they was gone, Gunner come back and attack one of Miz Rachel's students."

"What did Rachel do?"

"Miz Rachel, she just exploded. She'd come so far, Mr. Mark. She'd forgiven all them people, and she was feeling good about herself, and she was giving herself to help them students. Things was going real well for Miz Rachel. Then that Gunner come back and hurt one of her students real bad. I thought she was going to lose her mind. I thought she was going to kill him."

"Kill him? Rachel couldn't kill anyone," Mark protested. "She might say she was going to, but—"

"I tell you she was determined on vengeance, Mr. Mark," Lovey interrupted, and her voice rose as she remembered the intensity of that evening. "She took a rifle out of the closet, and she was gonna shoot that Garth Gunner to get even with him for killing her Grandmere and for attacking her student!" Suddenly Lovey fell silent, and Mark watched in amazement as a peaceful smile covered her face and her whole body relaxed. To Mark she seemed to have gone to another place in her mind.

Unwilling to shake Lovey's peace, but desperate for answers, he gently took the old woman's hand in his, "Lovey," Mark asked quietly. "What happened next? What did Rachel do, Lovey? You must tell me; I need to know."

"Something miraculous happened, Mr. Mark. When Miz Rachel had a chance to take vengeance on that awful man, she couldn't do it."

"I told you Rachel couldn't kill," Mark said flatly.

"It wasn't that, Mr. Mark. I think when she left the house with that rifle, she was so mad she could've killed that man, but God stopped her."

"I don't understand, Lovey," Mark confessed.

"I knows you don't. You see, God made her understand that He loved Gunner just like He loved her, in spite of all the bad things Gunner done. It was a miracle, I tell you. It was a miracle."

"I still don't understand, Lovey."

"I knows you don't, honey. Things like I's talking about you just got to experience. You ain't ever gonna understand them because we ain't got what it takes to understand God. All I knows is He give Miz Rachel a special grace that evening 'cause He make her understand how much He love her, and He make her know that she's worth something 'cause of His love. All her life she been going about it the wrong way. She been trying to get good enough to be worth something, but God showed her she never needed to do any of that stuff. Ain't nothing she ever done or ever could do gonna make her worthy or unworthy. God's love made her worthy from the very first second he thought of her."

Mark waited for Lovey to go on, but she said no more, so he prompted her. "And dealing with Garth Gunner somehow made

Rachel understand these things you're talking about?"

"Somehow it did, Mr. Mark."

"I'm totally confused," Mark admitted. "I just don't get the connection."

"That's the best way I can say it. You best talk to Miz Rachel; I imagine she can say it better."

"If I can get her to talk to me, really talk to me."

Lovey patted him on the knee as she encouraged him. "She gonna talk to you. You just wait till all this company be gone. Miz Rachel got her mind scattered in too many directions right now, but I know she loves you."

"Yes, she loves me, but is she in love with me? Maybe I waited too long. Now Rachel's got Louis and Billy Ray Snyder both after her."

"Miz Rachel ain't gonna marry Billy Ray Snyder. I can tell you that for certain sure."

"But what about Louis?"

"I ain't so sure about him," Lovey admitted. "He got a lot to offer Miz Rachel, but so does you."

"I just hope she sees it that way."

"Miz Rachel ain't ready to get married again, so you got a little bit of time." Lovey stopped speaking and watched his face intently. When she saw the despair he felt displayed across his handsome features, she intentionally changed the subject. "You ain't told me nothing about yourself. I knows you been traveling all over the world 'cause I seen your news stories in all the magazines. I even seen you on the TV news. But what's been happening inside you? That's what I want to know."

"A lot of years have passed, Lovey. It's kind of hard to sum it all up in a few words. In retrospect, it seems like I've just been running away and reaching for the wrong things. I guess I've kind of been on the same journey Rachel has, except I just ran further."

He paused and waited for Lovey to say something that would prevent him from more self-examination. She was silent.

"The truth is, I've been living hard and fast, Lovey, just trying to block out the pains of my life—the death of my parents, losing Miss Elinore—most of all, losing Rachel. I've been angry all these years about those losses, and I figured if I couldn't have what I wanted here in Louisiana, I'd go to the end of the world and find something I wanted more. The trouble is, I never could find anyone who meant as much to me as Rachel does."

"But something made you come home, Mr. Mark. Is it the

same thing that make you limp when ain't nobody looking?"

Mark sighed heavily. "I never could put anything over on you, Lovey."

"Best just tell me, Honey. I ain't leaving till you do. What hurt you?"

"A bullet…..a bullet from nowhere. I never even knew who fired it, but suddenly I was being dragged down a dirty street by my partner as pain tore through me so viciously I couldn't stay conscious. Finally I woke up in a steamy room, and I couldn't move. The medics told me there was a bullet in my back, and it was lodged so close to my spine that I had no chance of ever walking again. The most they could hope for was to try to get me to a good hospital where my life could be saved. So I decided that I just wanted to die."

"That don't sound like you, Mr. Mark. It don't sound like you to just give up."

"Actually, Lovey, it was the second time in my life I wanted to die. After my parents were killed in the car wreck, I wanted to die. I came so close to diving into the swamp and letting it close over my head." Mark hesitated, then added quickly, "but obviously I didn't."

"Why not?"

"It all sounds so crazy, but when I was about to dive into that black water, a white swan swooped down onto the water, and right before my eyes, it turned golden. I know, I know; it sounds impossible. I thought at the time I was crazy, but I felt so peaceful after I saw that swan…. I can't explain it."

"Sounds like God to me. That's what He does, Mr. Mark. He always give us what we needs, and at that time in your life you needed something you could see, something real strange-like that you wouldn't forget. Sounds to me like God was just reminding you that He was in charge of the world and could make anything happen, and He love you enough to give you what you gonna pay attention to."

"I didn't understand any of that then, Lovey. All I knew was that I felt at peace. I guess I was afraid I was crazy, so I told Miss Elinore about it. She basically said not to try to reason it out; it was just God's way of proving His presence. She called it 'a glimpse of splendor.' I never forgot that phrase. I felt better about my sanity. I can't say I understood what had happened, but I never forgot it."

"No, sir. I guess you didn't." Both fell silent as they considered the supernatural event.

"You know, Lovey, after I grew up, when I was in a dangerous situation, like when I was in Viet Nam, I would think of that swan turning golden, and I knew I wasn't really on my own in this world. There really was—and is—a power greater than me, and He really does have control of this world. But I didn't want to embrace Him. Isn't that strange?"

"You ain't no different from the rest of us, Mr. Mark. You just didn't want to give yourself away—not even to God."

"I guess that's it. But as I went around the world as a journalist, I saw what horrors people can cause, and I also saw God at work in the worst possible situations. We humans produce unspeakable situations because of our greed and hatreds, but God still remains with us. I don't understand how He could possibly love us so much."

"He made us, so as He could love us," Lovey said serenely. After a moment of silence between them, she added, "You's changed, Mr. Mark."

"I have. I don't know how to explain it, but when I was lying in that tent after I was shot, it just occurred to me, 'Mark, you've got to decide what you believe now because you may not make it this time. Either God is real, or He's not.' Well, I decided He's real. Then I thought, 'if He's God, He's got to be all powerful, and I better get myself in line with Him because I am sure weak and maybe my life is about to end.' Then I felt panicky because I didn't know exactly how to get myself in line with God. It was then that your letter arrived."

"Thank you, Jesus," Lovey murmured. "Thank you."

"Lovey, I have to tell you—" He stopped as tears filled his eyes, and he found it hard to speak. "There's no way that letter could have found me—no way at all—except God knew where I was. When my buddy told me I had a letter from somebody named Lovey in Louisiana, in that instant I knew that God loved me. And I remembered your way to God. I remembered Miss Elinore's way. I remembered all your talk about Jesus being the connection to God, and suddenly I knew, really knew who Jesus was, and I knew I needed Him. I had let so many angry years stand in the way!"

"We all got hard things in our lives, Mr. Mark, and maybe it's good we do 'cause they be the way we learn we ain't gods ourselves. Once we learn that, we's open to accepting the God who loves us more than we can imagine."

"The thing is, Lovey, I don't know what to do now. Back then I knew that I had to throw all my energy into getting well and pray that God would help me. And He did! It really is a miracle that I'm here with you, but I don't know what to do now."

"You just gotta trust God. You can trust Him, you know—"

Mark stood up suddenly and limped away from the bench a few paces. Nervously he ran his fingers through his hair and shifted his weight from one foot to the other. Finally, his voice full of tension, he confessed, "Lovey, I'm worried about everything. I don't know who I am anymore. I don't even know if I'm a journalist any more. I don't know if I ever want to go back out on a story. I've had too many years of war zones, but if I'm not a journalist, what am I? All I know for sure is that I love Rachel, but now that I'm back, I don't know if I can get her to marry me. And if I can't win Rachel, how can I build a life without her?"

Lovey stood up, walked to his side, and began to gently rub his back just as she had done when he was a boy. "You's rushing things, Mr. Mark. You's just cramming things all together just like you did when you was a boy. There ain't no need to hurry things so. Miz Rachel ain't going nowhere."

"I can't stand to lose her again, Lovey! The thought of it is driving me crazy, but there's more. I don't know who I am professionally."

"Answer me one question. Is your job or Miz Rachel more important?"

"Rachel, without a doubt. I now understand that life isn't about climbing some ladder of success. It's about love and growing inside, you know, in your heart, your spirit."

"Then you need to slow down and get quiet enough to hear God, and you need to talk to Miz Rachel. And don't you hold back, Mr. Mark. You tell her what you been learning about God. Miz Rachel been on a spiritual journey too, and if God wants you two to marry, he will bring your spiritual journeys together somehow, some time."

"I hope so, Lovey. I hope so. I know you're a wise woman, and I know I'm confused, so I'm going to bank on your experience with life. I'll talk to Rachel. I just hope I can get her to open up and show herself. I hope I can do the same."

"Things is gonna be better between you two after her company leave. And that reminds me, I better get on home 'cause it's getting close to suppertime, and they's gonna be some hungry men waiting for me."

"Thanks for talking to me, Lovey." Mark put his arms

around the elderly woman and hugged her gently.

"I loves to talk to you, Mr. Mark. I hopes you ain't gonna go off anywhere."

"I'm not going anywhere without Rachel."

Lovey laughed. "Then you's gonna be here a while, 'cause Miz Rachel can be real hard-headed." As Lovey headed out of the gate, she called back over her shoulder, "And so can you." Then she stopped and turned back to him. "Mr. Mark," she said quietly, "you can get me to tell you all kinds of stuff about Miz Rachel, but you ain't gonna fix nothing without God's help. This be a real good place and a real good time to sit down and listen up."

Mark nodded his agreement and turned back to the bench.

Chapter 7

The next morning, Mark stood on the verandah at his Uncle Philippe's house and stared gloomily at the dismal weather. The sun had risen over an hour earlier, but it still had not managed to evaporate the late December ground fog that draped itself over the pines and prevented Mark from seeing past the front lawn of his Uncle's house. Standing on the verandah, Mark felt that he, too, was draped in a fog. His talk with Lovey the afternoon before had stirred up a bitter stew of thoughts that had simmered on the front burner of his mind throughout the night, so he had slept little.

Foremost on his mind was his anguish about the years of suffering that Rachel had endured in her marriage. About three o'clock in the morning, he had finally confessed to himself and to God that he had never cared enough about Rachel's sufferings. He had been so embittered by her choice of Collins over him that he had silently and repeatedly said to himself, "she deserves what she gets." After talking to Lovey, however, he realized that he had had no real idea just how painful life had been for Rachel. Even in the light of morning, he could not tolerate visualizing Rachel unconscious on the floor with a gash in her head. He shuddered any time the image approached his mind, and when the shudders ended he shook himself, as if somehow that violent motion would ward it off.

"That's history," he muttered for what must have been the hundredth time. "You can't change it; it's over." He thought a minute longer, then admitted to himself silently: I'm still being totally selfish. I'm worried that what Collins did to her will impact the way she feels about any man now. It has to. Maybe that's why she's interested in Louis. He's totally controlled; I can't imagine him ever stumbling in life. He'll definitely take care of Rachel; he would consider it a dishonor and a blotch on his family name not to. Maybe she knows that about him—

"Oh, there you are, my boy!" Philippe exclaimed as he spotted Mark on the verandah. "I've been looking for you all over the house."

"What's on your mind?" Mark asked as he continued staring absent-mindedly out at the landscape.

"I want to talk to you about your future, my boy," Philippe answered cheerily, obviously expecting to spark a keen interest in his nephew. Mark, his back still turned to his uncle, remained lost in his own thoughts and made no reply. "Mark, are you listening to me? I said I want to talk about your future."

"What future?" Mark sighed tiredly and finally turned to face Philippe.

"Hmmm...." Philippe observed him a few seconds. "Sounds like woman trouble to me. Come on over here and sit down, Mark." Philippe walked over to a wicker chair, sat down, and motioned to a chair facing him. "I hadn't planned on talking about Rachel, but if you want—"

"I don't want to talk about Rachel," Mark said abruptly.

"Okay," Philippe agreed. "Whatever you say. Let's talk about politics then. Politics and your future, to be specific."

"Politics and my future have nothing in common."

"I don't agree." Philippe once again beckoned to the chair opposite him. "Just sit down, my boy. I need your help."

Mark settled reluctantly into the chair. "My help? What's up?"

"I'll make it short and sweet, Mark. I want you to run my public relations campaign."

"Don't you already have someone doing that?" Mark asked suspiciously.

"No one with your expertise, my boy," Philippe answered, then paused. When he went on, he was obviously choosing his words carefully. "They do the best they can, but frankly, my whole public relations program is just patched together. I need your level of sophistication."

Mark studied him a moment before answering, "I appreciate the offer, but I think you're just trying to manufacture a job for me."

"Not at all, my boy," Philippe insisted. "Sure, I would like for you to stay around, but frankly, I don't have the money to manufacture a job for anyone. I really need your help, Mark."

"You always win hands down," Mark observed. "Why

would this race be any different?"

"I'm going after bigger fish this time." Philippe grew more agitated before adding, "The governor's chair is not so easy to attain, you know, and frankly, I'm not running as far ahead in the polls as I'd like to be."

"I'm sure your people have plans to remedy that," Mark responded disinterestedly.

"Yes, but will I like the plans?"

"What do you mean? Don't you trust them?"

Philippe stood, turned away from Mark and walked toward the edge of the verandah before answering. "They are good politician makers, and they're well paid to control who becomes governor."

"Paid by whom?" Mark asked.

"The party, of course. And there's the rub—"

Mark stared at his uncle for a long, silent moment. An unidentifiable anxiety had flared in him, as he sensed his uncle was in some kind of danger. He leaned forward in his chair. "Get specific, Uncle," Mark demanded. "What's really going on?"

Philippe remained evasive, "They aren't family, Mark, if you know what I mean." When Mark said nothing, Philippe blurted out, "I'm not even sure they're Louisiana."

Mark stood and walked to his uncle's side so he could see his face. "I think I know what you mean by 'family,'" he said quietly, "but what do you mean by 'Louisiana'?"

"They don't care about the people around here—"

"Do you?" Mark demanded.

Philippe flushed as he studied his nephew for a long minute. Silently he returned to his chair and pretended to relax. When he spoke, his voice was conciliatory. "I know we've had our differences—deep differences." He waited for Mark to respond, but Mark said nothing, so he continued. "I know what you think of me, but I am a D'Evereau. There are some lines I won't cross."

"Such as?" Mark kept his voice cold.

"I don't sell out the people. I don't sell out the land. I need you, Mark. I make no bones about it. I need you. Something's wrong—" Suddenly the phone rang inside the house. "I've got to take that call," Philippe said as he rose hurriedly from his chair. "Don't go away, Mark. I'll be back."

Mark waited, his curiosity aroused. He had never been particularly close to his uncle. There had even been times when he disliked him immensely, and he wasn't at all sure about his uncle's ethics on many matters. He was sure, however, that his uncle would never disgrace the D'Evereau name. Also, there was the matter of the land. Mark stared out at some of the acres of D'Evereau land, knowing that its vastness was beyond anything he could see. He sat back down to wait, contemplating. We've been here two centuries, and my ancestors have paid for this land with their blood more than once. I know what that means to me, and it must mean even more to my uncle.

Philippe hurried back out the front door onto the verandah and sat down. Immediately he leaned forward, his face tense. "Will you help me, Mark?" he asked point blank.

"I'll think about it." Mark conceded. "If it's for the family, if it's for the land, I'll think about it."

Philippe settled back into his chair and sighed heavily. "Thank you, boy. Thank you." The two men sat silently, each thinking his own thoughts. Then suddenly Philippe observed, "It won't hurt your future either, you know."

"What do you mean?" Mark asked.

"You came back for Rachel, didn't you?"

"Yes," Mark admitted. "That's the only reason I'm here."

"I hope you know you've got quite a race on your hands. That Louis has been training for the job of Rachel's husband all his life. He's a real thoroughbred, that one. Sophisticated, aristocratic, lots of old money."

"Old money?" Mark asked. "I thought they were just entrepreneurs in the piano business. I mean, Andre was always coming to Belle St. Marie to tune Miss Elinore's piano."

"Don't you believe it!" Philippe laughed. "Andre came to Belle St. Marie because he loved Elinore and he couldn't stay away from her."

Mark's temper flared. "Are you suggesting—" He stopped himself, then commented as coolly as possible, "Miss Elinore would never—"

"No, no, of course not," Philippe agreed hurriedly. "Elinore was a saint all her life. But she did grow up with Andre in New Orleans, and her father always planned for her to marry him."

"He planned for her to marry a piano tuner? You've got to be wrong."

"Pianos are just Andre's little hobby. Something to keep himself busy. He never needed to work; the Simone family has been in New Orleans since before the American Revolution, and they had the good sense to move much of their wealth to France before the Civil War. Make no bones about it, Mark; the Simones are loaded."

"I never realized."

"Andre has never been ostentatious with his wealth. He's a gentle soul, a total romantic, but I warn you, Louis is not like his daddy. There's a ruthless streak in him."

"What do you mean?" Mark demanded as anxiety raced through him. "Get to the point, Uncle."

"I mean Louis will do whatever it takes to get whatever he wants, and he wants Rachel. Is that plain enough for you, boy?"

"Does he love her?"

"Every man loves Rachel just as every man loved Elinore. But in Louis' case I think he loves what Rachel is, which is not the same thing as loving who she is, if you know what I mean."

Mark's anxiety was suddenly replaced by intense anger. "You mean he loves her family name."

"Yes, Louis very much wants to marry a D'Evereau."

Mark slammed his fist down on the chair arm. "How does Rachel feel about him?"

"All I can tell you is, she has spent a great deal of time with him this fall. And she always seems very happy when he's around."

"I don't believe it!" Mark claimed. "Rachel's too smart to fall for this."

Philippe responded quietly, "She's fallen for this kind of man before, my boy."

Mark flushed angrily, but admitted, "Yes, she has. Collins Greyson. And look what he did to her. Surely she's learned something from that mistake."

Philippe shook his head sadly. "Don't we all keep repeating the same mistakes?"

Mark anxiously ran his fingers through his hair and said nothing, so Philippe continued, "Louis is smart, Mark. Smart and very smooth. He's hiding a great deal from her. In fact, he's hiding a great deal from all of us, even from his daddy, I'd say. I can't prove it, but I feel it in my gut. I know you want her. Don't leave this time. You'll never get another chance to make Rachel yours."

Mark said nothing, then suddenly changed the subject. "What's going on with this Billy Ray Snyder guy?"

"Don't worry about him. He isn't even on the racetrack when Louis is around."

"What about when Louis is not here?" Mark asked.

"Rachel's been known to spend time with him," Philippe admitted. "Why not? He reinvents himself to please her. Women like that, you know. He's a tough man—a real scrapper. Came up the hard way."

"He appears to have money.".

"Oh, he's got money and plenty more coming. That boy's a real money maker."

Mark said nothing and closed his eyes as he thought the situation through. Philippe chuckled quietly, "Yes sir, it's going to be quite a horse race, Mark. If I were a betting man though—and I am—I'd put my money on you."

"Why? I don't have the money or the sophistication Rachel obviously likes."

"Rachel loves you, boy. Besides, you don't like to lose. And you've already had one taste of what it's like to lose her. I don't figure you want to go through that again."

Mark shook his head.

"Then you better stay on the racetrack, boy," Philippe said, then grinned. "So, now, how about that job?"

Mark stared at his Uncle for a minute, then narrowed his eyes and said, "Nothing's changed, has it, Uncle? Things always work out to your advantage."

"I make them work out, my boy."

"Okay. You're on, Uncle. I'm not going anywhere."

Philippe laughed. "I didn't think so. I'll tell you what. You go on down to the campaign headquarters downtown and get Lisette to show you what's been going on in the public relations arena. I'll tell her you're in charge now." He sighed before continuing, "She won't like it, of course, but that's too bad, isn't it?"

"If you say so," Mark replied cautiously. He studied his uncle several minutes as a number of questions about Phillipe's relationship to Lisette ran through his mind.

Finally Philippe said, "Go ahead and ask, boy. Whatever's on your mind, we better get it cleared up if you're going to work for me."

Mark chose his words carefully. "It was my understanding that Lisette runs your campaign, but your mention of the Party financing things and running in their hired professionals makes me wonder. Exactly who is running things?"

"The party is, but ultimately they can't override me on any matter."

"Why not?"

"Because I'll quit, and they'll have no candidate."

"They could run somebody else."

"Not at this late date. How could they ever explain the switch?"

"So where does Lisette come in?"

"She's my personal assistant, schedules my whole life—you know, that kind of thing."

"And is it necessary to consult with her at three in the morning.in your bedroom?"

Philippe looked startled, then laughed loudly. "No wonder you're such a hotshot reporter! You don't miss anything!" When Mark didn't join in his laughter, Philippe turned serious and said, "Mark, you're not a kid anymore. Surely I don't have to be as discreet around you as I did when you were a boy living in this house. Besides, you'd figure it all out now anyway, wouldn't you?"

"I imagine so," Mark agreed as he stood to leave. Then, pausing to look down at his uncle, he added, "After all, I did when I was a boy."

Philippe turned red, then said, "Mark, I did the best—"

"Forget it, Uncle," Mark interrupted. "I just needed to know exactly who has what power around here."

After breakfast Rachel and Louis stood on the front verandah with Andre as he said goodbye for a few days. Louis gave his father a quick kiss on both cheeks and commented, "Give my best regards to the Montpelliers and tell Claude that I hope to see him soon."

"Yes, you definitely must see them before you return to France," Andre responded, clapping his son on the back before turning his attention to Rachel. "And you, My Dear, must allow Louis to pamper you totally today. I'm afraid that you wore yourself out yesterday giving all of us a wonderful Christmas."

"I'll take care of her, Papa," Louis answered as he smiled down at Rachel. "I am well aware how fortunate a man I am to have a whole day alone with Rachel. I don't plan to waste a minute of it."

Rachel smiled up at him, then turned to his father. "Have a wonderful visit with your friends, dear Andre," Rachel encouraged as she reached up to give him a good-bye hug, "and I'll look forward to seeing you back here at Belle St. Marie in several days."

"Don't worry, My Dear," Andre called back over his shoulder as he descended the steps. "I wouldn't miss a New

Year's Eve celebration at Belle St. Marie for the world."

"Now, drive carefully, Papa," Louis called after his father. "The fog hasn't totally lifted, and remember, you don't own the highway."

"Nonsense," Andre responded cheerfully. "I've paid enough taxes in my life to finance several highways."

Rachel and Louis stood on the verandah laughing as they watched Andre slip into the driver's seat, start the car, and drive off down the long, winding driveway. Once his father was out of sight, Louis put his arm lightly around Rachel's shoulders and asked happily, "How shall we spend the day, beloved?"

Rachel smiled up at him, and when their eyes met, she realized that she had never seen him so relaxed before. She was glad; now that Mark had returned, she was anxious to know more about Louis in order to prepare herself for the choice she would most likely face. "Whatever you would like to do," she answered. "I have no particular plans except that Billy Ray is coming by in half an hour, but he'll be gone by 11:00 at the latest."

"Billy Ray!" Louis shook his fist in mock anger. "That man has no sense of propriety."

Rachel laughed and asked, "Exactly what do you mean by that, Mr. Simone?"

"I mean it's my turn to have you all alone, and he should honor that fact."

"He's only coming by to show me some changes he wants to make on the school plans," Rachel said, "and it won't take long, I promise."

"He doesn't fool me; he's using the school project to spend time with you. And frankly, I don't blame him." Louis looked down at Rachel just as a sunbeam shone through the thinning morning fog and lit Rachel's bright blue eyes. "You are beautiful, Rachel," Louis said quietly. "The most beautiful woman I know."

Rachel blushed and lowered her head. Satisfied she had felt the compliment, Louis gracefully changed the subject. "The day is turning out to be quite fine. If you really have no plans, shall we take a drive? Perhaps Lovey will prepare a picnic lunch for us. Surely there are plenty of leftovers from Christmas. Would you like that?"

Rachel looked around at the pine woods as the brightening sunlight highlighted them, and thought about how tied to the house she had been for the last two days. The thought of a drive through the countryside was very appealing. "Oh yes, that would be very relaxing," she agreed. "And it would give Lovey time to rest, too."

"Then it's all decided. I shall finally have you all to myself, and—"

"Excuse me, Mr. Louis," Lovey called from the front door, "there's a phone call for you, some man wanting to talk about business."

"Oh, dear." Rachel sighed aloud.

"Don't worry, Rachel. It will take wild horses to drag me away from you today. I may never get another chance like this." He gave her a quick hug as he turned back toward the front door. "I'll handle this in no time."

Rachel walked the length of the front verandah, admiring the dew drops that were turning into short-lived diamonds on the trees and ornamental shrubs. Perhaps we could take the river road, she thought dreamily. I love the way it winds and winds—quite suddenly her serene thoughts were interrupted by the sound of Louis's raised voice as he spoke on the phone in the parlor.

"Don't forget who you're talking to," he angrily ordered someone. Then his voice turned icy cold. "I'm the one who conceived of this plan in the first place, and you can rest assured that I will get what I came here to get."

Suddenly anxious, Rachel turned back toward the front door. By the time she reached it, Louis came striding out. His whole demeanor had changed. His eyes were hard, and although he struggled to speak in the same easy tone he had used a few minutes earlier, his words were clipped.

"I'm sorry, Rachel," he began abruptly, then paused and with great effort softened his tone. "I'm afraid something has come up that necessitates my return to New Orleans. It can't be helped."

"Oh no—" Rachel began, but when she examined his hardened face, her impulse was to shrink away. "We'll have our drive another day."

"Rachel, I assure you that I need—I mean, I want to be with you today, but I must take care of business."

"We'll have another chance, I'm sure," Rachel said, trying to soothe him. "Please don't worry about it. Really, I don't mind."

"I do worry about it," Louis insisted. "My relationship with you is intensely important to me, but—I must go to New Orleans. I'm sorry. I'll make it up to you, I promise." He put his arms around her, and as he drew her close to him, she felt the hardness of his muscles and the rigidity of his body. There was no doubt that he was very angry, and Rachel had to force herself to suppress a shudder of fear. She tried to think of something to calm him down, but he released her and turned abruptly toward the front door.

Once he had left the verandah, Rachel's heart began pounding, and for an instant she actually felt faint. Rather than returning into the house, she descended the steps and walked out onto the serenity of the lawn.

In less than ten minutes Louis reappeared, his suitcase and briefcase in hand. He paused long enough to kiss Rachel lightly on the lips, but it was evident to her that his mind was already far away. "I'll be back before New Year's Eve," he promised as he turned to walk briskly toward his car.

Amazed at the change in Louis' demeanor, and more than a little relieved that he was leaving, Rachel watched as he drove away.

Lovey came out onto the verandah with a broom in her hand. "I thought you was spending the day with Mr. Louis," she said as she, too, watched his car speeding down the driveway.

"We were going to drive up the River Road and have a picnic lunch, but that phone call changed him into a different man. Suddenly he was all business."

"He ain't the only one catching that bug this morning," Lovey observed as she began sweeping.

"What do you mean?"

"Mr. Billy Ray called while you was having breakfast with Mr. Louis and Mr. Andre. I didn't think I better interrupt you since you was with Mr. Louis. I don't think he likes Mr. Billy Ray."

"What did Billy Ray say, Lovey?"

"He say to tell you he got to go out of town on business, that he's real sorry 'cause he can't come over here and go down to the school building with you, but he gonna be back in a day or two and he gonna call you."

"You're kidding!" Rachel laughed. "One minute I'm trying to juggle the two of them and keep them both happy, and the next minute I'm abandoned by them both. You know what, Lovey, I couldn't be happier. Thank goodness for business. I wanted the day to myself. Now I have it!" She laughed again. "I'm going for a solitary walk in the woods," she called over her shoulder as she turned away.

"Hmm," Lovey murmured as she watched Rachel. "I wonder where Mr. Mark is."

Even though it was the Christmas season, Lisette was busy

in the deserted campaign office. She was trying to decide whether to stop for lunch when her phone rang. She glanced at the phone number of the incoming call and immediately answered with an angry question. "Where are you calling from?"

"I'm on the interstate headed south," a male voice answered. "Just stopped for coffee."

"What?" Lisette demanded, then hurried on. "You're supposed to be with Rachel."

"I know."

"I thought we agreed that you were going to spend some time with Rachel, softening her up."

"I had to change my plans; I'm on the way to New Orleans."

"What on earth for? You need to be working on Rachel. Nothing could be more important than—"

"Some unexpected business came up."

"What business?" Lisette asked.

"You just handle your part, Lisette."

"I don't like being left out of the loop. I want to know—"

"I'll decide what you need to know," the man broke in harshly. "Leave the negotiations to me, and do your part."

Lisette scowled, but kept control of her anger when she spoke. "Speaking of my part, we're in trouble. Philippe is going to ask Mark to work on his campaign."

"How do you know that?"

"The same way I know everything about Philippe. I don't sleep with him for nothing, you know," Lisette replied sarcastically. "Anyway, I don't like it. Mark's too smart, and unlike his uncle, he's always sober."

"You're over-reacting, as usual. A guy like Mark won't stay around Louisiana. He's seen too much of the world."

"Don't be a fool. He's not staying around for the scenery. He wants Rachel, and he'll stay around until he gets her."

"No one gets Rachel but me," the man said flatly.

"I know you think you're God's gift to women and the greatest thing that ever hit Louisiana, but I've been around the D'Evereaus longer than you have. Besides, Philippe tells me everything, even about the family. I tell you, Mark has power over Rachel. She loves him. She just doesn't know how much yet."

"I don't care if she loves him as long as she doesn't marry him. I want Belle St. Marie, and I plan to have it."

"Then you better win Rachel. You're a handsome man, but

I'm warning you, you won't have an easy time getting Rachel away from Mark."

"I will if he's discredited. Rachel may love Mark, but she's a woman and just as susceptible to jealousy as any other woman. Every man alive has something to hide. Why should Mark Goodman be any different?"

"Oh yes, that'll solve everything, won't it? Look, Mark is not the kind of man who's spent his life hanging out in Paris brothels."

"Somewhere there's some dirt on him, and I'll find it."

"I'm warning you, it won't work. Mark isn't typical in any way."

"Mark is a man. No more arguments, Lisette. You do your part. You handle dear old Philippe. I'll handle Mark and Rachel."

"I want to know—hello? Hello, can you hear me? Hello?" Lisette waited for a moment, then slammed down the phone. "Lost the connection," she mumbled angrily. "He'll call back." She sat waiting for the phone to ring for three or four minutes before the truth occurred to her. "He hung up!"

Chapter 8

By noon Rachel had enjoyed a solitary, refreshing walk in the mist-enshrouded woods. All her anxious feelings generated by Louis' sudden departure that morning had dissolved as she watched the squirrels' hilarious antics and acrobatic feats as they chased each other through the treetops. Slowly the yellow sun began to filter through the pine needles, dissolving the mists into graceful plumes which danced for a moment or two, then disappeared. Leisurely returning home, she occasionally stopped to picked up a magnolia seed pod full of bright red, waxy seeds and marveled at its beauty.

After a light lunch, she settled on the east verandah to finish reading a novel she had started before her Christmas guests had arrived. Consequently, she was stretched out on a wicker settee, propped up with throw pillows, when she heard Mark call out from a distance. "Hi, Rachel! Don't let me startle you."

She sat up and started to stand to greet him, but as he walked up the stairs, he insisted, "No, just stay comfortable," and she obeyed happily and leaned back against the pillows. "I'm just looking for a casual visit if you're in the mood," he assured her. She pointed to a chair, and as he settled in it, he commented, "Hasn't this been the most unusual weather for the day after Christmas? One hour it feels like late fall, and the next it feels like early spring."

"It's been grand," Rachel answered through a yawn she was trying to stifle. "Sorry," she apologized. "I guess I just got too relaxed."

"You deserve it." They both remained comfortably silent, lost in their own thoughts, until Mark asked, "How many afternoon hours do you suppose we spent on this east verandah when we were growing up?"

"I couldn't even guess, but they were all wonderful. I can still see Aimee and me playing jacks on the floor over there while you teased us."

"And Justin was always sitting right about where we are now with his sketchpad in his hands," Mark added. "How many drawings do you suppose—" He broke off, looked closely at Rachel and asked, "Does it bother you to talk about Justin?"

"Not as much as when I first came back here," Rachel answered. "At first, I couldn't stand to look at any of the old pictures or even to open up the music room. All the missing loved ones....but slowly things have changed, and a lot of things about the family don't bother me as much as they did."

Aware that he had been fortunate indeed to find Rachel so relaxed, Mark reminded himself to proceed carefully or he would lose this chance to re-establish some type of intimacy with her. "It's been strange—and not altogether pleasant, either—to return to Uncle Philippe's house. I guess I had forgotten about all the painful memories there. You know how it is; things can be stirred up when you return to a place that was difficult for you."

"You're right, of course, but surely there are good memories at your Uncle's for you, too, just as there were good memories here for me at Belle St. Marie. I don't know why the bad ones seemed to take control at first—well, I guess I do know now."

"Why do you know now and not when you first arrived?"

Rachel shrugged her shoulders, then commented in an off-hand way, "I just don't see myself the same way. I mean, when I came here eighteen months ago, I had a particular view of myself....not a very good one actually....but I've grown past it. And thank God I have!"

Mark fell silent again as he pondered how open to be with Rachel, particularly about the things he had learned from Lovey. Finally he decided to be straightforward. "You know," he said, "I didn't just happen to wander over here. I've been waiting for a time to talk to you about the past."

"I don't want to get into all that stuff between us when we were in college," Rachel objected. "It was just too long ago, and there's no point in digging it all up."

"I agree; let's save that for another time."

"Let's leave it buried!" Rachel retorted. "I mean it, Mark. I don't want to—"

"Hey, girl, that's really not what's on my mind. I want—actually, I need—some answers I think you may have. You see, I talked to Lovey yesterday afternoon about you."

Rachel sat bolt upright and demanded stiffly, "Why? Why did you do that?"

"Take it easy, Rachel. It was just one of those accidental things that happen. I was at the cemetery thinking about the past, and Lovey came down there with some flowers. She was nice enough to take time for me....you know how she is. I had some things on my mind, and she was willing to listen." Rachel frowned and nodded slightly. "Rachel," Mark pleaded, "relax. You know Lovey is the last person in the world who would hurt you. Please, let's just talk like we used to when we were kids, and we had all those long, hot afternoons to while away. Remember?"

Rachel leaned back against the pillows and smiled. "Weren't we lucky to have those days here at Belle St. Marie with Grandmere and Lovey? Weren't we just the luckiest kids in the world?"

"We were," Mark agreed, then sighed as he slipped further down into the cushions on the chair and stretched his long legs out in front of him. "That's one of the things Lovey and I talked about —those summers. You know, Rachel, I was just a stupid kid. I never knew how much trouble you had at home in Texas during the school year. I just thought you were a spoiled brat who had to be straightened out by Miss Elinore at the beginning of every summer."

"Thanks a lot!" Rachel laughed.

"No, really, I didn't understand that you were upset when you arrived. Oh, I guess I must have heard bits and pieces about your mother's illnesses and Mammy Cassie, but I just never bothered to put it together. I certainly never considered what it was doing to your concept of yourself. I just thought you were a selfish kid. The pattern was always the same every summer—after a week or so, you seemed to fall more into the spirit of the place around here and become a gentler person. Looking back, I realize I didn't really try to understand you at all."

"Why should you have tried? You were just a kid yourself. Besides, when I was little, I couldn't have explained myself even if you had asked. I didn't understand why I felt so angry. By the time I was a teenager, I was too embarrassed to talk to you about my life in Texas. I just wanted to arrive at Belle St. Marie and pretend I was another person, a different girl who was treated all year long the way Grandmere treated me during the summer."

"I can understand that, but the fact of the matter is, your home life in Texas must have been shaping the way you viewed yourself."

"You better believe it. It was making me feel worthless." Rachel stopped talking, and Mark stared at his outstretched feet as he thought about her words. Finally Rachel added, "The truth is, I didn't know just how worthless I felt until Collins died and I dragged myself back over here to Belle St. Marie."

Mark shook his head in amazement. "It's crazy, isn't it, Rachel? Without a doubt you are one of the most successful people I have ever known. It seems almost impossible that in spite of all your successes you could feel worthless."

Rachel laughed bitterly. "All those successes came from my frantic attempts to earn a sense of worth. I may be a highly educated woman, but the sad truth is that I had to reach the lowest point in my life before I began to understand myself. I actually had to reach the point of sitting in the attic of this old house during a violent storm reading Civil War diaries before I could even define my problem. How weird is that?"

"Not so weird, really. It takes a lot for people like you and me to accept the idea that we can't force things to be what we want them to be. Tell me about those diaries. Lovey said they were very important and to ask you about them."

"They were important, "Rachel admitted as she sat up straight, clutched one of the throw pillows to her chest, and rethought that night of her life. "They provided a real breakthrough for me, Mark, but I suppose they wouldn't have impacted me so much if other changes hadn't already taken place in my spirit."

"A breakthrough," Mark thoughtfully repeated her words before asking, "How were they a breakthrough?"

"The first diary I found was written by a woman named Marie. She fell in love with my great-great-grandfather, and they were married before the Civil War. She was obviously a very positive, sweet personality with a strong faith in God, and when she fell in love with my grandfather, her life was all hearts and flowers. She recorded all the major events of her life before the war. The thing that struck me was that as soon as a wonderful thing happened, like the birth of a child, it was quickly followed by a tragic event like a death. That was exactly the way I saw my life. Her life seemed to embody all the false hopes and wrecked happiness that I was experiencing in life. And, of course, my despair was heightened as I read her words because I knew the Civil War was coming into her life."

"I can understand why you connected with her so much, but how did that help you?" Mark asked.

"It allowed me to express my anger. My life had battered me so much I was ready to explode, but I had always pushed down my emotions in an attempt to keep control of things. But suddenly, there I was, by myself in an attic in the middle of a lightning storm. I just turned my fury loose."

"And it really helped you?"

"It really did, but there was more to it. Marie's story really bothered me. You see, no matter what she suffered, she retained her faith in God and in herself. I just couldn't understand how she could do that. I had a slight understanding of how she retained her faith in God because I had known Grandmere. But how on earth did Marie continue to think well of herself? I simply could not understand that at all. All my life when things went wrong for me, I thought less of myself. Marie's troubles never seemed to shake her view of herself. I was amazed!"

"So am I, frankly. She sounds a little naive, to put it kindly."

"That's what I thought at first, but not after I read the journal of Jacques, her husband."

"Her husband was keeping a journal at the same time?"

"No, his story was altogether different. Apparently Jacques didn't feel compelled to record anything until after he returned home from the Civil War. In fact, there was so little left in the house that he ended up using an old ledger to write on. He didn't write often; really, he had no time to write because the plantation was damaged during the war, and he was fighting to bring it back to life."

"And Marie was struggling with him, of course."

"No, Mark, she was dead. She had died from a fever after burying all their children as well as her in-laws. All dead. Can you imagine? Jacques had fought for years and walked home from Virginia just to find that Marie and his kids and his parents—all were dead."

"I can't imagine surviving that," Mark admitted.

"And he couldn't even piece together a coherent account of his family. All Jacques knew was what a former slave couple could tell him. What he did learn, though, was how heroic Marie had been during those desperate years of the War. Later he found out that she had even managed to save enough assets to help him save the plantation."

"What an incredible nightmare for him! Obviously he made a go of it because here we are sitting on the verandah at Belle St. Marie."

"Yes, apparently he was very strong. He saved the

plantation and eventually remarried. I am a descendant of that marriage. He accomplished a great deal, but I found no evidence that he ever felt good about himself again. That's why I identified with him much more than I did with Marie."

Mark studied her for a moment before asking, "But you really wanted to be a Marie, didn't you?"

"Of course. I couldn't imagine how I could go on with my life believing that I had to earn my worth and that no matter how hard I tried, I would never succeed. I had been doing that all my life, and I was exhausted by the effort."

"So the diaries just raised the issues for you," Mark observed. "They didn't give you any answers."

"They started me down the right road. They showed me how Marie had handled the difficulties of her life and retained a sense of her worth, but Jacques—like me—never seemed to move past his anger. It was other events that kept me on the journey."

"Like what?"

"Several things happened. I don't know if I can place them in order, but I guess that doesn't matter. I knew I had to forgive a number of people from my childhood, and in order to forgive them, I had to come to some understanding of why they had acted the way they did."

"What people? That Mammy Cassie I heard about every summer when you arrived?"

"Mammy Cassie, for sure! But I think the most important one was my father. Mother, too, of course, but somehow it was my father who was the hardest to forgive."

"But you did it."

"Yes, after he came over here, and we had a terrific fight. It was really painful, but it cleared the air. It sounds so stupid, but suddenly I realized he was human and consequently capable of mistakes."

Mark nodded his head. "So forgiveness was the first step. Then what?"

"I found out that Grandmere's life was not what I had always thought it was."

"It wasn't?" Mark pulled his legs in, sat up and leaned toward Rachel. "What do you mean?"

"You wouldn't believe how hard her life was, Mark. She had so much trouble with my grandfather, and she lost several children. That just about killed her. I didn't know that she had been through so many painful experiences and that she had had to choose a path of peace repeatedly until it became the fabric of her being. It was stupid of me, but I had always thought that she was born with that remarkable serenity she had. The truth is, Mark, she had to choose it over and over."

"I am surprised, but when I think about it with the mind and experience of a grown man, what you say about Miss Elinore makes sense. I always saw her as living a charmed life, but, of course, no one does. So it was important for you to know about your grandmother's life?"

"Yes, immensely important because until I knew about all the hard choices she had made to gain her serenity, I would not embrace the fact that I had to do the same. After Andre told me her story, I knew that if I wanted the peace that Grandmere had had, I would have to do something with my past pains—not just resent them. Then several apparently unrelated things happened which seemed to have no relevance at the time. Now I see that they led me where I needed to go."

"What things?"

"I met two black girls in the woods, the girls we were talking about yesterday at the dinner table. They were playing hooky from school because their skills were so minimal that school was just making them feel like losers."

"So that's when you started the school?"

"I started tutoring them in an attempt to prepare them to return to the public school. Of course, the whole thing was meant to help them, but I received the most from the effort because my focus changed. I was thinking about them and others like them more than I was thinking about myself, and most importantly, I was investing myself in them because I believed in their worth."

"So, in spite of their race and poverty—the things that would make society consider them worthless—you thought they were worth something?"

"It seemed obvious to me," Rachel said simply.

"I see. And did believing in their worth make it possible for you to recognize your own?" Mark asked.

"Not until Garth Gunner returned." Rachel shook her head. "The last man I ever wanted to see, the man who had killed Grandmere--there he was, back in my life. I couldn't believe it."

Mark's face turned dark with anger. "I just wish I had been here."

"I know, I know how you feel. All I wanted to do was kill him, but for some reason I had to confront the person I hated most in all the world and recognize his worth before I could see my own."

"I don't get it, Rachel. How could confronting that trash again make you feel worthy?"

"He wasn't trash, Mark," Rachel answered softly. "It was truly remarkable how I suddenly knew that. I wanted to kill him myself, to rid the world of that snake until I saw him curled up on the ground bleeding. You see, the men who work the land had beaten him almost to death because he had attacked one of the girls I was teaching, Sassy. I should have hated him even more, but suddenly I realized that he was just a human being who had made horrible choices. Don't ask me to explain all of this, Mark. I don't really think I can. There was something spiritual about the whole experience, something that can't be reduced to logic."

"Something like the golden swan," Mark murmured.

"The golden swan? Oh, forgive me! That should have been the first thing I said to you. Thank you for that gorgeous present. It's breathtaking! Where did you find it?"

"In a bazaar in Sudan. I was just strolling through this dirty, poverty-stricken town and saw this pathetic bazaar. Most of the stuff was just junk, of course, but in one of the tents there was this guy carving animals out of wood. There was all the usual tourist stuff, but there was also this one carving of a swan; he only had one, and somehow he had managed to get his hands on some gold leaf and covered its surface. I bought it because it reminded me of something I really needed to hold on to during those depressing days."

"What was that?"

"You. Even after all those years had passed and I had traveled all those miles, I still needed you. Now that I've come home, I don't need a reminder of you. I need you."

"Mark, we agreed not to get into that."

"Rachel, I realize I haven't handled my return well at all. I shouldn't have just dropped into your life so suddenly. It's just that I've been in such a strange place in my head."

"What on earth do you mean by that?"

"I know....I know it sounds totally weird. Will you let me try to explain?" he asked. Rachel said nothing. Instead, she picked up the novel and absentmindedly looked at the cover. Mark stood and walked across the space that separated them. He knelt down on one knee, so that their eyes were on the same level. "Will you listen?" he asked. "Will you just hear me out?"

"I'd rather run," she admitted. "I'd rather just head for the woods and hide out until—"

"What would that accomplish, Rachel?"

"Peace! That's all I want, Mark. I've found my equilibrium, and I don't want you upsetting it by—by—"

"By reminding you that you still love me?" he asked quietly.

Rachel jerked her head away and stared out into the garden, but no matter how hard she tried to retain her composure, tears gathered in her eyes and ran down her cheeks.

Mark gently touched her cheeks and wiped the tears away. "There are things between us that have to be resolved, Rachel," he said quietly. "Please, look at me."

When she turned her face back and looked into his eyes, she saw the depth of his sadness and pain. "Give me a chance," he pleaded, "just hear me out."

Unable to speak, she nodded her head.

Mark stood. Raising her legs from the empty side of the settee just enough to slip beneath them, he sat down and placed her ankles in his lap. Rachel flushed and pressed the novel to her chest.

"We used to spend hours when we were teens sitting just like this," Mark murmured. "Remember?"

Rachel nodded.

Determined to bring things out into the open, Mark sat in silence, thinking out what he should say and absentmindedly stroking her knees. Finally he spoke. "I've made some major tactical errors, Rachel. I should have called you rather than rushing in here with no warning. I mishandled things. In fact, I should have contacted you as soon as I knew about Collins' death."

"Why didn't you?"

"I couldn't."

"You still couldn't forgive me...."

"No, it wasn't that, although I was really angry with you for a long time after you married Collins."

"If you love me so much, Mark, why didn't you call me or even come help me when I was in so much trouble? I don't understand...."

"For the last few years, Lovey's letters have been my only source of news about you, and those letters had to chase me around from hotspot to hotspot before they finally caught up with me. By the time Lovey's last letter found me—" Mark stopped as the memory of his agony stole his thoughts and made him break out in a sweat.

"What?" Rachel demanded as she sat up straight. "What stopped you from coming home? I needed you, Mark. Surely you knew that."

"I had...I had been...shot." Mark finally said the words. "The doctors were sure I would be paralyzed if I lived."

Rachel froze, her eyes glued to his face as her mouth fell open. "Mark! What....what are you saying? You almost died? Oh, my God! Why didn't you have someone call me?"

"And saddle you with a broken man?"

"Pride! Your stupid pride. This is the Viet Nam issue all over again. You just marched off to war and wouldn't even marry me before you left because you might be wounded or disabled in Viet Nam. You haven't changed a bit!"

"No, I haven't. I still love you too much to willfully ruin your life."

"Maybe I would have wanted you in any condition. Did you ever consider that? Maybe I loved you no matter what!"

"Rachel, be reasonable. You were just recovering from Collins' death; you were dealing with all these issues of your worth you've just mentioned."

"Maybe I would have felt worthy if I had known you wanted me, needed me!"

"Maybe you would have thought I only wanted you because I was broken. What would that have done for your self-esteem?"

Rachel said nothing. She sank back on the pillows as she tried to sort it all out.

Mark hurried on. "After I was shot, I had to fight with all my mental strength to survive. Then I had to push indescribably hard to get through the months of therapy to walk again. It was the thought of you, Rachel, the hope of attaining you that kept me going. You and I together for the rest of our lives became my new life vision. No more globe trotting for me; all I wanted—and still want—is for us to be together."

"Mark, please don't—"

"Okay. Okay, I won't push that right now. But please hear me out, Rachel. My point is that I had to work up an enormous momentum to get back on my feet, and I just kept pushing and pushing. I guess I should have contacted you and somehow helped you through—"

"No!" Rachel stopped him as tears sprang to her eyes. "No, you couldn't have. I see that now. God forgive me; I have been so self-centered."

"You didn't know," Mark said to soothe her, "and you were

pushing through a painful therapy all your own."

Her voice quivered. "I wasn't fighting to live. Oh, dear God! Why all this suffering? Is there no end to trouble? Can't we ever get free of the past and just live peaceably in the present?"

Mark reached for her hand and held it firmly in his own. "I wish I could have avoided telling you all this, especially at this time. You're worn out, and my return has just added to your stress. Maybe I should have waited to talk about the shooting, but I couldn't just go on fighting with you. I had to lay the facts on the table. If it's another tactical error on my part, forgive me. Please forgive me."

She nodded and tried to relax into the pillows. She lay there, silent, her white neck elongated, her golden hair draping over the pillow, and struggled against her brimming tears. Finally she murmured, "I feel so sad. I failed you."

"No, you didn't." Mark's voice was firm. "You are not responsible for something you don't know about. Besides, it was really you who kept me going. I thought of you constantly. I put that golden swan where I could see it, and I sweated my way through those painful days absolutely determined to bring that swan to you."

Rachel nodded as she whispered, "I knew there was something extraordinary about that gift. It seemed alive in my hand." She fell silent, sighed and closed her eyes.

Mark felt a wave of relief rush over him. With great difficulty he restrained himself from scooping her into his arms, and forced himself to wait a moment before speaking.

"The golden swan I gave you is wooden, of course, but there was a live one—right here at Belle St. Marie," he said quietly.

Rachel's eyes opened. "A live one? Here?"

"Down at the pond. Can you remember anything about when I first came here after my parents were killed?"

"I do remember that summer. I remember that you just suddenly showed up in my life, and Grandmere told me about your parents. I remember that I couldn't think of anything to say to you to help you."

"You were only nine. I was twelve, and I was so low I really wanted to kill myself. In fact, I tried to. Your Grandmere tried to reach out to me, but at first I wouldn't let her help me. I was totally shut down."

"Grief does that," Rachel observed quietly. "I don't know what I would have done without Lovey after Collins died. But you didn't really try to kill yourself, did you?"

"Yes, I did. I actually stood by the pond ready to jump in and drown myself."

"Why didn't you do it?"

Mark shook his head slightly. "You will find it hard to believe, Rachel, but a large, white swan flew in and landed on that black, glossy water. It startled me and made me pause, but it didn't change my emotional state. I still felt devastated by my loss." He turned his head, looked directly into her eyes, and added, "Then quite suddenly it turned golden, flapped its wings and lifted off the water. It was quite a sight!"

"I guess so!" Rachel exclaimed. "So, what did you do?"

"The fact that the swan turned golden was startling, to say the least, but what really surprised me was how my emotional state was completely changed by the swan's miraculous transformation. My grief was replaced by total peace."

"So, of course, you didn't go ahead with your suicide attempt."

"No, I was only twelve, but I knew something profound had happened. I didn't understand it at all, but I definitely felt it."

"Amazing," Rachel murmured. "It had to be some kind of gift from God. You know, something that would really get your attention and make you pause long enough...."

"Yes, something like that." Mark agreed. "But that wasn't the end of that special afternoon. Pretty soon I heard a girl singing. I sneaked through the underbrush, and I saw you balancing on a log. There was a ray of sunlight on you, and you reminded me of the swan."

"I don't remember..."

"No, you wouldn't. You never saw me there. But I did go back across the lawn at Belle St. Marie, and I talked to your Grandmere. She took me back to the kitchen. That's when I met you and Lovey and Aimee."

"You never told me about any of this before!"

"It's not the sort of thing a twelve-year-old would confess to a nine-year-old kid. And you know how it is later, when you're a teenager in love with a blonde-haired girl from Texas who shows up for the summers. Besides, I'm not at all sure I had much understanding of it during those years. It was really only after I had gone to Viet Nam and had lost you to Collins that I began to see that you were more than a beautiful, bright girl to me."

"What was I to you, Mark?"

"Once I was tramping through rice paddies with a gun in my

hand, I realized that you had always been my hope for joy in my life, my hope for meaningful human intimacy. Yeah, that's one of the two things that Viet Nam definitely taught me."

"And the other?"

"I discovered that Miss Elinore was my link to faith. I had been so embittered by my parents' death that I wouldn't let God into my life unless he was escorted by your Grandmere."

"That would have been just about the time she was killed," she whispered as she once again struggled to fight back tears. Mark held out his arms to her, and Rachel scooted across the space between them to sit in his lap and put her arms around his neck.

"It was," he whispered into her ear, "and that was the end of my relationship with God. But you, even though you were married and unavailable to me, remained my hope for joy in my life, Rachel. I know that I should have stopped loving you—you were another man's wife—but I didn't. And I haven't. And I won't."

Rachel just sat there, weeping silently into Mark's shoulder, and he held her tight and wondered how he would ever let go of her.

She answered that question for him quite suddenly when she abruptly un-wrapped her arms from his neck and stood up. She pulled some Kleenex out of her slacks pocket and wiped her face as she walked away from him. "The issue of God has been a tough one for me all my life," she admitted. "I grew up surrounded by religious people, as you know, but somehow most of the people got in the way between God and me. Except for Grandmere and Lovey. Losing Collins and coming back here have made me think about God again, but I don't know.... I can understand why you don't believe in God, Mark."

"But I do now, Rachel."

"You do?"

"Yeah, ever since I was shot. I thought I was going to die—it was one of those times you hear about when your life flashes before your eyes and you have to decide what you believe. I found out I believe in God. In the last six months I've been trying to understand more about what that really means."

"And have you?"

"I've still got a lot to learn," he admitted, "but one thing I know for sure. I don't ever want to live without God again."

Rachel sighed. "I just want peace, Mark."

"There's no peace without God, Rachel. Believe me, I've

traveled the globe looking for peace, and I never found it until I let God into my life."

"God never brought anything but strife into my life, Mark."

"That wasn't God, Rachel. That was people who brought strife into your life, people who called themselves 'believers.' God is another thing entirely."

"I don't know, Mark. My life is getting better day by day because of my own efforts. The God thing just confuses me and upsets me, just like it did when I was a kid."

Rachel waited for Mark to argue with her, to say something. Instead, he covered his eyes with his hand and rubbed his forehead as he thought.

Finally Rachel broke the silence, "Mark? Are you okay? I didn't mean to upset you."

He stood and came to her side. "I'm not upset," he said quietly as he placed his hands on her shoulders and looked down into her face. "You say you want what that Marie in the journal had, Rachel. You want to know your worth like she knew hers. You say that you're sorry to see that you're more like your ancestor, Jacques. You need to look at those old journals again, at what those two people wrote so long ago, because the difference in those two people is simple. Marie knew that she was a unique creation of God's, and she lived her life depending on Him and making the choice minute-by-minute to be that unique creation no matter what was happening in her life. Jacques believed in himself, and yes, he put the plantation back together, but apparently he never felt his worth because he never embraced His creator."

Rachel laughed nervously. "Goodness, Mark, when did you become such a preacher?"

"I'm not a preacher, Rachel. I'm a stubborn idiot who had to almost die before he would lay down his pride and admit he needed his Creator."

"So you think God sent a bullet to—"

"No. I don't think that. God didn't send the bullet. The bullet was meant to do me harm, to kill me; but God was there, and He made it plain to me that He always had been and always would be."

"How did He make it plain?"

"I was shot as I walked back to our camp after buying the golden swan."

"No!" Rachel exclaimed. "You bought it right before you were shot?"

"Yes, in the middle of nowhere God provided me with a visible, tangible sign of His presence by providing a gilded swan, a direct reminder of my attempt at suicide here in Louisiana. A direct reminder that God had not allowed me to end my life when I was twelve. I was mystified at His obvious intervention in my life again; that is, I was mystified until I heard the shot and felt the searing pain in my back."

"God must really love you...."

"And you. Not for anything you've ever accomplished, Rachel. Just for you. I've always loved you, too, but not the way I do now. Before, I loved your beauty and your mind and the way you made me feel. Now I love the unique creation God made, the one we humans call Rachel D'Evereau, the one who occasionally shines through these days. And I want her to see who she really is."

Rachel looked away and made no response, so Mark added, "I've worn out my welcome, I'm afraid—"

"No man has ever said anything like that to me. I don't know what to think."

"Listen, Rachel. I've messed up every time I've been alone with you since I got home. It's just too much too fast, I know. Facing death put me on a fast track that you're not on. I apologize for that. Let me make some simple statements; then I'll go. I love you, more deeply than ever, and I'm not going away again. I know you have other men interested in you, and I know they can offer you many things I can't offer. But they don't love you the way I do, Rachel. They couldn't because they don't know you the way I do. Please, just promise me that you'll take your time and not be pressured by any man, including me."

Rachel nodded. Mark waited, but she said nothing.

"That's all I ask," he reiterated. When she remained silent, he added, "I'll say good-bye now." He leaned forward and kissed her on the top of the head. Then he turned to leave.

"If you're not going away, what are you going to do here?" Rachel called after him.

"Help Philippe with his campaign."

"You are? Doing what? I mean, I know you have a lot to offer, but—"

Mark paused on the steps and turned back to face her, "Philippe's in trouble, Rachel," he said quietly.

Rachel laughed lightly. "Cousin Philippe's always needing to raise more money, Mark."

"I know that," he agreed, then added, "but there's

something else going on. Some other trouble, the kind of trouble that eats up a man's soul and destroys him."

Rachel was stunned, but Mark did not wait for her to ask questions.

Chapter 9

Philippe D'Evereau's New Year's Eve Party was exactly the kind of social event Rachel hated most—masses of swirling people drinking too much and boisterously exclaiming their delight at seeing each other. The women were always focused on the fashions of the evening, and the men were just focused on the female form and the readily available alcohol.

"What's the point?" Rachel asked herself gloomily as she sat at the organdy-skirted dressing table in the quiet of her bedroom. "All those exuberant greetings followed by empty conversations. Everyone trying so desperately to be noticed. It's depressing." She picked up her comb and made a final adjustment to her hair before sternly addressing herself in the mirror. "Philippe is family, and this annual event of his can't be avoided if you are going to live at Belle St. Marie. Besides, Andre will love it, and Louis wants to go, and they are your guests, so that settles that." She resigned herself to the evening's activities and dropped her comb on the dressing table.

A soft knock defused some of her annoyance because she knew it was Lovey, coming to help her into her evening dress. "Come in," she called quietly as she looked into the mirror. When she saw Lovey slip into the room and close the door behind her, she said to her own image, "You'll just have to do," and stood up from the dressing table.

"You'll more than do, Honey," Lovey insisted as she gazed up at Rachel's face. "You's grown into the most beautiful woman I's ever seen. Your Grandmere would be so proud of you if she could see you now."

"Thanks, Lovey." Rachel put her arms around Lovey's shoulders and gave her a little squeeze.

"Now be careful, Honey, and don't mess up your hair. It

looks real elegant all piled up on your head that way."

"I just hope it all stays up there. It's going to be a long night. I suppose Andre and Louis are pacing downstairs waiting for me."

"You don't need to be in no hurry. Mr. Louis just left to drive Mr. Andre over to Mr. Philippe's house," Lovey reported.

"He did? Oh, dear! Andre must have really been tired of waiting for me."

Lovey smiled mysteriously. "I don't think it had a thing to do with Mr. Andre."

"You don't?" Rachel asked. Lovey shook her head, her eyes sparkling from her own secret thoughts. "Lovey, what's going on?" Rachel demanded.

"I think those two men just making sure Mr. Louis get plenty of time alone with you. Besides, Mr. Louis want to arrive at that party as the only escort you's got. He don't even want to share the spotlight with his Daddy."

"Oh dear," Rachel said again. "I see. What am I going to do with that man?"

"Well, the first thing is we's gonna get you into your dress, then while you's waiting for Mr. Louis to get back, you can figure out what you's gonna do with this little problem." Lovey held out a small, velvet-covered box to Rachel.

"What's that?" Rachel asked, but before Lovey could respond, she exclaimed, "Oh, Lovey, it's not a present from Louis, is it? What am I going to do? I don't want to commit to—"

"It ain't from Mr. Louis, Honey," Lovey interrupted. "It's from his daddy, Mr. Andre. It's something that was his mother's, and he wants you to have it."

Rachel warily took the box and held it under the lamp on the dressing table to see it more clearly. The velvet was worn thin on the edges, and the name of the jeweler was so faded she couldn't read it. Slowly Rachel opened the lid, and even though she was prepared to find a ring, she was stunned by the brilliance of the sapphire set in platinum and surrounded by diamonds.

"Oh, Miz Rachel!" Lovey exclaimed. "That ring look like it come from another world."

"It did, Lovey, if it belonged to Andre's mother. Another world entirely. But I can't accept it. You know I can't."

"If Mr. Andre gave it to you, Honey, it must mean a lot to him for you to have it. I bet he been saving it for just the right lady—"

"That's the point, Lovey. He's saving it for his daughter-in-law. He expects me to marry Louis, and I just can't make that commitment now. I thought I could until...." Rachel's voice trailed off.

"Until Mr. Mark come home?"

"Yes. Mark changes everything. I don't know how much yet. I just know I can't make a commitment to Louis until I figure all this out."

"Well, you sure can't do that in the next few minutes."

"So what am I going to do? I can't bear to hurt Andre. You know how loving he's been to me since I came back to Belle St. Marie, and you know how much he loved Grandmere. He's like a grandfather to me."

Lovey took the box from Rachel's hands, closed the lid, and put the box in Rachel's evening bag. "You's gonna take this ring to the party and find Mr. Andre and tell him that you can't take his momma's ring 'cause it just be too dear to him, and you knows he shouldn't part with it."

"He'll be hurt, Lovey."

"I know that, so you's gonna soften the blow by saying you would love to wear it just for this one evening 'cause it's his momma's, but you just can't be happy unless he put the ring on your finger himself."

Rachel frowned down at Lovey for a minute, then a smile flashed across her face. "Lovey! You are quite a strategist! Someone will undoubtedly overhear the conversation, and in no time the whole party will be gossiping about it, and Mark will know why I'm wearing a Simone family ring and that it's not an engagement ring."

"He'll know why you's wearing this ring tonight, and he'll also know he better not do no foot dragging or he gonna lose you."

"Lovey, you are devious!"

"I's just practical. I can't seem to trust you or Mr. Mark to get on with things. You two wants to think too much, and I ain't getting any younger. Now let's get you into this dress, so you can make a grand entrance walking down the staircase when Mr. Louis get back."

"Are you sure you want me to impress Louis?" Rachel asked as Lovey walked to the closet and lifted down the evening dress which hung from the door.

"We gotta go through that part before we can get you to the party," Lovey announced as she held up the dress for Rachel to step into. "Then Mr. Mark can see you in this dress."

"It is gorgeous, isn't it?" Rachel smiled happily as she ran her fingers along the tissue-paper-thin, cobalt blue silk of the dress.

"It gonna be even prettier when you finally gets in it." Lovey shook the dress a little, and Rachel laughed as she stepped into it. "There you is," Lovey exclaimed as she zipped up the back of the dress. "Come over to the mirror and see yourself." Gently she pulled Rachel toward a full-length, freestanding mirror. "You's elegant, Miz Rachel, just elegant!"

"I love this dress!" Rachel exclaimed as she turned slowly to view herself from all sides. The blue silk had been fashioned into a graceful cowl neckline which framed Rachel's face before flowing over her shoulders and plunging into a deep, v-shape down her back almost to her waist. The bodice of the dress was closely fitted, emphasizing her tiny waist before flowing to the floor in a waterfall of shimmering blue silk.

"It be just the color of your eyes," Lovey observed. "You's gonna steal the show, Miz Rachel. All them other ladies gonna just disappear in all them black dresses they wears all the time."

"You may be slightly prejudiced," Rachel teased.

"I ain't prejudiced. I's been helping ladies dress for parties for over 50 years, and I knows quality when I sees it. You just wait and see. Mr. Louis gonna just about faint when he see you coming down them stairs."

"And what will Mark think?"

"He won't never get over it!"

Rachel laughed, walked over to the dressing table bench and started to sit down.

"Wait!" Lovey exclaimed as she hurried over to Rachel and picked up the back of her skirt so it would drape over the bench when Rachel sat down. "Ain't no need to start out with wrinkles," she said as she arranged the skirt. "You know, Honey, I seen you and Mr. Mark sitting on the verandah talking the other afternoon. You ain't told me nothing about it, but you two sure looked just like you used to when you was teenagers. I don't know how many times I seen you sitting on that same wicker couch with your legs draped over Mr. Mark's lap. The only thing missing was a Pepsi Cola in your hands."

"Lovey! I was an RC Cola girl; it was Mark who insisted on Pepsi."

Lovey burst into laughter. "I's getting old for sure. How could I ever have gotten that mixed up?"

"I can't imagine, but if you really are that out of your mind, you better sit down and rest. I'll get you a chair."

Rachel started to rise, but Lovey insisted, "Don't you move. I's got your dress all fixed. I'll get my own chair." She laughed again as she pulled a small chair closer to Rachel and sat down. "I can't believe I forgot about you and RC Cola. You and Mr. Mark used to fight about that all the time, and Miz Elinore and I ordered up them wooden cases full of both Pepsi and RC just to keep the peace."

"Oh, I remember those wooden cases. I haven't seen one in years. Whatever happened to them?"

Lovey sighed. "Seems like everything is paper or plastic these days."

"Remember the glass bottles with the bottle tops you couldn't open without a bottle opener?"

"Oh, I remember them all right, Honey, and I remember Mr. Mark showing off in front of you by popping those tops off using the drawer handles in my kitchen."

Rachel giggled. "That's the only time I can remember you ever getting mad at us, Lovey." She fell silent a minute, then sighed. "Those were fun-filled days. Our biggest problems were our disagreements over favorite drinks and who was the best rock-and-roll singer."

"I remember. All you kids used to sit on the verandah arguing over Elvis and Ricky Nelson. But that wasn't what you was arguing about with Mr. Mark the other afternoon, was it?"

"We weren't really arguing, Lovey; we were talking about some very serious issues. Mark has turned into such a deep thinker. It surprises me."

"He was always more serious than you realized, Miz Rachel. Now he's been through some tough times. He can't help but be changed by them, but that don't mean the changes is bad."

"No, they aren't bad, but they do surprise me. Would you have ever thought that Mark would be interested in spiritual matters? I wouldn't have."

"Oh, Miz Rachel. That boy been wrestling with God since he first came here, just like you has."

Rachel fell silent and stared into the mirror, looking far past her own reflection.

"I hears a car," Lovey announced as she jumped up and dragged her chair back to the wall. A few seconds later they both heard the front door open.

A wave of relief swept over Rachel. "I better get myself

downstairs. I've kept Louis waiting long enough."

"I'll tell him you's on the way down, Honey." Quietly she picked up the blue silk shawl that completed Rachel's ensemble and exited the room.

Before Lovey descended the staircase, she stopped and whispered, "Lord, she done come a long way. You know how she was when she come here. I's depending on You to be patient with her, Lord." Lovey started down the stairs, then stopped and added, "but not too patient, Lord." She thought about her words as she descended several steps, then stopped again and added another postscript. "I's sure you's gonna get it just right, Lord. You always does."

Satisfied with her understanding with God, Lovey hurried on down, found Louis in the drawing room, and announced, "Miz Rachel be coming down now."

He smiled at her and left the room to wait in the wide hall that ran the full depth of the house. Lovey followed him, Rachel's silk shawl still in her hands. She stood in the background and watched as Rachel descended the wide staircase, the blue silk of her dress vivifying her blue eyes and floating around her ankles.

Louis' face lit up with a proud smile, and when she reached the bottom of the staircase, he eagerly took both her hands in his, leaned forward and kissed them. When he straightened, his face was covered with a puzzled look which undoubtedly resulted from finding no sapphire ring embellishing either hand, but he said nothing. Instead he turned to Lovey and took the shawl from her hands. "We have a magnificent evening to usher in the New Year," he said to Rachel as he turned back to face her. "The sky is crystal clear, full of diamonds, but all of them put together can't compete with you tonight, Rachel." He gently placed the stole around her shoulders and leaned forward and kissed her.

"Shall we go?" Rachel asked when his lips left hers.

"I would rather not share you," he admitted as he put her arm through his and escorted her to the front door, "but I suppose I must."

"Good night, Lovey," Rachel called back as they left, "and Happy New Year."

"Good night, Honey," Lovey answered. After she had closed the door and was sure she was alone in the house, she announced, "Lord, I's ready for that man to go home to Paris. He ain't nothing but a roadblock for Miz Rachel. He ain't the right one, and You and I knows it. Besides, I don't trust him. You gotta put a whole ocean between him and Miz Rachel."

Mark impatiently circulated through the elegant downstairs rooms of his Uncle Philippe's mansion, pausing to make polite conversation only when he was absolutely required to. He had only one guest on his mind, and she had not arrived. The very thought of watching Rachel arrive with Louis made Mark bristle and tighten his hands into fists. To deal with his frustration, he tried to focus on inventing ways he would employ to move her out of Louis' reach during the evening and keep her to himself. More tense minutes ticked by as Mark came to the painful realization that he had little chance of being alone with Rachel.

"Mark." His Uncle interrupted his thoughts. "Would you greet our guests for a few minutes? I have some urgent business to attend to." Without waiting for Mark to respond, Philippe left his side and hurried up the staircase. Mark's tension doubled. He had no desire to greet Rachel and stand by helplessly while Louis controlled her attention; nevertheless, he was stuck with the job. Once again the door opened. Certain that Rachel would enter this time, Mark steeled himself for the encounter.

"Well, Mark, old boy!" Billy Ray Snyder called out from the doorway, much to Mark's surprise. "I see Philippe has you on door duty. No doubt he's got bigger fish to fry, if you know what I mean."

"I don't," Mark responded coldly.

"Sure you do," Billy Ray insisted. "Big spenders. Political contributions, that sort of thing."

"It's a New Year's party, Billy Ray. Just a party."

"Now, Mark, don't get your back up. You know everything is political with old Philippe. Why shouldn't it be? He's a politician."

"He's a D'Evereau, and this party is the continuation of an old D'Evereau tradition," Mark insisted stiffly.

"Whatever you say," Billy Ray taunted. "But if it's a party, where's your date?"

For a split second Mark considered stopping Billy Ray's mouth with his fist, but fortunately his maiden Great Aunt Emilie appeared at his side and slipped her hand into the crook of his elbow. "Oh, Mark dear," she said sweetly, "I see Philippe has stuck you with the door. That's no place for an active boy like you. You run along and have fun."

"Thank you, Aunt Emilie," Mark murmured as he reached over and kissed her on the forehead. "I do need to be relieved of this duty."

"Of course you do," she agreed as he started to walk away with Billy Ray Snyder close behind him. "One moment, Mr. Snyder," she called after them. "I don't recall dismissing you, and I'm sure I wouldn't think of doing so until I've had a chance to visit with you properly. You stay here." She pointed to a place beside her. Billy Ray stared back at her. "Right here," she insisted until Billy Ray reluctantly but obediently returned to her side. "Now, isn't this lovely," she asked as she smiled sweetly up into Billy Ray's face. "We shall have such a delightful chat."

Mark walked toward the staircase, trying his best to hide the grin that was blossoming on his face. He had changed his mind and decided that he preferred to be upstairs when Rachel arrived with Louis. He climbed the stairs two at a time until he reached the top and found himself in the relative peace of the upstairs hall.

As Mark wandered down the length of the hall, he suddenly heard his Uncle's angry voice behind a closed door. "I expressly forbade you to invite those men, Lisette! I won't have them in my house!"

"Don't be such an idiot, Philippe!" Lisette retorted. "We need them. You do want to be governor, don't you?"

"I would a thousand times rather lose this election than have their support!"

"And you will lose it, too," Lisette retorted, "if I leave it up to you. But I have no intention of doing that! I plan to—"

"I am the candidate—not you!"

"More's the pity," Lisette sneered. "I wouldn't be swayed by all your sentimentality. All your D'Evereau, family-name, useless baggage."

Icy silence suddenly replaced the raised voices, and Mark, confused and worried by what he had heard, turned to walk away. As he did, he heard Philippe say coldly, "You've demanded the name often enough, Lisette."

"And I will again, Philippe," she warned. "Don't think I won't. But I'm nobody's fool. I don't want to become a D'Evereau until after you become elected governor."

"So what you really want is not me. You just want to be the First Lady of Louisiana," Philippe concluded.

"It all goes together, doesn't it? Why shouldn't I want to be the governor's wife? You owe me that much."

"Perhaps I do, Lisette, perhaps I do," Philippe agreed wearily. "But I still won't do business with those men. We'll find the money somewhere else."

"I've found the money already," Lisette informed him. "Don't worry, you won't have to get your D'Evereau hands dirty." Again Mark heard nothing but silence. When Lisette finally spoke again, she had changed her tone completely, "Be reasonable, Darling," she pleaded. "We do need their money, and I hear that Billy Ray Snyder does some business with them. He's as 'Louisiana' as they come, isn't he? So you see they do have Louisiana connections."

"I thought you hated Billy Ray Snyder."

"I don't hate him, Philippe. I just find him uncouth and obnoxious, but he is a good businessman."

"A shady one, you mean. Heaven only knows where all his money comes from."

"And heaven can worry about it, too," Lisette snapped. "I certainly don't intend to. All I care about is that he contributes heavily to your campaign. Now, Philippe, you really have to be realistic. All you have to do is give these men a private minute or two this evening. That will satisfy them."

"It's New Year's Eve, Lisette. I have hundreds of guests to consider, guests I invited, and I did not invite these men!"

"What are you going to do? Throw them out? That'll make a fine scene for your guests and the news people."

"They can stay in the house for the evening, but I will not meet with them privately. I don't like this kind of connection. We could get hurt—"

Philippe's words were suddenly cut off for a long minute, then Lisette sighed and cooed, "Don't worry, Darling. You know how much I love you. I'll take care of everything, just like I always have."

"I still don't like it," Philippe said, but all the forcefulness had left his voice.

"But you'll keep quiet, my love," Lisette answered confidently, "and we both know why, don't we?"

Sickened by what he had heard, Mark turned and walked the length of the hall, opened the French doors that accessed the upper verandah, and hurried out into the fresh air. Once he reached the railing, he leaned on it as he fought his impulse to return to his uncle's room and jerk him out of Lisette's arms. Finally he muttered, "That settles it. The devil himself couldn't keep me out of this campaign now."

A Mercedes pulled up close to the steps of the lower verandah, and Mark watched as Louis stepped out, walked around, and helped Rachel out of the car. When Louis turned to give the keys to the parking attendant, Rachel raised her head, apparently looking up at the stars. Her eyes stopped when she saw Mark, and he was filled with an immeasurable longing to be at her side. Quickly she looked down as Louis came to her side and offered her his arm for support. Mark stood perfectly still, imagining the scene being acted out beneath him as Rachel made her grand entrance into the house. "She'll steal the show," he whispered, "but Louis won't steal her from me. She's mine!"

Mark impatiently waited for a reasonable amount of time to pass before he walked around the verandah and used the servants' staircase to descend to the first floor. Quickly he walked through the busy kitchen, determined on two things: to embrace Rachel and to spot the men his uncle so violently objected to.

He spotted Rachel first as she moved around the front parlor greeting everyone. Overwhelmed by her beauty and his feelings for her, he stopped to watch her. A moment later his concentration was broken by a bustling activity to his right and the sound of a woman's voice exclaiming, "Oh, there's Rachel D'Evereau. She's Philippe's niece. You must meet her." A man with a distinctly foreign accent responded, and Mark turned toward the sound. He saw two men, who bore all the characteristics of middle-eastern origin, smiling at an elderly lady who began to usher them toward Rachel. Mark was immediately struck with the conviction that he had seen the men before, but he couldn't place them. He watched as the lady directed them to Rachel's side and introduced them.

Alarms suddenly sounded off inside of Mark, alarms he did not understand. He could not resist them, so he began to move toward Rachel to protect her from some danger he could not define. He had only walked halfway across the room when, much to his amazement, he heard Louis say curtly to the men, "Rachel has many people to greet. Please excuse us." Mark watched as Louis put his arm around Rachel's shoulders and firmly led her away from the men. Her surprise was obvious. As Louis ushered her out of the parlor, she looked back over her shoulder at the men, her eyes filled with apologies.

Certain that Louis would take care of Rachel, Mark's alarm turned to intense curiosity, so he proceeded toward the men, eager to meet them. The elderly lady was only too happy to introduce him to the strangers, who identified themselves as Syrian businessmen. They expressed delight at meeting Philippe D'Evereau's nephew. Haunted by his feeling that he had seen them before, Mark intentionally talked with them in the most casual manner he could achieve. His years as an investigative reporter were shaping his conversation, but before he could learn much more than the fact that they were connected to the oil industry, Lisette suddenly appeared at his side.

"Now, Mark," she chided good-naturedly, "You mustn't monopolize our guests." She looked up into the faces of the men and dazzled them with her most charming smile. "You must come enjoy some of our Louisiana specialties," she insisted as she ushered them away.

Mark waited a moment, then followed the three across the hall into the dining room. He watched as Lisette picked up a plate for each man and shepherded them through the buffet line. As soon as their plates were filled, Lisette spotted Philippe in the doorway and exclaimed, "Oh, there's Philippe! He'll be so delighted you're here. Let me get his attention and then the three of you can sneak away to his library for a private drink." She hurried over to Philippe, forcibly ushered him to the men and then urged them all toward the library. "Don't worry," she called as Philippe, obviously unhappy, moved away with the men in tow. "I'll bring you some champagne myself." All business for the moment, Lisette took a tray of filled champagne glasses from a waiter and followed the men.

Mark desperately wanted to follow her into the library, but he could think of no pretense to do so. Instead he moved toward the buffet table himself, absent-mindedly filling his plate. Across the table two women were delicately choosing tidbits for themselves and talking gaily, but Mark ignored them until he heard the name "Rachel." Without looking up from his plate, he turned his attention to their conversation.

"Have you ever seen such a ring, Hilary?" one woman exclaimed. "It's positively fabulous."

"Awesome, totally awesome," Hilary agreed, "but I'm totally confused, Kristen. Are you sure the old man gave it to her? Are you sure it didn't come from his son?"

"I heard it myself, I tell you. Rachel told the old man—what's his name?"

"Andre Simone."

"Right. She told Andre Simone that she couldn't accept it as a gift, but she would wear it just tonight."

"I could accept it!" Hilary exclaimed. "Especially since you and I both know what it really means."

"You don't mean the old man wants to marry her!" Kristen laughed. "How ludicrous! Can you imagine her royal highness,

Princess Rachel, marrying—"

"Don't be an idiot, Kristen," Hilary snapped. "It's the son who wants her. You know, that gorgeous man from Paris named Louis. He's old Andre's son."

"Oh, I get it. You're right, I am an idiot. But why doesn't Louis just ask Rachel to marry him?"

Hilary sighed dramatically. "She's a D'Evereau, Kristen. These wealthy old Creole families still do things their own way. Don't worry. He'll ask her, and soon, I bet."

"Do you think she'll accept?"

"Wouldn't you?" Hilary demanded. "I mean, look at the man! And he's rich, too."

"Rachel D'Evereau doesn't need money," Kristen insisted. "In fact, the ice princess doesn't seem to need anything."

"She needs a man, Kristen," Hilary pronounced flatly, then changed the subject. "Oh-h, look at these French pastries!"

Mark left the buffet, abandoned his plate on the nearest table and went to find Rachel.

Chapter 10

Mark scoured all the reception rooms but could not spot Rachel. As he stood in the central hall, his anger and frustration grown to the volcanic point, the grandfather clock struck 11:00, and he heard the faint sounds of an orchestra as it began to play. Quickly he returned to the dining room and passed through it into the ballroom wing of the house that had been added at the turn of the century.

When he entered the ballroom, he found it half full of dancing couples. He moved to the side until he spotted Rachel moving gracefully around the floor in Louis' arms. She was looking up into his face, smiling happily, her golden hair gleaming in the light from the crystal chandelier. Mark's eyes moved from the golden curls on top of her head, down to her slender waist encased in blue silk, and finally to her graceful ankles. He was so mesmerized by the swaying of her full, silk skirt he was transported back over 15 years to their college days together. They had danced away many a night, and even now Mark could still feel the curve of her waist in the palm of his hand.

He shook himself back to the present and spotted Rachel's right hand gently joined with Louis' hand. Forewarned by the women's gossip about Rachel, he thought he was thoroughly prepared to find an elegant ring on her finger, but he wasn't. As Louis once again whirled Rachel around in the waltz, the sapphire and diamond creation embellishing her right hand caught the light from the chandelier and flashed rays of blue and white light. The sight infuriated Mark. Feeling totally outclassed, he turned away and strode out the open French doors onto the verandah.

Mark leaned against a pillar, looking up at the bright stars, but all he saw in his mind's eye was Rachel's sapphire-embellished hand. "What does it mean?" he murmured. Then as his own thoughts provided him with unwelcome answers to his question, his whole body stiffened. "Whatever it takes," he said aloud, "I will win. He can't have her."

Abruptly he turned back to the ballroom, and after entering the door, he once again spotted Rachel dancing in Louis' arms. Controlling his limp as much as he could, he boldly stepped toward Louis and tapped him on the shoulder. The couple stopped as Louis, his arm still around Rachel's waist, turned and coolly stared at him. When Louis made no movement to release her, Mark insistently tapped him on the shoulder again. White with anger, Louis turned back to Rachel, bowed, and excused himself.

"My dancing is slightly impaired, I'm afraid, but I can't resist a waltz with the only woman in the world for me," Mark said loudly enough for the departing Louis to hear, "and no ring from any man will ever keep me away from you."

"Mark, please," Rachel said as she moved into his arms to dance. He slid his right hand around her waist and silently vowed that he would do anything—even control his temper—to win her. However long it took, whatever tactics were necessary, he would fight until he won because there was no life for him without her.

He drew her closer to him and whispered in her ear, "Don't worry, Rachel. I'll stay calm, but I won't hide the truth. I love you, Rachel. I know you, the real you, and I love you. No other man could ever love you as deeply as I do. They don't even know you. Remember that. No one will ever love you like I do."

Rachel raised her head and looked intently into his eyes. Her eyes softened until they shone like luminous jewels. "I know," she said, then placed her cheek on his shoulder. Mark was content.

In far too short a time another partner tapped Mark on the shoulder, and he had to relinquish Rachel, but he did not fret about it. He left the center of the ballroom, walked to one of the French doors and stepped outside on the verandah. The cool air felt good, and the stars were still shining brightly overhead, but his star was dancing with a young college student, not with a serious suitor. Mark walked down the steps from the verandah to the grass and sat on a bench to collect his emotions.

He knew that in the next hour the ballroom would fill and the guests would begin to eagerly watch the clock for the magical hour that would turn the old year into a new start for everyone. He also knew that Louis would insist on his right to Rachel for the countdown to midnight. Silently he warned himself, I will have to watch Louis kiss her as the New Year begins, but I can handle that. I can let Louis have the first hour of the year because I plan to have the rest of her life.

Mark sat, thinking about his future with Rachel as the old year ran down. Patience, he told himself, and a steady temper. I know she loves me. I know she does. As he reassured himself, his thoughts were interrupted by a low, intense voice coming from the verandah he had just left.

"I don't like it, Lisette," a male voice very familiar to Mark insisted. "They should not be here."

"But they are so important to Philippe's campaign," Lisette insisted as Mark rose from the bench, determined to make certain that his suspicion was correct, that the man was indeed Louis. Mark made no attempt to hide himself, nor did he need to because Louis and Lisette were turned away from him and intent on their own words.

"I often wonder if you have any sense of class, Lisette, any sense of decorum at all," Louis said pompously.

"I haven't had the advantages of Rachel D'Evereau, if that's what you mean," Lisette retorted.

"Your behavior makes that fact so obvious you need not state it," Louis replied cruelly. "I don't want those men here. Remove them!" He turned his back and left.

Lisette stood for a few minutes, wringing her hands, obviously struggling to control herself. Then she lifted her chin and walked resolutely back into the ballroom.

Mark stepped back onto the verandah and followed her. Immediately he noticed that Louis had reclaimed his position as Rachel's dancing partner and was now gliding across the dance floor with her as he smiled down at her. For a moment Mark stood and watched Louis' expression, stunned by the quick change from black anger to light-hearted sociability. Who is this man really? Mark wondered. Cruel as he was to Lisette, or loving, as he seems to be to Rachel?

Thoughts of Lisette made him glance around the ballroom to find her. When he did, he saw her standing between the two Syrians, smiling vivaciously at them as she directed them from the ballroom. Mark followed at a distance. When Lisette had escorted the men into the dining room, she eagerly beckoned to the young women, Hilary and Kristen, and made quite a show of introducing them. Then she made some excuse and hastened off, but Mark noticed that from the entrance hall she watched the four carefully. Her efforts were obviously successful, for soon the taller man stopped a waiter and picked up glasses of champagne for the four of them. They broke quite naturally into two couples and wandered out onto the verandah.

Amazing, Mark thought. Louis commands, and Lisette obeys. But why? What hold could he possibly have over her?

The guests became more feverish as the midnight hour approached, and they gathered in the ballroom. Philippe took control of the microphone and made quite a gallant speech about the great hopes for the New Year. Then the whole party counted down the last 30 seconds, and suddenly the New Year had begun. The band struck up "Auld Lang Syne," and the guests sang, interrupting the song only long enough to kiss. Mark stood to the side and watched while first Louis and then Andre kissed Rachel.

"You should be kissing that particular lady," a female voice announced behind him. When he turned, he found Aunt Emilie looking up at him. "Go on over there," she insisted amidst all the tumult, "and kiss her. Ignore those Simones. Your mother was a D'Evereau, so you're a D'Evereau, and a D'Evereau man hasn't lost a woman to a Simone yet. Don't you be the first, or I'll have to turn you over my knee!"

Mark laughed heartedly, then took her gently in his arms. "You're the first lady I'm going to kiss in the New Year," he announced. He leaned over and brushed his lips lightly across hers. "Happy New Year, Great Aunt Emilie."

"Happy New Year, darling boy. Your mother would be so proud of you. I hope you know that. So proud and so glad you're back in Louisiana. Now go kiss Rachel." Just as she stopped speaking, the noise in the ballroom was overshadowed by the fireworks going off outside, and the guests began to move out the French doors. "Go on, boy, go kiss her," she insisted.

"I will," he promised, "but not until I can create some fireworks of my own." She nodded her understanding, and he added, "Let's go see the fun," and escorted her outside.

When Mark returned to the house after the fireworks, he could not spot Rachel in any of the crowd. His heart sank at the prospect that she and Louis had slipped away during all the noisy celebration. He knew Rachel well enough to know that she would prefer quiet, and he was certain Louis would be delighted to accommodate her. Methodically, but without drawing attention to himself he searched all the public rooms of the house. He ended his search on the eastern verandah, the place where he could stare into the woods and know that less than a mile away along the path he knew so well Rachel was probably sitting with Louis.

"You're right," a male voice said behind him. "She's not here."

Mark turned halfway to give Billy Ray Snyder a look that clearly communicated, "Go to hell!"

"He's got her to himself, old boy," Billy Ray continued, his voice depressed, as he walked up close to Mark and slapped him on the shoulder. "I guess we both lost this race." Slightly unsteady on his feet, he put a hand on Mark's shoulder to keep his balance.

"You've had too much to drink, Billy Ray," Mark replied coldly as he brushed Billy Ray's hand off.

Billy Ray laced his words with profanities as he brightened up and announced, "No need to get down about it though. What we got to remember, Mark, old boy, is that the trophy hasn't been lost. This is just one little race."

"I don't know what you're talking about, Snyder," Mark tried to walk past Billy Ray, but he reached out and grabbed Mark's arm.

"Sure you do, old boy, we're talking about the prize of all prizes, Rachel." Billy Ray laughed quietly. "Don't pretend with me, Mark. I know who my competitors are, and I'm not as drunk as you'd like to think. That's not my style. I run a race to win, and drunks don't win."

"Rachel isn't a prize in a horserace," Mark replied stiffly. "Let go of my arm."

"Sure, sure." Billy Ray released him. "Just remember that after tomorrow, when Louis returns to Paris, there will only be two horses running on this track: you and me."

Mark stared angrily at him for a moment before silently turning to leave.

Once again Billy Ray put out an arm to stop him. "What have you got to offer her, Mark? You can't even take care of her. Unless, of course, you're idiot enough to think you can wrap her up in one of your Time magazine covers and keep her warm."

"Get out of the way, Billy Ray," Mark warned.

Billy Ray moved closer to Mark's face and sneered. "Or maybe you don't need to take care of her, now that I think of it. She's got plenty of money and sure to inherit more. Maybe you're just planning for her to take care of you—"

Mark's fist shot out and caught Billy Ray's chin, knocking him against the railing of the verandah. For an instant it appeared that Billy Ray would right himself and come back swinging, but then he laughed as he wiped the blood off his lip.

Mark turned and stalked off the verandah, but not quickly enough to miss Billy Ray's parting shot. "Yes sir, it's gonna be quite a horse race."

Furious with himself for allowing Billy Ray to goad him into violence, Mark walked the grounds of his uncle's plantation, trying to cool off. "The truth is, I didn't even hit the man I want to hit," Mark muttered angrily. "It's Louis I want to smash to a pulp. He's the only real competition here; Rachel wouldn't give Billy Ray Snyder a serious look."

He walked down the long driveway, then stopped and looked back at the mansion, which now seemed to be bursting with merrymaking. The band played loudly, and the crowded ballroom could not contain the exuberant dancers. They had flooded the verandah and even spilled onto the lawn. "No wonder Rachel left," Mark murmured. "This just isn't her kind of scene."

"You need me to get your car, mister?" a voice from someone behind Mark asked. "What kind is it?"

Mark turned away from the mansion as he answered, "No, no, I don't need a car."

"Oh, Mr. Mark, I didn't know it was you. 'Course you don't need no car—"

"We need our car," a woman called gaily from somewhere up the driveway closer to the house. "In fact, we need two cars."

When Mark turned toward the voice, he recognized the woman named Hilary, who was staggering down the driveway clutching the arm of one of the Syrians.

"We need ten cars!" her friend, Kristen, announced loudly as she approached with the other Syrian. "Twenty cars! One in every color—"

"Mr. Mark," the valet said, turning to Mark, "I can't let them drive. Mr. Philippe will fire me if—"

"I will drive," the taller Syrian announced. "I am quite capable. Bring the silver BMW."

"I want to drive!" Kristen insisted. "I can drive!"

"Bring the car," the Syrian ordered. The valet looked at Mark for confirmation, and Mark nodded his approval before walking away.

As Mark walked back up the driveway, he moved his thoughts about Rachel to the back of his mind and reconsidered the events of the evening that related to the Syrians. He remembered overhearing Philippe and Lisette arguing about some guests she had invited and whether or not to accept their financial support for Philippe's campaign. He had assumed that these two men were the guests Philippe couldn't stomach, an assumption that had been strengthened by Louis' overt disapproval of them and his insistence that Lisette get them out of the house. He stopped and looked back at the men helping Hilary and Kristen into the car. Lisette set this all up, Mark thought; she provided the girls to get rid of the Syrians. Why did she act so quickly on Louis' order? What power does he have over her?

Certain that something devious, and probably injurious to his uncle, was going on, Mark chose not to return to the guests. Instead he stepped off the driveway and walked across the lawn to circle the house so he could enter through the kitchen.

I need to think about all this, he thought as he climbed the servants' stairs to the second floor and walked to his own bedroom. When he had arrived, he closed the door behind him although there was no way to shut out the noise of the party. He walked through the French doors out onto the upper verandah off his room and settled in a rattan chair.

It doesn't surprise me that Lisette is unscrupulous, he thought, especially when it comes to funding Uncle Philippe's campaign. It also doesn't surprise me that she does what she wants whether Uncle wants her to or not. She knows she can get away with anything because she's having an affair with him. He's always had a weakness for beautiful women, but Lisette is more than beautiful. She's smart and conniving and totally selfish. She wants to be the first lady of this state, and she doesn't even bother to hide her ambition from Uncle. I wonder why he puts up with her; there are plenty of women he could have, a lot of them more beautiful than Lisette.

And how does Louis fit into all this? Mark considered that question a moment. What hold has he got over Lisette that she would jump to do his will? And why does he object so much to the Syrians being here? Does he know them? He has to know them; otherwise he wouldn't object to them so violently. Louis is a snob, no doubt about that, but his objection to these men is more than snobbery.

Mark pondered all these questions for a few minutes, then whispered insistently, "I know I've seen those guys before. Somehow they were connected to some story I did, but it's been a number of years back, and they couldn't have been principal players in the story, or I would remember them. Who are they?

That's got to be a priority of mine; I've got to find out."

The thought of Louis made Mark suddenly re-focus on Rachel. She's with him right now, he thought, probably in the car, so close to him he can just reach out and touch her....The thought made Mark spring from his chair and walk to the railing. He peered through the woods in the direction of Belle St. Marie. "That Andre is a crafty old man," he whispered, "trying to give Rachel that family ring. They're setting her up, and I'd bet my last dollar that tonight is the night Louis will pop the question."

Chapter 11

It was a few minutes after 1:00 when Rachel and her guests returned to Belle St. Marie from Philippe's New Year's Eve party. As Louis opened the front door for Rachel, Andre trailed behind insisting, "Louis, you must take Rachel back to the party. I refuse to cause her to miss all the merry making."

"Really, Andre, I've had enough celebrating," Rachel assured him. "It was a wonderful party, but I think the best of it is over now."

"But, My Dear, it's not fair to the other guests," he argued gallantly, "to remove your golden beauty and sparkling charm from the group just because your ancient house guest is tired. Think how dismal the party is at this very moment because you have left."

"Andre, Andre," Rachel laughed softly, "you are hardly ancient, and I'm sure the party is going on more boisterously than ever."

"Impossible!" Andre insisted. "How can a party survive when the very light of it has left?"

Rachel moved closer to his side, stood on her tiptoes and kissed him on the cheek. "You are wonderful, my dear Andre. God threw away the pattern after He made you, and oh, how the world has suffered because of that loss! We could have used so many more Andres in this world."

"Thank you, My Dear." He took her hands in his, leaned over and kissed them. When he did, the light from the chandelier flashed off the sparkling sapphire and reminded Rachel that she must now return it.

She waited for a moment as Louis stepped up behind her and slipped off her silk stole. Then she removed the ring and held it out to the older man. "Wearing this exquisite ring of your mother's has been the highlight of the evening, dear Andre. I felt like a princess every time I saw it on my finger—"

"No, no, My Dear. You made the ring extraordinary. It is, after all, only a cold stone, but you carry a light that no jewel could hope to match."

Rachel smiled at his flattery, but she refused to be diverted. She drew the small velvet box from her evening bag, opened it and slipped the ring back into its safe spot. "Thank you, Andre, for honoring me this way, but the evening is over." She held out the box to him.

He leaned over and kissed her on the cheek. "It is I, and indeed all the Simones, who have been honored, My Dear. Isn't that true, Louis?"

"Rachel's mere presence in my life honors me, Papa," Louis replied smoothly. "She is the true jewel."

"Well said!" Andre exclaimed and suddenly turned toward the staircase. "Good night, dear ones," he called back.

"But Andre, wait—" Rachel held out the ring box and started to follow him. Louis gently pulled her back. Turning to him, she insisted, "I can't keep the ring, Louis. Really, I can't."

"Not as a gift, I know," Louis agreed, "although Papa would gladly give it to you. Here, let me have it." She placed the velvet box in his hand. "I'll take care of it." He began to draw her into the parlor where bright coals were smoldering in the fireplace. "Let's enjoy the new year in peace," he suggested as he led her toward the hearth.

She stood watching as he added several logs to the fire, then took out a white handkerchief to wipe his hands. The dry bark of the logs burst into a multitude of tiny flames, which sent sparks of light and dancing shadows around the otherwise dark room. His task finished, he turned toward her; silently looking down at her, his face became a picture of contentment. His dark eyes softened as he placed his hands on her shoulders and said, "Rachel, now is our time....right now."

She instinctively knew where he was leading the conversation and tried to veer it off his intended path. "It was difficult to talk at the party, wasn't it? It was so crowded!"

"That's not what I meant, my darling. I meant that this is our time in history, our time to live life to the fullest. You are perfection in my eyes, you know."

Uncomfortable, Rachel tried to pull away and turn to the sofa, but he gently held her. "I know it's embarrassing for you to listen to such praise, but what I said is still true. You are beautiful and intelligent. What more could a man ask for?"

Rachel raised her head and looked intently into his face. "Character, perhaps? Even spirituality?" she asked quietly.

He was unperturbed. "I don't know anything about God," he admitted, "but neither does anyone else. That's why they fight about Him all the time." Rachel could not deny the truth of what he said. Her own family had been embroiled in religious warfare as long as she could remember. When she remained silent, he continued, "I do know that life belongs to the strong, the ones willing to live it fully."

"I don't know if I agree," Rachel replied hesitantly.

"It's true, my darling. We humans make our own reality. You and I are the lucky ones because we have the wealth and power to create a pleasant reality for ourselves." He stepped closer to her, dropping her hands as he reached out and cupped her face in his palms. "The world is ours, Rachel," he insisted. "Let's take it together."

"What are you saying, Louis?"

"I'm asking you to marry me. Let me slip this ring of my grandmother's back on your finger as my pledge to you of my love, and let us move forward from this minute planning our lives together. Will you marry me, Rachel?"

She had known this moment was coming, but now that it was here, she didn't know what to say. There had been times in the previous year when she had had little difficulty imagining herself as Mrs. Louis Simone. Those times always came after she and Louis had enjoyed a symphony or ballet together or had simply walked the streets of New Orleans, arm in arm silently enjoying the beauty. Life with Louis would undoubtedly provide her with a serene existence filled with all the positive experiences life could offer. But was that enough to make her happy? She didn't know, and there was the question of Mark.... "I can't make that kind of commitment now, Louis," she finally said. "I need time."

"I understand," he said, so easily that he startled her. "You are a wise woman. You need to learn more about what life with me will be like. I anticipated your need, my darling, so I reserved two tickets to Paris."

"Paris?"

"The social season is just beginning in Paris; we will have missed little of importance, and I know you will love every minute of it."

"But Louis," Rachel objected. "I can't just leave Louisiana."

"Why not? There's nothing here to hold you."

"You don't even know me if you can say such a thing," Rachel protested. "There are people here I love!"

"Of course, of course, and you can return to visit them as I visit my father. But, Rachel, you must face facts. Your life is not here. You were not made to spend your days in some backwater town. You are too beautiful, too intelligent, too elegant. You were made to grace the stages of the world, and as my wife, you will be able to do just that."

"But I have made commitments here, Louis."

"What commitments? What are these commitments that are so significant they should hold you here?" he asked gently.

"This plantation!" Abruptly she pulled away from him and walked several paces before turning to face him. "The school," she added, "yes, the school. I have dedicated myself to improving the lives of poverty-stricken young people in this area by raising their level of education. Doesn't that seem important to you?"

"Absolutely." He strode to her side and gently stroked her neck. "Your concern for such people is one of the things I admire in you. And I understand how helping them has helped you to recover from your husband's death, but Rachel, you don't need that work anymore. I can give you anything you want, everything you need."

"Can you?" Rachel asked doubtfully. "Can you really, Louis? Can you give me the fulfillment that comes from helping others?"

"Rachel, darling, fulfillment comes from enjoyment of life, not from struggle. Why surround yourself with other people's difficulties? The whole world would like to have what you have. Enjoy it."

"I've never lived my life that way, Louis. I don't want to. I don't even know if I could."

"I know. You've always taught college even though you never needed money, but what has it gotten you? What painful price have you paid for the way you lived your life during your first marriage?"

Stunned, Rachel stared up at him, her mind galloping in all directions. When she finally found her voice, she could do no more than whisper hoarsely, "Are you blaming me for the pain in my marriage?"

"Of course not! I know what kind of man Collins was. I know about his drinking, his affairs. What I am saying is that you deserve better. Even you don't seem to know what you deserve. You don't need to save the world—or even a portion of it—to deserve happiness, Rachel. I adore you, and I can give you the world. We are alike, darling. I understand you; I can make you happy, I promise."

Rachel walked to a sofa and sat down slowly. Lost in her own thoughts, she stared across the room at the fire without speaking. Louis did not press her for a response; he simply seated himself by her side and took her hand in his.

"You say you understand me, but I wonder…. Even I don't understand myself these days," she murmured. "I thought I had my direction all settled, and then—" She stopped, thinking it better not to say what was on her mind.

"Then Mark returned," he finished her sentence for her.

Hurriedly she glanced at him, expecting to find bitterness on his face.

He smiled at her. "Of course, you feel confused. Who wouldn't? But I promise you, Rachel, when you have time to sort things out, you will remember the many wonderful hours we have spent together in the last year. You will remember all the things we have in common."

"Yes, it has been a wonderful year; we have shared many happy times, and I have grown very....very fond of you. But, Louis, the question is, do I have the kind of love for you that will sustain a marriage?"

"I think you do, Rachel. I know I love you so much I can't imagine life without you." He leaned forward and kissed her tenderly on the lips. "My darling, isn't it true that you had no doubts about our future together before Mark came back?"

She hesitated but finally nodded her head guiltily. "I thought it was just a matter of time. I thought we would be married—" Rachel hesitated, "in time, but I never dreamed you would expect me to abandon my work here."

Louis put his arm around her shoulders and pulled her close to him. "Rachel, I understand. I'm asking you to make huge changes, and now there's also the question of Mark. It's all right. I can't pretend I like it; I can't pretend I don't want to kill Mark Goodman, but I know you will move past this time of confusion. I know you love me and that we will be married."

"I'm just asking for time, Louis. I know we could have a good life together—"

"We will have a great marriage, Rachel, because great marriages are built on compatibility infused with love."

"But, Louis, I can't cheat you or myself by not examining my feelings for Mark. Fifteen years ago I loved him more than I can describe."

"But you married Collins."

"Totally on the rebound, Louis. I was furious with Mark when he enlisted. I could not understand why he would choose to involve himself in Viet Nam, and then when he refused to marry me before he left, I was so hurt I told myself that I hated him."

"Frankly, I don't see any excuse for his enlistment," Louis commented as casually as he could.

"Honor," she whispered reverently. "I see it now, but I was too young then to understand. I didn't want to understand! Now I see that Mark has always been about honor."

"Admirable, I'm sure," Louis commented dryly. "I can only say that I would never have left you. Not for any reason."

Rachel studied Louis' face intently before responding. "No, you wouldn't have. You and Mark are two entirely different men. I have to have more time, Louis. I have to sort through my past feelings for Mark. But there's more—"

"What is this 'more'?"

"I'm not whole yet; I'm not healed from the wounds inflicted by my family. It's embarrassing to have to admit such a thing, but it's true. There are still things I need to settle in Texas, or I'll never be free."

"I can't agree, darling. Why dig up the past? We are going to make a new life, separate from the pains of your past. Why agonize over the stupidity of others? They didn't appreciate you—why, I can't imagine—but they are not worth one minute of your present life."

"I am talking about my parents, Louis!"

"I know. I know. But their previous behavior makes them undeserving of your attention now."

"They are still my parents."

"Not all relationships can be fixed, Rachel, because it takes more than one person trying."

"You're right about that. My father and I have made great progress in mending our relationship, but Mother—"

"You have tried long enough, Rachel. I am glad for the new relationship you have with Jack, but the only solution for the ugliness of the past is to move on."

"Without resolving things with Mother? Without at least forgiving her?"

"Forgiveness is highly overrated, darling. Just move on."

"I don't know. I just don't know." Rachel fell silent as she stared at the flames. "You may be right about Mother, but even if I agree with you that my relationship with her is permanently broken, there are other responsibilities here. What about the school I've started? I'm only now beginning to make a difference for the children here, and I love doing it."

"Why limit yourself to the few children here? As my wife you will have a global platform. Think of all you could accomplish for children."

"But these children need me."

"Your current "hands on" approach is admirable but misguided. It's a waste of your talents. Others can do what you're doing now, but others can't understand the bigger pictures, organize the national or even international efforts. Others simply don't have the presence or position to run things. Face it, Rachel. More children are cared for as the result of an elegant society fundraiser than you'll ever help by going down to that little school and teaching. You weren't made to get your hands 'dirty,' if I may use that word. Look at you, darling, you were made to draw together the wealthy, the powerful—those are the ones who make policy changes in the government and fund the charities of the world. Darling, they don't live in rural Louisiana."

"But I love it here, Louis!"

"I know, darling. Don't worry. We'll keep Belle St. Marie, of course. Naturally we'll keep the Simone mansion in New Orleans and my house in Paris. I'll sell my New York apartment, and together we'll buy a truly grand place there, a place to entertain. That can be the base for all you want to do as well as for our personal lives. Think of it, darling. All the great music and dance and theatre you adore as well as the perfect setting for your philanthropic efforts."

"I've never thought of a larger scope for my efforts. I've always just done what's at hand—whether that meant helping a college student or one of the children here."

"And no doubt you've learned a great deal from those efforts. Now it's time to capitalize on what you know. You have a magnificently loving heart, Rachel. Don't limit its possibilities."

"I don't know what to say except what I said before. I need time, Louis, a great deal of time, to ponder all you've said."

"I'll wait, my darling. I love you. But I do ask one thing of you."

"What?'

"I ask you to keep my grandmother's ring—"

"No, Louis, I can't. It wouldn't be right. I haven't agreed to marry you."

"I'm only asking you to keep it as a reminder of my love and the life I'm offering you. After all, Rachel, it's only fair. Mark will be here in person; I should at least be allowed to leave a symbol of my love. You needn't wear it; just promise to look at it often and remember me." Gently he pressed the box into the palm of her hand and closed her fingers around it.

"Louis, please remember—"

"I know, my darling. You've made no commitment." He kissed her quickly before she could say more.

Rachel lay in bed staring at the top of the canopy and listening as the clock downstairs chimed out 3:00 am. I've got to get some sleep, she fussed. New Year's Day has already begun, and I promised to bring Louis and Andre to Billy Ray's New Year's Day brunch. He's been so supportive of the school, and he's talked about nothing but his new house for all these months he's been building it. We just can't disappoint him.

Once again she closed her eyes and tried to clear her mind of all thoughts, but the best she could do was just skim the top of sleep. Finally, when the clock struck 5:00, she threw back the covers and slid out of the high bed. "I'd rather be up," she grumbled. "In fact, what I really want is to take a walk, but I guess that won't be possible until the sun is up."

She pulled on a warm robe and slipped her feet into her slippers. Pausing by the dressing table, she ran a brush through her hair, then demanded irritably, "What difference does it make anyway? The rest of the house has the good sense to be asleep. The whole country is asleep!" Quietly she left her room and descended the stairs.

When she reached the kitchen, she turned on only the light over the stove. "What's it going to be?" she asked herself as she lit Lovey's old-fashioned gas stove. "Warm milk that won't help you sleep, or caffeine-laced tea that will keep you awake?"

A few minutes later, she pulled out a chair and set a cup of tea on the table. "I just wish I could quit thinking," she murmured. "My mind is so muddled I don't know why it doesn't just shut down from sheer exhaustion."

Slowly she sipped the tea and stared out the window at the darkness. Minutes ticked by until Rachel's attention was arrested by a tapping sound. Confused, she sat in the semi-darkness and listened to it for a minute. Then she realized someone was quietly tapping on the door. When she got up and looked out the window, she saw Mark standing on the back verandah.

"What on earth are you doing here?" she demanded as she opened the door.

"I've come for my New Year's kiss," he announced as he walked past her. "It's still New Year's Day, you know."

"You are certifiably insane, Mark Goodman."

"I know," he said. Then he took her in his arms and kissed her until she pulled her lips away in an effort to get air.

"Do you know what time it is?" she asked.

"Somewhere around 5:00, I'd say," he answered without releasing her.

"Turn loose of me," she demanded. "I'm not even dressed."

"I don't mind."

"Mark, turn loose!" Finally he dropped his arms, and she went back to sit at the table. "Where have you been?"

He shrugged. "Nowhere really. Just wandering around waiting for light." She sipped her tea and did not respond. "Aren't you going to ask me to sit down?" he asked.

"No."

"Thank you, I believe I will sit a spell." He settled in the chair next to her. He stared into her eyes until she grew uncomfortable and looked away. "Louis asked you to marry him, didn't he?"

"None of your business."

He took her left hand in his and examined it. "Well, I don't see the ring. What does that mean?

"I don't want to talk about it."

"Either you didn't accept his proposal or else you don't think gigantic sapphires go with your robe."

"Mark," Rachel growled warningly.

"Rachel," he growled back. "Talk to me."

"I don't want to."

"Why not?"

"Because I can't."

"Why not?"

"Mark! You sound like a two year old."

"Talk to me, Rachel. I'm not going away."

Rachel glared at him, then suddenly blurted out, "I'm so confused."

"Confused is good," Mark announced. "I like confused."

"Thanks a lot! I'll have you know that being confused is painful."

"Not as painful as marrying the wrong man," Mark said flippantly. When she said nothing in response, he leaned close to her and changed his tone. "Listen, Rachel, I know this is a difficult time for you. I know I've made things difficult for you, but I can't say I'm sorry because I'm not. I'm glad I'm back here, and I'm grateful to God that I got back before you married Louis or anyone else." He took her hand in his. "I love you, you know."

"I know, but I'm still confused."

"Hey, it's been a stressful week. The holidays are always like that. Too much going on and not enough sleep. You just need to give yourself some time. Time to rest, time to grow, time to understand yourself a little better."

"Louis says I'm perfect now. I don't need to change. According to him, all I need to do is grab hold of the world and live. You say I need to grow."

"Louis is wrong. You know how much I love you, Rachel, but you're not perfect. You never will be; you'll always be on a journey."

Rachel jumped up from the table and walked to the window to look for the beginnings of dawn. "I want to arrive, Mark! I'm tired of struggling to understand. I just want peace. Louis can give me peace."

Mark rose from the table and walked over to stand behind her. "No, Rachel, he can't. Neither can I. To find peace you're going to need someone bigger than both of us."

Rachel ignored his remark. "He wants me to go to Paris with him. To go experience the world."

Mark wrapped his arms around her. "Rachel, I've experienced the world. Trust me, it won't satisfy your most basic need. Only God can do that. When you're dying, you won't care how many places are stamped on your passport."

Rachel's face contorted at the idea of Mark dying, and without another thought she turned and wrapped her arms around him. "Thank God, you're alive," she murmured as she stood on her tiptoes and buried her face against his neck.

Mark held her for a few minutes before saying quietly, "I'm going to go. Promise me you'll go back to bed and sleep now."

"I'll try," she agreed.

He leaned down and kissed her lightly on the lips before leaving.

"Lord, a mercy!" Lovey exclaimed when she entered the kitchen about 6:00 on New Years Day and found Rachel still sitting at the kitchen table in the dark. "What's you doing in here at this hour?"

"Just thinking," Rachel answered as she lifted her cold

teacup to her lips.

"Why you sitting in the dark? Don't you want some lights on?"

"I didn't want to wake up anybody," Rachel said vaguely. "I just needed space to think, and I couldn't seem to clear my mind upstairs."

Lovey turned on a light, then moved to the stove, turned on the burner, and placed the teakettle on it. "It don't sound to me like you's just thinking. You's fretting. What's got you so worked up?"

"Lots of things," was all Rachel would confide.

"Hmm." Lovey returned to the table and sat down across from Rachel. "Would one of those things be a proposal from Mr. Louis?"

Rachel nodded.

"And you's interested?"

"I might be. I don't know, Lovey, that's the problem," Rachel confessed. "Suddenly I can't decide what I want out of life. I can't even remember who I am. I'm afraid maybe I'm taking giant steps backwards."

"What do that mean?"

"I can't explain it. It's just a feeling." Rachel jumped up impatiently and went to the sink to rinse out her teacup.

"Honey, did you get any sleep last night?" Lovey asked.

Rachel sighed tiredly. "No. After I talked to Mark, I just couldn't quit thinking." She reached for the tea canister. "You want some tea, don't you?"

Lovey nodded then asked, "When was Mr. Mark here?"

"Actually it was early this morning. Very early. I went to bed, but I couldn't sleep, so I was sitting in here drinking tea."

"And Mr. Mark just showed up?" Lovey asked.

Rachel shrugged. "You know Mark. He had made up his mind to come, so he did."

"He knowed Mr. Louis gonna propose," Lovey concluded. "Sounds to me like that ring of Mr. Andre's worked just like we thought it would."

"Like you thought it would."

Lovey ignored that comment. "What did Mr. Mark say? Did he propose too?"

"Not really. He just asked me to wait before I made any decision. Then he started talking about life and—Oh Lovey! I just need to get away from both of them and think. I had finally found some peace in my life, and then Mark showed up and

Louis started proposing. Louis says I'm perfect, and Mark says I need to grow. I don't know what to do!"

"You gotta do just what you said. You gotta get away and think."

"But how? I've got company, and it's New Year's Day, and Billy Ray is having a big party for all the bowl games. He wants to show off his new house."

"You don't care nothing about them football games, and I knows it. Besides, Mr. Louis ain't gonna want to spend the day with Billy Ray Snyder."

"Oh dear! You're right, Lovey. I think he actually hates Billy Ray. But, on the other hand, Andre really wants to see the games."

"That Mr. Andre, he just like a party—any party, and Mr. Billy Ray, he be sure to put on a good party."

Rachel sighed. "I'd give a million dollars to have today to myself. I really need some space to sort things out, but I can't abandon my guests, Lovey, and what about Billy Ray? I don't want to hurt his feelings. He's so proud of that house. Oh, how do I get myself into these messes?"

"You gets yourself into these messes trying to please everybody and can't nobody do that, so you got to give it up." Lovey stared off into space for a moment, then said quietly, "Miz Elinore always visit the housebound on New Year's Day."

"The housebound?"

"Those folks she knew that was too frail to get out. Miz Elinore always take them some kind of special treat."

"Treat? Lovey, I'm lost. I don't understand what you're saying. You just said not to try to please everybody—"

"I'm saying that you's the mistress of Belle St. Marie now, and you's gotta keep up the traditions of Miz Elinore. You's gotta go visit the housebound and take them some sweets and things. They's God's children, too, and He want you to show them some love. Ain't your fault you can't be with the men folk all day today. 'Course, when you's through with your visiting, ain't no reason you can't drop by about supper time to see Mr. Billy Ray's new house and visit a spell."

Rachel burst out laughing, "Lovey, you're the most devious person I know! How did you get so smart?"

"Just lived a long time, Honey."

"I just hope Louis doesn't want to accompany me on these visits."

"No need to worry about that, Honey. Mr. Louis ain't got

that kinda heart."

Sobered by the truth of Lovey's judgment, Rachel nodded her agreement, then said, "I don't know what I'd do without you, Lovey. Promise me you'll never leave me."

"Oh, I's gonna have to leave one of these days 'cause I sure want to see Jesus and all my family that gone before me. But don't you worry, Honey, God gonna send just the right people into your life at just the right time."

"I sure hope so."

"You can count on it, Honey. I been watching Him work all these years. He's a faithful God, and He loves you. Now why don't you just put your fretting away and go on upstairs and catch a long nap. Those men won't be up and about for a good while longer. Later on while they's watching all that football, you can have you some time alone."

"Boy, that sounds like a plan to me." Rachel hugged Lovey. "Thanks. Suddenly I feel like I could sleep all morning."

Chapter 12

After New Year's Day, Rachel's guests scattered back to their individual lives. Louis and Andre Simone returned to New Orleans. Louis had tried one more time to convince Rachel to go with them and then to continue on to Paris with him, but Rachel held firm in her conviction that she needed time to decipher her feelings for Mark. His unexpected arrival had presented her with a whole new option for her future, an option she wanted to explore more than she was willing to admit even to herself.

When Mark also temporarily left town to begin his duties for Philippe, Rachel welcomed the opportunity to turn her attention to the after-school tutorial program she had established and to the renovation plans for the school building. It was her hope that this temporary distance from Mark and this concentration on matters other than her personal life would enable her to calm down enough to sort out her feelings.

The work at the school did indeed prove to be consuming, at least during the daytime hours. It was no small task to move the existing schoolrooms into a smaller wing of the building and to cordon off the remaining space so that the returning children would not be harmed by the construction on the facility. She had little time to think of either Mark or Louis. Her evening hours, however, were too solitary and inactive, and she found herself tossing and turning as she struggled to decide what she wanted, and whom she wanted, in her future life.

At last the school building was as ready for the returning students as she and her crew could make it, and Rachel sighed with relief and gave herself a day off, a day just for herself. She had long wanted to visit Claire for a quiet day of sharing thoughts. Every time she had been in the presence of this remarkable woman, who was married to Rachel's distant cousin,

Robert, she had yearned for some time alone with her. She instinctively knew that Claire was one of those special beacons of wisdom who had been placed in her life, and Rachel desperately needed someone less prejudiced than Lovey to discuss her future with.

Claire Carlyle was many things—a middle-aged mother of three college-age children, and a very active patron of education and the arts. Most important to Rachel, Claire was a practicing artist, a painter and sculptor, who thought deeply about life. In fact, Rachel considered her to be something of a mystic, a woman much like her beloved Grandmere. There were other things about Claire, which Rachel envied. She seemed to make no obvious effort to be attractive or to impress people. She wasn't the least bit materialistic. In short, Rachel sensed that Claire was comfortable with herself, and Rachel longed to be the same way.

Right after breakfast Rachel called Claire to invite her to lunch, but she was thrilled when Claire countered her invitation. "Today is one of my studio days," Claire explained, "so I'll be painting all day. Why don't you come over here and keep me company? Rather than coming to the front door to the main house, just take the brick path that wanders off to the left, and you'll find me out in the old carriage house."

Rachel's expectations were high later that morning as she walked up the brick path that was softly flocked with velvety moss. She strolled through a welcoming garden, now dominated in January by towering camellia bushes. A light mist from the night before had left the glossy, dark-green leaves decorated with crystal rain drops which reflected in the mirrored surfaces of the leaves. The large, rosy flowers glistened as the morning sunlight touched their dew-drenched petals, and Rachel could not prevent herself from stopping for a few moments to enjoy the stunning beauty all around her.

"They make me feel like I've fallen into a bowl of sparkling rubies and emeralds." Claire's gentle voice interrupted Rachel's thoughts.

"What a perfect description!" Rachel exclaimed as she turned to greet Claire. "They're truly amazing; you must be quite a gardener on top of all your other talents."

Claire laughed. "I would be quite an egotist if I took any credit for these beauties," she answered as she gently traced her finger down a glossy leaf. "They've been here longer than I've been alive. Certainly much longer than I've lived in Louisiana."

"How long have you lived here?"

"Over thirty years now. I can hardly believe it myself. Come, let me show you my studio." Claire motioned her forward.

"I feel very light hearted," Rachel confessed, "like a little girl being led to a new friend's playhouse."

"Oh dear, you've pegged me, Rachel!" Claire exclaimed. "You're right on target; this studio is most definitely my playhouse."

Rachel laughingly shook her head, "You can't sell that notion, Claire. I've seen some of your paintings. You are definitely doing more than playing out here."

"Doing any creative thing you are passionate about is play, Rachel," Claire insisted. "Here, come in and make yourself at home." Claire stood aside and waved Rachel through a set of French doors. "There's a dying fire in the fireplace, but if you're chilly, we can build it up."

"No, no, this is fine," Rachel answered absentmindedly as she stared at the two-story, stone fireplace, which was full of glowing embers. Slowly she turned around to survey the studio. "Goodness, this is quite a place, Claire! What a history it must have."

"I confess I often find myself wishing these walls could talk; I know such a small part of their story, and I'm greedy for more. Have a look around, Rachel." Claire swept her arm in a circle. "This all started as a carriage house built before the War Between the States. That's why it's placed away from the house."

"I guess the owners weren't too keen on smelling the horses," Rachel laughed.

"Who can blame them?" Claire joined her laughter. "When automobiles came along, rather than convert the carriage house—which was so far from the main dwelling—into a garage, the family built a new structure right behind the house. After that, as far as I can tell, nobody paid much attention to this old place until I came along."

"But wasn't the house damaged during the War?"

"Partially burned. The back half of it went up in smoke, but for some reason the fire didn't spread throughout the house. My guess is it started raining cats and dogs, one of our famous Louisiana deluges, and the Union troops just moved on."

"Thank God for Louisiana monsoons! So you think the troops just left the carriage house intact?"

"They must have. I know that the remnants of the family who were left after the war, mostly women and children, of course, moved out here."

"What a mess. I read some old journals of my family a few months ago. It's really impossible to imagine the deprivation they suffered through."

"And to understand the kind of strength they had," Claire added. "The Yankees may have given up on burning the house, but you can be sure they took every valuable they found and certainly all the foodstuffs."

"I can't imagine how I would have coped…." Rachel mused, then turned her thoughts back to the present. "So what brought you out to this old building?"

"I was the mother of three lively children under the age of five, and I desperately needed a space of my own. Robert and I had moved back here and taken up residence so we could take care of his mother after his dad died. Between the children's needs and my efforts to please my mother-in-law, I was totally frazzled. One day I got the idea that my only hope of sanity lay in painting again, but of course, I had no quiet space. I remembered this old building, but Robert's dad had kept it so boarded up, I had never seen inside it."

"So when you came out here for the first time, what did you find?"

"I pulled away a few boards blocking those huge doors." Claire turned and pointed to the large openings on the front of the structure, openings which were now converted into windows with imbedded French doors. "I was barely able to squeeze my way in. Inside I found this fabulous, two-storied, open space just begging to be converted into a studio. It took weeks to clean it up, of course."

"Was this old fireplace here?"

"It was, believe it or not. And that loft area toward the back was there, of course. Even the brick floor was here. The men who drove the carriages apparently lived here."

"So it was the natural place for the family to camp out until the house could be rebuilt."

"Yes, and as you know if you've been reading old journals, houses around here weren't rebuilt for quite a few years. The first priority was getting the fields producing again—and without slave help. I think the women and children must have lived here about 5 years. That's probably when the brick floor was put in and when some of the windows were added, although they wouldn't have had glass, of course, just shutters."

"Just think of the summers they endured…."

"It must have all been awful, but nothing was worse than

waiting for their men to return, wondering if they were alive, praying, praying. Lord, how those women must have prayed!"

"And buried. They buried a lot of children and elderly," Rachel added bitterly. "You would think all the burying would have stopped the praying."

"Why would you think that?" Claire asked softly.

"Eventually they would just give up on God, wouldn't they? I mean, wouldn't you?" Rachel demanded.

"Would you, Rachel?" Claire turned the question back on Rachel as her gentle green eyes caught and held Rachel's bright blue ones. "Have you, Rachel?"

Tears gathered in Rachel's eyes so suddenly, she turned away and abruptly changed the subject. "So what are you working on? It looks like you keep several things going at once. I see three standing easels and over here you seemed to be working on something in clay. "

"I think most artists probably move from project to project," Claire answered quietly, having obviously decided not to push the question. "But this morning I'm beginning a portrait of the Sanders girl, Karen. Do you know that family?"

"No, I don't think so."

"They've been around this area for several generations, but they're not one of the 'old' families by D'Evereau standards." Claire winked at Rachel as she picked up her brush. "Initially I'm working from these photographs I took over the Christmas holidays." Claire pointed to some photos she had clipped to her easel. "Later I'll have her in here for several sittings."

"She's lovely, isn't she?" Rachel commented.

"She's going to be quite a beauty," Claire agreed, "but I love the challenge of painting her at this age. She's 12. You know, half child, half budding woman. I hope I can capture that time in a girl's life. I want this painting to be more than just a portrait of a particular child; I want it to illustrate that first breaking through the cocoon that we all have to go through. You know, that time when we begin to see ourselves as separate from our parents and begin to imagine the infinite possibilities of our lives."

Claire's musings made it obvious that her artistic mind had already taken on the challenge ahead of her, so Rachel stepped back so she could focus on Claire rather than on the painting. Her friend had graying red hair that was gathered at the nape of her neck with a simple tortoise shell barrette. She was tall and slender and dressed in pine-green corduroy slacks and a matching pine-green sweater. Her dark green eyes contrasted dramatically with the translucent white skin of her face, and they sparkled with enthusiasm as she applied the preliminary strokes that would soon become her vision of another person.

"Will it bother you if I watch you work?" Rachel asked.

"Heavens, no! After all the years I've taught painting, I'm certainly accustomed to having someone hanging over my shoulder watching. Just get comfortable wherever you like."

Rachel dragged a chair into a position where she could see the canvas and watched in silence as Claire applied quick strokes of gray paint to outline the girl's face and began concentrating on positioning the eyes, nose and mouth. Several times she snatched up a cloth, wiped away her work and started over. Finally she had a pose she liked, and as she stepped back to view it, she seemed suddenly to remember Rachel's presence.

"So how are things going with the school renovations?" She glanced up at Rachel before concentrating on her palette, where she began to mix paint. "Are you as ready for the kids to start again as I am?"

"I'm ready; in fact, I've missed them."

"Not all teachers would be saying that!" Claire laughed.

"True, but remember I'm only tutoring them for a few hours in the afternoon."

"I would hardly call it tutoring," Claire said as she reached for a tube of paint and squeezed a little onto her palette. "The program you set in motion last summer is very extensive—all those different kids working at their own paces. I don't know how you keep up with them."

"It's fun, really. Instant gratification for me. I really get to see a change in their lives—" Rachel paused and the tone of her voice changed to worry—" for some of them at least."

"Sounds like you're worrying about someone."

"I am," Rachel admitted, "and she's very special to me."

"Sassy?" Claire asked as she turned to Rachel, palette knife in hand.

"How did you know?" Rachel demanded.

"I know you've struggled to keep her in the program since last spring, since she was..." Claire paused to choose her words carefully and settled on "hurt."

"I feel so responsible for that girl, Claire."

"What happened is not your fault, Rachel. You aren't blaming yourself, are you?"

"Of course I am! Garth Gunner would never have attacked her if she hadn't been connected to me. You know that;

everybody around here knows that. He hated all of us D'Evereaus and especially me after I set the Sheriff on him."

"What else could you have done?" Claire asked. "He was threatening you; he actually tried to hit Lovey and would have succeeded if you had not been there. He was wandering around Belle St. Marie at all hours of the night, destroying things whenever he liked."

"I don't know—maybe I should have held my temper better and dealt with him in a more reasonable way."

"Rachel." Claire put down her palette knife and concentrated totally on Rachel's face. "Garth Gunner hated black people. He was—and probably still is—a totally irrational racist. No one could have reasoned with him."

"I just know that most of my actions toward him were exaggerated because I hated him so much for running down Grandmere. If I had been able to forgive him, maybe I would have dealt with him more successfully, and things would not have become so violent."

"Forgiving him frees you, Rachel, and it's true that you could have freed yourself years ago if you had understood the power of forgiveness and chosen it regarding Gunner. But your forgiveness would not have made Gunner less hate-filled, less violent. It was inevitable that he was going to hurt some black person on your property, and being the coward that he is, he would naturally pick a young teen."

"I can't argue with any of that, but somehow I've got to help Sassy now."

"And you will," Claire encouraged. "I know you will, but remember that Sassy has more to overcome than what Gunner did to her. She has to overcome all the neglect and abuse she's suffered from her family all her life."

"I know, I know," Rachel sighed. "If I could just get her to return to the school, I might have a fighting chance."

"She's not attending at all?"

"Before the Christmas break she only showed up about once a week."

Rachel fell silent as she pondered the problem, and Claire quietly returned to mixing paint on her palette.

"I'm determined to change that girl's life!" Rachel suddenly blurted out. "I'm going to go find her and talk to her. I'm going to buy her some new clothes, take her to the beauty shop—maybe I'll even find a better place for her to live."

"And none of that will work—not ultimately."

"Why not?" Rachel demanded.

"Did it work for you?"

Confused, Rachel stared at her friend before asking, "Claire, what are you talking about?"

"Did all your clothes and beauty and accomplishments make you feel any better about yourself?"

Rachel stood up and walked over to the fireplace as she considered what Claire had asked. "Not really," she finally admitted. "Those were just temporary fixes; they weren't what I really needed."

"What was?"

"To finally understand that I didn't need to make myself worthy—that God had already taken care of that." Rachel raked her fingers through her hair in frustration. "You're right. Fashionable clothes, a nice house, an education, a man who loves you—they can all make you feel good for a while. But that feeling wears off, and you have to face your own impression of yourself all over again."

"And if your impression is that you must earn your basic worth, you're back at square one," Claire observed.

"Actually you're back at zero!" Rachel shot back. "That's how it feels—empty, hopeless. That's how it really feels."

"And that's the way Sassy feels. Rachel, you know that the true problem here is that Sassy feels worthless."

"I know."

"Her life before she ever met you had already made her feel worthless. What happened last spring when Gunner attacked her, that just added the extra burden of feeling hopeless."

"I know! I know!" Rachel's voice rose to match her frustration. "So how can I help her? How can I help any of my students for that matter?"

"Not by dealing only in the externals of their lives."

"Externals? What do you mean by that?"

"You can work to give them a better education; maybe you can even improve their living quarters or their clothes. If you're really lucky, maybe you can improve their everyday home life. But none of that is enough. Look, let me show you something." Claire laid down her brush and beckoned Rachel to follow her over to a window. "Look at this table."

Rachel looked down at an exquisitely shaped, small table, which Claire was obviously refinishing. "It's going to be beautiful when you finish," Rachel commented.

"It is finished, Rachel."

Surprised, Rachel glanced up at Claire and then back down at the table. It was a mess; Claire had started removing paint and old varnish from about half of it, but it definitely was not a finished project.

"I don't understand, Claire. It doesn't begin to look finished to me, and what's this table got to do with Sassy or me?"

"Look at this end of the table." Claire pointed to a 6-inch-long piece of the top. "It's solid walnut. Look at the beautiful grain in the wood. It's completely unadorned, completely natural wood, and it's solid."

"It is beautiful. I hope you're planning to return the whole table to this."

"Why?" Claire asked softly.

"Because it's beautiful. For heaven's sake, Claire, it's a solid walnut table. Walnut is a gorgeous wood—beautiful color, beautiful graining."

"Apparently others have not thought so," Claire answered. "Look at the next section; someone covered this solid walnut table with an elaborate veneer of mahogany, ebony, and beech. Someone, some artisan, decided the table needed this fantastic design glued to it to make it more worthy. Then, of course, he decided the wood should be sealed and shiny, so he applied tung oil."

"Yes, I see that, but I don't understand your point."

Claire moved her hand further down the table, pointing to another area. "Later still, someone applied a stain and a heavy coat of varnish. Do you see it over here?"

"Yes, but what has this table got to do with Sassy and—"

"Look at this last section," Claire interrupted. "Someone decided the table was worthless without a new look, so he painted it white and antiqued it. Then he decided it wasn't durable enough, so he finished it with a coat of polyurethane."

"Frankly, Claire, I almost feel sick just looking at that end of the table."

"Why, Rachel?"

"It's ruined. All the beauty of the wood has been covered up. Veneers, stains, varnishes and finally paint and polyurethane. The table is ruined!"

"No, Rachel, you're wrong. The original, walnut table is still here. All the work of the original craftsman is still here. I just have to remove all the misguided attempts to make this walnut table worth more than its original, inherent worth—the worth its creator gave it."

Rachel knelt down by the table and ran her fingers along its surface, carefully feeling each of the layers Claire had removed, slowly moving back in time, back in the history of this creation of wood. Her fingers felt the raw walnut of the original table; once again she admired its color, its graining, and once again she was certain it was most beautiful in its original state. At last she looked up at her friend and asked, "What has this to do with Sassy?"

"What has this to do with Rachel?" Claire answered. "What has this to do with me? What has this to do with all the people God has created?"

Rachel struggled with Claire's question as she turned back to study the table. Finally she whispered, "I don't know. Tell me, please tell me."

"We are all the strong, beautiful, completely worthy people God made. We don't need any embellishments, any accomplishments to make us worthy. We don't need one thing the world can offer us to make us worthy. We simply need to accept that fact."

Rachel sighed heavily. When she rose to face Claire, there were tears in her eyes. "For just a moment last spring I thoroughly understood that fact," she admitted. "At times since then I've remembered it in varying degrees. Why—oh why—can't I keep it firmly placed in my mind?"

"Because the world doesn't want you to, Rachel. The world manipulates us all by making us feel we are worthless, by convincing us that we need their approval and their products to be worthy. But that's a lie."

"Yes," whispered Rachel, "a damnable lie. Oh dear God! Just think how much pain that lie has caused in human psyches throughout the generations. But what can we do to stop it, Claire? How do we repair the damage?"

"We begin where we are. We struggle with our personal doubts about our worth. We help each other by reminding each other of the truth. Most of all, we see the truth in each other; we see the inherent, God-produced worth, and we give testimony to it."

"So will you strip all these layers off this table?"

"No, I need that table just as it is to remind me what the world does to all of us. I need to come over to this table and contemplate all the layers of so-called improvements the world has encouraged me into. I need to see that I started out in this life as a beautiful creation, a worthy one."

Rachel nodded her agreement.

"It is in my life that I need to strip away the false additions that have supposedly made me worthy."

"Yes, I understand." Rachel nodded as she spoke. "That's what I need to do, too."

"And so what do you need to do for Sassy? For all those kids?"

"I don't need to encourage her or them to acquire things or attain accomplishments as a means of knowing their worth."

"The things and accomplishments are not bad if they make life more comfortable, more joyful, but they do not add to anyone's worth. You can't earn your worth, Rachel, and you can't lose it. God gave it to you. That's the truth we must all help each other embrace."

Claire walked back to her easel, back to the painting she had started. Rachel brushed her fingertips across the table once more. This is why I am here today! This is why I am here today! That thought replayed itself over and over in her head, and her smile grew.

In time she walked over to the fireplace, added a log and sat down to stare into the dancing flames while Claire painted quietly.

When Rachel returned to Belle St. Marie that afternoon, she stopped the car before she entered the wrought iron gates that marked the beginning of the property, which her family had called home for generations. She left the car, and leaning against its hood, she read the words on the arch over the entrance. . . . Enter in Peace.

"I remember that desperate night 18 months ago when I first returned," she confided to a cardinal, which was foraging among the ivy entwining the old brick posts that supported the ornate gate. "I remember how worthless I felt, and I remember how healing this piece of land with its memories and beloved people has been for me." She paused and thought about Sassy and the other children who lived on this property, her property now, because their ancestors had been born here for generations. "They deserve the same," she concluded simply.

Chapter 13

Grateful for the beginning of the new semester and its accompanying return to normalcy, Rachel welcomed the children and teens back to the after-school program the next Monday. She devoted her attention to them, glad for the additional distraction from her confusion about her feelings for Louis and Mark.

Billy Ray continued the restoration of the empty classrooms, and his crews arrived early in the morning so they could finish their workday by 3:00 p.m. before the children arrived. Rachel eagerly watched the restoration proceed, even though she was forced to spend more time in Billy Ray's presence than she cared to. The best part of her day was when the school bus stopped at the old school building next to the church; she ran to meet the students, and all her personal dilemmas were quickly forgotten. Children of all ages descended the steps of the bus, hurrying because they knew they would be greeted by Rachel's army of tutors and be given after-school snacks. They also knew that the price for those snacks would be the necessity of settling down a half an hour later to some learning.

Some of the after-school students were genuinely motivated to study by either their own dreams or their parents' dreams for them. Others were motivated only by the prizes they could earn with the points they gained for each lesson finished. Either way, Rachel figured that the kids would improve their basic skills, and surely that improvement would bear fruit in their public school classroom performances and hopefully in their adult lives.

One afternoon in early February, Rachel watched as the school bus stopped and the doors opened. As usual a stream of kids emerged, but Rachel was particularly waiting and watching for Chelsey, one of her first students. Chelsey had been Rachel's greatest success story thus far because she was determined to be the first girl from her family to graduate from high school and go on to college. On the other hand, her friend, Sassy, was just as bright but only motivated by the prizes she could attain from studying with Rachel. Both girls were from desperately poor and dysfunctional families. They both obviously enjoyed earning points for a new t-shirt or some make-up, but Rachel sensed how driven Chelsey was to change her life.

All through the fall term Chelsey had worked hard while Sassy had more and more often decided not to get off the school bus at Rachel's school. In fact, since school had started again after the Christmas break, Sassy had not even been riding on the bus. Obviously, she had dropped out of the public school almost entirely, and Rachel was worried. Today was no exception; even though Rachel waited, Sassy didn't appear, and Rachel decided it was time to take action.

"Hi, Chelsey," Rachel greeted as the girl approached. "Can I talk to you a second?"

"Sure, Miz Rachel." Chelsey threw her book bag down on the sidewalk and joined Rachel as she walked away from the building toward a private place under the pines.

"I'm worried about Sassy." Rachel came right to the point. "She has dropped out of school entirely, hasn't she?"

"Yes, ma'am." Chelsey offered no further information.

Rachel sighed as she glanced up at the sky. "Chelsey, I could ask you a bunch of questions and try to drag information out of you, but I'd rather save us both the time. You know I care about Sassy, so please just tell me what you know. Have you seen her?"

Chelsey looked down at the ground and dragged one of her bulky jogging shoes through the accumulated pine needles. Rachel waited as patiently as she could until Chelsey sighed heavily and finally began to talk. "I's seen her, Miz Rachel, but I don't like what I's seen."

"What do you mean?"

"She just ain't interested in school anymore. She ain't interested in anything she used to care about."

"Do you know why?"

"Not really," Chelsey answered, but she wouldn't look Rachel in the face.

"I think you know more than you're telling me."

"All I know is she's still real upset about what happened last spring."

"You mean with Garth Gunner."

"Yeah. She's still just real messed up about that."

Rachel strongly suspected that Chelsey wasn't even beginning to tell her all that she knew, but she needed to tread carefully. Neither girl was likely to snitch on the other. "Chelsey, would you give Sassy a message from me?"

"Sure."

"Just tell her I asked about her. Tell her I miss seeing her."

"Yes, ma'am, I'll sure do that." Chelsey looked relieved, waited for Rachel to say more, then eagerly asked, "Can I go to class now? I's got a lot to learn today."

"Yes, go ahead." Rachel watched as Chelsey quickly crossed the yard back to the sidewalk, jerked up her book bag, and hurried into the building.

A strong sense of apprehension rose in Rachel; she felt the presence of something truly threatening, and she felt helpless. Shaking her head firmly, she took herself in hand. This is all totally predictable and understandable, she thought. No one quickly gets over the kind of brutal attack Sassy endured last spring. I certainly couldn't, and she's just a young teenager. The answer is obvious; I've got to get her more counseling. Yes, that's what she needs! That mother of hers is useless to her. If it weren't for Sassy and her siblings, I wouldn't even have that woman on my property. But never mind that. I can help Sassy; I'll get that psychologist back on the case. Having reasoned her way to what she considered an answer, Rachel marched back to the building to teach.

When Chelsey left the school that day, she avoided the other children and headed down a barely visible path in the woods. It was a shortcut to Sassy's house that very few people knew about. After trudging along for 10 minutes, she walked into a clearing in the woods and saw the place where Sassy had spent her fourteen years. Chelsey stopped and appraised the rusty trailer. "Thank God I don't gotta live like that," she muttered. "At least Mama's got a real house made outta wood, even if it is half falling down."

Chelsey stood a few minutes longer; she knew better than to approach the trailer too suddenly. There was almost always something going on inside that she didn't want to mess with, and Sassy's mother could be brutal if she was interrupted at the wrong time. Chelsey scanned the dirt yard around the trailer and saw no cars except the wreck Sassy's mother owned. It was parked in the same spot it had occupied for months because it wouldn't even start. "At least there ain't no men around," Chelsey encouraged herself, but she continued to watch rather than move forward.

The door scraped open, and Sassy appeared in the doorway.

When she saw Chelsey, she stepped down onto the cinder blocks that served as a doorstep and ambled over to her. Chelsey sized her up as she walked, making sure she was sober.

"What you doin' here, girl?" Sassy greeted her friend. "Ain't you supposed to be at Miz Rachel's fancy school getting ready to catch you a rich husband?"

Chelsey couldn't refuse the bait. "I ain't after no husband," she retorted. "I's going to college and get me a good job. I ain't gonna depend on no man."

"Sure you is," Sassy taunted. "Girls like you and me ain't got no choice about that. Don't you know nothing?"

"I knows if I wants a man, I's gonna pick him. I ain't gonna settle for no trash like that Jamal you's hanging with."

"Don't you go talking 'gainst Jamal. He's a super stud, girl. You's just jealous. Besides, he got plenty of money."

"Yeah, for drugs. That what he got money for."

"He got money for me!"

"Oh yeah. What you spending it on? I don't see nothing new 'round here. Where's all them new clothes you say he buying you?"

"You just come over here for a fight? Is that why you's here?" Sassy demanded.

"No, I come with a message from Miz Rachel."

"I don't need no message from Miz Rachel."

"Well, you gonna get it anyway. She say to tell you she misses you."

"Sure she do. She misses me like a hole in the head."

"She want you to come back to school and—"

"You tell Miz Rachel D'Evereau I ain't coming back to no school no time. I don't need no school. I got me a man."

"That ain't no man you's got. That's just trouble!"

"Well, if he be what trouble be, then bring it on, sister!"

"That Jamal gonna hurt you, Sassy. You's my friend, and I don't wanna see you hurt by that trash."

"Jamal loves me! You's just jealous 'cause you ain't got no man."

"I can't even talk to you anymore. We used to be friends, but since you started hanging with that Jamal, you ain't acting like anyone I wants to be friends with."

"Then you just get your fat—"

"I ain't gonna stand here and listen to this," Chelsey interrupted. "I's outta here!" She turned around and stomped back into the woods. The farther she got from the trailer, the angrier she became until she finally made up her mind to drop Sassy as a friend. "She ain't never gonna make nothing of herself," she exclaimed to the woods. Who needs her?"

Shortly after 2:00 the next morning Chelsey sat up in bed with her heart thumping wildly. There was someone shaking the window frame, trying to open it. Chelsey panicked. There was no lock on that window, and she was alone with the younger children since her mother was out with her boyfriend. Nauseated with terror, Chelsey jumped out of bed and began frantically fumbling around in the dark for a weapon to defend herself. The first thing her hands found was a heavy book she had been reading before she fell asleep. Without pausing to think, Chelsey seized it and threw it at the window. It missed the glass but thumped loudly as it hit the wall next to the window frame.

Immediately a high-pitched voice cried out, "Chelsey! It's me—Sassy!"

Chelsey stopped in her tracks and drew in a deep breath as she struggled to understand that she was in no danger.

"What's wrong, Chelsey?" her youngest sister demanded from the bed.

Chelsey looked back and saw both her little sisters sitting up in bed, their eyes shining in the dark as they shivered with fear and cold.

"Nothing," Chelsey answered. "It's just Sassy; go on back to sleep." She watched as they both settled back into the meager comfort of the bed.

Her legs shaking, Chelsey stumbled over to the window and pulled up the tattered shade. On the other side of the glass she saw Sassy's face peering in. Chelsey jerked the window open and demanded, "What you doing here? It's the middle of the night; you 'bout scared me to death!"

"Let me in," Sassy demanded. "I ain't got no place to sleep." She started hoisting herself up on the windowsill but fell backward onto the ground.

"Go home," Chelsey ordered. "You's gonna wake up the kids."

"I ain't never going home again!" Sassy declared from her position in the dirt.

"Then come around to the door, Sassy. You ain't never gonna get in this way. You's too big."

"I ain't too big!" Sassy argued as she tried to stand back up. "I's just too dizzy." She broke into uncontrolled giggles as she fell back down in the dirt.

"You's too drunk! That's what you is, and you can just stay out there in the dirt where you belong." Chelsey slammed the window shut and jerked the shade down. "I's going back to bed."

Chelsey threw herself onto the bed and lay there utterly exhausted from the scare she'd had. All she wanted to do was to sink back into sleep and forget Sassy and the whole miserable condition of her own life. "I ain't gonna live like this the rest of my life," she muttered. "I ain't!"

Suddenly Sassy yelled, "Hey, Miz High and Mighty. You ain't gonna go back to sleep and leave me out here in the cold. I ain't gonna let you!"

A minute later Chelsey heard pounding on the window and knew that Sassy had no intention of simply passing out and giving her some peace. Angrily she sat up and threw her legs over the side of the bed again. This time she left the room, cautiously picking her way around the pallet on the floor where her younger brothers slept. When she reached the front door, she paused and struggled with herself. The last thing she wanted to do was to get involved with Sassy when she was drunk. She knew from experience that the little girl she had played with in the woods had become a very angry, nasty—even violent—teenager, especially if she was drunk.

"Chelsey!" Sassy sang out at the top of her voice. "Hey, Chelsey!"

Before Chelsey could answer, she felt someone tugging on her arm. Without even looking down she knew it was her baby brother. She picked the three-year-old up and held him in her arms. As he snuggled against her neck, seeking comfort, she heard Sassy call out again, "Chelsey! I's getting cold out here!"

Chelsey clutched her baby brother more tightly to herself and made her decision. She opened the door and yelled, "Shut up, Sassy. I's coming." Then she turned back to the bedroom, settled her brother back on the pallet, soothed him a few seconds, and returned to the front door. This time she stormed across the porch, down the steps and around to the side of the house, where she found Sassy staggering around.

"What you mean keeping me waiting like this?" Sassy demanded. "I could catch the pneumonia out here and die."

"Ain't no such luck!" Chelsey retorted. "You's got all the kids awake, and they's good and scared. Now what do you want?"

Sassy giggled and lurched toward Chelsey. "I just needs a place to sleep. That's all." She threw her arms around Chelsey. "That ain't too much to ask of my best friend, is it?"

"I ain't your best—"

"You's always been my best friend," Sassy interrupted her angrily.

"I ain't your best friend anymore, Sassy. The way you's been acting—I don't even know who you is anymore. You's changed, and I don't like—"

"Oh, Chelsey. Save the lecture till daylight. I's tired." Sassy pushed past Chelsey and headed toward the porch.

"You ain't gonna sleep in the house," Chelsey insisted. "I don't trust you. You's drunk and maybe worse." She raced to beat Sassy to the door, but Sassy shoved her aside and went into the front room.

"This will do just fine," Sassy announced as she threw herself on a broken down sofa. "You got a quilt? I's cold."

"My mama gonna kill me if she finds you here when she comes home."

"Your mama ain't coming home, and you knows it," Sassy retorted.

"Why can't you just go home?"

"Cause my mama is home, and she don't want me 'round 'cause her man friend just might like me better than her. Now, shut up and let me sleep." Within seconds Sassy started snoring.

Chelsey recognized the hopelessness of the situation and returned to her own bed, but she couldn't fall asleep. For the rest of the night she lay staring at the ceiling, spending half the time crying over the condition of her life and half the time planning her escape from it.

When Chelsey finally heard the first birds begin their morning calls, she knew that dawn was arriving and her long, sleepless misery was over. She slipped out of bed, careful not to awaken any of the children, snatched up her clothes and went into the front room of the three-room house. As she expected, she found Sassy still snoring on the couch. Chelsey stood staring down at her, filled with a mixture of disgust and fear—disgust at the way Sassy was behaving and fear that her life might take her down the same path.

The room began to lighten as the morning started, and Chelsey noticed a gash over Sassy's eye. Horrified, she dashed to the kitchen area of the room, lighted a kerosene lamp and brought it back to the couch. Holding the lamp high, Chelsey squatted and peered at her friend. She saw then what she couldn't see in the wee hours of the morning. Sassy's face was thoroughly battered.

"Sassy!" She shook the girl. "Sassy, wake up! What happened to you?"

Sassy continued snoring despite Chelsey's efforts to awaken her. Finally Chelsey placed the lamp on the dirty floor and sat down herself. She was face to face with the sleeping girl, face to face with the future she feared. Tears streamed down Chelsey's face as she looked at her friend, then stared around her at the grim poverty so evident in the room. "I ain't gonna live like this," she whispered, "God, if you care for me half as much as Miz Rachel say you do, you gotta help me!"

"Why you crying, Chelsey?" a small, familiar voice asked. "Sassy ain't dead, is she?"

"No, baby girl." Chelsey pulled her youngest sister, Crystal, into her arms. "She ain't dead, but she might as well be 'cause she's just walking dead."

"What's 'walking dead'?" the five-year-old asked.

"Never you mind. You and I ain't gonna ever live like that." She stood up and began ordering their day. "Now, you go get your clothes on and wake up Charlene, and the two of you dress your brothers. We's gonna have to take them to stay with Aunt Mathilde before we go to school."

"Where's Mama?" Crystal asked.

"I don't know. I figure she'll be back when she gets ready. We ain't gonna wait for her, that's for sure. Now, you go on and do what I told you. I's gonna light the stove and see what we got to eat. Go on now! We ain't gonna be late for school. Do you hear me, Crystal? From now on we ain't never gonna be late for school, and we ain't gonna miss a single day."

"I hear you, Chelsey." The little girl started toward the kids' room. When she got to the door, she turned back and asked, "Is you crying again, Chelsey?"

"No, I ain't!" Chelsey quickly dragged her hand across her face. "I ain't gonna cry; I's gonna act. Go get dressed!"

As the little girl disappeared into the kids' room, Chelsey turned toward the black stove, picked up some wood, angrily thrust it in, and stirred up the coals. "I ain't gonna cry," she muttered, "'cause I ain't gonna feel nothing 'bout this place. This just be a place to get out of." She paused as she heard the kids talking in the other room. "Lord, I can't leave them; I gotta take them with me. How's I gonna do that?" She began rummaging around for food.

The kids had nothing for breakfast except bread smeared with bacon grease, but Chelsey did manage to get them dressed, fed, and out the door. She dropped the boys off at Aunt Mathilde's and hurried the girls to the school bus stop.

As the day wore on, Chelsey did her best to concentrate, but her mind kept returning to a picture of Sassy's face. First, she wondered who beat Sassy up. Then she wondered why violent things kept happening to Sassy. Next she worried about her own safety and that of her brothers and sisters.

By the time the last school bell rang, Chelsey knew she had to make one more attempt to help Sassy. She rounded up her sisters, boarded the bus with them, and when the bus stopped at Rachel's school, she stayed seated.

"Ain't you gonna go to Miz Rachel's school?" Charlene asked.

Chelsey sighed heavily. "Not today. Ya'll get on off, and I'll see you later at home. I got something I got to do."

When Chelsey exited the school bus further down the road, she hurried to her house. As expected, she found that Sassy had awakened some time during the day and gone. Also as expected, she found her mother asleep. She left the house, determined to find Sassy and talk some sense into her.

After winding her way through the woods, she approached Sassy's house cautiously. She stopped to size up the situation before stepping out of the woods. Just as she feared, Jamal's car was parked in the dirt in front of the house. "I ain't going near that place," she muttered as she turned away.

She hadn't taken more than a few steps when she heard Sassy scream. Seconds later Jamal started yelling at Sassy, his words peppered with obscenities. Chelsey froze and listened to Jamal's furious accusations that Sassy was cheating on him with other men. "I knows all about it," he screamed, "and I's gonna teach you right now that you ain't gonna make no fool of me!" Chelsey heard a loud slapping sound, followed by a scream.

"Oh, Lord," she cried out, "what's I gonna do?" As she hesitated, she heard Jamal's continued yelling followed by slaps. She couldn't stand it; she had to act. She raced to the door of the trailer, jerked it open and stepped into the dim interior. "Stop it!" she shouted at Jamal. "Don't you hit her again!"

Jamal was so surprised he fell silent, and Chelsey seized the moment. "Come on, Sassy! Let's get outta here," she cried as she rushed to her friend's side to help her up off the floor.

Much to her amazement Sassy started laughing and taunting her. "What you so scared of, Miz High and Mighty? The fun is just starting."

"Are you crazy?" Chelsey demanded as she stared down at Sassy's swollen face. "He's gonna kill you!"

Sassy starting laughing so hard she rolled around on the floor. "Chelsey, you's the stupidest girl I ever seen," Sassy finally choked out. "Don't you know that mens always acts like this before they get to making love?"

Chelsey drew back in shock. "You really is crazy!' she exclaimed. Then she took a hard look at Sassy, and she finally understood. "No, you's just good and drugged up. That's what you is."

Sassy broke into giggles. "Why don't you hang around, Miz High and Mighty, and we'll show you how it's done. You needs a real education—not the kind Miz Rachel gonna give you."

"I ain't gonna try to reason with you. You's coming with me!" She grabbed hold of Sassy's arm and started pulling her to her feet.

"She ain't going nowhere!" Jamal lunged toward Chelsey. "Turn her loose."

"She's going with me!" Chelsey tried to stand her ground.

Jamal backhanded her across the face. Chelsey instinctively dropped Sassy's arm and covered her face to ward off further blows. Jamal slapped her again, then jerked her up off the floor and threw her out of the trailer.

Chelsey landed so hard on the packed, red dirt that she was knocked senseless for a minute. When she could finally think again, stark fear surged up in her, fear that Jamal would come after her. She struggled frantically to her feet and staggered toward the woods. As she reached their cover, she broke into a full run. Sheer panic driving her on, she dashed down the overgrown path until she finally burst out onto the road close by the church and the school.

When she saw the school, she finally felt safe enough to collapse under a tree and catch her breath. She sat there for a long time, tears running down her face, as she considered her options. With all her heart she wanted to run to Rachel, but for some reason she could not understand, she felt ashamed. "She couldn't never understand," Chelsey whispered, "and I gotta have her help to get outta here."

Her mind turned to Sassy, still back in the trailer with Jamal, and she both grieved for her childhood friend and boiled with fury at Sassy's behavior. Finally she just gave up on her. "She done made her choices," Chelsey muttered. "I can't fight for her and me both. And I gotta fight for me. I just got to!"

The shadows lengthened as Chelsey rested, and soon the school door opened. All the kids came pouring out, chattering happily as they clutched the "prizes" they had earned that day. Chelsey called her sisters, pulled herself up off the ground and stared at the school for a moment.

"That's my only hope," she said. "Ain't nothing gonna stop me from being there tomorrow." She turned back into the woods and took her time getting home.

Chapter 14

As Rachel walked among her students' desks the next afternoon, watching them work, she noticed that Chelsey never raised her head from her work. At first she thought the girl was simply concentrating, but then she began to sense that Chelsey was avoiding looking at her. When the class was finally over and Chelsey rose to leave, Rachel was stunned by what she saw. Chelsey's right check was lacerated and badly swollen. Rachel hurried across the emptying classroom, and when she reached the teenager's side, she demanded in a whisper, "What happened?"

Chelsey stared down at the floor and said nothing.

Rachel waited until the remaining students had left before saying, "Just give it to me straight, Chelsey. What happened to your face?" When Chelsey still remained silent, Rachel added, "You're not leaving here until you tell me what's going on."

Chelsey settled heavily into a desk and looked up at Rachel. Finally she spoke, her voice draped in sadness. "I went over to talk Sassy into coming back to the school, and Jamal was over there."

"Who's Jamal?" Rachel asked.

"Just a guy, a real mean guy....real mean."

"Okay. So you went over there to find Sassy. Then what happened?"

"They was doing drugs, and he hit me and threw me outta the trailer into the dirt." She paused and looked down at her lap. In spite of Rachel's instant fury, she managed to wait for the girl to continue. "Now I feels like dirt," Chelsey whispered as tears rolled down her face.

Rachel immediately squatted down next to Chelsey and stared intently into her eyes. "Listen to me, Chelsey, and hear what I say. You're not dirt. No one can make you into dirt. You are God's child. He gives you the kind of worth that nobody can take away from you. I know you don't understand that right now, so you're going to have to trust me and believe what I'm saying. In time, I hope you will understand who you really are. I'm going to do everything I can to help you understand, but you have a part to play too." Rachel stopped and waited for a reaction from Chelsey; when the girl said nothing, she asked, "Do you at least hear what I'm saying?"

"Yes, ma'am. I hear you." Chelsey murmured as the rivulets of water continued to stream down her face.

Rachel reached up and stroked the top of the girl's head as she explained, "We're going to have to work on these feelings of yours, and it's going to take time. Right now, I'm worried about Sassy. Do you know where she is?"

"Probably at her mama's trailer."

"Do you think Jamal's there?"

Chelsey nodded slowly, then looked up at Rachel. "He gonna kill her, Miz Rachel, it just be a matter of time."

Rachel struggled to take in the unbelievable words. Suddenly they registered, and she stood up abruptly. "Not today he's not!" she exclaimed as she walked back to her desk for her coat.

"What you gonna do, Miz Rachel?"

"I'm going over there and throw him off my property!"

"You can't go over there, Miz Rachel." Chelsey rose hurriedly from the desk and came to intercept Rachel. "It ain't safe. Jamal's dangerous, and you can't get messed up in all that filth over there."

"I'm not going to get mixed up in anything. I'm just going to send Jamal packing!"

"You can't do that, Miz Rachel. He's dangerous, I tell you!"

"He wouldn't dare harm me, Chelsey," Rachel declared as she started for the door. "A bully like that only picks on people he thinks are helpless."

"But Miz Rachel!" Chelsey's voice rose as she ran after her. "He ain't thinking at all if he's drunk or doped. You gotta call the Sheriff. You can't go by yourself!" Chelsey grabbed her arm to stop her. "Please, Miz Rachel, don't go!" the girl begged as she started crying again. "You ain't got no idea what you's getting into."

Rachel stopped and looked into Chelsey's tear-stained face. The raw desperation she saw in the young girl's eyes, coupled with her scraped and bruised face turned Rachel's stomach. All she could think was, This is real, and it's happening on my property! How could I have been so blind? God forgive me! Children are being battered on my property!

Chelsey's tears had turned to sobs, great choking sounds that brought Rachel back to the needs of the girl in front of her. "Okay, okay, Chelsey." She struggled to make her voice soothing. "Just calm down. I promise you if Jamal's there, I'll call the Sheriff, but I can't call him before I know there's a problem. Jamal may not even be there, and I can just sit down and talk to Sassy."

"Please don't go, Miz Rachel. It's so dirty and ugly, and you ain't never seen nothing like it. I just know you's gonna get hurt, and it'll be my fault."

Rachel's conscience shook her thoroughly as she listened to the girl trying to protect her. Where have I been? How could I not know? Then she remembered that Sassy was in danger, and she had to act.

"I'll be fine, Chelsey, I promise," she soothed. "Now you wait here—"

"No! I ain't gonna let you go over there by yourself."

Torn between her sense that Sassy was in terrible trouble and her certainty that Chelsey was very upset, Rachel made a swift decision. "Okay," she agreed. "You go with me, if that'll make you feel better."

Chelsey nodded, and Rachel hurried out the door with Chelsey close behind.

When they reached the edge of the woods, Chelsey ran ahead of Rachel, calling back over her shoulder. "I knows a short cut."

"Good," Rachel agreed. "The sooner we get there, the better."

Rachel diligently followed Chelsey's turnings through the dense, pine trees, and in a matter of minutes she saw a clearing ahead of them. Suddenly Chelsey stopped and grabbed Rachel's arm. "We gotta go slow here," she whispered.

"And I'm going first," Rachel insisted as she moved ahead of the girl.

"Wait, Miz Rachel!"

Rachel ignored her and hurried toward the very edge of the clearing. When she reached it, she stopped to survey it, but her eyes were immediately drawn to a bright red car parked haphazardly in the dirt yard. "Jamal," she said under her breath.

"Miz Rachel, he's here!" Chelsey whispered intently. "Miz Rachel, we gotta call the Sheriff."

"Yes," Rachel agreed. "Go to the nearest phone and call him. Tell him I said to come at once."

"You come with me," Chelsey pleaded.

"No, I'll just wait here. Now go on—"

"Stop, Jamal! You's hurting me!" Sassy suddenly yelled from inside the trailer. Rachel sprang forward and strode across the yard as Sassy's frightened voice continued to ring out from the trailer. "Please, I told you I don't want to do that no more!"

"Sassy!" Rachel shouted as she walked. "Sassy! I want to talk to you!"

The whole clearing suddenly became silent.

Chelsey raced up behind Rachel. "No, Miz Rachel, no," she begged. "Jamal gonna kill you."

"Sassy!" Rachel shouted again as she approached the trailer. "Get out here this minute!"

Rachel stopped twenty feet from the cinder blocks that served as a step for the trailer, her hands on her hips, her fury mounting. The rusty door suddenly banged open, and Jamal stepped out and shouted at her. "Get outta here, white lady. You ain't got no business here!"

"This is my property, Mister, and Sassy is my business," she informed him coolly, "and you're the one who is leaving—not me."

"Lady, I could break you in half without even trying," he snarled at her as he jumped off the cinder blocks.

Rachel stood her ground, but her mind raced. What am I going to do? What am I going to do? Much to her surprise she found that her next question was, What would Grandmere do? The answer came roaring back. Pray!

But Rachel ignored the answer.

Jamal slowly began to walk toward Rachel and Chelsey, taunting, "You better listen up, white lady. I can fix you so you don't never bother me again."

At that moment Rachel heard Chelsey's shaky voice plead, "Lord, help us!"

"Ain't no use in callin' on the Lord, little girl," Jamal sneered at her. "He ain't been round here in a long time, and he ain't likely to show up for you." Jamal turned his furious eyes on Rachel and announced, "I's gonna break you in half just for the fun of doin' it, white lady."

Fear flooded through Rachel as the hulking man approached her. "Jesus...." she whispered, "Jesus. . . ." She had not willed the word to come; it had just risen from somewhere deep in her spirit. The instant she uttered it, a commanding calmness permeated her. She relaxed her posture and spoke quietly. "You won't hurt me, Jamal."

He stopped. "How you know my name?"

"That's irrelevant," Rachel informed him. "I'm not here for a social call. Get in your car and leave my property."

Confused by her apparent lack of fear, he sized her up. "You can't tell me what to do," he argued, "I told you. I can break you into little pieces and feed you to the—"

"But you won't," she interrupted calmly as she stared into his furious eyes.

"Oh, yeah, why not?" He took one more menacing step toward her.

"Because you don't want to pay the consequences," Rachel replied casually. "You touch me, and you'll be the one praying—praying the Sheriff gets you before some mob does."

The slightest flicker of fear flashed in Jamal's eyes, but he hardened his gaze further and tried to stare her down. When she refused to blink, he muttered a string of obscenities, then announced with false nonchalance, "You ain't worth the trouble, white lady." He turned and slouched toward his car.

After he had thrown himself into the driver's seat, he looked back at Rachel one more time. She was still staring coolly at him. He turned on the ignition, revved up the motor to create a horrendous noise, and then raced out of the clearing, leaving a cloud of dust to cover Rachel and Chelsey.

"Oh, thank God! Thank God!" Chelsey sobbed as she sank to the ground.

Rachel turned her attention back to Sassy and hurried toward the trailer. Sassy met her at the door, and when Rachel saw her bruised face and the gash on her forehead, she drew the girl into her arms. "Thank you, Jesus," she breathed. "Thank you."

"You can't come in here, Miz Rachel." Sassy interrupted her litany of thanks. "I don't want you to see this place."

"I think it's way past time I see what's happening on my own land," Rachel replied as she released Sassy. She entered the dusky, stinking interior of the trailer with both girls following her.

Inside Rachel found complete chaos, and the peace she had felt seconds ago was replaced with indignation. It was impossible for her to believe that anyone could live in such disorder and filth. She wanted to rant against what she saw, but she held her tongue by reminding herself she had come to rescue Sassy, not to condemn the condition of her trailer.

Rachel had no desire to stay one second longer than necessary to get the girl's things and get her out of there. She intentionally softened her voice as she insisted, "Sassy, you are worth so much more than this." She waved her hand around to include the filthy interior of the trailer. "And you are worth a million times more than what Jamal is giving you. You deserve a life without fear and beatings. You deserve more than the kind of pain that makes you reach for alcohol and drugs and someone like Jamal."

Sassy shook her head as tears welled up in her eyes. "You don't understand, Miz Rachel. There ain't no way you can understand."

"I want to understand, Sassy. Talk to me. Tell me why you're doing the things you're doing. I care about you."

"Why?" Sassy suddenly lashed out. "Why you care 'bout a black girl ain't got nothing, ain't worth nothing? What's there to care about? I's nothing!"

"That's a lie! You're God's child, Sassy—"

"Oh yeah? Is that why He let that Garth Gunner beat me up? Did your God let that happen 'cause I's His child? Well, I don't need no God like that!"

"Garth Gunner is one person, a crazy person who chose to do many evil things, and he's going to pay for them for the rest of his life."

"So am I! I's gonna pay for what he done for the rest of my life."

"You don't have to, Sassy. God is giving you choices every day, but you're reaching for the wrong things."

"Oh yeah, I got heaps of choices. Just look around here at all my choices."

"You do have choices, Sassy! You can come to the school and get the education to get yourself out of this hole. You can let me help you—"

"I ain't worth helping! What's wrong with you, lady? Can't you see I ain't worth it?" Sassy screamed at her.

Rachel stepped closer to Sassy, looked her in the eye, and said decisively, "No, I can't." She waited for Sassy to calm down, then continued. "What I see is a very young woman who has been so abused that she doesn't even recognize who she is. It doesn't surprise me that you have embraced Garth Gunner's treatment of you as the true definition of you."

"In my whole life ain't no one treated me like anything but

dirt."

"No one?" Rachel asked quietly.

"Not my mama, not my daddy—whoever he is. No one 'round here."

"No one?" Rachel asked again.

Sassy looked into Rachel's eyes and began to cry. "No one but you, Miz Rachel. You's treated me good," she admitted, "but I don't know why."

Rachel reached up and gently cupped Sassy's battered face in her hands. "I know you don't know why. Somehow I've got to make you understand that you're worth it. I know that it's going to take time, and you're going to have to cooperate with me. Will you do that, Sassy?"

"I guess you means I got to come back to school."

"There's something even more important than that."

"What?"

"When you think about Garth Gunner or your mama or anyone who makes you feel worthless, I want you to remember that I think you're worthy."

"So do I, Sassy." Chelsey walked toward her friend. "So do I."

"You see, Sassy," Rachel said, "there are at least two of us, and you must choose to define yourself the way we see you and not the way the hurtful people in your life see you. Do you understand?"

Sassy nodded as tears trailed down her cheeks. Rachel put her arms around the girl and reached out to pull Chelsey into the circle. "It's going to take time to adopt a new vision of yourself—time and a lot of effort. But it can be done, and when you see how worthy you are, you won't need to turn to someone like Jamal to fill the holes in you. You won't even have those holes anymore."

Sassy began to sob uncontrollably as Rachel and Chelsey held her tight.

"We can't leave her here, Miz Rachel," Chelsey said. "That Jamal gonna come back."

"I know. I'll take her to stay with Alice for a few days until I can figure out a more permanent solution. Alice took good care of her last spring after Gunner attacked her. Is there anything she needs to take with her?"

Chelsey looked around her, then shrugged her shoulders helplessly, "She ain't got nothing to take."

"Then let's just go. Come with us, Sassy." Rachel gently led the crying girl to the door. "You're going to spend some time with Alice."

As they stepped out of the door, a battered car pulled into the yard, and Sassy's mother, Norene, slowly got out of the passenger side. Obviously well on the way to being drunk, she ambled over to Rachel, and ignoring her daughter completely, she flashed Rachel a big smile. "How you doin' today, Miz Rachel?"

"Not too well," Rachel answered brusquely. Then she turned to Chelsey. "Take Sassy back to the school. I'll be there in a few minutes."

She watched as the girls moved off. Then she confronted Norene. "Sassy will be staying with someone else for a while because she needs someone to take care of her, and you are obviously not going to do it. There are a good many things I want to discuss with you, Norene, but this is obviously not the time. I'm too angry, and you've been drinking."

"I ain't drunk, Miz Rachel!"

"You're sober enough to understand and remember what I'm about to say, so listen up! If you let that boy, Jamal, back on this property, you won't be living here. Do you understand?"

"I can't keep that boy away from Sassy," Norene said, "he say he in love with her." She giggled and puckered her lips in an exaggerated kiss. "In lo-o-ove.....you even know what that mean, Miz Rachel?"

"It doesn't mean beating up a girl!" Rachel retorted. "Norene, you've already lost your younger children to the state, and you probably don't really care if you lose Sassy—"

"You got that right. I don't care! What she ever done for me anyhow? She come into this world when I's fifteen and just give her daddy an excuse to hang around and beat on me. If she gettin' beaten now, serves her right!"

"How can you even think that way? She was a baby! She didn't ask to be born."

"But she was, wasn't she?" Nora moved closer, her greasy face contorting in anger. "If the army didn't get her daddy and get him killed, he'd a killed me sure thing. He never touch Miss Sassy. Oh no! She's his princess. I's the one he be beating on all the time."

Rachel struggled to take in the barrage of information coming her way, the explanation of how a woman like Norene came to be and how she could watch—even want to see—her own daughter repeatedly beaten. Words of protest, of reason rose to her lips. She wanted to shout "You can't blame a baby!" until

Norene finally heard her, but she realized that Norene was beyond reason, even beyond her help. She had to focus on Sassy.

"Do you want to live here on my property or not?" she demanded quietly.

"Course I does. This be my home."

"Not if I catch Jamal back over here," Rachel warned. "I'll have the Sheriff evict you if you allow him to stay over here."

"But Miz Rachel, it ain't my fault—" Norene protested.

Rachel stepped toward her and locked eyes with her, "Norene, you listen carefully to me because I mean what I'm saying. Things are going to change here, or people are going to leave my land. If you don't remember anything else from this afternoon, you remember that, and you spread the word."

"It's all 'cause that Sassy born!" Norene suddenly shouted. "It ain't my fault!"

"Nothing is ever your fault, is it?" Rachel retorted, then thought better of starting an argument with a drunk woman. "I'll talk to you later, Norene. Oh, and by the way, just in case you care, remember that your daughter will be staying with a friend of mine for awhile."

"Sounds real good to me," Norene drawled as she grinned at Rachel. "Far as I'm concerned you can keep the garbage. I ain't got no use for her."

Rachel resisted the temptation to slap her and simply replied, "This conversation is ended…. for now."

After Rachel had taken Sassy to the doctor and settled her into Alice's spare bedroom, the surge of adrenaline that had supported her through her frightening confrontation with Jamal suddenly plummeted, and she felt physically and emotionally drained. Using the last ounce of energy she could summon and giving herself a non-stop pep talk, she numbed her mind and drove the short distance to the plantation house. All she wanted was space and time alone, but as she turned the last curve in the driveway, she spotted Lovey hovering anxiously on the front verandah. "News travels fast," Rachel murmured.

The minute she parked the car, Lovey appeared outside the driver's window. "What is you thinking of, getting into an argument with that crazy boy? I already heard all 'bout it, and you's lucky you ain't killed."

"I'm fine, Lovey," Rachel responded as she exited the car and soothingly draped her arm around the beloved housekeeper's shoulders. "Jamal is mean, but he's not crazy enough to hurt me."

"You don't know what he gonna do when he's all doped up."

"I know what he did to Sassy," Rachel answered sadly. "You should have seen her, Lovey. It makes me sick." Rachel dropped her arm from Lovey's shoulders and walked off toward the house.

"Miz Rachel, you can't be messing with a boy like that," Lovey continued, following as fast as she could. "He gonna hurt you!"

"What do you expect me to do? Nothing?" Rachel exploded as all the fear and fury she had been suppressing surfaced. "He hit Chelsey, too. Right here on my property, on Belle St. Marie! I won't have it!"

Lovey refused to back down. "Miz Rachel, this be too big a thing for you to handle by yourself. You gotta have help. You gonna have to get the Sheriff or get Mr. Mark to deal with this."

"Mark? What's Mark got to do with this?" Rachel demanded. "I can handle my own affairs, Lovey! Belle St. Marie is my job, and I don't need any help from—"

"We all needs help sometimes, Honey," Lovey countered. "I know you's plenty smart, and I knows you likes to be independent, but that Jamal be twice your size. That's a fact you can't change. Besides, he ain't gonna listen to no woman, but he would listen to Mr. Mark."

"I'll handle this myself, Lovey!" Rachel insisted as she strode away from the housekeeper and up onto the verandah. "Besides, Mark is in Baton Rouge. He has his own life to deal with. Now I'm tired and cold, and I want a cup of tea." She stalked down the center hall of the plantation house, turned into the kitchen, and grabbed the tea kettle.

"I'll make the tea, Miz Rachel," Lovey said quietly when she reached the kitchen. "You just settle down at the table and calm yourself."

"I'm perfectly calm," Rachel retorted as she slammed the tea kettle on the burner.

"I can see that. You's just as calm as a hound that done been turned loose from its pen."

"Lovey, Jamal is nothing but a bully." Rachel jerked a chair away from the table, scraping it on the stone floor. "I ought to know; I just faced him down half an hour ago."

"You just faced him down? Just like that? You just told him to leave, and he just whined and left like a little whipped puppy. Is that what happened?"

Rachel hesitated, then told the truth. "No, actually he argued with me and—"

"And what?" Lovey demanded. "What did that boy do?"

"He threatened me, and for a moment there I thought he was going to—" Rachel stopped in mid-sentence as she realized how upset Lovey would be if she knew the whole truth.

Lovey pounced on Rachel's hesitation, left the stove and came to stand over her at the table. "Going to what?" she demanded. "You ain't tole me everything that happened, has you?" When Rachel didn't respond, Lovey pulled out a chair and sat down and leaned across the table. "Miz Rachel, I knows you. I's known you pretty near all your life, and I bet you ain't even told yourself what really happened. But now you's gonna tell me what really happened 'cause I ain't leaving this table 'till you do."

Rachel's anger collapsed in the face of Lovey's concern. She replayed the confrontation with Jamal in her mind, remembering his fury and the way he'd loomed over her. Finally, she spoke, her voice shaky. "I thought he was going to hit me, Lovey, but then he stopped."

"What made him stop?"

"I don't know. I honestly don't know. I had already said everything I could say, but he just seemed to be getting angrier and angrier. Then quite suddenly he just stopped." Rachel fell silent.

"That don't make no sense to me."

"Nor to me," Rachel admitted. "There was something surrealistic about it."

"I ain't got no idea what that word mean, Miz Rachel, so just say it plain. And remember, I's sitting right here till you do."

"Something unreal, something unpredictable happened. I don't know why Jamal suddenly changed like that...." Rachel's voice trailed off as she thought. "Maybe I do know," she finally added. "I'm just not sure."

Lovey waited a minute, then encouraged her to go on, "Say it, Honey. Say what you's thinking."

"Chelsey prayed." Rachel spoke the two words reverently. "That's really all that happened. Chelsey prayed. When Jamal threatened me again, I prayed. I didn't even think of it as praying, Lovey. I just said, 'Jesus.' Then everything changed. It all just changed. Even Jamal changed; the fight just seemed to go out of him."

Lovey nodded as tears filled her eyes. "Praise the Lord," she whispered. "Thank you, Jesus. There's the answer. God rescued you, Honey; that's what happened."

"I just don't know, Lovey. It seems so farfetched. Why would God even notice what was going on?"

"He notices everything, Honey—"

"I know you believe that....I'm glad you believe that because it gives you peace. But for me, it just doesn't seem possible. On the other hand, Jamal was obviously furious enough to beat me into pulp; he had been doing drugs.... he wasn't thinking straight—"

"So God stepped in, and now He expect you to use some common sense. You's not gonna handle this thing no more." Lovey announced as she suddenly rose from the table. "I ain't gonna have it."

"I have to handle it!" Rachel insisted.

Lovey ignored her and walked to the stove to take the boiling tea kettle off the burner. She methodically poured the scalding water into the waiting teapot and swished it around to warm the pot. As Rachel fidgeted at the table, Lovey emptied the teapot, added the loose tea leaves and poured the hot water over them. She took her time covering the teapot with a cozy, positioning it on a tray she had pulled from a cupboard and adding cups and saucers, a creamer of milk and the sugar bowl. By the time she carried the tray to the table, Rachel had calmed down a bit.

"I's gonna tell Mr. Mark if you don't turn this over to the Sheriff," Lovey said quietly as she placed the tray in front of Rachel.

"You can't tell Mark, Lovey. He'll have a fit."

"Of course he will. He oughta have a fit. You's gonna get killed, and I ain't gonna stand by and wait for it to happen."

Shaking her head, Rachel jerked up a teaspoon, took the tea cozy off the teapot and stirred the tea aggressively.

"You ain't the only one in danger here, Miz Rachel. That Jamal gonna come looking for Sassy at the school or wherever she be. He gonna get hisself all drugged up, do something stupid, and hurt somebody for sure."

Rachel stopped her vigorous stirring. "You're right," she admitted. "I'm just so angry!"

"And what about Sassy?" Lovey asked as she took the tea away from Rachel and poured it. "You think she gonna stay away from him? She got her part to play too, you know."

"I'm worried about that; I can't deny it. She's scared now, so I know I've got a little time to work on her, but I just don't know how far he's gotten her into drugs. I don't know how addicted she is."

"Miz Rachel, this be more than you can handle. You's gonna have to have help. Ain't nobody but the Sheriff can handle Jamal, and Sassy need one of them head doctors."

"I know she needs professional help. I also know I must call somebody at Child Welfare Services, although I don't know that they'll do anything different from what I've already done. I took her to stay with Alice, and I just hope to get her to stay there long enough to get her the kind of help she needs and to break whatever hold Jamal has over her—"

"Ain't none of that gonna do her no good if that Jamal kills her. You gotta call the Sheriff." Lovey watched Rachel closely, and when she made no move toward the phone, Lovey added, "Honey, this ain't no time for you to let your pride get in the way. I know you likes to be independent, but they's too much at stake."

Rachel nodded, stood and walked out into the hall to the telephone. When she returned a few minutes later, she said, "The Sheriff is on his way out here. I have to file a complaint."

"You gotta do what you gotta do, Miz Rachel," Lovey encouraged. "Don't fret about it too much; just do it and get it off your mind." Rachel said nothing; instead she crossed her arms and lowered her head, so Lovey added, "You know, I sure would like to hear you play the piano."

"Not now, Lovey," Rachel murmured. "Maybe later. I'm just going to go sit on the verandah and wait for him."

After Rachel left the kitchen, Lovey whispered, "Lord, I needs your help here." She waited, still and intensely focused. Then quite suddenly she gathered up the tea things as she said, "You's right, Lord. That be just what I's gonna do."

The Sheriff came, and as Rachel had expected, he said that since Jamal had not injured her there was little he could do unless Sassy or Chelsey filed a complaint. Rachel knew that neither Sassy nor Chelsey would dare file. The Sheriff promised to try to find Jamal and warn him to stay off Belle St. Marie and away from any of its residents. In the meantime he encouraged Rachel to seek a restraining order against Jamal. As soon as he left, Rachel called Claire's husband, Robert, and asked him to start the process the next morning. She also called Child Welfare Services, but she felt sure she had done nothing that would make any real difference.

Shortly after Rachel had eaten what little supper she wanted, she heard someone knocking at the front door, and when she answered it, she was grateful and pleased to find Claire standing there.

"I was concerned about you," Claire said as she held out a bouquet of camellias to Rachel. "Robert told me a bit about your day, and I thought you might need a few of the rubies and emeralds around my studio. Are you too beat to talk?"

"No, come on in, and thanks for coming." She hugged Claire with one arm as she accepted the bouquet. "Your timing is perfect. It has been a horrible day, and I could definitely use a friend right now." She motioned her toward the drawing room. "Want some coffee or something?"

"Not really," Claire answered as she sank into a comfortable chair close to the fireplace. "But I wouldn't mind a bit if you lit that fire; that wind you hear starting up is blowing down from the north. I think we're about to have one of our few frosts, hopefully a light one. I can't possibly cover up all those camellias."

"No, I guess not. A fire does sound good. I'd enjoy the comfort of the crackling sounds even if it wasn't getting cold. Just let me grab a vase for these beauties, and then I'll set a match to that kindling."

"Go ahead; I'll light the fire." Claire stood up and walked toward the fireplace.

When Rachel returned with the camellias in a vase, the kindling in the fireplace was snapping and the edges of the dry logs were starting to spark with tiny explosions of cheerful gold. "I do love a fire," Rachel murmured. "I always have."

"Yes, all that vibrant color and heat have a way of holding the problems of the world at bay, don't they?"

"If anything can...." Rachel sighed as she settled into a comfortable chair.

"How badly hurt is Sassy?"

"Her face looks horrible, and she's got bruises all over—some new, some old. Obviously these beatings have been going on for some time."

"And what does the doctor say?"

"'Just superficial.' Those were his very words, Claire! 'The girl's injuries are just superficial.' Can you believe that?"

"Unfortunately, yes. I can."

"I don't know what to do! I know what I want to do; first, I want to find Jamal and kill him! Then I want to assemble everyone in this county and lay down the law about how my students are to be treated."

"You would have to undo years of prejudice, Rachel—"

"I know! I can't even control what's going on right here on my own land, and that's making me crazy. Of course, Lovey just wants me to call Mark and fall helplessly into his arms."

"She wants to protect you."

"I know, but I don't need protecting."

"Yes, you do, Rachel. You do need protecting."

"Not by Mark!"

"Why not? Why does the idea of Mark send you into such a tizzy?"

"Why does everyone assume I can't run my own life?"

"Is everyone assuming that?"

"Yes! Lovey wants to call Mark, who obviously thinks he can just show up whenever he pleases, fan the flames of passion a bit and marry me. Louis wants me to marry him and run off to Paris, so he can take care of me—"

"Rachel, what does either Louis or Mark have to do with Sassy?"

"Oh, I don't know! Well, maybe I do......at least a little. Louis is offering me the easy way out. Life without responsibility. Just beautiful dresses to wear to elegant parties. No up-close encounters with kids like Sassy, like Chelsey, no needy people at all."

"No Rachel?"

"What?"

"Isn't that really Louis' appeal? He is offering you a life where you don't have to confront yourself. You don't have to deal with your past—not the pain of your childhood, not the pain of your break-up with Mark, and definitely not the pain of your marriage to Collins. The only problem with Louis' offer is that you know it's not valid. You know you can't just marry Louis and suddenly feel happy, because you know you have to deal with your past and grow in your present to be happy. Louis can't just cover you with happiness, with a sense of your worth. No man can."

"Mark certainly can't! He dumped me, for heaven's sake!"

"Mark did not dump you; he went to war. It's your parents who dumped you, Rachel."

"I know....I know. Oh, why can't I get past that?"

"You can, but not by running off to Paris. You've already figured that out; that's why you didn't go. You know you must stay here and face the difficulties that are here; you can't move on unless you do just that. You don't have complete resolution with your past yet, Rachel. In a way Sassy is a blessing to you because her problems remind you of your own."

"How can you say such a thing, Claire?" Rachel demanded as she jumped up from her chair. "How can that girl's battering help me? We shouldn't even be talking about me! We should be trying to help Sassy!"

"We are trying to help Sassy; you have even risked your own safety for her. But we can also learn whatever God is trying to teach us—not just about children like Sassy—but also about ourselves."

"Are you suggesting that God is letting Sassy be beaten so I can learn something?"

"No, I am not! Sassy is being victimized by her mother's choices, by our society's choices and by her own choices. God is grieved by what He sees in that girl's life. That's why He's positioning us to see it and to help her and others. But don't underestimate God, Rachel. He can help Sassy, bring change to our society's sinful devaluation of poor people, and teach you something at the same time."

Rachel sighed, walked to the fireplace and mechanically stirred the fire as she tried to calm down. Finally she asked the waiting Claire, "So what does God want to teach me?"

"You should be asking Him that, Rachel." Claire's gentle voice robbed Rachel of her anger, and she turned from the fire and sat down.

"Okay. I'll try asking Him....later. But what do you think I'm supposed to learn from this?"

"Sassy's mother doesn't value her, and you feel that your mother didn't value you. Am I right?"

"Yes, but I'm grown now, Claire, and all that is in the past and can never be changed. All I can do now is help Sassy."

"There's still a hurting little girl inside you, Rachel, a little girl who feels worthless in spite of all she's done and all she owns. God can help you heal while He helps you help Sassy. And then there's the matter of Mark. You still have strong feelings for that man. You've tried to bury them, even to obliterate them, but you have not succeeded. I don't know what your final decision about Mark will be, but I do know that if you don't walk through your current confusion about Mark and heal the wounds from your past, you won't ever be able to move forward."

"It seems like a lot to ask of God...."

"God is the great multi-tasker. You just let the Sheriff handle Jamal. You work on Sassy, on the other children and on yourself. And pray, Rachel. Open yourself to God's wisdom. You don't have to do this on your own. You have more than mere human strength and understanding available to you."

Tears filled Rachel's eyes, but she nodded her acceptance of Claire's words.

"Now you need some rest," Claire said as she rose from her chair, "so I'm going to say good night."

Rachel brushed her tears away as she stood to accompany Claire to the door.

"Stay here," Claire said as she gently hugged Rachel. "I can find my own way out, and you need to just sit here quietly, let the silence soothe you, and pray. You know where I am any time you need me."

Rachel sat back down as Claire left the room, and she stared at the flames until she could finally manage to utter the words, "I'm listening."

Chapter 15

Mark struggled to keep his exhausted, drooping eyes open as he drove the last few miles to Philippe's estate. It was long past midnight, and the woods rising up on each side of the car were so dark and still on this moonless night that he felt like he was hurtling through a tunnel. After three days of intense campaign work in Shreveport, he had been so tired he had returned to his motel room planning to simply crash and sleep until he woke up refreshed, no matter how long it took. That intention had been quickly de-railed by the phone call he had received from Lovey just after he had settled under the blankets. Her report of Rachel's encounter with Jamal had sent a surge of adrenalin through Mark that made him leap from the bed and start throwing his belongings into a suitcase while he still held the receiver.

The miles back to Philippe's seemed to have doubled as Mark sped along, his thoughts racing in fear for Rachel. Finally the road made the familiar curve leading to the gate of the estate, and Mark sighed heavily as he slowed the car, turned off the highway and drove through the gate. "Another five minutes," he murmured, "and I'll be home. I'll catch a few winks and see Rachel and the sheriff first thing in the morning." As he made the final turn of the long driveway, he noticed that the house was completely dark, so he cut the headlights and made the decision to park away from the house to avoid waking up anyone.

Wearily he dragged his briefcase and small suitcase from the car and began to walk toward the back of the house where he could make the quietest entrance. Just as he turned the corner toward the back, he heard the sound of a car racing up the long driveway, and seconds later its headlights pierced the darkness. It roared to a stop near the house. Car doors slammed loudly as two men jumped out, strode to the front door and knocked.

Mark's fatigue vanished instantly as he recognized the two foreigners who claimed to be Syrians. As lights came on in the house, Mark hurried around to the back, dropped his bags in the kitchen and moved stealthily toward the front of the house. The men had already been admitted into the huge center hall, so Mark paused in the shadows and watched as Philippe, struggling to put his robe on, vigorously protested the men's presence.

"You have to talk to them sometime," Lisette insisted sarcastically as she stepped in front of him and motioned the men into the library. Then she turned back and said coldly, "If you won't talk to them in the daytime, Philippe, you'll talk to them in the middle of the night. One way or the other you are going to take what they have to offer."

"I've told you repeatedly," Philippe said, raising his voice, "they have nothing to offer that I would touch with a ten foot pole. I want nothing to do with them!"

"Don't be stupid. They can win this election for you. Now quit being a stubborn old man and get yourself in there and talk to them." She raised her arm—Mark noted that she was fully dressed—and pointed to the library door.

Philippe didn't move. Instead he commented dryly, "I see, my love, that you are dressed for company. You were expecting them."

"What of it?" Lisette demanded. "Someone has to do the dirty work it'll take to get you elected."

"I had hoped to be elected on my record of service to the people," Philippe answered as he strode past her into the library. Lisette followed him, and Mark, anxious for his uncle, moved to the library door where he heard Philippe's formal, frozen fury directed toward the men. "I regret that you have been encouraged to pay me a visit at this time of the night or indeed at any time of the day or night. Apparently I have not made myself sufficiently clear on several matters of grave importance. First, I and only I decide who will contribute to my campaign. Second, your contributions are not welcome, and indeed they will not be accepted under any circumstances. Have I made myself plain enough now that you will cease and desist from attempts to buy my future political favorsl?"

"You are a fool, Philippe!" Lisette exclaimed. "A stupid old fool. You need these men; you need their help. Without them, you're going to lose this election."

"Lisette is right," the taller man said coldly. "We can make or break your campaign, Senator, and we will."

"I don't need your money," Philippe asserted.

"Perhaps not," the other man replied, "but you need our good will, if you know what I mean."

"Are you threatening me?" Philippe demanded.

"I see that you are beginning to understand. That's good. You can accept our help now or later, but one thing's for sure—in the end you will work with us."

Philippe stared at the man a long moment before uttering flatly, "Never."

Both men laughed lightly, and one said, "There are ways, old man; there are ways."

Mark's fury, which had risen steadily throughout the encounter, boiled over, and he stepped into the light of the room and ordered, "Get out, you two! Now!"

"Mark!" Lisette exclaimed as she whirled around. "What are you doing here?"

"Watching either your stupidity or your treason in action, Lisette," Mark responded without taking his eyes off the men. "I told you to get out." He addressed the men again.

The taller man nodded to the other, then said lightly as they walked toward the door, "This isn't over."

Philippe, Lisette, and Mark listened as the men's footsteps echoed in the hall and across the porch. A moment later they heard the sound of the car starting, turning in the gravel drive and tearing out.

Mark turned to Lisette and demanded, "Tell me who they are."

"Would-be, wealthy backers of Philippe's campaign!" Lisette shot back, "and I'm tired of both of you treating me like some kind of conspirator for trying to get the man I love elected to the office he says he wants to hold."

Mark waited for Philippe to say something, but when he remained silent, Mark quietly asked, "Would the man you love by any chance be the 'stupid old fool' you tricked into a post-midnight meeting with men he obviously despises?"

Lisette bit her lip and stared furiously at Mark.

"Tell me who they are, Lisette."

"Find out for yourself," she answered as she turned on her heel and stomped out.

"Let me handle this, Mark," Philippe said wearily.

"Lisette or those men?"

"Both." Philippe raised his head and locked eyes with Mark.

"Both," he repeated with emphasis. "Your job is public relations. Stick to it."

As Philippe left the library, Mark glanced around him at the shelves of leather-bound law books, the antebellum mahogany desk, the portraits of former D'Evereau politicians—all the things that had made this library the center of D'Evereau political power for generations. He was mightily moved to protect the tradition he had only slightly valued previously. This land, as well as his powerful family that had guided it faithfully for well over 150 years, had become more precious to him than he had realized since his homecoming to Louisiana. He was certain now, more than ever, that his instincts of danger were correct. Louisiana and the D'Evereaus were at risk.

Whenever Mark was troubled, as he was this morning, he took a brisk walk in the woods, a walk which inevitably ended at the pond on Belle St. Marie. The stillness of the inky water always transformed it into a shiny mirror, which reflected and consequently doubled the draping greenery fringing its edges. There was an otherworldly quiet, which aided the soothing visual effect, and together they produced a mental space where Mark could ponder and usually resolve what was bothering him.

Ever since Philippe's New Year's Eve party he had lost countless hours of sleep trying to remember the identity of the Middle Eastern men he had seen at the party. In the days immediately following New Year's, he had done some practical sleuthing by checking out their hotel and car rental registrations. He had, consequently, discovered that they were carrying Syrian passports, but his many journalistic assignments in Syria told him they were definitely not Syrians; they were far more aggressive. Even that judgment of his, that they were aggressive, puzzled him because he had seen no aggression from them—until last night.

Being present when those men arrived long after midnight to pressure Philippe had changed the game for Mark. Now he had to find out exactly who they were and what they wanted. He was convinced he had seen them before and that some actual memory of them was niggling around in the back of his mind, but whether or not he was right about that, he had to uncover their true identity and motivations. Lisette was obviously acting as their connection to Philippe, but Mark felt sure that even she had no accurate idea of their identity.

Mark sank onto a decaying log and stared into the depths of the black water, trying to force his mind back in time—back to the correct location, back to his previous encounter with those faces. All he could drag to the present was a definite sense of danger, a sense so strong he felt his muscles involuntarily flex for fight or flight. His body responded to the tension with increased heartbeat and ragged respiration, and he soon felt as spent as if he had been running for his life. Surprised by his extreme mental and physical responses, he stood and walked away from the log as he made a conscious effort to slow his breathing.

"Who are they?" he demanded aloud. "Why can't I remember them?" Frustrated, he picked up a pebble and threw it into the glassy, black water. Circle after circle rippled out from the spot where the pebble sank as Mark reached beyond his own powers for help. "God," he whispered. "I need to know. We're in trouble; I can feel it." For a moment longer he stared at the pond, watching the last ripples disappear, struggling to remember.

He was no closer to an answer than when he had begun his walk, so he abruptly turned back to the path. Checking his wristwatch, he hurried home.

Later that morning Mark arrived at the main political event of his day, a rally outside a sugar cane processing plant. The event was scheduled for noon, but as was his custom, Mark arrived at the rally several hours ahead of Philippe. He had his routine down pat. He always quickly looked over the preparations the local party members had made and sent people scurrying around to make whatever changes needed to be made. Today, however, was no typical rally. Today was planned as a special photo-op that Mark hoped would gain positive national exposure for Philippe. After all, Mark reasoned, if Louisiana voters saw Philippe highlighted in the national press, it was only natural that they would see him as a winner who would some day make Louisiana proud on the national stage. Mark had chosen the day and the place carefully. The plant owner was a major supporter of Philippe's, and he had agreed to give the workers a full hour at lunch and even to allow a few carefully chosen workers to linger behind to talk enthusiastically about Philippe to the press.

Mark's first actions were to increase the amount of free food and drink for the workers and to make changes in the platform. Quickly he re-arranged the risers that made up the platform until he had created wide steps from the ground to the top. He had provided Philippe with a portable microphone, which would allow him to move down into the crowd and turn the event into a cozier affair. The image Philippe needed splattered all over the media was one of a born leader whose powers were instinctively recognized by those he gave his life to serve.

According to Mark's plan, the statewide and national press would arrive shortly before Philippe's entourage; then, just after the workers had come out of the plant and had had time to fill their plates and settle in the shade, Philippe would arrive like a conquering hero. He would mount the platform and begin his fiery remarks immediately with his hallmark challenge to the workers, "Who among you is ready to step up and save our beloved Louisiana?" The elegant way Philippe delivered the challenge immediately painted him as a pure Louisiana thoroughbred, and the workers always stopped chewing the minute they heard his voice. Today, for the benefit of the press, Philippe would maintain his aristocratic tone but surprise everyone by abandoning the flag-draped podium and descending a level or two to engage the audience more intimately. It was this "in touch with the ordinary people" Philippe which Mark wanted the press to record and disperse through the state and country.

From that point onward, Mark's job was on hold, and he would step down from the platform while his uncle ranted about the sorry condition of the current regime in office and the dire necessity of electing him governor. Philippe was a born orator; rousing a crowd to a feverish pitch was second nature to him, and Mark could relax a few minutes, certain that the workers would gulp in Philippe's rhetoric as enthusiastically as they gulped down the free food. As the noon hour wound to a close and the workers became skittish and started to go back to their work, Philippe would bring his remarks to a thundering close by pointing his finger at the crowd and demanding in his most aggressive tone, "Do you have the guts to save Louisiana?" Here he paused for a full 15 seconds as he looked around the crowd, pointing his finger and meeting voters eye to eye. A marvelous stillness always fell over the mass, and when Philippe had them in his grip, he raised his right hand to heaven and pronounced with quiet assurance, "God knows you do." A lesser man would raise his voice, but Philippe was a D'Evereau, and he knew the power of playing the gentleman, so he would raise his face to heaven and finish with quiet confidence, "God knows you will."

At this point the crowd would always begin to cheer, and Mark would hustle around making certain that every cameraman got his shots and every reporter had a chance to ask his questions. That was the way the political rallies always went...every time...until today.

On this day Philippe's arrival befitted an emperor, and he mounted the platform with stately vigor amidst the cheering workers. He began with his hallmark challenge to the workers, "Who among you is ready to step up and save our beloved Louisiana?" Unexpectedly a voice boomed back, "I will!" and a rock came flying through the air, barely missing Philippe's head.

Carefully placed hecklers began shouting as more missiles were thrown at the platform. Almost instantly the workers turned on the hecklers and tackled them. As Philippe struggled to regain control from the platform, party members in the crowd fought to silence and remove the hecklers, but in mere seconds, fists were flying, women were screaming, and the press was gleefully closing in with cameras and microphones. Food tables were turned over, and dust rose quickly as the melee escalated into a free-for-all.

Stunned, Mark watched from below the platform as the crowd swirled like a flood-swollen river. When he saw angry men bolting onto the platform and grabbing at Philippe, he forced his way through the crowd and tackled one of them. Other dignitaries on the platform fought with the intruders as Mark struggled to reach his uncle. When he finally reached him, Mark slugged the man who was forcing Philippe to the floor, shuffled his uncle off the back of the platform and hurried him to his waiting chauffeured car.

"Get in, Mark!" Philippe commanded when Mark turned back to the crowd. "Get in, boy! There's nothing you can do."

"I can't just leave!"

"Trust me," Philippe insisted. "The sooner we're gone, the better it will be for everyone here."

Mark hesitated, but when he saw Philippe step out of the car to pull him in, he complied. In seconds they were roaring away from the crowd.

Struggling to breathe, Mark watched in amazement as Philippe composedly pulled a spotless white handkerchief from his pocket and quietly patted his brow. "What on earth happened?" Mark demanded.

"We had a bit of a riot."

"A bit of a riot? Are you sure you want to be the governor of people who can turn on you like that?"

"It wasn't their doing, Mark. Those people love me. And why shouldn't they? I've represented them well for years. I've kept that factory going; I've kept their jobs and consequently their lives intact ."

"Well, something's wrong with their memories then," Mark retorted.

"No, my boy. You'll see when we get a look at the video.

Those weren't locals throwing rocks and mounting that platform. That's why we had to leave; we were the target. The fight will stop now that their target is gone." He fell silent as he receded into serious reflection. "I should have expected this," he finally murmured, obviously to himself.

Mark stared at him in amazement. "Why?"

Philippe seemed to recollect himself abruptly. "Why? Well.....a politician's sure to have a few people disagree with him occasionally, isn't he?"

"That wasn't a little disagreement, Uncle. They meant to hurt you!"

"No, no, my boy." Philippe laughed lightly but insincerely. "You're mistaken. Oh, things got a bit out of hand, but they meant no real harm."

"No real harm." Mark echoed his uncle's words as he stared down at the blood on his clothes without a clue whether it was his or someone else's. Philippe handed him his handkerchief as if that action closed the discussion.

But nothing closed the event for Mark—not Philippe's manufactured nonchalance nor any explanation he heard from Lisette and others when they returned to headquarters. Local party members phoned in reports that the men who had stormed the stage had disengaged from the fight as quickly as possible after Philippe's departure and that they had been seen driving off together. Eagerly Mark sought the first video he could lay his hands on, and when he found it, he played it for Philippe and Lisette. His uncle was quick to point out that the aggressors were not dressed like workers, that obviously they were agitators hired by the opposition. To Mark, he seemed overly eager to dismiss the affair as "unfortunate."

Lisette made no comment, a fact that spoke volumes to Mark and spurred him into action. He killed some time making phone calls until Lisette had turned her attention to other matters. Then Mark stood up, yawned, and slowly left the office. Once he had pulled away from the building and left the immediate area, his whole demeanor changed. He hurried toward the hotel where the self-defined Syrians were staying, and once he had parked on the street across from the entrance, he reached into his camera bag on the backseat. He had a long wait, but eventually the men came back to the hotel and Mark caught them on film.

"I hope Nick hasn't lost that incredible memory of his," he muttered as he pulled away from the curb, intent on developing the images and sending them to his journalist sidekick, his photographer, before the day ended.

When Mark finally fell into bed shortly before midnight, he struggled to turn off his thinking and fall into the sound sleep he desperately needed. Sleep finally came, but so did dreams. At first he dreamed about the violent disruption of the rally that morning. Once again he felt himself scrambling through the crowd toward the platform, intent on saving Philippe from harm. Over and over he saw Philippe falling to the platform and a dark-haired man dragging him back up and shoving him around. In time the face and figure of Philippe morphed into another face, a blue-eyed American who was being dragged toward Mark. The number of people increased, and Mark saw frightened American faces, a small group of Americans being roughly shoved around by dark-haired men. Slowly he understood that these Americans were in danger, and he began to fight his way forward to reach the Americans to help them while his photographer, Nick, followed, wildly clicking pictures.

Quite suddenly two men grabbed Mark and stopped his progress toward the Americans as other dark-haired men pummeled Nick. As Mark grappled with the men assaulting him, he saw their furious faces up close. Quite suddenly he was back at the rally that morning struggling with the agitators on the platform, and he saw the same faces. They were the "Syrians," the men Mark had instinctively feared. Mark struggled so violently to free himself from the men in the dream that he lunged in the bed and woke himself. Sitting upright, he swung his feet off the bed and held his head in his hands as he concentrated on normalizing his breathing.

"This is crazy," he muttered as he shook his head to clear it. "Those men, those supposed Syrians, were not even at the rally this morning. Man, the power of the subconscious to roll things together and confuse—" Mark stopped speaking abruptly as his mind began to piece things together. "That's right!" he whispered triumphantly. "They weren't at the rally this morning, but they were in Tehran when the American Embassy staff was dragged away. I remember! Nick and I rushed to the front—half thinking about getting the best shots and half thinking about rescuing the Americans. We were caught up in the struggle, and I started shoving and throwing punches, but Nick just kept shooting pictures until those men knocked him down. I turned away from the embassy staff to rescue him. He was bleeding badly from the head and clutching his camera to his chest like a baby he would protect at all costs. I almost never got us out of there, but we made it, and we made it with some of the best pictures of the day. Those two men were part of that mob; they were up front, inciting others to fury against the Americans. It all makes sense. They are Iranians! No wonder they're traveling under false passports! The US has absolutely no relations with Iran now that the Shaw has been deposed."

In his excitement Mark leapt up from the bed and paced the room. "But why are they here?" he demanded. "What's so important to Iran about Philippe's campaign?"

"If only I could go to Rome. Nick never throws away a negative. A few days of rummaging through his files and I know I could identify those men. I couldn't go to Iran, of course, but I could talk to our contacts—" Mark stopped. "And leave Philippe alone here? No, I can't do that.... But if those men are Iranian agents—and they must be—why else would they have been up front in that mob in Tehran?"

Mark walked to the window and stared out blindly as he struggled to think things through. Two Iranian agents trying to gain control of Philippe.... Why? Why bother?

God, what's going on? If I'm right—and I know I am—Philippe's in danger. God, you gotta show me. Just show me why they would bother with Philippe, with this race.

A man who tended to throw his requests at God and then act on his own, Mark resolutely turned from the window, dressed quickly and slipped out of the house. Something, or Someone, warned him against using the house phone and reminded him that Lisette was asleep nearby, so he left the estate as quietly as possible, found a pay phone and placed a call to Nick in Rome.

Quickly Mark filled his friend in on his dilemma, told him the pictures were coming; and asked him to identify the men.

"Man! You don't want much, do you?" Nick commented wryly.

"If anyone can do it, you can, buddy," Mark encouraged, "and it's really important. I need their names; I need to know their connection to the current regime. I need any and all info you can get me."

"I'm on it," Nick agreed, "and it's gonna make one helluva story. Who are we gonna sell it to?"

"Haven't thought about it. Right now I'm just trying to save my family."

"Still....it'll make quite a story if we can prove there really are Iranian operatives struggling for a foothold in Louisiana—"

"Not 'if'!" Mark shot back. "'When'!"

"How do I get in touch with you?"

"Call my office," Mark said, giving him the number, "but just say we've been offered a great assignment. I'll call you back from a pay phone."

"Got it. Be in touch soon."

"Thanks, man. I owe you," Mark said before hanging up.

Driving back to Philippe's, Mark pondered the possibility of Lisette's involvement in any scheme with international implications. "She's just not that sophisticated," he thought aloud. "She's not a player on the world stage. Plenty smart enough, but definitely just local. Just Louisiana. Besides, why would she involve herself? What's in it for her? She says she wants to be the governor's wife. That's all she wants. But Philippe can become governor without foreign help. She's smart enough to know that, so what's she up to? Or maybe a better question is, who else is involved in this scheme?"

Chapter 16

Several weeks after Rachel had rescued Sassy and taken her to live with Alice, she eagerly welcomed the teenager back to her school. She had allowed the Sheriff to handle Jamal, and he seemed to have disappeared from the neighborhood.

Sassy's body had healed from the battering it had taken at his hands, but Rachel wasn't naïve enough to believe all was well with the girl. Nevertheless, she did feel hopeful that they were making progress. It was a joy to watch Sassy sitting safely next to Chelsey, struggling with her math lesson. It was obvious the girl still hated school, but she was present and trying. Rachel smiled contentedly and glanced out the window. Much to her amazement she saw Lovey rushing—half walking, half running—across the schoolyard. Rachel's pulse fluttered wildly as she realized that something was terribly wrong. Abandoning the class without a word, she hurried to the door and met Lovey on the schoolhouse steps.

"What's wrong?" she demanded as her heart raced faster and faster.

"Oh, Miz Rachel, you better sit down," Lovey gasped out as she struggled for breath. "I gotta talk to you."

Rachel gathered Lovey into her arms. "Just tell me, Lovey! What's wrong? Tell me!" As Lovey looked up at her with tears gathering in her eyes, Rachel suddenly felt sick to her stomach. She released Lovey, sank down on the school steps and bowed her head before asking, "Is it Mark? Has something happened to Mark?"

"No, Honey, it be your daddy," Lovey said simply as her tears spilled over and coursed down her face.

Rachel's head shot up, "Daddy? I just talked to him early this morning about the plantation accounts! What's happened?"

"He had a heart attack, Miz Rachel. Must have been about mid-morning, best I can tell."

Rachel sprang to her feet, her eyes wide with fear. "Is he....Lovey, is he....?"

"He's alive, Honey. I couldn't get the pastor to tell me much, but he told me to come get you. You supposed to call him at this here number." Lovey held out a slip of paper, which Rachel immediately snatched from her hand before turning and bolting into the building to the phone.

"Fr. Deering? Rachel demanded the minute she heard a voice on the other end of the line. "This is Rachel. What's happened?"

Lovey sank into a chair, and holding her breath, she watched her beloved Rachel's face straining with anxiety as she listened. "Why didn't someone call me?" Rachel shouted into the phone. "It's been six hours! Why didn't you call me?"

Her fury obviously mounting, she listened to the response, then turned to a nearby wall and banged on it with her fist. "Of course!" Rachel exclaimed, her voice shrouded with sarcasm. "What did I expect? How utterly stupid of me to think Mother would want me to come! Well, you tell Daddy I'm coming. I'm on my way right now. And as for Mother—tell her anything you like!"

Rachel listened for a few more seconds before commanding, "Stop it, Fr. Deering. Just stop it! No sermons. They won't do any good. Obviously nothing has changed over there. But here's a truth you can take to the bank. I've had a lifetime of their outrageous behavior, and believe you me, I know how to handle them. I'm on my way!" Rachel slammed the phone down.

"Miz Rachel, you gotta calm down," Lovey insisted as she rose hurriedly from the chair. "You can't go driving off to Texas in your state of mind."

"Lovey, Daddy had a heart attack about ten o'clock this morning, and no one called me! And do you know why no one called me? Because Mother wouldn't let them! And she wouldn't let them call a pastor either. Finally Daddy regained consciousness and asked for Fr. Deering. Otherwise, I wouldn't even know now that my father is close to death. Don't tell me to calm down!"

"Honey, I don't care what they done; it ain't gonna do you no good to be this angry. You's only hurting yourself."

"I have a right to be angry!"

"I ain't arguing with that. I's just saying—"

"Don't bother!" Rachel snapped back. "I'm out of here. I've got to get to Texas."

Lovey stepped over and took Rachel's arm. "Okay, Honey. We'll just pack a few things and get on the road, and then we can talk."

"I'm going alone, Lovey, and I'm going now." Rachel shook off Lovey's soothing hand as she opened a drawer and pulled out her purse. "Marge will take you home."

"But you can't go by yourself!" Lovey protested. "It ain't safe. Besides, you ain't got no bag.You gonna need clothes and all kinds of things."

"Lovey, my father is dying! I don't care about anything else. I'm leaving now. Marge will take care of the students and you." Rachel snatched up her purse and stormed out of the room.

Lovey hurried to a window, and seconds later she saw Rachel jump into her car, start it and tear out of the parking lot. "Oh Lord," Lovey pleaded, "You gotta help her. You got to, Lord! She ain't gonna drive safe, and when she get there, she gonna kill somebody. And even if she don't, what's gonna happen to her? You know how they tears her to pieces every time she go around them." Lovey closed her eyes and continued praying fervently; then suddenly her eyes popped open, and she announced, "I gotta call Mr. Mark! He be the only one Miz Rachel gonna listen to, and I ain't even sure about that."

Lovey picked up the phone and called Philippe's house, looking for Mark. They directed her to call the campaign headquarters where she was connected to Lisette. Lovey soon found out that Mark was on the other side of the state campaigning with Philippe, but Lisette listened sympathetically and promised to find Mark immediately and have him call Belle St. Marie.

Lovey paused only long enough to tell Marge why Rachel had gone before she hurried back to Belle St. Marie to wait for Mark's call.

Rachel raced along the curving, hilly highway as fast as she dared drive. As she whizzed through tall, dense pine forests, she was totally oblivious to the fairyland around her: a world of white-blooming dogwood trees intermingled with frothy, raspberry-colored redbud trees, all of them glowing in the shade. She noticed nothing except the yellow stripe down the center of the two-lane road.

All her thoughts were fear-laced anger. One minute she agonized over the actual condition of her father….had Fr.

Deering told her the whole story? How close to death was her father really? The next minute she stormed aloud at her mother. "How dare you not call me! Do you really hate me this much? Why? Why? What did I ever do to make you hate me so much? For heaven's sake, I was just a child! What could I possibly have done to make you hate me so?"

Thoughts of her mother's past and present behavior toward her sent Rachel's mind reeling back to the last journey she had taken down this road. "What a different person I was then," she muttered. "How vulnerable, how hurt! I swore I'd never return to Texas, certainly never back to Pinewood. I was escaping, running away from my pain. How strange that now I am so desperately eager to get back to the very place I fled only eighteen months ago. The answer is obvious, isn't it? There has been reconciliation between Daddy and me. How has that happened? Simple, really. I just opened my mind and tried to understand more about the struggles of his life, and when I did, I was able to forgive him for not being more than human.

But nothing has changed with Mother, has it? She still resents me, and no doubt she's being encouraged by that champion cheerleader of hatred, Mammy Cassie. And why? Why does Mammy Cassie hate me so? For being born! Does she actually think I chose to be born to her beloved Patsy? Does Mammy Cassie think at all? Or does she just strike out?

I know one thing for sure; Mammy Cassie better understand that the Rachel who's returning to Texas tonight is not the victim who left. And Mother better get something straight too. She can reject me the rest of my life; she can even hate me, but she is not going to make me feel worthless again! That's over, finished!

When Rachel finally turned into the hospital parking lot shortly after 7:00 in the evening, the car was running low on gasoline, and she hadn't eaten a bite or swallowed a drop of liquid from the moment Lovey gave her the news. Undeterred, Rachel jumped from the driver's seat and ran across the parking lot. Once inside the building, she quickly found the intensive care unit and barged through the double doors that were clearly marked "Do not enter."

If Rachel had been less worried than she was, she would have been appalled by what she saw. All the intensive care units opened on to a centrally placed nursing station; each unit was fronted by double doors that were wide open so the nursing staff could continually watch the patients. The result was that Rachel received a horrifying view of suffering patients. She also quickly spotted her father and immediately marched toward the cubicle where he lay. She had almost reached the wide doors when a nurse grabbed her arm and demanded, "What are you doing in here?"

"I've come to see my father," Rachel replied curtly as she shook the woman's hand off her arm.

"This is not a designated visiting time!" The nurse grabbed her again. "You'll have to leave and wait until 8:00 o'clock."

"I'm Rachel D'Evereau, and I have driven from Louisiana—"

"I don't care who you are, Miss. We have rules around here, and everybody abides by them. Even you," she added for emphasis. "Now go back to the waiting room." She dropped Rachel's arm, and Rachel looked at her coolly, sidestepped her and stalked off in the direction of her father's cubicle.

"Call security!" the nurse ordered an LVN at the desk.

"Cancel that," a white-frocked doctor behind the station said. "I want her to see her father."

The nurse opened her mouth to protest, but then thought better of it and moved aside as the doctor followed Rachel. "Ms. D'Evereau," the doctor called softly after Rachel. "Just a minute, please."

Rachel whirled around, clearly ready to do battle again, but before she could speak, the doctor hastily said, "Don't worry. I want you to see your father. I'm Dr. Hanson, the cardiologist who was called in on his case. I just want to make you aware of a few things before you see him. Then I ask you to keep your visit short and come back to the desk. I want to talk to you more at length."

Rachel nodded, and the doctor pulled her over to the side of the unit. "Your father has had a serious heart attack, and his condition is critical. I'll go into more details later. Here's how you can help. He has been quite agitated all day; apparently he's worried about your mother. He's been asking for you, but I had no way of finding you until I called Fr. Deering."

"Why didn't you simply ask my mother how to contact me?"

Dr. Hanson averted his eyes for a second, and Rachel understood his dilemma.

"She wouldn't let you call me. Is that it?"

"Yes. Ms. D'Evereau. I don't need to know about the existing frictions in your family. I just want to save your father's life and do what we can to give him many more healthy years. So what I need you to do is to go in to see your father and ease his mind about whatever is upsetting him so much. Leave the family difficulties out in the waiting room. Do you understand?"

"You can count on me, Dr. Hanson. My father's life is more important to me than anything else; I'll do whatever it takes."

"Okay. For now, as I said, just bring him as much peace as possible. A good night's rest could do wonders for him. Do keep your visit brief—and above all else, keep it non-stressful, non-emotional."

"I can handle it," Rachel insisted.

"He looks quite weak, and there are lots of tubes and—"

"I can handle that, too, Dr. Hanson." Rachel cut him off. "I'll be back to talk with you in a few minutes." She turned her back on the doctor and hurried into her father's cubicle.

Rachel took one deep breath before approaching her father's bedside and made a conscious decision to ignore all the medical paraphernalia, including the steady beep of the heart monitor. Gently she moved forward and leaned over the bed, placing her face close to his. "Daddy, it's Rachel. I'm here." She took his hand in hers, and his eyes fluttered open. "Everything is going to be fine," she assured him. "You're going to come through this and be yourself again, and I'm going to take care of Mother and anything else that needs to be handled."

"Rachel," he sighed. "Thank God, you're here."

Rachel bit her tongue to keep from shouting, "I would have been here hours ago if Mother had called me!" Instead she kept her voice level and stroked his head. "Yes, I'm here. I'm going to take care of everything. Do you understand?"

He nodded weakly, and she continued, "Dr. Hanson says you will come through this fine if you get plenty of rest, so you need to relax and sleep. Will you do that?"

"Yes," Jack breathed, "but....Rachel...."

"What is it, Daddy? You mustn't worry about anything. I told you. I'll take care of everything."

"I know you will, baby." Jack hesitated as a look of deep sadness covered his exhausted face. "Rachel," he whispered, "Rachel, forgive me."

"There's nothing to forgive," Rachel answered. "Daddy, please—"

"There's so much more than you know," Jack insisted, "I've made such horrible mistakes, and you've paid the price for them." He struggled to sit up, and Rachel, frightened for him, gently pressed him back on the pillow.

"Now you listen to me, Daddy." She spoke firmly but

quietly. "The past is the past. It's over, finished. If you made mistakes, you made them because you are human. I understand because I'm human, and I've made mistakes too."

"Will you forgive me?" he asked desperately.

Rachel finally understood that he needed to hear the words, so she spoke emphatically. "With all my being I forgive you, Daddy, for any hurt you ever caused me. I forgive you for the hurts I know about and those I have yet to learn about. They are all in the past; they are all forgiven."

He nodded, and the tension evaporated from his face. A slight smile softened his features. "Sleep," he sighed and closed his eyes.

"Yes, that's right," she agreed. "Plenty of sleep. That's what you need now. I'll be close by." She squeezed his hand, waited for his breathing to become steady, and when it did, she slowly withdrew from the cubicle.

Dr. Hanson was waiting for her. "There's a private conference room off the waiting room. Let's go talk there." Rachel nodded her agreement and followed the doctor out the double doors.

Lovey paced up and down the center hall of Belle St. Marie as she kept a running, one-sided conversation going with God. At the same time she kept her eyes glued to the phone. Occasionally she stopped in front of it, wrung her hands and agonized over whether to take further action. Finally at about 7:30 the phone rang and jarred every one of Lovey's nerves. She snatched it up and exclaimed, "Mr. Mark! Miz Rachel need you. She's gone to Texas 'cause Mr. Jack, he had a heart attack."

There was dead silence on the other end of the line until a man finally answered, "Lovey, this is Andre Simone. What's all this about Rachel and Jack? What's happened?"

"Oh, Mr. Andre! What am I gonna do? Miz Rachel be in a terrible fix, and I can't find Mr. Mark nowhere. I talk to that Miz Lisette, and she supposed to find Mr. Mark, but he ain't called, and it been hours now. Miz Rachel, she over in Texas all by herself, most likely already at the hospital, and you knows how that mother of hers and that awful Mammy Cassie upsets her—"

"Calm down, Lovey," Andre insisted. "Let me get this straight. Jack has had a heart attack, and Rachel has gone to Texas—"

"And I can't find Mr. Mark!"

"Now, now, Lovey, calm yourself. This calls for clear thinking and heroic action; Rachel is in trouble. I'll handle everything; you just hang up the phone, and let me get to work. I'll call you back as soon as possible. Don't worry anymore, Lovey; you know I won't leave Rachel in distress."

Lovey heard the click of the phone as Andre cut the connection, so she slowly replaced the receiver. She looked up at the ceiling and announced, "I ain't gonna worry, Lord, but I ain't gonna leave You alone either." She sat down in a chair next to the phone. "I's gonna sit right here until You gets things fixed." She crossed her arms and bowed her head in prayer.

In less than ten minutes the phone rang again. Lovey snatched it up, but before she could say a word, Mark's voice came through the line loud and clear. "Lovey, I'm at Uncle Philippe's, and I'm leaving for Texas right now."

"But, Mr. Mark, that Miz Lisette supposed to find you—"

"I know, I know, Lovey. Don't you worry. I'll deal with that situation when I get back. All I want to know now is, should I take a bag for Rachel? Did she take any clothes?"

"Miz Rachel ain't got one thing with her. She just run out of the school and drove off like a crazy woman."

"I'll be at Belle St. Marie in a few minutes, Lovey. Throw together some things she might need."

When Lovey heard the phone click, she went into action. She hurried upstairs, grabbed a small suitcase from a storage closet and began to snatch items of Rachel's clothing from the closet and bureau. Minutes later she heard Mark calling from the front door, "Lovey!"

"I's up here," she called down the staircase as she raced to the bathroom to find Rachel's toothbrush.

Mark bounded up the stairs two at a time and almost ran into her as she hurried back to Rachel's bedroom. "I just know I ain't got everything she need," Lovey worried aloud.

"Anything will be better than nothing, Lovey. I've just got to get on the road; it's three hours to—"

Suddenly the phone rang, and Mark ran to Rachel's bedside table to snatch up the receiver. The minute he realized it was Rachel calling, he demanded, "Are you all right? Where are you?"

Lovey immediately hurried to his side, and Mark leaned over and shared the receiver with her.

"I'm fine, Mark," Rachel answered sharply. "I'm mad as—never mind, I refuse to be angry until later."

"You ought to be spanked for dashing off by yourself! What were you thinking? You could have been—"

"Mark, I'm here, and I've seen Daddy. That's what counts."

"How is Mr. Jack?" Lovey called into the receiver.

"The doctor says his condition is critical, but he's hopeful that with a good night's rest, he may be stronger in the morning. They really don't know much at this point; they've just spent the day stabilizing him, but they're guessing he needs bypass surgery when he's stronger."

"Is you there by yourself?" Lovey asked.

"Yes. By the time I arrived, Mother had already left."

Mark handed Lovey the phone, went to the bed and closed up the suitcase. "Tell her I'm on my way," he called over his shoulder as he left the room.

"Mr. Mark say he be on the way, Miz Rachel."

"Wait a minute! Tell him he doesn't have to come. I don't even know if I want him to come. Let me talk to him."

"He on his way out the front door, honey."

"Go stop him, Lovey!"

"I ain't gonna do that. You needs him."

"Lovey, listen to me. He shouldn't come over here. He's just going to get mixed up in a painful, family mess. Go stop him!"

"It be too late, honey. He already gone. But it don't matter anyway. That man gonna come whether you wants him to or not. Besides, you needs him."

Rachel fell silent, then sighed loudly. "Maybe I do, Lovey. I'm going to need somebody to keep me from blowing up the minute I see Mother. I've just got to keep a lid on myself; the doctor says that Daddy must be protected from stress of any kind."

"You can do it, Honey. I's gonna be praying for you. You can do anything you needs to do to help your Daddy."

"You're right, Lovey, if I stay totally focused on Daddy—"

"Just leave the past in the past, honey. You can't change it anyhow."

"I know, I know. The problem is, the past is still very present when I'm over here in Texas."

"I should've come with you. I just knowed I should've come when you went dashing out the door. I can't stand to think of you being around that Mammy Cassie again."

"You can stop worrying about that right now, Lovey. I'm not a child anymore; I can handle Mammy Casssie. It's Mother I'm worried about. Daddy needs me to take care of her, and I'm not sure she's going to cooperate. She never has."

"Just get through tonight, Honey, and know the Lord ain't gonna give you more than you can stand."

"I just hope he hasn't over-estimated my abilities, Lovey."

"He don't make no mistakes, Honey. You knows that."

"So I've been told. Well, it's almost 8:00, and I can go in and check on Daddy. That's when they let the families of ICU patients visit. I just hope he is fast asleep and stays that way through the night. It's going to be a long night."

"Have you eaten anything?"

"No, I'm not hungry."

"You gotta eat, Honey, and you can't wait until you gets hungry. You gonna have to keep up your strength."

"I'll grab something after I check on Daddy," Rachel said.

"You promise?"

"I promise, Lovey."

"And you call me when Mr. Mark get there."

"You'll be asleep by then," Rachel protested.

"I ain't going to sleep until I know Mr. Mark be with you, and that's a fact. So you call me, or I's coming over there myself."

"I'll call, I promise."

"Everything gonna be all right, Honey. Just trust the Lord to get your Daddy and you through this."

"Yes, Lovey. Good-bye now."

Rachel hung up the phone and hurried back toward the double doors to join family members of other ICU patients who were gathered at the doors, waiting to be invited into the area Rachel had barged into earlier.

When she once again approached her father's bedside and found him fast asleep, she smiled wearily. "Thank you, God," she whispered. Standing by his bedside, she watched his regular breathing and listened to the beep of the heart monitor as she tried to pray. No eloquent, prayer-worthy words came to her mind; instead, the word "help" seemed to rise from her being with every beep of the monitor. Finally the nurse signaled that she had to leave.

As Rachel exited the ICU unit, her eyes filled with tears, and to her horror she realized that she was about to break down. She hurried toward a ladies room, but she heard a man call her name. Before she knew what had happened, someone had wrapped his arms around her and pulled her close. Rachel tried to regain control of herself, failed, and began to sob on his shoulder. Through her own sounds she heard soothing words, and took the handkerchief that was offered to her.

When she finally managed to stop sobbing, she lifted her tear-drenched eyes to look up into the face of her comforter.

"Billy Ray!" she exclaimed as she took a step backward. "Billy Ray Snyder, what on earth are you doing here?"

"Why, what a question, Rachel! I came to help you, of course." Billy grinned down at her, quite pleased with himself. "How's your daddy?"

"He's asleep, but the doctor says he's in critical condition," Rachel answered hurriedly as she swabbed her face with the handkerchief. "How did you find out about Daddy? And how did you get here so fast?"

"Lovey told me what happened, and I just headed for the airport and my little Cessna. Didn't take any time at all to get here. Then I paid some guy at the dinky little airport here to drive me into town. But enough of that, come on over here, sweetheart, and sit down. We gotta take care of you."

Rachel allowed him to hustle her over to a couch in the waiting room. She wearily sank down on it and wiped her eyes again. "I must look a mess," she muttered.

"Not to me, sweetheart." He pulled her hands into his. "Now, let's take care of Rachel. Have you eaten anything?"

"You sound like Lovey."

"That's because we both care about you. Don't dodge the question. Have you eaten?"

"No," Rachel confessed.

"Okay, that's where we start. We'll get something to eat, then we'll get you over to your parents' house and get you—"

"Wait!" Rachel interrupted him. "I'm staying here tonight. I'll go get something to eat, but then I'm coming right back here and spend the night in this waiting room."

Billy studied her for a minute, then announced, "You're the boss. We'll both stay here tonight. Now let's get some food. Where do we go in this town at this time of the night and find a decent meal?"

"I hope you like the Dairy Queen," Rachel answered, "but, Billy Ray, you really don't need to stay here tonight. I appreciate your coming, but after we eat, I think you ought to go home to Louisiana."

"Not likely, sweetheart, not likely," Billy replied. "I'm not about to leave you here alone, and I don't exactly see a horde of family gathered around you."

"That's a long story," Rachel sighed.

"Which can wait until later," Billy added, "or never be told at all. Only one thing concerns me, and that's you, right now, in the present. I have no use for the past. Let's go eat." He pulled her to her feet and escorted her out of the waiting room.

Chapter 17

When Rachel returned to the ICU waiting room an hour later, a young woman timidly approached her. "Are you Rachel?"

Rachel's pulse quickened. "Yes!"

"Oh, nothing bad has happened," the young woman quickly assured her. "It's just that you had two calls, one of them all the way from Paris, France."

Still struggling with her racing pulse, Rachel slumped down on a nearby couch and struggled to catch her breath.

"I'm sorry; I didn't mean to scare you. Here are the phone numbers." The young woman held out a piece of paper. "I wrote them down for you. I sure hope I got that foreign one right."

"Thank you, ma'am." Billy Ray stepped forward and took the paper. "That was very kind of you. I'll take it from here."

Rachel looked up at the young woman and smiled weakly. "Yes, thank you."

"No problem," she replied. "By the way, I'm Lily Ann. My mom is in ICU tonight 'cause of her diabetes acting up again."

"I'm so sorry." Rachel pulled herself together and tried to extend friendship to the young woman. "Are you staying here tonight?"

"Actually, I'm not sure. It depends on whether I can get a ride home. They've got Mom stabilized, so I guess I could go."

Rachel stood up and patted Lily Ann's shoulder. "Just let me return these calls, and I'm sure we can figure out a way to get you home."

"Oh, you don't have to do that," Lily Ann insisted. "I don't want to be no trouble. You've got enough trouble as it is."

"Let me return these calls, and then we'll talk." Rachel turned and reached for the paper. "I know the Paris call must be from Louis," she said to Billy Ray, "but who is the other one from?"

"Probably from Andre," Billy Ray answered. "Let me take care of this, Rachel. It won't do you any good to rehearse what you've been through."

A picture of Louis' reaction if Billy Ray called him flashed through Rachel's mind, and she stammered out, "No! No, that wouldn't be a good idea, Billy Ray. I'll call them; just give me the paper." She held out her hand until Billy Ray reluctantly handed over the slip of paper.

She called Andre first and insisted that he did not need to drive up from New Orleans. Louis was harder to persuade, partially because Andre had told him that Mark was on his way to Pinewood. "If things are so serious that you need Mark's help, Rachel, then obviously you need mine. I've already booked a flight from Paris to Houston."

"I don't need Mark's help!" Rachel insisted. "And by the time you arrive, I'm sure Daddy will be out of danger. Please, please, Louis, just wait until morning. The doctor is hopeful that a good night's rest for Daddy will pull him back from danger."

"I don't like this, Rachel, but I'll wait on one condition. Promise me that you'll call Papa if you need him. He can charter a plane and fly over in no time."

"I really don't need anyone—"

"Promise me, Rachel, or I'm coming tonight."

"I promise, I promise!" Rachel instantly agreed. When she put the phone down, she leaned wearily against the wall and murmured a quick prayer, "Lord, please help me contain this mess. I don't want all these people to know about my family. But oh! More than that, just please, please heal Daddy. Yes, that's what I want the most."

As she returned to the waiting room, she wondered what was going to happen when Mark arrived and found Billy Ray there ahead of him. "He'll just have to deal with it," she muttered. "The only man I care about at the moment is Daddy. That's all I can handle. I just hope I can get Billy Ray out of here before I have to deal with Mother. I know full well that Mark won't leave, no matter what I say." She stopped and thought about that and realized that she was glad.

Mark arrived at the hospital a little after midnight. Rachel saw him coming down the corridor and ran to meet him. When he threw his arms around her, she suddenly felt a little safer; nevertheless, unwelcome tears sprang to her eyes. By the time Mark released her and looked down into her face, her cheeks were stained with rivulets of water. He reached up and tenderly tried to brush her cheeks dry, but it was a losing battle.

"How is he?" Mark asked.

"Still critical, but he's resting well now."

"Now that he knows you're here," Mark surmised.

"Yes, apparently he was quite agitated all day because he was worried about Mother, as usual."

"Is that all he said?"

"No, he apologized to me. Some kind of general apology about everything from my birth on. Oh Mark! I don't care about any of that. I just want—" Rachel broke into quiet sobs, and he pulled her to him and held her tight.

"Rachel, Rachel," he comforted. "We're going to get through this, and somehow we'll get everything sorted out. Whatever it takes, we'll do it. Right?"

Rachel nodded her head in agreement and snuggled her face close to his neck.

"All we can do now is wait," Mark added.

"And assure Daddy that everything is okay," Rachel mumbled. "That's what the doctor said, and he was very specific about it too. He said to bury whatever family trouble there is."

"Then that's what we'll do." Mark held her tight as his gaze shifted to the waiting room. "I want you to go back into the waiting room and lie down on one of the couches."

"Okay," Rachel whispered. "All of a sudden, I'm exhausted."

"Let's go." Mark gently pushed her away from him and put his arm around her waist to support her.

Rachel suddenly remembered Billy Ray. "Oh Mark, I completely forgot. Billy Ray—"

"Is here. I know; I spotted him. Don't worry about it. Just come lie down."

After Mark had settled Rachel on one of the couches and covered her with his jacket, he walked over to confront Billy Ray.

"What are you doing here?" he demanded.

"Protecting my territory, old man," Billy Ray responded cheerily, "just like you."

"You don't have any territory here, Billy Ray. You're not needed, and you're not wanted."

"On the contrary, when I arrived here, Rachel was all alone and very upset. I have been her pillar of strength. Where have you been all this time?"

Mark ignored his question and posed one of his own. "How

did you find out about Jack's heart attack anyway?"

"Why, Lovey told me, of course."

"Lovey called you?" Mark demanded. "I don't believe you."

"Well, as it happens, I called Belle St. Marie to talk to Rachel, and poor old Lovey was beside herself with worry about Rachel. Seems she couldn't find you 'cause you were off politicking somewhere. So I just jumped in my plane and headed to Texas."

"You're a liar," Mark said quietly.

"Now, Mark, old boy, that's not a nice thing to say." Billy Ray grinned at him. "You're not being a very good sport about all this."

"This isn't a sport, Snyder. This is Rachel's life, Rachel's pain."

"Well, we all lose our daddies some time, don't we? The story is that you lost yours pretty young."

"My life is none of your business."

"Everything about you is my business, Mark, old boy. I make it my business to know everything about my rivals."

"You're not even in the race, Snyder."

"Well, we'll see about that. We'll just see about that. I hate to keep bringing up painful facts, but you don't have what it takes to make Rachel happy. In fact, you don't have much of anything to offer her, do you?"

"I'm not going to discuss Rachel with you, Snyder. You just make your plans to leave in the morning." Mark walked away from Billy Ray and went to sit close to Rachel.

Billy Ray followed him, pulled Rachel's car keys out of his pocket and announced tauntingly, "I've got to do a little errand for Rachel. Seems she wants someone to take this young woman over here home. But then, you wouldn't know about that, would you, Mark? 'Cause you haven't been here."

Mark's jaw stiffened as he watched Billy Ray approach a young woman, help her gather up her things and leave with her. Rachel's eyes fluttered open, and she whispered, "Don't fight with him, Mark. Please don't fight with him."

"Don't worry," Mark answered as he leaned forward and stroked her head. "I wouldn't give him the satisfaction. Now you go to sleep."

She closed her eyes, and Mark slipped down in his chair and stretched out his long legs in front of him.

He had some thinking to do.

How did Billy Ray find out about Jack? Mark wondered

silently. Lovey would have warned me if Billy Ray was on the way to Pinewood. So who told him? Who could have told him? Lisette? She could have, but it's not likely; she hates Billy Ray's guts. Philippe? He didn't know about Jack until Andre called him, and I was standing right there when he got the call. Besides, Billy Ray must have already been on his way to Pinewood by then.

Maybe someone on the campaign staff called him. But why would anybody do that? Why would anybody even think to do it? In fact, did anyone on the staff know about Jack, other than Lisette? So that leaves Lisette. But she really hates Billy Ray; it's obvious every time they're even in the same room. Remember Christmas day and at Philippe's on New Year's Eve. Both times Lisette was openly and aggressively furious with Billy Ray. It was really quite a show! A show? A show...maybe it was just a show. Maybe she was just pretending. But why would she do that?

Good question. Why would she pretend to hate Billy Ray? He pondered that for a while; then another question popped into his head. Why didn't Lisette make a genuine effort to find me and give me Lovey's message? She knew exactly where Philippe and I were. Why didn't she call me? Didn't she want me to come to Pinewood? No, that makes no sense. Lisette would use any excuse to get me away from Philippe, to remove me from the everyday running of the campaign. She'd send me to Mars if she could.

So why didn't she hunt me down and send me to Pinewood? Granted, she's obviously jealous of Rachel, but why would she want to keep me away from Rachel? After all, she's got Philippe in her pocket.

I'm going in circles here! I need more info.

Mark folded his arms across his chest, closed his eyes and slipped into a light sleep.

The next morning brought good news for Rachel. After the doctors examined Jack, they offered her a cautiously positive projection of his future. He had survived the first 24 hours since his heart attack without any further episodes of heart malfunction, and he was stronger in general. To be on the safe side, they chose to keep him in ICU for another day, but they were hopeful that he could be moved to a room in the cardiac unit by the following day.

Fr. Deering stopped by the waiting room a little before 8:00. Rachel hugged him, introduced Mark and Billy Ray, and tried her best to express her thanks for his call to her in Louisiana. He accompanied Rachel when she went into ICU to visit briefly with

Jack at 8:00. When she saw how much better her father looked, Rachel broke into a big smile, which Jack noticed immediately.

He grinned at her and quipped, "All I needed was a good night's sleep."

"You need a good deal more, and I'm going to stay here and see to it that you behave yourself," Rachel playfully warned him.

"Better listen to her, Jack," Fr. Deering said. "You know how stubborn she can be."

"And I know where she got that stubborn streak, too," Jack said as he held out his hand to Rachel, and she grasped it. "She's a D'Evereau. She'll always be a D'Evereau."

"Now, Jack, I wouldn't count on that," Fr. Deering warned. "That waiting room out there is fairly teeming with suitors for Rachel's hand. At least half the eligible men in Louisiana are out there, determined to take care of her."

"I'm the one who had the heart attack," Jack said, as he playfully squeezed Rachel's hand.

"Oh, they don't care a flip about you, Jack. You just gave them a great opportunity to take care of helpless, little Rachel here."

"Is one of them Mark?" Jack asked Rachel.

"Yes, Daddy."

"And who else is out there? Louis? Don't tell me Louis came all the way from Paris."

"No, Daddy, Louis called and so did Andre."

"Louis? Andre?" Fr. Deering broke in. "You mean there are more? The only other one I met is Billy Ray Snyder."

"Not Snyder!" Jack retorted. "Get rid of that one, Deering!"

"Whatever you say, Jack. But it may take me a while; the man flew over here in his private plane to take care of our fragile, little Rachel."

"Will you two stop it?" Rachel laughed. "You're both incorrigible. We're going to get thrown out of here in a minute, so let's get serious. Daddy, promise me you'll cooperate with the nurses and sleep all day."

"Depends on how good-looking the nurses are, baby," Jack quipped.

"That's the spirit, Jack!" Fr. Deering cheered.

"Daddy! Be serious. You've had a close call, and the doctors are hopeful about your future, if you behave yourself. Now promise me!"

"I promise, baby," Jack answered solemnly. "Now you promise me you'll go over to the house and get some rest. You've had a long night of it out in that waiting room while I slept in here."

Rachel leaned over and kissed his forehead. "I promise."

"And send that Billy Ray Snyder back to Louisiana."

"Gladly," Rachel agreed. "I'll see you later today."

"See you tonight, Jack," Fr. Deering promised as he waved good-bye.

Once they had exited the ICU, Fr. Deering pulled Rachel aside to talk to her, and she could tell from his expression that she was in for some religious instruction. "Now, Rachel, you and I need to have a little discussion about the power of forgiveness. I know you must be angry with your mother; it's only natural. But she was in quite a state yesterday, and you must forgive her for not calling you. For your father's sake and for your own sake, you must start the day with a clean slate."

"I know. The doctors warned me to keep things calm. I've thought about it all night, and no matter what I have to do, I will not fight with Mother."

"Or with Mammy Cassie," Fr. Deering added.

"That will be harder, I confess, but I'll do my best. I'm well aware that upsetting Mammy Cassie will only upset Mother. You're just going to have to trust me to handle this. I can do it."

"Of course you can. I just know it would be so much easier if you could just forgive—"

"I have forgiven her for the way she treated me when I was growing up. Really, I have. That's what I've been working on the last 18 months."

"And have you forgiven her for not calling you yesterday?"

"No."

"And what about all the things she's sure to do in the coming days that will anger or hurt you. Are you ready to forgive her for those?"

"No, not really. I guess I'm just hoping for kind, or at least fair, treatment from her."

"Rachel, I don't like to be saying this, but you know your mother is a sick woman."

"I know she's selfish."

"She's sick, Rachel, and recognizing that truth is the fastest way to learn to forgive her on the spot every time she hurts you. Can't you see the wisdom in what I'm saying to you?"

"I don't really want to see it because I still want to believe that she can make choices about her behavior, and she could choose to treat me differently."

"Ah, but she can't, my child. Maybe years ago, she could have made different choices, but as she's aged, she's become enshrouded in a confusion of mind. Sometimes she can cover up that confusion, it's true. Sometimes she can put on a pretty good show and still be that belle of the ball she used to be. But more and more she resorts to anger and hurtful behaviors because she can't cover her confusion any other way."

"I'm sorry. I just don't believe what you're saying. I know you do, but I don't. She's choosing to be whatever she is—just like we all do!"

Fr. Deering sighed. "You would be wise to believe what I'm saying, Rachel, and to remember it. It's you who will be having to do the bending. Your mother will never admit she's wrong."

"I know that, but somehow I'll handle it, for Daddy's sake."

"Even better to forgive her for your sake and her sake."

"There's got to be some way to fix our relationship. I just want to fix it!"

"Not everything is fixable, Rachel. There's great wisdom in knowing when to let go of your dream for a relationship because you can't control the other person."

"But if only I knew why she's always disliked me so much! Maybe I could fix it."

"Perhaps you will find out her reasons, perhaps not. We don't always learn the why of things in this life. Either way, though, you'll have to forgive her."

Rachel sighed heavily. "Well, it won't be long now before I have to do something. Surely she'll come to see Daddy at the 10:00 visiting time."

"Yes, surely she will."

"Does she even know I'm here?"

"She knows. I called your Uncle Lloyd last night. I'm sure he passed on the news."

"Well, after I see her, the first thing I've got to do is find a place to stay and get some rest."

"You won't consider going to your parents' house to stay?"

"I don't think I'll be invited, but I'll go out there first, of course."

Fr. Deering nodded his agreement. "Good, and maybe you'll be surprised. If not, we have a new hotel, you know."

"That'll do. Now I think I'll go do my very best to get Billy Ray Snyder to go home. I don't mind Mark being here; he at least knows the family situation. I'd just as soon Billy Ray didn't learn about it."

"You'll be in my prayers. There's just one other caution I want to give you. I know you pretty well, and you have a wee tendency to be hard on yourself, to hold yourself to too high a standard. Be good to yourself, Rachel. If you slip up a little and give in to the temptation to be angry or hurt, just forgive yourself and move on. And remember we have a chapel in this hospital for a very good reason."

"Thank you." Rachel hugged him. "Thank you for helping Daddy and for being here for me."

"And I will be here! In fact, you won't be able to get rid of me," Fr. Deering laughed.

"I wouldn't want to. Now let's see if I can get rid of Billy Ray."

When Rachel reentered the waiting room, she put on her cheeriest smile for Billy Ray and Mark and delivered an excessively positive report. "Great news!" she announced. "Daddy is much, much improved. The doctor's prognosis is very positive. One more day in ICU, just for safety sake, and then a few days in the cardiac unit before they send him home. Isn't that grand?"

"Wonderful!" Billy Ray exclaimed.

"That's good news, Rachel," Mark said quietly as he peered down at her, studying her face.

"All he needed was to see you," Billy Ray said. "Any man would recover at the sight of you." He turned to Mark, "Don't you agree, old boy?"

"I do," Mark murmured, still watching Rachel closely.

"I could never have made it through the night without your support, Billy Ray," Rachel said. "And yours too, Mark," she added in an apparent afterthought. "But now that Daddy's prognosis is so positive, there's really no need for you to stay, Billy Ray, and I know you must have very pressing business responsibilities." She intentionally paused, then added, "and the same goes for you too, Mark."

"I wouldn't think of leaving you, Rachel," Billy Ray insisted, "not for several more days."

"But, Billy Ray," Rachel countered, "with your private plane you could return in an hour if anything awful happened and I needed you."

"True, true," Billy Ray agreed, then gave Mark a pointed look as he added, "I wouldn't have to take hours driving over here."

"Exactly. Besides, I'm going to go home to my parents'

house and sleep the day away. The doctor was so positive about Daddy's recovery I think I can finally calm down and rest. So what good is it for you to hang around Pineview?"

"You've convinced me," Mark suddenly announced. "I do need to get back to Philippe's campaign. We have several major media events coming up tomorrow, and I'm not at all confident the staff is ready. You can always reach me through campaign headquarters, if you need me."

"I don't know, Rachel." Billy Ray hesitated, then barely concealing an expression of triumph, looked disparagingly at Mark. "I'm not the kind of man to just walk out and leave you here alone."

"But I won't be alone," Rachel assured him quietly. "My Uncle Lloyd stayed at the hospital yesterday with Mother, and I'm sure they'll both be returning this morning. He'll be here, and you'll only be an hour away by plane."

Mark didn't wait for Billy Ray to respond; instead he leaned over and kissed Rachel lightly on the lips and said, "Promise you'll call me if you need me?"

"I promise," Rachel assured him.

"Then the truth is, I really do need to go back to Louisiana," Mark admitted.

"Go, Mark. I'll be fine, really I will."

"Call me tonight. Okay? I'll be back at Philippe's by 7:00."

"I'll call you," Rachel promised.

She and Billy Ray watched as Mark hurried out the door; then, knowing full well that Billy Ray wouldn't leave until he was certain Mark was gone, Rachel went to a sofa closer to the windows, plopped down, laid her head back against the sofa and closed her eyes. When Billy Ray followed her, he had a clear view of the parking lot, and Rachel gave him plenty of time as she feigned utter exhaustion and said, "I'm going to go now, too. If I go on over to the house, I can check in with Mother before she leaves for the hospital. Then I'm going straight to bed and sleep away the day."

"Sounds like a good plan," Billy Ray said as he continued to look out the window. Silence fell between them as Rachel continued to "snooze" for a few minutes. Finally Billy Ray leaned over her and said, "You better get up and go on home, Rachel, before you pass out completely." He pulled her to her feet and added, "If you absolutely swear you'll call me the minute you need me, I'll take a taxi out to the airport and fly on home, at least for today."

"I promise, Billy Ray. I'll keep you posted on everything. But maybe I should drive you to the airport before I go home," she offered.

"No way. You're far too tired; I know this is a small town but surely they have a cab service."

"They do," Rachel encouraged, "but why don't you go call one before I leave? That way I'll feel less like I'm abandoning you."

"Don't you worry about me, sweetheart. I can take care of myself. I got here last night, didn't I?"

"You sure did," Rachel agreed, "and just when I needed you."

"And I'll always be here when you need me, sweetheart." He leaned down and kissed her lightly on the lips. "Now I'm going to walk you to your car first, and then I'll call a cab."

Once Rachel had driven out of the hospital parking lot and turned the car in the direction of her parent's home, anxiety gradually replaced her exhaustion. She was fast approaching a moment she had avoided for 18 months, the moment she would come face to face with her mother and Mammy Cassie again. Inevitably her mind filled with destructive phrases hurled at her by Mammy Cassie when she was a child. You's a devil chile! You's ruined your mother's life. She ain't been happy since the day you's borned. Rachel shook herself, gripped the steering wheel harder, and sternly corrected her thinking. "You're not a child any more, Rachel. You don't have to be wiped out by Mammy Cassie's hatred." But the minute she stopped talking to herself, the words shouted back in her head. I hope you's happy. You's gone and made your mother sick again! You don't care 'bout nobody but yourself!

Nausea began to churn in Rachel's stomach, and she pulled the car onto the shoulder of the road. She barely made it out of the car and to the weeds on the roadside before she was overwhelmed with a series of dry heaves. Exhausted by the effort, she turned back to the car and leaned on the back bumper for support as she waited for her heart to stop its pounding and tried to talk some adult sense into herself. "Rachel, you've got to get in touch with who you are now. You're not a child. You're not even the adult who fled this place 18 months ago. You've healed and grown so much. Be who you are now; don't let them drag you back into the misery. Take control! You don't have to be hammered and hurt by Mammy Cassie's words. Just tell her to shut up!"

Rachel thought about that advice for a minute, then modified it. "I can't just tell Mammy Cassie off; she'll go straight to Mother, and I must keep mother calm for her sake and for Daddy's sake. Besides, shutting up Mammy Cassie won't keep Mother from saying hurtful things." She considered her mother. "You can't shut Mother up; she's going to strike out at you if she's upset, and she's sure to be upset now. Fr. Deering is right; she always uses anger to cover her fear."

Rachel sighed hopelessly and returned to the driver's seat. "What am I going to do?" she asked herself as she started the car and pulled back onto the road. "What am I going to do? I'm trapped."

By the time she turned into the gates of her parents' estate, her anxiety had turned to panic. "I'm not ready! I'm not ready!" she muttered. "I thought I could do this, but I just can't!"

She stopped her car about half way up the driveway and actually considered turning around. "I can't, I just can't," she whispered as tears ran down her cheeks. "What am I going to do?" Slowly she grew angry with herself. "For heaven's sake, Rachel, your father has suffered a heart attack! He needs you; you've got to help him. For heaven's sake…" Rachel stopped as the phrase echoed in her mind. "For heaven's sake," she murmured, "for heaven's sake. I'm supposed to be God's child. Lovey says I am; Grandmere used to say I am. Why isn't He helping me?"

She sighed as she wiped her face with the back of her hand, "It just never seems to work for me," she whispered as she put the car back into gear and drove around the last curve in the drive. The first thing she saw was Mark's car parked a short distance from the front porch. He was leaning against the car, waiting for her. Rachel began to cry again, this time with relief. "Oh, thank you, God!" she whispered. "Thank you."

When she pulled her car in front of his and turned off the ignition, he came to the door and helped her out. He pulled her close, and she snuggled gratefully against him. "I'm so glad to see you," she managed to whisper. "You just don't know what this means to me."

"You didn't think I would actually leave, did you?" he asked quietly.

"I guess I did," she admitted.

"I'll never leave you again, Rachel. I told you that; I don't know why I can't get you to believe me."

"But how did you find the house?"

"I just asked for directions. Everybody in Pineview knows where Jack D'Evereau lives."

Rachel pulled back from him and reached for the soggy wad of tissues in her purse. "Here," Mark said as he handed her a handkerchief. "I think we need to retire those."

"I seem to have done nothing but cry all the way out here. I'm so afraid. I just can't believe how afraid I am. I'm embarrassed. Here I am a grown woman—"

"It's going to be okay, Rachel," Mark assured her.

"But I don't know what is about to happen, Mark, and it could be very ugly."

"Whatever is going to happen is going to happen. We'll get through it. No doubt, Lovey has half of Louisiana praying for you, and I've been throwing a few requests at God myself."

"The fact that you're standing here tells me that the prayers are being answered."

"So let's get on with it." Mark put his arm around her shoulder. "Are you ready?"

"As ready as I'm going to get."

Chapter 18

When Rachel and Mark arrived at the front door of her childhood home, she paused, not at all certain whether to ring the doorbell or simply walk in. Finally she rang the bell and gritted her teeth. Mark put a reassuring hand on her shoulder as they waited, but he could not stop Rachel's pounding heart or ease the shallow, useless breaths she drew.

An eternity seemed to pass as Rachel began to feel the distinctive disorientation, the light-headedness of acute anxiety. Mark moved his hand to support her rigid elbow. Finally the door opened, just a crack at first, and Rachel was greeted with, "I might of knowed you gonna show up. Poor Miz Patsy! She already half dead, and now she gotta deal with you."

Rachel gulped in one last breath of fresh air, and pretending to ignore Mammy Cassie's words, she pushed the door completely open and forced her way past the bulky, shapeless form. Once inside the entrance foyer of the elegant home, she faced her lifelong enemy and quietly asked, "Is Mother going to the hospital this morning?"

Mammy Cassie focused flat-black, hateful eyes on Mark and said nothing.

"Answer my question!" Rachel demanded, resorting to her often-used tactic of covering her fear with anger.

"Course she is. Why, I don't know. She ain't gonna do Mr. Jack no good sitting 'round no waiting room. She just gonna make herself sick; that's what she gonna do."

"Does she know he's better this morning?" Rachel asked.

"How she gonna know that? She ain't been to the hospital yet."

"She might have called ICU," Rachel replied curtly. "Go tell her that Daddy is much improved this morning. That should relieve her mind. And tell her I would like to see her."

"I ain't sure she gonna want to see you 'cause you always—"

"I'll be in the parlor," Rachel interrupted as she took Mark's hand and led him into a meticulously decorated room off the hall.

"Beautiful room," Mark commented.

"Yes, yes it is. Mother always hires the best decorators." Rachel slowly turned and looked around the familiar room. "It seems like I've been away for a decade and at the same time it seems like I never left."

"It must be strange to return, especially since so much has changed in your life since you left. You know, that's what you've got to remember, Rachel. You don't have to react to things here the way you used to."

"I know. Believe me, all the way out here from the hospital I've been counseling myself to remember that I can choose the way I react. Inside, though, I'm still pretty shaky. I feel like a child, a helpless child."

"Part of that has to be fatigue, and you haven't eaten a thing this morning."

"Right, and that reminds me. After I see Mother, I'm going to check into a hotel."

"Then you're not going to stay here?" Mark asked. When Rachel shook her head, he agreed. "Probably just as well. You do need to eat, so we should—"

"Good morning!" an absurdly cheerful voice called from the doorway, and Rachel turned to see her mother, Patsy Longwood D'Evereau, standing in the doorway in an elegant, satin dressing gown. "Do forgive me for not getting dressed," Patsy exclaimed, "but I simply couldn't bear to wait to see you. My darling, darling Rachel! How are you?" Patsy swept across the room and threw her arms around Rachel. "How I've missed you! But here you are and don't you look wonderful," she chattered while she sized-up Mark over Rachel's shoulder.

Rachel was stunned into silence by her mother's exaggerated, positive welcome, but Patsy went right on exclaiming, "And who is this handsome, young man? Rachel, darling, you've been keeping secrets from me!"

Before Rachel could formulate an introduction, Patsy turned to Mark and, beaming up at him, said, "Welcome, welcome to my home. I'm Patsy D'Evereau. Of course, I used to be Patsy Longwood, and most people around here still think of me as a Longwood, but you, of course, are probably from Louisiana. One of Rachel's charming friends, I'm sure."

"Mother." Rachel finally found her voice. "This is Mark Goodman. He is Philippe D'Evereau's nephew. I'm sure you remember his name. During my childhood summers at Belle St. Marie I used to play with him and—"

"Oh, those wonderful summers at Belle St. Marie! I was simply thrilled that Rachel was able to spend her summers with dear, dear Elinore. Oh, how we miss Elinore! She was a saint, an absolute saint, and I don't know how we've gone on since her death. You must have loved her, Mark. Everyone—absolutely everyone—did."

"She was a very special influence in my life, Mrs. D'Evereau," Mark replied quietly.

"Of course she was! She was an absolute saint. But goodness me," Patsy said, taking Mark by the arm and leading him toward a sofa, "where are my manners? You must think I'm perfectly awful. I haven't even asked you to sit down, and you both must be famished. Do sit down, Mark, and I'll ring for Florence. She'll fix you the very best breakfast you've ever eaten....and something for Rachel too, of course." Patsy glided across the room and reached for a crystal bell while Rachel, still completely mystified by her mother's behavior, sank down on the sofa by Mark.

When Patsy returned, she descended gracefully into an antique French chair, struck a poise certain to give the impression of gentility, and gaily directed Mark, "Do tell me all about yourself, Mark dear, and tell me all about Louisiana. Such a beautiful state! How I miss seeing it!"

"Mother," Rachel intervened quietly, "did Mammy Cassie tell you that Daddy is much better today?"

"She did." Patsy smiled sweetly at Rachel. "How relieved I am! Of course, I knew the minute you arrived Jack would perk up."

"Would you like some more details? I spoke to the doctor after he examined Daddy this morning."

"Well, of course, Darling, if you feel the need to tell me." Patsy smiled at Rachel, then abruptly turned to Mark and asked, "Isn't she just the most beautiful little thing you've ever seen? I shouldn't brag on her, of course; after all, she is my daughter, but you must admit she's a beauty, and some people do say she takes after me."

"She is beautiful," Mark agreed, "the most beautiful woman I've ever laid eyes on....present company excluded, of course."

"Oh, how sweet you are!" Patsy exclaimed with a tiny giggle. "Rachel, I should just spank you for keeping this wonderful man a secret. How could you do such a thing to me?"

A door opened at that moment, and Florence, the cook, shyly entered the room. "Miz Patsy, did you need something?"

"Florence, look who's here," Patsy called out gaily. "Our darling Rachel has finally come home. Isn't it wonderful?"

Florence beamed at Rachel. "Miz Rachel, you's a welcome sight."

Rachel rushed to the white-haired black woman's side and threw her arms around her. "Oh Florence, I'm so glad to see you."

"Florence has been with us forever," Patsy confided to Mark. "She's just one of the family, just like Mammy Cassie. In fact, I think they're sisters. Well, whatever. We couldn't survive without either one of them. Now, Florence, I'm just sure these two young people haven't had any breakfast, but you'll take care of that, won't you?"

"Yes ma'am," Florence agreed.

"Something light for me, please, Florence," Rachel requested.

"Nonsense!" Patsy countered. "You need your nourishment, and Mark deserves a hearty breakfast. Just think of it, Florence, they both stayed up all night in the waiting room at the hospital. Don't you think they are absolutely heroic?"

"Yes ma'am," Florence agreed. "It won't take me no time at all to get breakfast ready."

"Tell Mammy Cassie to help you, Florence," Patsy ordered. As the cook hurried out, Patsy turned her attention back to Mark. "Now I won't wait another minute, young man. I want you to tell me all about yourself. I don't approve of my darling Rachel running around with just anyone."

"Mother, I'm not running around with—"

"What else would you call it?" Patsy's demanded, her tone turning acid so quickly that Rachel was stunned into silence. "You show up over here with this man. Heaven only knows what you've done during the ride over here." She turned her back on Rachel and focused on Mark. "I'm sure you're from a fine, Louisiana family, Mark, but our standards here are quite high. Higher by far than those in Louisiana."

"Mother!"

"As I indicated earlier," Patsy ranted on, "I'm a Longwood, and whether Rachel likes it or not, so is she. Being a Longwood requires a certain level of genteel behavior which, I fear, is not always appreciated by Rachel, though, Lord knows, I've tried hard enough to teach her."

Stunned, Rachel stared at her mother, then insisted. "Mother, I drove over here by myself—"

"Oh, of course you did," Patsy replied sarcastically.

"Mrs. D'Evereau," Mark intervened. "Rachel did drive over here by herself. Personally I don't think she should have because she was too upset to drive. I should have driven her myself, but I was in eastern Louisiana, and frankly I'm having a difficult time forgiving myself for not being available when she needed me."

Patsy gave him a long, hard look, then laughed nervously. "Oh, how sweet," she murmured, backing down. "Well, don't be too hard on yourself, Mark. We all make mistakes. Besides, I'm sure it's all Rachel's doing." She turned her attention back to Rachel. "Now Rachel, you mustn't let your father find out about all this. Why, he'll be so disappointed in you. You know how your father feels about your maintaining a sterling reputation, and you haven't exactly pleased him on that score in the past."

"Daddy has never said one word—"

"Well, of course not, Rachel! You know your father. He leaves all the unpleasant tasks to me. Besides, he's not well right now," Patsy continued. "You know it wouldn't be good to upset him. So that's all settled. We are not even going to discuss the matter. It's settled. Just try to behave like a lady in the future."

Rachel's mouth flew open to defend herself, but a clock on the mantel struck the hour, and Patsy suddenly became aware of the time. "Goodness me!" she exclaimed. "I must get dressed. There was something very important I was going to do today. What was it? Oh yes, I remember. I must go to the hospital. Now Rachel, you see to it that Mark has a good breakfast; then you two need to get some rest."

"Mother, I thought—"

"No, darling, no arguments." She rose from her chair, and Mark immediately stood up. "We all must take care of ourselves. I know you're young, but you've been at that dreadful hospital all night." She turned to Mark. "Now, young man, you will stay with us, of course."

When Mark started to object, she declared firmly, "No, I won't hear of any objections. It's the least I can do. To think that you've stood by my darling Rachel so heroically. Why, I simply don't know how to express my gratitude! I'll have Mammy Cassie prepare a guest room for you, and by the time you've had your breakfast, everything will be ready. Now, I do apologize, but I must go finish dressing. You see, my husband is in the hospital."

"I understand," Mark said quietly. He stepped forward and took Patsy's hand. "I'm sure he's going to be fine. The doctor was very encouraging this morning."

"Well, of course he was!" Patsy stretched and kissed Mark on the check. "Aren't you a darling boy to come encourage me this way." She turned to Rachel. "He's just like our adorable Justin, isn't he?"

Speechless, Rachel simply stared up at her mother, but Patsy didn't seem to notice. She turned gracefully and walked toward the door. Just before leaving, she stopped and turned sharply back to Rachel. "Now remember, not a word about your indiscretions to your father. He would be devastated. And what would people say? You know you've given people plenty of room to gossip about this family in the past. I can't bear a re-run of all the pain you've caused."

Rachel jumped up, instinctively ready to defend herself.

"No, Darling." Her mother cut her off with a wave of her hand. "You can't undo the past. You must make a fresh new start. We'll simply have to hope that our neighbors have forgotten all the scandal you caused by your treatment of Collins." Before Rachel could object, she swept from the room.

As soon as Patsy was gone, Rachel exploded. "How dare she suggest—"

"Keep calm, Rachel," Mark said firmly as he took her by the arm and pressed her down on the sofa seat.

"Why does she act like that?" Rachel demanded as her anger mounted, and her breath grew shallower. "She's all sweetness and light one minute and absolutely vicious the next."

"She's clearly a volatile person, Rachel. In fact, I hate to say it, but she sounds incoherent at times, and the way she switches moods so suddenly suggests to me....but let's not jump to the worst conclusions. She's been under enormous strain since Jack's heart attack; perhaps the doctor gave her something for her nerves which has made her more irritable and incoherent than normal."

"This is normal, Mark!"

"Rachel, try to ignore her."

"I'm not a reporter on a story," Rachel snapped at him. "That's my mother who automatically assumes I've done something wrong, who automatically assumes I'm going to do something to embarrass the family."

"You're not a reporter," Mark agreed as he sat down next to her, "and that is your mother hassling you, but you are a rational human being. You can choose to restrain yourself as well as to protect yourself. Blowing up won't do you or anyone else any good. Besides, your father has to be your priority."

Rachel swallowed hard and agreed resolutely, even though she continued to shake inside. "Right. You're right. I need to stay calm. For Daddy's sake I have to stay calm. But I'm sick of this! I want to know why Mother treats me this way. There has to be a reason, and I want to know what it is!"

"I don't blame you," Mark said, trying again to calm her. "Maybe you need to try to talk to your mother—not now, but after your father is better."

"I need to talk to someone now, Mark! I've had a lifetime of this. I can't keep shoving this down. I've swallowed so much abuse I'm going to choke. But who can I talk to? Mammy Cassie will never tell me the truth. I obviously can't ask Daddy."

"What about Florence?' Mark suggested. "How much would she know?"

"Everything." Rachel breathed more normally at the thought of Florence. "She doesn't miss a thing that goes on in this house."

"She's our answer. As soon as your mother leaves, we'll talk to Florence. That is, presuming Mammy Cassie goes with your mother."

"Oh, Mammy Cassie will go with her," Rachel retorted sarcastically. "You can count on that; she never lets Mother out of her sight. She's always had total control of her precious Patsy, and she plans to keep it."

"Rachel, take some normal breaths. You're overreacting."

"I'm not overreacting!" Rachel snapped. "You have no idea how controlling and mean Mammy Cassie can be. You have no idea—"

"You're grown, Rachel," Mark countered. "Whatever Mammy Cassie throws at you, you can handle. Right?"

Rachel lowered her head and said nothing.

"Don't agonize over this, Rachel," Mark insisted. "You've had enough years of this pain. If things can be resolved between you and your mother, then I'm sure you'll take whatever steps are necessary. If they can't be resolved, then you have to let it go. You can just move through it logically, if you try to."

"I'm not sure I can be logical about this, Mark. I feel just like I did eighteen months ago. I was an emotional and physical wreck; I was still recovering from my head injury, and of course every time I thought of Collins I was furious and grieved all at the same time. The doctor had me thoroughly medicated, but no matter how many pills I took, I couldn't stop the emotional pain. Every time I was conscious at any level, I could hear my mother's angry voice."

"Why was she angry?"

"She thought that somehow I had shamed her and the family."

"By doing what?" Mark asked.

"She blamed me for Collins' behavior."

"For his drinking?"

"Yes, and for his affairs."

"That's ridiculous," Mark asserted. "Surely you see how absurd that is, Rachel."

"I do now, but I confess I didn't then." Rachel sighed. "And if the truth be told, now that I'm back in this house, I feel ashamed and inadequate all over again. That ugly voice in my head has returned."

"What voice?"

"The one that keeps telling me that I failed, that somehow I'm responsible for all the unhappiness around here, that it is my fault that Collins ran to other women and drank so much."

"Rachel, when you were growing up in this house, you were the child. Your parents were the adults. If they were unhappy, it was because of choices they made, not because of you."

"It sure didn't feel that way at the time."

"But it was that way. And the same is true with Collins. He made his choices too." Mark stared at her solemnly for a long moment before adding, "Live in the present, Rachel. Don't let the past control your present." He sighed tiredly. "That's going to be the real battle for you while you're here in Texas. You're going to have to choose to keep your mind in the present."

Something about his tone made Rachel stop and study his eyes. Finally she asked, "Mark, are you talking about me or yourself?"

"Both of us. We both have pasts we need to leave behind."

"And we can just choose that? To leave them behind?"

"We must," he answered firmly. "If we don't, they'll suffocate us. They'll strangle all the joy from our present."

Rachel was surprised at his intensity and shamefully aware that she had never considered the pains in Mark's past. She had always been totally self-absorbed when she was around him.

"Your pains." She quietly began to name the few she knew about. "Viet Nam, whatever you suffered when you were shot—"

Mark waved a hand, as if to dismiss what she was saying. "Those were easy compared to the deaths of my parents and being the totally unwelcome ward of Uncle Philippe."

Rachel could think of nothing to say. Right before her eyes he was becoming a real, flesh-and-blood person, and she was horrified to recognize that he had never been an independent soul, someone totally separate from her before. He had always been someone to lean on, to enjoy, to push away when he hurt her feelings. "Oh, Mark!" She barely breathed the words. "Forgive me. I've never even considered what you've suffered."

"Don't start beating yourself up about that, Rachel. You were a child when I came to Louisiana."

"But I've been so selfish!" Rachel's voice rose. "How could I have been so selfish?"

"Cause that's just the way you is!" Mammy Cassie exclaimed as she flung open the door and loomed in the doorframe. "And you ain't ever gonna change." Before Rachel could gather her wits, Mammy Cassie ran on, "Miz Patsy say for me to tell you we's goin' to the hospital. Your Uncle Lloyd be here to take her. She say she see you when she get back, but I hope to heaven she be wrong. I hope you ain't even here when we get back 'cause you ain't gonna 'cause her nothing but grief."

Rachel flinched at the words and struggled to take control of the situation. "You may go, Mammy Cassie," she said weakly.

"I ain't finished with what I come to say." Mammy Cassie sneered at her. "I knows you, Miz Rachel. When things get tough, you just turns tail and runs for Belle St. Marie. This time ain't gonna be no different. I's gonna win in the end just like I always does." She smiled triumphantly and left.

Rachel jumped to her feet to follow Mammy Cassie, but Mark grabbed her hand. Furious, she turned on him. "Let go! This is the present you said I have to deal with, and I'm going to deal with it."

"This is the present, and Mammy Cassie is in it," Mark conceded as he stood, towering over her. "But she's not important unless you make her so. Rachel, you're going to have to choose your battles carefully. If you do the same thing the same way, you'll get the same results."

Every instinct of Rachel's was pushing her to snatch her hand from Mark's grip and go after the woman who had tormented her throughout her youth. She wanted, needed to fight back, but just as she thought the temptation would overcome her, she heard a sweet voice behind her. "Miz Rachel, I got some breakfast ready for you and your guest."

It wasn't the first time Florence had pulled her back from a useless confrontation with Mammy Cassie. Rachel forced herself to calm down and finally managed to respond, "Thank you, Florence."

When she turned toward the dining room door, Rachel suddenly realized that no one had introduced Mark to Florence. "I'm sorry, Florence," she said as she walked over to the cook. "I don't think you've met Mark. He's a longtime friend from Louisiana." To Mark she said, "Mark, I want you to meet the lady who kept me sane throughout my childhood."

"It's a genuine pleasure to meet you, Florence." Mark walked toward her to shake hands, but much to Mark's obvious surprise, Florence shyly ducked her head, and mumbling something about breakfast, hurried back into the kitchen.

"She's just very shy, Mark; she wouldn't hurt your feelings for the world," Rachel encouraged him. "You can count on Florence. When the chips are down, she always comes through."

"And she was in your childhood, too," Mark reminded her. "Just as your Grandmere and Lovey were in mine."

Rachel's eyes filled with tears, but she managed a small smile. "That's true," she conceded. "I need to remember that. But I'll tell you one thing, Mark. Before I leave Pineview again, I'm going to find out why Mother thinks I'm such an awful person. I don't know how, but I'm going to find out. I may have been a mischievous child, but I have never been the trouble-maker she thinks I am. Something about all of this does not add up."

"Nothing about this adds up."

Chapter 19

Mark's presence seemed to keep Patsy on her best behavior for the next three days. Whenever they were together, she beamed up at him and chatted gaily in her best southern belle mode. Mammy Cassie had obviously been warned not to misbehave while Mark was in the house; nevertheless, whenever she found Rachel alone, her geyser of abuse erupted. Rachel managed to clamp down on her own temper and curtly dismiss the woman from her presence. At Mark's suggestion, she made a point of noticing every victory and congratulating herself. In spite of her sense that she was walking on eggshells, she knew she was making progress in her ability to manage her reactions to painful encounters. "I can only control me. I will control me!" she kept telling herself, "for Daddy's sake as well as my own."

Mark received constant calls for help from members of Philippe's campaign team. Refusing to leave Rachel, he did his best to assist by phone, but he was growing more and more concerned about the campaign time he was losing. In addition, he was worried about leaving Philippe alone while Lisette was undoubtedly pressuring him to accept funding from the Iranians.

Rachel received calls from Louis twice a day, but since Jack was improving so rapidly, Louis cancelled his plans to fly to Texas. She had a harder time keeping BillyRay in Louisiana, but she managed to do so.

As the days passed, Jack continued to improve; he was moved out of ICU and into a room in the cardiac unit. By the fourth day, the doctor enthusiastically predicted that Jack could go home in another 48 hours as long as he had plenty of bed rest and good nursing. Rachel was relieved and delighted.

On the other hand, Patsy was upset by this positive news. "I can't be expected to take care of an invalid," she announced to

Rachel. "I'm practically an invalid myself, and don't you go thinking that Mammy Cassie is going to nurse him. She has to take care of me."

"I'll hire a nurse," Rachel responded. "You won't have to do a thing."

"No, I think your father should just stay in the hospital."

"He can't, Mother." Rachel tried to reason with her. "These days, once a patient is well enough to come home, the hospital moves them out."

"Well, what if they don't have a home to come to?" Patsy demanded.

"I suppose they go to some nursing facility."

"Then that's what Jack should do," Patsy said.

"Daddy is not going to a nursing home, Mother!" Rachel responded furiously, then thought better of it and continued more quietly. "Daddy has a home; he has all of us to take care of him. He will recover better and faster in his own home. And that's what you want, isn't it?"

"Well, of course it is!" Patsy retorted. "I just want life to get back to normal. This has not exactly been fun for me, you know."

"I know it's been hard on you, Mother, but the best way to hurry Daddy's recovery is to bring him home, where we can take care of him."

"I'm not going to nurse him, Rachel. I'm not strong enough, and that's that."

"I agree," Rachel soothed. "I wouldn't think of allowing you to endure any more stress than you've already had. That's why I'll find a nurse."

"And who's going to take care of him at night?"

"I will," Rachel answered quietly.

"Oh, you'd love that, wouldn't you?" Patsy sneered. "You and your precious Daddy talking about Louisiana and the grand D'Evereau family all night long."

Rachel was embarrassed by the obviousness of her mother's jealousy, but she swallowed hard and bargained, "Mother, I'll get two nurses, one for daytime and one for evening. You won't have to do a thing, and neither will I."

Patsy arched her eyebrows triumphantly as she responded, "Then you won't need to be here at all, will you?"

"No," Rachel conceded. "I won't be needed."

Patsy smiled brightly. "By all means, do find the nurses, Rachel. We mustn't let your poor father languish in that hospital a moment longer than necessary."

Rachel felt tears stinging at the back of her eyes, but she forced them back. She simply nodded and left to begin her search.

That evening a call came from Philippe himself. Another political rally had been disrupted by agitators who had infiltrated the crowd, and the news media had spread photos of the melee across the state. This time Philippe openly expressed concern and asked Mark to return as soon as possible.

"You have to go help," Rachel insisted when Mark told her about the call. "Daddy is out of danger, and we'll be bringing him home day after tomorrow."

"And you'll be taking care of him by yourself," Mark added. "I'm not leaving."

"I've found several agencies that can supply nursing care. In fact, I'm going to interview prospects tomorrow."

"And what if you don't find the right ones? You'll be here by yourself trying to nurse Jack back to health. I'm not leaving you."

"I'm sure I'll find someone, Mark," Rachel reassured him. "And Florence will help me for a day or two if necessary. Besides, you can always come back, if I need you."

"What about your mother? I don't want to take any credit, but she seems to behave herself when I'm around."

"I'm sure you're a calming influence on her, but I've been here for three days now and managed to keep my cool. I think I can just walk away from any confrontation that might arise. After all, I'm thoroughly focused on Daddy now."

Mark paced around the room, obviously struggling with his different loyalties. Finally he said, "I'll leave about 5:00 in the morning. That way I can get a whole day's work in over there, but if you don't find some help, I'm coming back."

"I'll find help, Mark," Rachel reassured him. "It's all going to go smoothly."

Shortly after five o'clock the next morning Rachel stood on the front porch of her parents' home, kissed Mark good-bye, and watched as he settled in his car and drove off. She sighed tiredly and, looking up at the dark sky, tried to decide whether to go back to bed or stay up to greet the first nurse who would arrive for an interview at 8:00. Finally she muttered, "I won't be able to fall back asleep anyway," and stepped back through the front door.

"Just as I thought!" a sharp voice greeted her. "Right here under my very own roof. I'm appalled! Have you no sense of decency, Rachel? Is this the thanks I get for trusting you and that man?" Patsy demanded.

"What are you talking about, Mother?"

"What am I talking about?" Patsy's voice rose. "What am I talking about? Isn't it obvious?"

"Sh-h-h!" Rachel tried to quiet her mother.

"Don't you try to silence me!" Patsy exclaimed. "This is my house. I won't have you sneaking around and sleeping with that man in my house."

Cold anger began to rise in Rachel, but she checked her tongue until she was certain she was in control of herself.

"Well, say something!" Patsy demanded.

"I refuse to discuss this. Your accusation is preposterous. Nothing inappropriate has been going on between Mark and me."

"Apparently we don't have the same definition of 'inappropriate,' young lady."

"Mother, I refuse to fight with you. If you want to fight with someone, go find someone else. I'm going to dress and prepare to interview nurses. My only concern at the moment is finding the right nurses for Daddy."

"Oh! Suddenly you're concerned about your father. How touching!"

"It just be too bad you can't think about your mama once in a while," Mammy Cassie boomed from the kitchen door. "Especially when you decide to start carrying on with all these mens."

"You're both being totally absurd, and I refuse to discuss this," Rachel said as she turned away to leave.

"We ain't absurd. We just knows you for what you is. You's the same devil child you was when you was little. You ain't never gonna change neither."

"And we are going to discuss it, young lady," Patsy insisted as she grabbed Rachel's arm. "Don't think I don't know what you're up to. Don't think I don't know what kind of woman you are. Carrying on with Mark in my house, and some other man calling you from Paris."

"And don't forget that Billy whats-his-name," Mammy Cassie threw in. "Insistin' on flying all the way over here from Lousiana. He don't be doing that for no reason."

"What?" Patsy demanded. "You mean there's another one?"

"Course there's another one. He already been over here once; one of them nurses at the hospital told me all about it. Now he wanting to come back."

"How do you know that?" Rachel demanded.

"I got ears, ain't I?"

"Oh, Mammy, what am I going to do?" Patsy wailed. "Whatever will the neighbors think? Oh, my head is beginning to throb." She turned loose of Rachel and held her head in her hands. "I need my medicine, Mammy."

Mammy Cassie rushed to her side, took her in her arms and began to soothe her like a child. "Now, now, Miz Patsy, your Mammy Cassie be right here. I's gonna take care of you just like I always done. Ain't nobody in the world love you like I does."

Mammy Cassie glared at Rachel as she began to help Patsy down the hall. "I hope you's happy!" she called back over her shoulder. "You's made your mother sick again."

As the familiar, sickening, guilt-producing words rolled over Rachel, she turned toward the kitchen, determined to run out the back door, to flee the house and the hate it sheltered, just as she had done when she was a child.

When she dashed into the kitchen, Florence turned from the sink and uncharacteristically commanded, "Don't run no more, Miz Rachel. Ain't no need. You's all growed up now."

The force of Florence's voice startled Rachel so thoroughly she stopped and stared at the elderly cook. She had never heard Florence raise her voice. Apparently Florence had surprised herself because she immediately ducked her head. Her words, however, had had their intended effect; all instinct to run disappeared from Rachel.

In her usual quiet tone Florence added, "Besides, you ain't done nothing wrong."

"Then why do they think I'm so bad?" Rachel demanded.

Florence shook her head wearily. "Ain't got nothing to do with you, Honey."

Frustrated by her lifelong, bewildering conflict with her mother, Rachel jerked out a chair, sat down at the kitchen table, and dropped her head into her hands.

"I fix you a cup of tea, Honey," Florence said as she turned back to the sink. "That fix you up, a nice cup of tea." She filled a kettle with water, and as she carried it to the stove, she encouraged, "You gotta think about Mr. Jack now. You can put up with anything for your daddy. I knows you can. And it ain't gonna last much longer. Ain't gonna be no time 'fore you get nurses hired and you get on back to Louisiana. You gotta hold on to that thought. You's gonna get away from here."

You's gonna get away from here. Ain't no need to run 'cause you's all growed up now. You's gonna get away from here. Ain't no need to run. Get away from here. The conflicting statements sang in Rachel's mind, whirling around like a tornado threatening to touch down and destroy. No need to run. Get away. No need. Get away. No. Revelation broke through the storm in Rachel's mind, and the tornado disappeared into a harmless breeze. She raised her head and said, "If you do the same thing the same way, you'll get the same results."

"What, Honey?"

"If you do the same thing the same way, you'll get the same results," Rachel said more forcefully. Florence stared at her, and Rachel announced, "I won't be going back to Louisiana, Florence. Not until this thing between Mother and me is settled."

"How you gonna settle it, Honey?"

"I don't know," Rachel admitted, "but I know that if you do the same thing the same way, you'll get the same results. And I won't accept the results I've been getting all my life anymore." Rachel stood and walked toward the door.

"Don't you want your tea, Honey?"

"I don't need it, thank you. I'm going to get dressed."

Rachel saw no more of her mother that day because Patsy was confined to her bedroom with one of her frequent migraines. As Mammy Cassie ran back and forth from Patsy's bedroom to the kitchen, she took every opportunity to scowl at Rachel and attempt to make accusatory comments. Rachel, who spent the day interviewing nurses, ignored her.

By evening Rachel was satisfied that she had found excellent nursing care for her father, and after a simple supper alone, she hurried to her room to grab her purse and keys so she could visit her father. Almost immediately she heard the phone ring, but after one ring it stopped, and assuming it was not a call for her, Rachel made no effort to answer it. A few minutes later Mammy Cassie opened the door and announced, "That man from Paris calling you again. Louis something-or-another. Lord knows, I can't keep them all straight."

Rachel dismissed her with a wave and picked up the phone. Fully aware that Mammy Cassie might well be listening, she guarded her remarks to Louis, but he was not aware of the need to be judicious.

"I'm flying to Texas in the morning," he announced. "I love you, Rachel, and I'm too concerned about you to stay away any longer."

Rachel panicked at the thought of Louis meeting her mother, especially given her mother's most recent response to Mark's presence. "No, Louis!" she heard herself saying far too sharply. She scrambled for ideas. "Actually, Daddy is coming home, and I've just hired nurses to take care of him. I know you mean to be helpful, but please believe me, I don't need anyone else here. It will take my entire concentration to settle Daddy in."

"That's exactly why I'm coming, Darling; you need help."

"Trust me, Louis," Rachel pleaded. "What I need is the freedom to focus on this one task. If I do that, I'll be able to leave in several days and return to my life. If you come, I'll just be worried about entertaining you."

"I don't need to be entertained...."

"Louis, please....I know myself. I'll be so much more anxious if non-family members are here. Please....just let me walk through this my way."

There was silence on the other end of the line.

"Please understand, Louis," Rachel tried again. "I can handle this, but I can't handle more."

"I love you, Rachel. Why won't you let me help you?"

"It's complicated; I can't explain all the family dynamics that are involved. It would just be too exhausting, but please believe me. I know you love me; I am so grateful that you care about me. It's just that sometimes we can best help those we love by staying away. Does that make any sense to you at all?"

"No, it doesn't. The only thing that makes sense to me is for me to come get you and bring you to Paris—after we place your father in the best possible institution, of course."

"Daddy is not going to any institution!" Rachel retorted. "Not now, not ever! I will take care of him."

"Darling, calm yourself. Whatever is best for your father, that is what we will do."

Rachel bit her lip as she struggled to drag her temper into submission.

"Rachel? Are you all right?"

"Yes," she forced herself to answer quietly. "I think that you just don't understand how well things are going here. I have everything organized, and I'll be returning home very soon. Please just let me do it my way."

"I want to see you. I must know you are really okay."

"Then plan to come to Belle St. Marie this weekend because I'll be home by then, and I will actually be able to enjoy your visit."

Louis sighed. "Very well. I'll change my reservation, but I will see you this weekend one place or the other. Wherever you are, I'll be there too."

"I'll see you in Louisiana this weekend," Rachel reiterated stiffly, then tried to soften her voice as she added, "Thank you for caring about me so much."

"I love you, Rachel."

"Yes, I know, and I am grateful. Now I must go to the hospital. I haven't seen Daddy today, and I want to tell him about the plans I've made."

"Of course. I'll call tomorrow. Good night," Louis answered, and after Rachel said her good-byes and heard the phone go dead, she realized she had been breathing far too shallowly and actually felt faint. Pausing only long enough to take several deep breaths, she hurried out the front door. The fresh air was welcome, and as she started her car and drove down the driveway, she wondered again how it was possible that her childhood home could be so deficient in oxygen.

Thirty-six hours later Rachel brought her father home from the hospital and began the process of settling him into a routine with the nurses she had hired. In spite of her promises to return to Belle St. Marie that weekend and in spite of the strain she endured at her parents' house, she couldn't tear herself away from her father's side. He seemed to be progressing well; the doctors were pleased, yet Rachel stayed. She called Louis and spent an hour begging him to postpone his flight once again. Through the whole conversation she was certain that Mammy Cassie was listening in and that there would be a price to pay.

Her guess was right. When Rachel left her room and returned to the parlor, Patsy, with Mammy Cassie at her side, awaited her, and the minute Rachel entered, Patsy unleashed her fury.

"Rachel, I simply won't tolerate any more of this immorality under my roof! I want you to pack your things and leave."

"Mother, there has been no immorality under your roof. You know that. I've been right here taking care—"

"What kinda fool you think your mother be?" Mammy Cassie demanded.

Rachel stood silently, considering the impact a fight might have on her father. Mammy Cassie mistook her silence for weakness and proceeded, "We wasn't borned yesterday, and we knowed you since you's borned. You's always been trouble. The day you was borned was the worst day of your mother's life and—"

"Be quiet!" Rachel commanded coldly. "And get out of here."

"Rachel!" Patsy exclaimed angrily. "This is my house, not yours, and I'll not have you talking to Mammy Cassie that way. She's absolutely right. Men don't fly all the way from Paris to Texas to make a simple courtesy call on a woman."

Rachel temper began to heat up. "And exactly who is flying from Paris, Mother?"

"Why that Louis Simone, of course. Mammy Cassie heard him on the phone."

Rachel stared angrily at Mammy Cassie before saying, "So you've added eavesdropping to your armory of destruction."

Mammy Cassie opened her mouth to respond, but Rachel stopped her before she could begin. "I don't owe you an explanation of my behavior, Mammy Cassie, and I won't give you one." Rachel turned to her mother and spoke to her, "On the other hand, Mother, I am concerned because you continue to be upset by the fact that I have male friends, so I will tell you what my relationship is to each one."

"I don't want to hear about it!" Patsy exclaimed. "I'm humiliated enough by your behavior without hearing the sordid details."

"There are no sordid details, Mother. That's what—"

"Of course there are!" Patsy exclaimed, her voice quaking. "I know you, Rachel. I know what kind of vile things you're capable of! Poor Collins! How that wonderful man endured you I'll never know. No wonder he drank!" Patsy's voice rose in volume and pitch, and in seconds she was clearly on the verge of hysteria. "No, Rachel, you can't fool me. You broke that dear man's heart, the way you carried on. How could you do such things? My own flesh and blood!"

"Mother, please calm yourself. You mustn't—" Rachel reached out to stroke her mother's shoulder, but Patsy jerked away.

"Don't touch me, you slut!" Patsy cried. "Stanton Berry was a wonderful man, a husband made in heaven! He deserved better than you. All that time he was fighting for his country, you were cheating on him! Why couldn't you have controlled yourself and waited for him to come home? Plenty of other women had to wait. Why couldn't you?"

Patsy dissolved into tears and sobbed, "I'm so ashamed of you. I'm so ashamed!"

Shocked by the virulence of her mother's tone and mystified by what Patsy had said, Rachel was stunned into silence. She stared at Patsy while Mammy Cassie rushed to her side to soothe her. "Of course you's ashamed of her. The way she carry on behind Mr. Collins' back. Poor Mr. Collins, poor Mr. Collins. He don't deserve for Miz Rachel to treat him that way."

"Oh Mammy! How could she?" Patsy cried. "How could she treat Stanton that way?"

"You means Mr. Collins, Honey. You's just upset. That Miz Rachel, she always upset you."

Who is Stanton Berry? Rachel's mind demanded. Who is Stanton Berry? I have to know! But then she thought of her father, lying in his room down the hall, hopefully still sleeping, and she knew she could not risk any more uproar in the house. She pinched her lips together to keep from asking.

"You got to go lie down, Miz Patsy," Mammy Cassie insisted.

"Yes," Rachel agreed. "Take her to lie down."

Mammy Cassie supported the crying Patsy as she helped her from the room, and for the first time since Rachel was a small child, a wave of sympathy for her mother washed over her.

Once she was alone, Rachel sank down into a chair and stared into space. In time, Florence's words wafted through her mind. "Ain't got nothing to do with you." She considered the words and repeated them aloud.

"Ain't got nothing to do with you."

A smile born of sheer gratitude began to blossom on Rachel's face. She was free. At last.

There were many answers she wanted and needed and hoped to get, but she knew the essential truth. All that she had endured from her family had nothing to do with her. It had never been her fault. It had never even been her story.

There was another story.

Chapter 20

When Patsy had left the room, Rachel went straight to the kitchen where she found Florence scrubbing the countertops so vigorously she seemed to be trying to remove the tile. It was obvious she had heard the fight.

"Who is Stanton Berry?" Rachel asked quietly.

"I….I don't exactly know, Miz Rachel," Florence answered as she kept her back to Rachel and continued to scrub.

Rachel stepped up to the counter and firmly placed her hand on top of Florence's to make her stop scrubbing. "You do know, Florence," she insisted. "And I need to know. Tell me. Who is Stanton Berry?"

Florence stared down at the counter and said nothing.

Rachel silently removed her hand, releasing Florence's. The old cook's shoulders slumped, and she hung her head, and Rachel understood.

"I'll ask someone else," she said quietly.

Florence didn't move a muscle, and a wave of sympathy swept over Rachel. "It's okay, Florence. It's okay." She turned to leave the kitchen, but Florence stopped her.

"Miz Rachel," the cook called out, and Rachel turned back. "Miz Rachel, this gonna take a heap of forgiving."

Rachel felt the press of anxiety growing in her. "No doubt," she replied.

"You got to ponder on how much you been forgiven, Miz Rachel. That be the only way."

"Forgiven by whom, Florence?"

"Forgiven by God. You just be human, Honey. We all just be human; you ain't no different from the rest of us. God gotta forgive us all for something every day we lives."

Tears suddenly stung Rachel's eyes. "I don't want to fight

anymore, Florence. I don't want to be angry and hurt anymore. I want to be free, and I don't want to have to run away to be free."

Florence stepped over to Rachel's side and cupped Rachel's head in her clumsy hands. "Then you listen to Miz Patsy's story, and you see how human she be and how mixed up humans gets, and you forgive her, and you forgive your Daddy, too."

Rachel nodded, but Florence wasn't finished. "Ain't gonna be just a matter of forgiving the past, Miz Rachel. You gonna have to keep on forgiving every day of your life 'cause we's all just human and we ain't ever gonna be able to get things right. We's always gonna be indebted to each other and need forgiveness."

"I'll try, Florence. I promise I'll try."

"Talk to your Uncle Lloyd, Honey. He been around through the whole story."

Rachel nodded again. "Uncle Lloyd. Yes, he would know everything about Mother. Thank you, Florence." She hugged the cook. "I love you."

"And I loves you, Honey."

Rachel waited until five o'clock before she approached her Uncle Lloyd at his office. Her appearance there startled him so thoroughly he leapt to his feet, concern flooding his face. "Is everything all right?" he demanded. "Is Jack okay?"

"Everything is fine," Rachel assured him. "Daddy is resting; Mother has one of her headaches."

Lloyd Longwood sighed as he sank back into his chair. "Another headache. So, what's new?" he asked sarcastically. "I can't remember a time when she didn't have those headaches."

"Mother has always been high strung, hasn't she?" Rachel asked casually as she sat in a chair across from his desk.

"I guess it's not her fault," Lloyd answered, "but I've often wondered if she brings them on herself sometimes. Not a very nice thing to say, is it?" He looked guilty and lowered his eyes. "Especially about your baby sister."

"I have wondered the same thing all my life," Rachel admitted. "Then sometimes I blame Mammy Cassie for the way Mother behaves."

Lloyd's head shot up angrily, "That woman is evil," he said.

"Why was she given so much control over Mother when Mother was a child?"

"I was a child myself at the time, but looking back now I see that our father was absolutely wiped out by his grief when Mother died. He blamed himself because she died in childbirth.

You probably don't know many details, Rachel. We've never talked about it, but the truth is that my father had to be institutionalized for a year after my mother's death. All three of us boys were sent off to boarding school. I suppose the family was just grateful that Mammy Cassie was there to step in and take care of the new baby, Patsy."

"But when your Father returned home...."

"He never re-established a meaningful relationship with any of us kids. He kept us boys away at boarding school and just spoiled Patsy by giving her everything he could buy."

"He must have seen what Mammy Cassie was doing to mother."

"Maybe. Maybe not. My father was a man who only saw what he wanted to see. Besides, he wasn't strong enough to argue with Mammy Cassie. Nobody was strong enough to argue with her....at least, not until you came along. By the time you were five, you were giving her hell." Lloyd chuckled. "I have to admit I was delighted to see you taking her on."

"You might have helped me," Rachel replied coolly.

"Yes, I might have. I should have. Your Daddy should have, for sure. But you see, by then it was really too late. We were all trapped in it. We still are. Mammy Cassie has control because she can make Patsy sick with just a few words."

"Sick and dependent," Rachel said.

"Right. So it's just been, keep the peace at all costs. You understand, don't you, Rachel?"

"I understand, but I don't approve. Daddy and I talked this out well over a year ago when he came to Belle St. Marie. At that time I accepted the fact that he had done the best he could do when I was growing up. The best he knew how to do."

"Yes, I think he did. We could all have done better by Patsy when she was a little girl, but by the time you came along, things were set in stone. Mammy Cassie had total control. Anything we did would have damaged Patsy more. At least that's the way we saw it."

"So who's Stanton Berry?" Rachel slid the question in as casually as if she had asked to use the phone.

"Oh, he and Patsy—" Lloyd stopped abruptly and stared hard at Rachel.

"Someone is finally going to tell me the truth," Rachel said simply. "I advise you to do it because you will, no doubt, tell it in a way that casts the most favorable light on my mother."

"Rachel, just leave it alone." Lloyd said firmly.

"I can't." Rachel stood abruptly. "I won't."

She turned to go and walked halfway across the office before Lloyd called out. "Wait." When she turned back to face him, he stood and said, "You will do no one any good by digging up the past."

Rachel walked back to his desk and leaned across it to look him squarely in the eye. "I will do me some good. I will finally know why my mother has disliked me all my life, and I strongly suspect that I will discover that her dislike has nothing, absolutely nothing to do with me. Yes, Uncle Lloyd, I will do me some good, and I'm worth it."

"Sit down, Rachel," he said. "Please sit down and listen to me."

"Only if you're going to tell me about Stanton Berry. Otherwise, I would be wasting my time."

"Rachel, it was so long ago."

"No, it's today. It was this morning when Mother accused me of betraying Stanton Berry, and if she's not drugged into oblivion at the moment, it's right now. She's stuck in the past. I don't know if she can be rescued or not, but I know that I can. I can find out what happened years ago that has made her dislike me so much."

"You can't fix it."

"I don't have to fix it! I have to forgive it. I can't do that if I don't know what it is."

"Rachel, you have no idea what you're talking about—"

"I know that forgiveness is what will free me, and forgiveness is a choice I have to make. Right now you are all, every one of you, denying me that choice by keeping me in ignorance."

"It won't do your mother any good—"

"For once I'm not trying to fix Mother. I'm trying to fix me. Tell me the truth!"

"Okay, okay! But promise me…."

"I won't use the information to cause any harm to anyone. I swear, I won't. I don't want to cause trouble. I just want peace."

"Well, first you've got to understand that it was during World War II. I don't know how I can make you understand what those days were like for us, those of us who were young then."

"I can only listen, Uncle Lloyd, and try to get in your shoes."

"Yes, well, it really seemed like the whole world had gone crazy, and I guess it had. I guess I don't need to get into all that.

Maybe the major thing you need to understand is that we had gone through our teens with the Great Depression hanging over us like a suffocating cloud. Our family didn't suffer the horrible deprivations so many around here suffered, but we just didn't get to have any of the fun that young people should be having. When we finally got old enough to really start living and the Depression was starting to let go of its stranglehold on our lives, all of a sudden we discovered that we weren't going to be allowed to live our private lives.

"Don't get me wrong, Rachel, we supported our country; we knew we had to fight. We also knew we might well die or be crippled for life. My point is, young people just felt like they had to grab happiness anywhere they could. Yes, that's what I'm trying to make you understand. All of a sudden, none of the rules counted anymore. If you thought you could find some comfort, some love, or even just a soft place to land for a few minutes....well, you just grabbed it."

"I understand, Uncle Lloyd, as best I can. Daddy told me that he married Mother too soon after he left the Veterans Hospital. You still haven't told me who Stanton Berry was....or is."

"Stanton Berry was the oldest son of the Berry family in Tyler. They did a lot of business with your Grandfather Longwood, so it was inevitable that he and Patsy would be thrown together frequently as she grew up. Stanton was five years older than Patsy, and she fell in love with him the minute she hit her teens. He was an absolute god in her eyes. She was determined to marry him, and of course both the Longwood and the Berry families were very supportive of that idea. It took Patsy quite a while to get his attention, I admit. After all, she was just a kid to him, but Patsy always got what she wanted.

"Anyway, she was engaged to Stanton the summer she turned eighteen. Daddy insisted that they wait a full year to marry; he knew how immature Patsy was. That didn't stop Patsy though. She began making elaborate plans for the wedding of the century. It was to be in June of 1942."

Lloyd paused and Rachel added, "But the Japanese bombed Pearl Harbor in December of 1941."

"Yes," Lloyd said, "and that changed everything, of course. Stanton enlisted; we all did. Patsy begged him to marry her before he left, but he refused to do it. Remember, he was older than she was and much more of a realist. He loved her, and he refused to make her a widow or, worse in his mind, tie her to a cripple."

"He sounds like he was an extraordinary young man," Rachel murmured.

"Stanton Berry was the best, Rachel, absolutely the best. The cursed war! It ruined Patsy's life."

"So he died?"

Lloyd hurried on without answering her question. "Anyway, Stanton and a whole lot of East Texas boys shipped out right after Pearl Harbor. Patsy was furious! I know because I was unfortunately stuck here for a few more months. For the first time in her life she had been told 'no.' She couldn't have what she wanted, and to make matters worse, our father agreed with Stanton's decision and defended him. In no time Patsy was sneaking out at night and staggering home drunk, or worse still, not coming home at all. She and father fought constantly, and we did everything we could to keep her behavior a secret."

"Did she stay in touch with Stanton Berry?" Rachel asked.

"No, but he stayed in touch with her. He considered himself engaged to her. Of course, he didn't know how she was behaving. Father finally sent Patsy away, to get her away from the crowd she was running with. He sent her back East to a girl's college. She wasn't the slightest bit interested in education, but she was surrounded by other girls who were waiting for fiancés. She began to see it as a romantic thing to do, so she put Stanton's ring back on, started writing him, went with the other coeds to volunteer at the Veterans Hospital and enjoyed the part of the martyred young lady awaiting the return of her only true love."

"At least, that's what we thought she was doing. As it turned out, she was also happy to stay at college because she had met a certain Jack D'Evereau of Louisiana. He had been wounded in the European theater of the war and returned to the Veterans Hospital where Patsy was volunteering."

"I see," Rachel said solemnly.

"Before you judge her, Rachel, remember how young she was and how unsure she was that Stanton would return. Try to put yourself in her shoes, in all our shoes. If there was any happiness close by, we just grabbed it. That's what having death so prominent in your life does to you, and we were surrounded by death and suffering."

"Uncle Lloyd, I'm sure I would have behaved the same way. In fact, I guess I did in a way. When Mark Goodman, who seemed to be the love of my life, was drafted and refused to marry me because he was going to Viet Nam, I just looked around for the most comfortable situation I could find. I found

Collins."

"See," Lloyd said, "it's not such an unusual thing."

"No, it's not," Rachel agreed. "What happened to Mother after she met Daddy?"

"She started having an affair with him, to put it bluntly. I don't think she could have loved him because the minute she found out that Stanton was on his way home, she dropped him. She went to Father and persuaded him that she and Stanton should marry immediately. Father agreed, and Patsy put together a small wedding, which was to take place a week after Stanton arrived.

"So she married him?" Rachel asked.

"Stanton came home to a big welcome, looking forward to being married, but Patsy had made one mistake. She had invited her best friend from college to come down to be her maid of honor. That girl had been engaged to a soldier who didn't make it home; the love of her life was dead, and she was pretty unhinged about it. She knew about Patsy's affair with Jack, and she told Stanton."

"So Stanton cancelled the wedding?"

"Yes."

"And Mother married Daddy."

"Yes."

"She just gave up without a fight? She just accepted the public humiliation of being dumped by Stanton without a fight?"

"There was no public humiliation. She eloped with your father and later told everybody that she was really in love with Jack and that Father was forcing her to marry Stanton, so she had eloped."

"And Stanton kept quiet?"

"He did."

"Why?"

"He was a gentleman."

Rachel rose, turned and walked toward the door. She reached for the doorknob, then dropped her hand and turned back to face Lloyd.

"Mother was pregnant with me, wasn't she? That's why Stanton wouldn't marry her. That's why she eloped with Daddy."

Lloyd stared at her grimly. "I had hoped to spare you that fact," he finally admitted.

"But don't you see?" she demanded, her eyes blazing. "You should not have spared me that fact. That's the one thing I needed to know. What were you people thinking? I needed to know that there was nothing wrong with me!"

"How do you tell a child such a truth, Rachel?"

"Oh, no! You won't slip out of this that easily. There was plenty you could have done. You could have stepped into my life, and even though you couldn't give me the brutal facts, you could've told me I was a good kid, that my mother was sick. You could've told me something, for heaven's sake, that provided a balance for the negative I was enduring. You certainly shouldn't have left a woman like Mammy Cassie in charge of me!"

"Surely all that was your father's job."

"That's the job of every adult for every child, but especially a child in your own family!"

Lloyd crossed his arms and stared tiredly down at his desk.

"It all makes sense now." Rachel's voice was draped with sarcasm as she imitated Mammy Cassie's voice. 'You's a devil chile and you ain't never gonna be nothing else 'cause you's conceived in sin. You's ruined your Mother's life. Your Mother ain't been happy since the day she knowed you was coming.' Oh yeah, now it makes sense!"

"Dear God!" Lloyd slumped into his chair, and his eyes filled with tears. "Oh Rachel! What can I say?"

"Nothing now!" she retorted. "It's too late!"

"Please....I know I shouldn't even ask, but....be merciful to Patsy. Try to understand—"

"Stop!" Rachel held up her hand. "Maybe I could understand if I thought about it long enough, but would that really change anything? Would that eliminate the painful experiences of my childhood? Would it make my mother respond to me any differently now?"

"Patsy isn't capable of change, not any more—"

"Precisely. She can't change, but I can! I can quit caring about all you crazy people. I can just refuse to give a damn. And that's exactly what I'm going to do!"

With those words Rachel turned and slammed her way out of the office. When she reached her car, she jabbed the key into the ignition and raced out of the parking lot and down the block. She had absolutely no plan, no idea where she was going. All she knew was that her head felt like it was going to blow off if she didn't scream at someone. But who? Her father, who was recovering from a heart attack? Her mother? What good would that do? Mammy Cassie? As if she'd even care?

When Rachel was forced to stop at a signal, her fury mounted even further as she whipped her head from side to side, wondering if she dared just run the light. It was then that she saw the church. It was then that she knew exactly whom she wanted most to yell at. Abruptly she turned left and drove into the parking lot. Within minutes she was storming down the center aisle, glaring at the altar.

She didn't kneel as her Grandmere had taught her or offer any reverence whatsoever to God. Instead she demanded in the silence of the vast church, "Where were You? Why didn't You help me?" When no response came, Rachel took several steps forward, raised her voice louder and demanded more belligerently, "Why didn't You help me?"

Without warning, she was overwhelmed with such vertigo she fell to her knees, and she distinctly heard two simple words, "I did." Rachel whipped her body around and scanned the church, looking for the source of those words, but she saw no one. Instead she saw the luminosity of the windows, the gleaming wood of the pews, the metal pipes of the organ. All these things she saw from the height of a five year old, just as she had first experienced them when she had entered this church for the baptism of her baby brother, Justin.

Rachel turned back to the altar and slowly raised her eyes to the huge, wooden crucifix hanging above it. As she had so long ago, she saw the suffering on the face of Jesus. Once again she felt the sorrow and confusion of a little girl trying to understand the adult world, and just when she thought she would burst with grief, she felt a presence beside her, and all the pieces came together for her. "Grandmere!" she breathed the name in utter awe as she lowered her gaze to the altar. "Oh, Dear God! You didn't desert me! You brought Grandmere and Lovey into my life to carry me through all those painful years. Only they weren't really doing the carrying; You were. You just used their voices and their loving arms."

Rachel sat down on the polished marble floor and stared up at the altar topped with its snowy white linens. She intentionally emptied her mind and waited. Some indeterminate amount of time later...she had no idea how long...she turned her gaze to the closest window, and there depicted in vivid glass she saw the gospel account of Mary's day of choosing to be an instrument in God's hand. It was the concept of choice—that amazing gift from God—that held her attention. She thought about herself and various choices she had made—some without sufficient understanding, many absolutely selfish. Her focus moved to her parents. God had given them choices, and they had made grave mistakes. They had chosen wrongly, but really, no more wrongly than she had. They had lived painful lives because of the choices of their youth, because they had never tried to right their bad choices, because they had never forgiven themselves or others and simply moved on.

"But I don't have to do the same," Rachel whispered. She stared up at the crucifix and said more boldly, "I don't have to do the same. God has shown me a different way. He kept my head above the murky waters of my childhood, He gave me living examples of a better way to live, and He has empowered me to change. And I will change, Father! I will forgive them because I know I could have made the same bad choices. I will stop being a victim of my past and live in the present. I will—"

Rachel stopped in the litany of her promises as she was struck by the implications of what she had just said. "This is downright scary, Father," she whispered. She swallowed hard, took a deep breath to steady herself and once again turned her gaze upward to the crucified Christ. "You see, the thing is, I could just run away. I could marry Louis and live a grand life. If I did that, I wouldn't have to deal with pain—my own or anybody else's."

Rachel allowed her gaze to fall to the base of the shiny marble altar. In its mirror-like surface she could see her own image—an obviously grown woman sitting in the posture of a confused, frustrated child. "But you're not a child," she whispered to the replica of herself. "That time is over; you can't recapture it. You have responsibilities. People need you, and there is joy in the struggles of life, isn't there? And what about love? Real love? The kind Mark offers. It will be a ragged, uneven life of great joy and deep sadness. But it will be real, Rachel."

She leaned back against the altar rail and rubbed her aching forehead. "I don't know what to do," she finally admitted. Stiffly she rose to her feet and stared back up at the crucifix. "You know, Lord, and You're going to have to show me. And please....make the message so dramatic I can't miss it....and....so compelling I can't ignore it. Please!"

A different Rachel left the church building and walked to her car. She was no longer angry; she was tired, but thoroughly gentled by her experience with God.

She took her time returning to her parents' house. When she finally entered the house, she went to her father's room to check on him, to be certain he was sleeping soundly, but Jack was sitting up in his favorite, overstuffed chair waiting for her. The minute she saw him, she knew that Uncle Lloyd had foolishly called him. Going to his side, she sank down on the ottoman in front of him and looked up into his eyes. They were filled with sadness, with remorse.

Rachel made her choice. Love meant remaining silent, allowing the pains of her parents' youth to remain buried, and that's what she chose. "Let's live in the present," she murmured. "What do you think, Daddy? Shall we do that?"

His eyes filled with tears as he nodded. They both fell silent, and Rachel became aware of a ticking clock in the room, a regular rhythmic sound that counted off the seconds of her life....time she was losing....time that would never come again. A commanding desire to move on overwhelmed her. "You know," she said quietly, "you are getting such excellent reports from the doctor, and starting tomorrow you'll be going into the physical therapy unit daily. Well, I think—"

"Go home, Rachel," Jack broke in. "Go home to Belle St. Marie. It's time for you to live your own life again. In another week I'll be up and about completely."

"You won't rush it? Promise me."

"Don't worry. I've had a good scare. I'll behave myself, but the truth is I'll be healthier if I know that you are getting on with your own life."

"There is a lot to do with the school," she confessed, "and I miss it."

"And Mark? What about Mark?"

Rachel sighed and smiled feebly. "Good question....very good question. We'll see."

"He's a good man. He loves you."

"You're as incorrigible a matchmaker as Lovey." She rose and kissed him on the forehead. "I'll leave in the morning."

The next morning as Rachel drove away from her parents' house, she was apprehensive about her father but terribly eager to get home. She had slept well for the first time since she had arrived. Uncle Lloyd's revelation, as painful as it was, had freed her from her lifelong struggle to fix her relationship with her mother. She now knew that Patsy's unhappiness had never been her fault and had never been in the realm of things she could control. Thanks to her experience in the church, she had more than mere knowledge to move her forward. She now understood that God had valued her so much He had never left her to fend for herself, and she felt confident that God would lead her in the weighty decision she had to make....if she would just listen.

Rachel intended to drive straight to Louisiana, home to Belle St. Marie, without stopping, but as she drove through downtown and approached the church, she felt a great longing to stop and go inside for a quick visit. The morning was bitterly cold with low-hanging, charcoal-colored clouds, and the thought of the candles and beautiful jewel tones of the church drew Rachel in. After parking, she raced across the frigid asphalt and into the foyer. She halted abruptly when she realized a service was in progress, wondering whether she should barge in, but an usher took her firmly by the arm, guided her down the left side aisle and seated her on the front row.

Embarrassed, but grateful to be enveloped in the spiritual warmth of the sanctuary, she knelt and offered up her prayers of thanksgiving for the renewed health of her father, as well as her own new emotional equilibrium. She rose when the pastor came to the pulpit to read the gospel, and it was at that moment that she saw the Lenten wreath with its circle of mostly violet candles. Quickly her eyes moved around the ring of lighted candles until they stopped at the one rose candle, so much brighter in color than the others. Today it was lit, and the golden flame bounced off the rich rose color. Rachel's mind filled with images of spring—of masses of azaleas and the first flush of roses—and she found herself weeping for joy.

The pastor held up the large, golden-covered Bible above his head and proclaimed, "The Gospel of the Lord," and Rachel choked out "Praise to You, Lord Jesus Christ!" in unison with the congregation. Still mesmerized by the color and light of the rose candle, Rachel struggled to listen to the sermon, but the priest's words could only float into her mind and find a resting place in its outskirts. Nevertheless, the message was clear: this rose candle marked the turning point of Lent. The long, dark, difficult days of fasting and penance were drawing to a close. The rose candle was lit to give the people hope that the darkness would indeed pass, and the Resurrection would come soon. What a gift! What a gift! Those words sang in Rachel's mind as the service continued, and when she left the church after longingly looking back one more time at the rose candle, she stepped out into a different world. The dark, oppressive clouds were dropping huge white snowflakes. They lazily floated to the ground, where they clung to a blade of grass.

Rachel walked leisurely to her car, laughing quietly as she stuck out her tongue trying to catch a few of the frozen delights. When she drove out of the city limits of Pinewood, she felt tired, but totally freed and strangely cleansed. The anger, the bitterness, the hurt of her life had been replaced with the purity of snowflakes. All the way to the Louisiana border, Rachel, warm in her car, watched the snowflakes fall and catch in the long needles of the pines towering beside the two-lane highway. Nature was decorating the landscape, turning every pine tree into a sugared confection.

Rachel laughed repeatedly and informed the empty car, "It never snows here! Just look at this! Thank God the asphalt is too warm to freeze."

Since she had driven more slowly than normal, she reached the gates of Belle St. Marie much later than she had planned; nevertheless, she stopped, left her car and stood out in the falling snow and gazed up at the black wrought iron. The words that had comforted her so many painful times in her life were still there. "Enter in peace," she read aloud. A tired, but happy smile slowly covered her face as she watched the white, fluffy snow gathering in the crevices of the iron letters, giving them a new elegance.

"Once more, a new beginning," she murmured. "Thank you."

As she cautiously steered the car around the icy curves of the long, gravel drive, she turned her mind to the future. Her father's heart attack had made her painfully aware of the brevity of life, of its uncertainty. "It's time to makes some decisions," she whispered, "to take a chance on love. It's time to build. What exactly does that mean? I don't know the specifics, but I do know that if I watch carefully, God will show me what to do. And when He does....I'm sure going to try to do it!"

Chapter 21

During the short flight to New Orleans, Mark closed his eyes and recounted the events of the last several days. The most important to him was the return of Rachel to Belle St. Marie after her extended stay in Texas. A wave of happiness washed through him as he remembered the moment she had opened the front door and had held out her arms for a hug. She had looked tired, but quietly victorious, and as she had recounted the happenings of her last day in Texas, he knew why. She had found a truth she had needed all her life, and even though it was not the truth she would have chosen, still, it had set her free. Best of all, she had confided it to him and she was safely home. Now he no longer felt separated from half his heart.

"If only that phone call hadn't come," Mark muttered. It had been a call from Louis, who announced he was in New Orleans. He would drive to Belle St. Marie the next morning. Mark's contentment dried up at the thought.

He's probably on the road right now, Mark concluded. Just as I have to leave town, of course. Irritation and anxiety washed over him.

The flight attendant's voice crackled over the speaker near his head and broke into his thoughts. Mechanically he followed her orders—seatback up, seatbelt buckled, tray table back in place—and reached into his coat pocket to extract his agenda for the day. Pushing his thoughts of Rachel to the back of his mind, quickly he scanned the page as the plane landed and taxied to the gate. He had a busy day ahead, full of arrangements for Philippe's scheduled media stops here in two days, and he was already running behind. That was the very reason he had decided at the last minute to take the shuttle flight to New Orleans rather than driving down.

One of the first passengers off, he headed to the rental car desk, his mind now full of the activities ahead. Philippe was scheduled as a guest on the upcoming weekend talk shows two days hence, and it was imperative that Philippe perform well. The continued harassment at his rallies was negatively impacting the polls, and the press was raising all kinds of doubt about Philippe's viability as the future governor.

Mark lived in fear that the press would discover what he now knew: that the violent eruptions at the rallies were the work of two Iranians who were trying to frighten Philippe into accepting their financial participation in his campaign. If the press discovered that fact, they would have a field day speculating about the connection, and Philippe's name would be forever linked with Iran as the truth quickly got lost in all the reporting. A few articles and a few broadcasts would reawaken the fury with Iran that was barely dormant in the voting public, and Philippe's campaign would flounder.

Mark moved quickly through the check-out process at the rental car desk, claimed the keys to his car and hurried toward the door. Just as he approached the exit, he glanced up and was so startled by what he saw, he stopped in his tracks. Outside the automatic glass door, Mark recognized a very familiar female figure. Lisette? Can that really be Lisette? His mind filled with questions as he stepped back from the exit and watched.

What is she doing here? She left campaign headquarters this morning to drive north; she's supposed to be in Shreveport today. Mark watched as Lisette paced up and down on the sidewalk. She refused a cab, obviously waiting for someone to pick her up. A very long five minutes later a black sedan pulled up to the curb, and Mark watched in fascination as Billy Ray Snyder emerged from the driver's seat. After a quick verbal exchange, Billy Ray helped Lisette into the car, joined her, and slowly pulled away from the curb. Mark waited 30 seconds, bolted out the door, hailed a waiting cab, and ordered the cabby to follow at a discreet distance.

Lisette and Billy Ray? Lisette and Billy Ray? The two names replayed over and over in Mark's mind. What are they doing here together? They hate each other. They can't even tolerate being in the same room. Every time they are, they verbally shred each other. Everybody knows—Mark stopped in mid-thought. "Of course," he said aloud, "that's just what they wanted us to think. I'm the world's biggest sucker!"

"What's that?" the cabby asked.

"Nothing," Mark snapped. "Just don't lose that sedan and don't be too obvious."

"You got it buddy." The cabby shrugged as he spoke.

Mark's mind raced as he struggled to understand Lisette's involvement with Billy Ray. What kind of relationship is this anyway? Just personal? That would explain her pretending to hate him and her sneaking down here to meet him. Poor Philippe! Mark's heart sank at the thought of his uncle's pain and embarrassment when he found out about the affair.

Maybe it's not personal at all, Mark conjectured, arguing against his first conclusion. Maybe it's business, but the only business Lisette is involved in is Philippe's campaign. What's Billy Ray got to do with that? He has contributed money to the campaign, but beyond that he's never shown the slightest interest in Philippe's victory....and now that I think of it, that's very odd. He's a real estate developer; all business logic would dictate that he would be aggressively supporting the local candidate, Philippe, in a campaign for governor of the state.

Mark went back to trying to understand Lisette's behavior. But if Lisette is in New Orleans to meet Billy Ray just to gain his support for the campaign—no, no, wait a minute. She doesn't have to come all the way to New Orleans, and she certainly doesn't have to sneak around. Philippe would be glad to have Billy Ray's public support. What's going on? Why the secrecy? They're having an affair; there's no other logical answer.

Suddenly Mark thought of Rachel, and his face flushed with fury. He's courting Rachel, even flying to Texas to be by her side, at the same time he's having an affair with Lisette? "Damn him to hell!" he muttered. "It's one thing to hurt Philippe; it's another to hurt Rachel."

"What's that?" the cabby asked.

"Nothing." Anxiously Mark leaned forward as the black sedan ahead slowed and carefully pulled into the curb in front of a small, exclusive hotel. "Hang back, hang back," he commanded, even though that's just what the cabby was doing. Then he changed his mind and ordered, "Pass on by and pull into the curb up ahead." Mark craned his neck to watch out of the back window as they passed the black sedan. Billy Ray and Lisette exited the car and slowly walked toward the front entrance. The cabby had parked a block away, and Mark leaned over the seat and handed him a fifty dollar bill. "Follow them inside and see if they check in."

"Man, I ain't leaving my cab. I don't know you from—"

Mark added another fifty dollar bill. "Go! What do I want with your cab?"

The driver paused a few seconds, then snatched the money and opened the door. "What do I say if they notice me?" he asked.

"You're a cabby. Ask if anyone called for a cab."

"Got it." The man looked both ways, then strode across the street.

Mark waited.

After what seemed like an eternity, the cabby slid back into the front seat. "They're eating in the restaurant, a table way in the back. You ain't gonna have no trouble slipping in without the couple seeing 'cause they're sitting with their backs to the door."

Mark slapped him gently on the shoulder. "You're good at this, man. What's your name?"

"Joe," the cabby said as his eyes met Mark's in the rear view mirror. "Hey, are you some kind of cop or something?"

"No. This is personal."

"I don't get it. Can't be that broad. She don't look like your type."

"She's not." Mark picked up his briefcase and grabbed the door handle to exit.

"Nah, I didn't think so," Joe said, then added, "Hey, I bet it's all about those two dark-skinned guys with them. Right?"

Mark froze and stared at Joe's face in the mirror. "Something like that. Listen, I need you to stay here and wait for me. Keep the meter running; I'll be back."

"Sure, sure, but hey, I got an idea. I've picked up guys here lots of times, and sometimes I got to go in and haul 'em out and take 'em home. If you know what I mean...."

"I do. What's on your mind?"

"Well, the thing is, I can show you a back way in, and there's this kind of a lattice thing dividing the service area from that back table where the broad is. What I mean is, you could hear them without them seeing you."

"Sounds good. Let's go."

With Joe leading the way Mark hurried around to the back of the building. They entered a back door into the kitchen, and as Joe waved at the chefs, Mark followed and wound his way through the work stations until they finally pushed through a swinging door and stopped just outside it. Joe pointed to the left, and Mark peered through the lattice divider and quickly spotted Lisette and Billy Ray sitting at the back with the Iranians. As waiters and busboys hustled by, Mark watched Lisette's repeated attempts to tuck her arm into Billy Ray's elbow and his determined effort to resist her. He also saw her give the Iranians a large brown envelope. In exchange they gave her a plain white business envelope. Mark's temper flared as he fought the temptation to charge out and confront her.

Finally the Iranians rose to leave, and Mark instructed Joe to follow them and meet him at the cab. Obviously enjoying his part in the espionage, Joe nodded and trailed behind the Iranians, acting like he was looking for someone. Mark turned, intending to retrace his steps out the back door, just as Billy Ray rose, left money on the table and beckoned for Lisette to follow.

Mark stopped and waited as they exited the dining room. Then he followed them cautiously and saw them climb the staircase together. Once again he saw Lisette wrap her arm around Billy Ray's, and this time Billy Ray rewarded her by putting his arm around her shoulders.

Disgusted, Mark left the lobby and hurried toward the cab.

"The men are in the bar," Joe reported eagerly the minute Mark slipped into the back seat.

"The others are upstairs," Mark answered quietly.

"You want their room number? I can probably get it. We could go up there and—"

Mark slumped tiredly against the back seat and thought about Philippe for a few seconds. Finally he answered, "We don't need to go up there to know what they're doing, do we?"

Joe sneered. "Nah, man. Don't take no genius to figure that out. So what you want to do?"

"Wait. We just have to wait." Mark leaned his head back against the seat and considered changing hotels himself in case he was being watched, then dropped that idea as a dead give-away that he knew too much. Next he mentally rolled through the meager list of private detectives he knew in the area, discarded them all as untrustworthy, and decided he needed help from a good lawyer with connections. He sat pondering the men he knew, trying to think of someone who was totally trustworthy because he was absolutely committed to the D'Evereau family. There was only one—his cousin, Robert Carlyle.

An hour later, Mark sat up straight as he saw Billy Ray and Lisette come through the front door. Once again he set Joe the task of tailing them; this time they returned to the airport. Lisette jumped out of the sedan and waved to Billy Ray as she hurried into the terminal. Mark waited until he was sure she was well past the door; then he paid Joe off and slipped into the airport to call Robert.

His requests to Robert were complicated: he wanted private detectives following Billy Ray, Lisette and the Iranians. He also wanted Robert to look into all of Billy Ray's various businesses for something that would logically link him to Iran.

By the time Mark returned home three days later, he was exhausted. He had been on edge through all of Philippe's events and media appearances, but everything had gone well. In fact, there had been no disruptions at all, and Mark had no problem guessing why. Through Lisette's hands, Philippe was now accepting illicit campaign contributions from the Iranians without even knowing it. In time, once Philippe was governor, they would quietly come forward and make their demands of him. Thanks to Lisette and the envelopes she was passing them, they undoubtedly had the power they needed to blackmail Philippe.

Robert's detectives had been working around the clock, but they couldn't work fast enough to please Mark. His frustration was further enhanced by the fact that Louis was still at Belle St. Marie, so Mark couldn't see Rachel.

He and Robert had agreed not to contact each other until Robert had made significant progress. Mark waited, his patience growing thinner and thinner, as the early days of the week dragged by. The hardest thing he had to do was remain silent around Lisette, especially when she was draping herself all over Philippe.

Finally on Wednesday morning, as a meeting between staffers broke up and everyone headed for the coffee, the secretary at campaign headquarters breezily informed him, "Oh, by the way, Mark, your cousin Robert called." She dangled a pink message in the air, which Lisette, who was standing next to her, snatched and glanced at before passing it off to Mark.

"What do you need a lawyer for, Mark? Is there something you're not telling us?" Lisette joked.

"Probably some woman suing him for child support," the secretary joined in.

"Nothing that interesting, ladies." Mark kept his voice even. "Just a cousin looking for an excuse to have a drink." He forced himself to walk toward the coffee pot, fill his cup and stop to chat with other staffers for a reasonable amount of time. In spite of his nonchalant movements, his mind raced ahead eagerly to a meeting with Robert His first problem was where they should meet. He needed a place that raised absolutely no suspicions but also provided total privacy. It didn't take him long to realize that Belle St. Marie was the one place where neither Lisette nor anyone who worked for her would go. And no one would question Mark and Robert both going there, especially if Claire came along. But what about Louis?

At lunch time Philippe was speaking to the combined Rotary Clubs of the area, and Mark took that opportunity to call Rachel. His spirits soared when Lovey answered and told him that Rachel was on the front verandah saying good-bye to Louis. When she finally came to the phone, he asked her to invite both Robert and Claire over early that evening.

"This evening? Tonight?" Rachel's surprise was evident.

"I apologize, Rachel, really I do. I know you need some space, but believe me this is really important. I wouldn't ask if—"

"I'll be glad to invite them, but it's not likely they're available on such short notice."

"They'll come," Mark insisted. "Just keep it simple; no need for dinner. I don't think anyone's going to want to eat anyway. I'm sorry I can't be more specific."

"What's going on? You don't sound like yourself."

"I can't explain right now, Rachel, but it's very important. In fact, it's critical." He struggled with himself, forbidding any questions about Louis to come out of his mouth. "Why don't I come by early and fill you in a bit?"

"Sure....okay....just remember I'll be down at the school until 5:30 or so." When Mark said no more, she added, "Well, I'll call Claire, and Lovey and I'll pull together something light for everyone to nibble on."

"Great. And by the way, if anyone asks, this was your idea. Just an impromptu get together you wanted to have. You know, that kind of thing. Okay?"

"Okay. Got it....just an impromptu get together. Mark, are you sure you're—"

"I'll explain when I get there. Just trust me."

"Consider it done."

When Mark drove up to the front verandah of Belle St. Marie a little before six, Rachel opened the front door before he could leave his car. As she waited for him to mount the steps, she sipped the cup of tea she had been drinking as she watched out the window. "I'm worried about you," she said the minute he reached her side.

Mark noticed that she did not offer him the usual hug, and his anxiety about his future with her shot through the ceiling.

"I'm not the one you need to be worried about," he finally answered. "Let's go in, and I'll tell you what I know so far. Robert is coming with more information, hopefully all we need to know."

As Mark quickly recounted what he had seen in New Orleans, Rachel's tired eyes began to blaze with growing fury, but before she could explode, Robert and Claire arrived. The four of them gathered in the drawing room in front of the fireplace. Robert's dark expression was a direct contrast to the cheerful fire, so Rachel eliminated the usual social niceties, and after giving Claire a quick hug, she quietly placed trays of hors d'oeuvres and iced tea on the large table between the sofas. Then she perched on one sofa next to Claire while, opposite them, Robert spread out his papers in front of Mark.

"Hold on to your tempers," Robert warned Mark and Rachel. "What I've got to tell you isn't pretty, especially not for the D'Evereau family. First of all, our supposed friend and neighbor, Billy Ray Snyder, is more ambitious than any of us suspected, and he's perfectly willing to destroy this family to get what he wants."

"Money, I presume!" Rachel retorted.

"I wish it were that simple; it would be safer for us. There are plenty of ways he can make money, but the truth is that he wants power."

"You're wrong, Robert," Claire said quietly. "What Billy Ray wants is social acceptance. He sees himself as an outsider, and he wants to be at the top of the social heap. He thinks money and power will—"

"Frankly, I couldn't care less what Billy Ray wants," Mark interrupted. "I just want to stop him from destroying Philippe's reputation, and I want to see to it that he never—and I mean never—approaches Rachel again. Give us the facts, Robert!"

"Okay. Here's what he's been doing for several years now. First, he's been buying up tracts of land."

"We already knew that," Mark said impatiently.

"Yes, we did, but we believed him when he said he was going to build a high end retirement area on a few hundred acres. What we didn't know was that he's systematically bought thousands of acres."

"Thousands?" Rachel exclaimed.

"Go on!" Mark ordered.

"At the same time, Billy Ray has quietly bought controlling interest in a company called Louisiana Southern Energy, and also a company that manufactures drilling equipment for the natural gas industry. The question is, where did he get the capital to buy all this, and the answer, as you're no doubt guessing, Mark, is that he is being financed by a cartel of Iranian financiers. Since they can't invest in the USA legally now, they're investing through Billy Ray."

"I don't understand," Rachel said. "Why is he buying all this land and these companies, and where does Philippe come in? Mark says these Iranians are trying to force Philippe to accept their contributions. Why?"

"Apparently Billy Ray is setting everything up to make a fortune on natural gas, Rachel," Mark answered. "He's got the land now and the equipment. As for Philippe, at the moment I don't know exactly what they need him for because I don't know exactly what laws they are planning to circumvent in the future."

"Or what laws they want changed," Robert added. "The point is, if they have Philippe in their back pocket, they can force him to cover for them, whatever they do. That's a simplistic summary of the Iranians' motivation for seeking power over Philippe, but it's accurate."

"And Billy Ray's motivation is power, particularly power over this family," Mark added.

"Surely it's not as personal as that, Mark," Claire said. "Isn't it more likely that any Louisiana family as powerful as the D'Evereaus would be his target?"

"I suppose it's easy to guess Lisette's motivation;" Rachel added. "She just wants to be first lady of this state and is willing to use anyone to get the job. Of all the players in this little game, she's the hardest one for me to forgive. To think that she would use Philippe the way she has.... I can't bear the thought of Philippe's finding out what she's been doing!"

"Heaven knows I have no sympathy for Lisette," Mark said, "but it's Billy Ray I'd like to kill."

"But he hasn't hurt anyone personally like she has—"

"Only because you didn't fall in love with him!" Mark retorted.

"Mark's right," Claire agreed. "Think about it, Rachel. He's courted you every way he could. Money for the school, flying to Texas to be with you when Jack had his heart attack. You could have been profoundly hurt if you'd cared for him."

"He's used you!" Mark declared. "He's used you, Rachel!"

"But why? Everything else was going his way. Why did he want me?"

"He needed you," Robert answered. "The proof is right here on this map. All that property he's bought up encircles Belle St. Marie. Now he needs the land Belle St. Marie sits on. The geologist I consulted says the natural gas that Billy Ray's after can best be extracted from wells on your land, Rachel. He needs to tap into the gas from here."

Rachel caught her breath and turned white.

"He would destroy this plantation—the land itself and all the people who depend on it—in order to get what he wants, and he would court and marry you to get Belle St. Marie," Mark said, summing up the situation, and then turned to Claire. "A man who just wants social acceptance would never do that, Claire. Billy Ray Snyder wants revenge."

"What have we ever done to him?" Rachel demanded.

"We prospered." Mark answered. "He hates us for being successful, for surviving—"

"It's not that simple, Mark." Robert interrupted him. "Billy Ray's not just a poor boy who resents the upper class. He specifically resents the D'Evereaus because.....well, I wish I didn't have to say this." He paused, then blurted out, "He believes he is Philippe's son."

"No!" Rachel exclaimed. "Surely not!"

"Why would he think that?" Mark demanded.

Robert sighed. "Probably because that's what his mother always told him."

All four of them fell silent and avoided looking each other in the face. The clock ticked. A log crashed down in the fireplace, sending out a shower of sparks, and Rachel moved forward mechanically to sweep them back.

Mark finally asked the question they were all avoiding. "Is it true? Is Philippe his father?"

"Highly unlikely," Robert assured him, "highly unlikely."

Rachel turned back to the group, her eyes full of tears. "Then why would she tell her son such a horribly unfair thing?"

"Because it's easier to tell your son that you were the mistress of a wealthy man who fathered him and then abandoned both of you, than it is to tell your son that you were a prostitute in a New Orleans brothel and don't have a clue who his father is," Robert answered quietly.

Mark walked over to Rachel's side and put his arm around her. She turned her face into his shoulder and murmured, "I'm so sick of the ugliness of the world."

"What is Billy Ray's real last name?" Mark asked.

"I don't think anybody, perhaps even his mother, could answer that," Robert said, "but I can tell you that Snyder is the name of the man who owned the brothel."

"I could almost feel sorry for him...." Claire murmured.

"Don't!" Mark exclaimed. "Millions of kids grow up poor, but they don't resort to this kind of vengeance."

"The 'sins of the father,'" Claire said. "The children always seem to pay."

"Sometimes it's the sins of the mother," Rachel whispered hoarsely as her tears flowed down her cheeks. "Sometimes it's the sins of the mother and the father."

Mark held her tight. "Everyone gets to choose, Rachel, at least in this country. Remember that. Even the children, certainly when they're grown, they get to choose. Billy Ray had the same choice you have, the same choice we all have."

Robert jerked up his folder of papers and slapped it back down on the coffee table. "He's chosen. Over and over, he's chosen. He's planned and schemed and worked to ruin this family."

"And he's conspired with enemies of the United States," Mark added, "but that part we'll leave to the government to handle. The question for us is how to stop him from ruining Philippe."

"Isn't that a question which Philippe must answer?" Claire asked.

"I'm afraid it is, Honey," Robert answered his wife. "We've got to call him, Mark, and the sooner the better. Do you know where he is?"

"The critical question is, where is Lisette? Philippe is in town tonight, so he's probably at home. I have no idea if Lisette is with him." Mark paused, then added, "And I guess there's only one way to find out." He released Rachel and walked out of the room to the phone in the hall. The others sat perfectly still, trying to hear Mark's side of the conversation.

"We're in luck," Mark announced as he strode back through the door. "Lisette's speaking to some women's club. Philippe's coming over to join us."

His words were met with complete silence and downcast eyes as they all considered what lay ahead for Philippe. "Maybe we should have some of that coffee," Robert finally said.

"Yes," Claire agreed, "and let's give Philippe a few moments to relax before you spring this on him."

"Poor Philippe....heaven help him!" Rachel threw herself

down on the couch beside Claire. "Lisette's treachery.... This is going to kill him!"

"Philippe is strong," Mark said gently. "He's been in politics all his life; he's seen it all."

"And heaven will help him," Claire assured her.

"And so will we," Robert added.

"I know he's taken his share of political knocks," Rachel said, "but his relationship with Lisette....surely that's a different thing....a different kind of hurt entirely."

"Should Rachel and I even be here when you men talk?" Claire asked. "Won't our presence make it more....well....embarrassing for Philippe?"

"But I want him to know we love him no matter what, that we've all made mistakes in our lives, that we won't abandon him!" Rachel exclaimed.

"Claire's right," Mark said, "Philippe will be mortified if you are here, Rachel. I know you want to support him, but I think you must leave him a shred of pride."

"I agree," Robert said. "Philippe has put you on quite a high pedestal, Rachel. But even if he hadn't, he's old school. He would not want to discuss his follies in front of ladies."

Rachel's eyes once again filled with tears as she hung her head and sighed heavily. "You're right, I'm sure. There's nothing I can do that will make any difference. That's the way things are. That's just the way they are."

The other three exchanged quick glances of concern.

"We can make a difference, Rachel," Mark insisted, "and we will. You're worn out. You've been through too much in the last few weeks."

"Mark's right," Clare agreed. "Let's go make a pot of tea, Rachel. Right now that sounds much better to me than coffee."

"Nothing sounds good," Rachel said as she stood up, "but I don't want to make things harder for Philippe. He will be humiliated when he discovers how Lisette has used him, and no words or hugs from us will make a bit of difference."

"I'm afraid you're right," Claire agreed. "Let's go sit this out in the music room."

Philippe was visibly surprised when he arrived and discovered Mark and Robert alone and obviously upset. They sat him down, gave him a cup of coffee and approached their business directly. He was furious when he heard about Billy Ray's secretive efforts to gain control of his candidacy by connecting him to Iranians, so furious that he jumped up and paced the room.

"Who does he think he's dealing with?" Philippe demanded. "Some political babe in the woods? Amateur! He's strictly amateur! Why, I'll cut the legs out from under him. When I get through with him....the very idea that I would ever be stupid or weak enough to take money from—"

"You already have." Mark cut him off as he rose and went to his uncle's side.

"Absurd! How can you think it?" Philippe demanded.

Mark faced his uncle head on and gently put his hands on Philippe's shoulders. "Lisette has sold you out. I'm sorry, but there's no easy way to say this, so here's the truth. Lisette has been working with Billy Ray; in fact, she's been....having.... an affair with him."

Philippe stared into Mark's face, and Mark watched helplessly as a string of painful emotions played across the older man's face. Shock turned quickly into hurt as Philippe muttered, "Fool, you old fool, you should have known." He broke away from Mark's hands, and to Mark's horror, he staggered a few steps to a sofa and sat down.

Mark and Robert stood helplessly and waited as seemingly endless minutes dragged by. There was no sound but the ticking of the clock and the hissing of the coals as Philippe, his shoulders slumped and his head bowed, stared into the fire. Mark's mind flashed back to the moment when he realized he had been shot and could not move his legs, and he broke into a sweat. Feeling utterly helpless, he began to pray silently, to beg God to help his uncle....indeed, to help all of them.

It was Philippe who spoke first, and to Mark's misery he asked the question Mark never wanted to answer. "Why has this happened?"

"Billy Ray wants money, of course," Robert quickly answered, "and power."

Still gazing into the fire, Philippe shook his head. "Not enough. That's not enough of a reason to take these risks. Billy Ray's no fool; he knows he's playing with fire, with men who would just as easily kill him as look at him. And to involve Lisette in this, a woman he presumably cares about on some level—no, there's more to it. He's after more...." Philippe looked up at Mark and quietly demanded, "Tell me, boy. Tell me the truth."

Mark flinched, his stomach turning so violently that he feared he would start heaving.

"Tell me," Philippe repeated.

Mark's face mirrored the grief he was feeling, but he exerted himself and said simply, "Billy Ray thinks you are his father and that you abandoned him. His mother was a prostitute in New Orleans; apparently she has told him all his life that you are his father."

"That's a lie!" Philippe bellowed as he sprang to his feet. "Let him have Lisette, if she's fool enough to want him. Let him stop me from being the governor of this state. But I'll be damned if he will bring disgrace on my name! I am not his father! God knows I've sowed more than my share of wild oats, but as God is my witness, I've never been to a brothel anywhere. Not because I was too virtuous to go, but because I've never needed to go. Why would I?"

Mark grinned briefly and shook his head in wonder as all traces of anxiety disappeared. This was the Philippe he had always known; this was the man who, for better and often for worse, had guided him through his teen years. This was the unsinkable Philippe D'Evereau—born politician, shrewd manipulator and yes, womanizer extraordinaire. Mark had no idea how Philippe would recover from the mess he was in, but he knew he would recover. "So what do you want to do about all this?" he asked quietly.

"Take the high road, of course!" Philippe shot back. "I'll take the story to the press myself, express my utter contempt for the scum who've tried to highjack our beloved state, and then I'll drop out of this campaign and pray the public sees my actions in a positive light."

"You'll drop out?" Robert exclaimed.

"Only because he hopes the public will draft him back in," Mark explained. "And what if they don't, Uncle?"

"Next time, my boy. Next time. The main thing is, I'll still be deserving of the D'Evereau name."

"What about Lisette?" Robert asked.

"That's history, of course!" Philippe shrugged his shoulders nonchalantly. When neither Mark nor Robert commented, he added, "Oh, all right, it hurts but....well....Lisette is one of a long list of women I've had affairs with. Ask Mark; he knows, I'm sorry to say. In the past I've always walked away from them before they left me, but this time I'm the one who got burned. Kind of makes me think that God may be watching after all. Some kind of justice at play, I guess."

"I guess," Mark said. "What do you want me to do?"

"You set up a press conference for tomorrow afternoon, in

time for the story to make the evening news. No fireworks, just a simple press conference. The fireworks will all explode after I make my remarks."

"Will you have time to talk to Lisette by then?" Robert asked.

"Not likely." Philippe's sarcastic tone made it plain he had no plans to talk to Lisette.

"And Billy Ray?" Mark asked.

"I'll be talking about him—not to him! And when I get through, he'll be mighty busy saving his own hide. Robert, I want you to contact the District Attorney and all the other entities who will want to investigate this. I'll meet with them after the press conference. We'll give them every shred of evidence we have."

"What about the Party?" Mark asked. "Don't you need to consult with them?"

"There's no point in asking questions I don't want the answer to."

"I don't understand."

"They'll resist my decision every way they can, but the truth is that I've got to stand on the bedrock of integrity because the D'Evereau name is at stake here, and I refuse to be the first man who publicly sullies that name."

"You won't be standing alone, Uncle. We'll be by your side."

"Absolutely," Robert agreed. "Now, I'm going to take Claire home. Mark, let me know about the timing tomorrow. I'll have the authorities ready to jump into it." He slapped Philippe on the shoulder affectionately. "Somehow it'll all work out," he said as he left.

"I'm going, too," Philippe announced. "To tell the truth, I can't face Rachel." He paused, than added, "I guess she knows everything."

"She does," Mark said, "and we had a hard time keeping her in the other room. She wanted to be in here supporting you."

"No, no, I couldn't stand that." Philippe took a few steps toward the door, then turned back to Mark. "Listen, Mark..." He choked up and stopped, obviously struggling. "I've hurt you, boy."

"Nonsense," Mark declared. "This isn't about me."

"Yes, it is. My behavior over the years....well, I didn't make you feel welcome all those years ago when you came to live with me. Too selfish—that's what I was." He paused and cleared his throat. "I just want to say that you're....you're the best." Philippe stopped and swallowed hard. Finally he managed to whisper, "If

I'd had a son—"

"I hear you, Uncle. I hear you, and it feels good." Mark's eyes brimmed over, and he swiftly wiped away his tears.

Silence reigned in the room as the two men stood there struggling to suppress what they could not seem to express.

"Okay....okay....son. You set up that press conference for tomorrow afternoon. It won't be easy, but...."

Mark walked to his uncle's side and embraced him. "I'll be standing by your side."

"I'm grateful for that, boy." Philippe patted Mark's cheek for the first time in their lives. "More than I can say. Right now, though, I've got some thinking to do, and I have to do that alone. Who knows? Maybe I'll even say a prayer or two."

Mark jerked his head up in surprise; Philippe nodded at him, turned and walked hurriedly out the door. Mark stood in the empty room, his mind staggering under all the heavy information he had received.

Rachel, followed by Lovey, cautiously came into the room. "He's gone home?" Rachel asked as she peered up into Mark's exhausted face. "Is he okay?"

"He's gone." Mark paused. "He's wounded, but he's not down. You know Philippe. He always comes out on top."

"Are you okay?" Rachel asked quietly.

"Yes, of course—no, actually I'm sick with grief for Philippe and ready to kill Billy Ray and...worried that I could lose you to Louis."

"Let's not complicate things by talking about that now," Rachel murmured as she turned toward the fireplace and began sweeping the hearth.

"Would it be a complication?" Mark asked.

"Yes." Rachel turned to face him. "I'll tell you the same thing I told Louis today. I've been through too much trauma in Texas to make life-defining decisions right now. You'll both just have to wait."

Mark made no reply.

"Frankly, I'm sickened by this mess with Philippe, Mark." Rachel's eyes filled with weary tears. " Surely that's enough stress for both of us right now."

"More than enough," he agreed reluctantly before giving her a hug and leaving.

Rachel stood in the hall staring at the closed front door as she listened to Mark's car driving away.

"Miz Rachel?" Lovey's voice barely penetrated Rachel's

mind. "I don't wanna have to tell you this, but I got to. Alice came to the back door to tell me that Sassy done run away with that Jamal."

Rachel slowly lowered her face into her hands. "Of course," she whispered. "Of course she has. Why did I ever think we could make a difference?"

"Don't give up, Honey. Call the Sheriff. Maybe he can find her.

"And what good will that do?" Rachel muttered. "She's just going to make the same choice over and over."

"You don't know that."

"Yes, I do. I've lived with it all my life." Exhausted and void of hope, Rachel turned and walked back down the long hall to the phone. She watched her fingers mechanically dial the number she now knew by heart, and she heard her voice speak to the Sheriff. When she had finished, she turned toward the staircase and began the arduous climb.

"Ain't you gonna eat nothing?" Lovey's voice seemed to travel for miles before it drifted into Rachel's mind. "I's gonna bring you some supper."

Rachel shook her head and continued. When she reached her room, she lay down on the massive mahogany bed She felt like she was balancing on the edge of a chasm of depression, a bottomless abyss into which all the equilibrium and understanding she had gained in Texas could disappear. "How could we have been so fooled by Billy Ray? Could he really hate us this much? And why oh why has Sassy chosen Jamal? It's too much, Lord!" She crossed her arms until she was hugging herself and rocked herself to sleep.

Chapter 22

"What is this press conference all about?" Lisette demanded the minute Mark walked into campaign headquarters the next morning.

"Ask Philippe," Mark answered curtly.

"What does that mean? You don't know what it's about? You're refusing to tell me?"

"Ask Philippe," Mark said again as he walked past her.

"I can't ask him because I can't find him!" Lisette raised her voice as she grabbed Mark's arm. "I'm asking you. Tell me!"

Mark glanced around the office and noticed that Lisette's angry tone had brought the work of the office to a halt. The whole staff was staring at her and obviously waiting for Mark's response. As much as he wanted to tell her off, he forced himself to remember the necessity of surprise and controlled himself. "All I do is what Philippe tells me to do, Lisette. If you can't find him, I guess you'll just have to wait like the rest of us."

"Not likely!" she spat, then turned on her heel and headed out the door.

Mark shrugged as nonchalantly as possible and walked to the back of the room, where his cubicle stood waiting to give him a modicum of privacy. Once he had seated himself behind the partitions, he allowed himself the luxury of slumping in his chair and leaning forward to hold his head in his hands. Sharp pain, the product of a sleepless night, ran up and down his spine, and he was worried about his uncle, whom he had not seen since their last words at Belle St. Marie. "Where is he?" he whispered into his hands.

"Mark?" A young female voice startled him, and he jerked himself up straight and began pushing papers around on his desk. "Are you okay?" the pretty intern asked.

"Yeah, sure....uh....just got a bit of a headache," he lied.

She grinned flirtatiously at him. "Too much to drink last night?"

He tried to smile back at her. "Yeah, something like that. What can I do for you?"

"Oh, nothing for me. I just wanted to tell you that some old lady named Lovey called first thing this morning and said to tell you not to worry, that she found what you're looking for at the church early this morning."

When Mark just stared up at her, she shrugged and added, "Doesn't make a whole lot of sense, does it?"

"Just enough," Mark murmured. "Just enough. Thanks."

"Sure!" She tossed the word over her shoulder as she left.

Amazed and relieved, Mark leaned back in his chair. "What do you know," he murmured, "Philippe actually did go pray. Unbelievable! Of course, maybe he was just hiding out. Either way, he's in the best possible hands now; Lovey, in spite of her un-worldliness and because of her other-worldliness, will know just how to help him through the morning." The ringing phone on his desk jerked him back into the realities of his job, and he began to field calls from a seemingly endless stream of reporters trying to pry an exclusive about the news conference out of him.

About eleven o'clock Mark picked up the ringing phone again and discovered Philippe himself on the other end of the call. "I've just gotten to the house," his uncle reported. "Dropped by just long enough to clean up."

"Lisette's looking for you," Mark warned.

"Figures. Well, she'll see me soon enough. Is everything in place?"

"Yes, the word has spread like wildfire, and I've spent the morning fielding press calls. A few vehicles have arrived outside the press room. I'll get on over there and be sure things are set up."

"Good. I don't want to walk in until just before noon."

"We'll be ready for you....or at least, the equipment will be ready. I don't know about the people."

"Not likely. See you soon."

Mark felt the tension rising in him again as he left his cubicle and headed through back hallways to the press auditorium, which Philippe had set up months ago when he had begun his campaign. As he walked through the building, he felt the stares of workers boring into him. They all knew something big was up, but even Mark did not know how big.

When Philippe strode onto the platform less than an hour later, Mark was amazed by the peace he saw in his uncle's tired face. Under the glare of the television lights Philippe stood ramrod straight and looked directly into the cameras as he prepared to speak. Mark held his breath as his uncle began.

"Last evening I learned that my campaign has been tarnished by the receipt of financial support from morally unacceptable and possibly illegal sources. To be more specific, I learned that a member of my staff has accepted donations from operatives working for an Iranian energy cartel. I totally repudiate any connection to these supporters. Such a connection is repugnant to me. I have taken the following steps to right this grievous wrong. First, I have notified federal authorities of these attempts to infiltrate my campaign. Second, I have instigated an investigation into the exact amount these operatives have donated, and I have given orders that every penny be returned. Third, I have fired the offending staff member who accepted these monies."

Philippe paused for these disclosures to sink in, and the room exploded into a mob of reporters shouting questions. Mark raced to his uncle's side, thinking he should try to bring order to the pandemonium. Philippe gently pushed him away and simply held up his hand. The room instantly fell quiet as reporters eagerly shoved microphones toward the podium.

"Let there be no room for doubt." Philippe's voice boomed with conviction. "I, Philippe D'Evereau, refuse to gain office or profit in any other way from monies that come from enemies of this great country. Consequently, I am withdrawing my name from the race for governor. I apologize to all who have worked for my campaign and to all the legitimate donors who have financed it. I had no knowledge of these illegal donations prior to last evening; I did not accept this money personally. Nevertheless, this breach of ethics and legality happened on my watch, and I take responsibility for it.

"No one but the Almighty knows what the future holds, but this much I can guarantee: should I ever be honored by the people of Louisiana with any political office in this great state, my independence and ability to act solely in the interest of the people will not be compromised by unethical donations from any source."

With those simple, direct words Philippe ended his run for the governorship, turned away from the cameras and strode off the podium. Questions were hurled at him from all directions, but with his shoulders squared, he refused to look back as he marched toward the exit. Bedlam mushroomed in the room as reporters scrambled toward the door with their photographers lugging their equipment behind them. In the midst of all the activity Mark saw two people standing perfectly still. On one side of the room, Rachel stood, staring up at him with tears running down her cheeks. On the other, Lisette stood, her face flushed scarlet with anger as Philippe walked right by her without even meeting her gaze.

Mark's first instinct was to rush to Rachel's side, but as reporters rushed toward him he was swept after Philippe, repeatedly answering "No comment" to the questions thrown at him. When he reached the office area, he was stunned to find several armed guards and the police awaiting them. Obviously everyone in the room was confused and somewhat fearful. Philippe held up his hands to silence the talking staffers.

"My dear friends, as you no doubt have just heard, my campaign is now finished, and this office must now be closed until the proper authorities have finished whatever investigation they choose to make. I must ask all of you to leave immediately and take nothing but your personal belongings with you. The guards you see are here to guarantee that no papers, which may later be needed as evidence, are removed from the premises. I assure you that you will all be paid a fair severance pay. Some of you, of course, may be questioned by the authorities. Please cooperate as completely as possible and know that we will untangle this situation and see that justice is served. Finally, please accept my profound thanks for all you have done for my campaign. I deeply regret that it has ended this way."

With those words, Philippe followed several federal officers into his private office, the guards took up their positions at the door, and Mark walked toward the front door to comfort those leaving. It was then that he saw Lisette's car tearing out of the parking lot. He joined Philippe in his office and said simply, "Lisette has just driven away. I suppose we know where she is going."

"If she's looking for Billy Ray, she'll have to look at police headquarters," Philippe answered. "He was picked up for questioning shortly before the press conference began. Now," he said, turning back to the men in the room, "let's move this along as fast as possible.

A tidal wave of frenetic action swirled around Rachel as waves of press people seemed to roll out the door. She fought against that tide, struggling to move toward the elevated stage that held the podium Philippe had just abandoned. Even though she had expected Philippe's announcement, his resignation from the race had sucked her deeper into her quicksand of depression. Her throat tightened and tears splashed down her face as she coupled his failure with what she perceived as her own with Sassy.

"You can't win," she whispered as she sank down on the edge of the stage. "There are Billy Ray Snyders and Jamals everywhere. If Philippe, with all his power, can't beat them....how could someone like me ever succeed? I've just been fooling myself. I can't help the children here. I couldn't even see what was going on right in front of me!" Overtaken by a total exhaustion of spirit, she couldn't continue.

Minutes of despair crept by as Rachel sat in the empty press room with salty tears running down her face. Finally she warned herself, "You can't just sit here crying: someone will come in and see you. Haven't you made a big enough fool of yourself already?" She pulled tissues out of her purse and blew her nose. "Not that it makes any real difference, I suppose," she murmured as she stood up. Letting her purse bump around her ankles, she went to the exit.

Outside she was greeted by a rumble of thunder, gray churning clouds, and pelting rain, but she made no special effort to stay dry. Instead she moved like a sleepwalker toward her car and lethargically inserted the key into the lock.

By the time Rachel reached the gates of Belle St. Marie, she had driven through one of the quick, flash storms that signal the beginning of a Louisiana spring. Neither the streaks of lightning nor the booms of thunder had registered with her; what little mental energy she possessed had been focused on peering through the streaming windshield. She left the highway, drove toward the gates, and turned off the engine. The rain continued to drum on the roof and slam against the glass as Rachel slowly lowered her head to the steering wheel. She was all cried out; there was nothing left in her but throbbing sadness.

Finally the storm moved further south, and a streak of sunshine began to pierce the windshield and play across Rachel's face. She raised her head and watched the light filtering through the trees and reflecting off the puddles in the gravel. She had no desire to proceed to the house, so she opened the car door and stepped out into cooler air. The sunshine brightened so suddenly that she looked skyward, where she found patches of cerulean blue escaping the clouds. When she looked down again, her gaze fell on large azalea bushes planted around the gate. They were drenched, bent over by the force of the rain, and the lower branches were smothered in mud. Rachel walked over to one, leaned over, pulled a heavy branch out of the mud and shook it. Muddy water sprayed all over her, but the tips of the branch suddenly emerged and revealed a mass of tiny jewels….countless rosy red buds.

"You probably go through this every spring," Rachel said as she picked up another branch and shook it. Once again, dirty water drenched her, but this time the branch snapped, and Rachel held a muddy mass of foliage in her hand. "Sorry," she murmured, "I didn't mean to..." She shook her head, dropped the branch in the mud and wandered off into the dripping woods.

When Rachel drove up to the house several hours later, she found Lovey waiting for her on the verandah with a broom in her hand. "Where has you been?" Lovey demanded. "I's been worried sick about you. I's about swept the boards off the hall watching out the door for you." She peered at Rachel. "You's been crying, and you's covered with mud!"

Rachel nodded. "They've beaten Philippe—even Philippe."

"He's quit running for governor. I know, Honey."

"You must have had the radio on...."

"No, he told me real early this morning when he's sitting in the kitchen drinking coffee." Lovey shook her head sadly. "That poor man, he was sure tuckered out after spending the night in the church, but he and the Lord had a good talk, and I think he finally found some peace. I 'spect he gonna be a different man from now on."

Rachel nodded. "Disillusioned, maybe even broken."

"Not broken, Honey."

"He'd have to be broken to spend the night in the church, Lovey. You know Philippe. He doesn't set foot in the doors of the church except on Christmas Eve and Easter."

"Well, he ain't no different from the rest of us. When our problems get too heavy to carry, we finally admits we's just human and goes looking for God. 'Course we don't have to look far 'cause He's always just standing right next to us, waiting for us to notice."

Rachel, unwilling to consider spiritual things, looked down at the floor rather than meet Lovey's eyes. "Well, it's done now, nothing left but the investigation. I'm sure he's not looking forward to going through all that."

"'Course not. We humans just want to be able to say we's sorry and move on, but there's always consequences to what we done and we gotta fix them."

Rachel raised her face to meet Lovey's eyes. "Fix them? Exactly how do we do that?"

"We changes what we can change, Miz Rachel."

Rachel shook her head. "And there's always somebody out there who's going to undo any good we might do. Lovey, I'm tired of trying to save the world."

"It ain't your job to save the world, Miz Rachel. You just gotta make the place where you is better. That's all."

Rachel sighed loudly and looked down at the mud covering her clothes. "I'm tired of that, too. I'm tired of fighting. I just want peace. I want life to be simple and pleasant."

Lovey put her broom down and wrapped her arms around Rachel. "You ain't even describing life, Honey," she said gently. "They's always trouble in the world, even here. I think you's just had too much trouble lately, and it remind you of the way you's raised. We's talked about this before; you gotta choose to think on the good in life."

Rachel said nothing.

"The Sheriff called," Lovey added, "he's got a good lead on finding Sassy."

"I'll never get through to that girl."

"You can't just quit, Honey."

"Why not?"

"'Cause God ain't given up on you."

"I'm not God, Lovey! I'm just a human being."

"That's right, Honey. You ain't God, and you gotta quit trying to be, but that don't mean you turns away from everything that's got trouble attached to it. You's the hands and feet of God on this earth, Honey. You gotta do your part. The end result ain't up to you, but you gotta do your part."

"Why?"

"'Cause you's put on this here earth for that purpose, and you ain't ever gonna be happy no other way. They's times to rest and rejoice, and they's times to work and grieve, Miz Rachel. It always be like that."

"If you say so. I'm going upstairs now."

"I'll bring you some tea. I bet you ain't eaten a thing—"

"No thanks. I just want to sleep."

Rachel had barely settled on her bed when the phone rang.

Louis' cultivated voice edged with anger greeted her.

"Rachel? Papa called me and told me about Philippe's public announcement. I don't like the sound of any of it, especially the part about his affair with Lisette."

"Philippe didn't even mention Lisette."

"He didn't have to. She's been talking to the press, trying to paint herself as Philippe's victim. It's hitting all the news services; apparently you don't have the television on. Well, that's just as well. I won't have you troubled by Philippe's tawdry affairs. I'm in New York, but I'm flying to New Orleans this afternoon, and I'll be at Belle St. Marie about noon tomorrow."

"That's not necessary, Louis. Things are crazy here, it's true, but I plan to withdraw and rest as much as possible.Fortunately I don't have to teach this afternoon because the children are out of school for Easter vacation, so unless Mark needs help—"

"Mark's a grown man, Rachel, who has worked his way through much more difficult things than the end of a politician's career. I don't want you carrying any of Mark's current burden, and I'm sure he doesn't want you to either."

"You're probably right," she agreed. "Poor Philippe....I just feel so...."

"Rachel, Philippe has made his bed. Now he must lie in it. You can't help him."

"But all the good he could have accomplished is ruined, Louis!"

"That's not your responsibility, Rachel. I don't like anything I'm hearing. I am not going to sit still while Philippe, who has clearly created his own problems, burdens you."

"Philippe hasn't said a word to me, Louis. Really, he hasn't. I just feel down because of my own inability to cope with the troubles around here."

"Troubles? What else is going on?"

"One of my students, Sassy—you remember her name probably—has run away, and I've completely run out of answers."

"Because there are no answers for people like that!" Louis retorted. "Of course I remember hearing about Sassy. That girl has actually put you in physical danger in the past! I won't have it! Philippe's disreputable behavior is bad enough, but for you to be confronting violent, drugged teenagers—no, absolutely not! I won't have it!"

"Surely that's my decision, Louis."

"But are you capable of making good decisions now? Rachel, you're not yourself; I can hear it in your voice. I can tell you are trying to carry the weight of the world on your shoulders just like you always do. You've been through a great deal with your father's heart attack, and you need to be recovering from your own ordeal—not exposing yourself to violent teenagers or Philippe's vulgarities. Someone has to take care of you now, and I am going to do just that."

"I don't need to be rescued, Louis. I need to rest. You and Andre are already scheduled to come this weekend for Easter. I'm looking forward to seeing you then."

"I am worried about you, Rachel, and I will make my plans accordingly."

"There's no need to worry. I plan to withdraw until I regain my equilibrium. Good bye for now."

Rachel hung up the receiver with more than usual vehemence. "Space!" she exclaimed. "I need space."

The sun was setting when Rachel went downstairs to arrange for the Simones' visit.

"When is they coming?" Lovey asked.

"Louis is so upset about the problems here he wants to come tomorrow, but I told him to stick to the original plan, so they should arrive Saturday after lunch."

"Should? That don't sound too sure to me."

"As I said, Louis is upset. There's no telling what he might do."

"Well, whatever he does, we's gonna have the best Easter dinner ever. You gotta invite Mr. Mark and Mr. Philippe and all your friends. I's had enough of Lent! Seem like it been going on forever."

Lovey's unusual vehemence surprised Rachel. "Maybe we should just keep it simple, Lovey. I'm so tired, and there's so much trouble—"

"Trouble ain't gonna keep us from celebrating Easter! What would Miz Elinore say? She'd say, 'We ain't gonna lower our standards 'cause of nobody or nothing.' I knows you needs to rest, and I ain't gonna let you do nothing else. I's gonna call Alice, and we's gonna cook up a storm and do Miz Elinore's memory proud."

Rachel studied Lovey's face for a moment and clearly saw worry etched across it, so she didn't argue with her. She just nodded tiredly.

"I's gonna fix you some supper now—"

"No, thanks, Lovey. Really, I'm too tired to eat." Rachel turned back toward the staircase. "I'm going to bed for the night."

"At 6:00?" Lovey asked as Rachel dragged herself up the lower steps.

"Whenever," Rachel said dully without looking back. "I just want to sleep. I don't want to ever feel anything again."

"Honey, I's gonna call the doctor for you."

"I just need time, Lovey," Rachel called back. "Just time. And maybe some distance."

When Rachel had totally disappeared, Lovey sank down on the hall chair next to the phone. "Distance? Did she say 'distance'?" she whispered. "This ain't good, Lord, I gotta have some help here."

Chapter 23

Rachel's tear-drenched face remained the primary image in Mark's mind in spite of the chaos of the day caused by Philippe's withdrawal from the campaign. That graphic image remained front and center as he answered calls from journalists and party operatives, as well as did what he could to forward the investigation into Billy Ray's and Lisette's illegal activities. Finally, around seven that evening, he could stand it no longer; his concern for Rachel forced him to walk away from campaign headquarters and turn his car toward Belle St. Marie.

I know how fond she is of Philippe, he thought as he drove, and I know she has a heart far too tender for her own good. Still...Rachel never breaks down in public, and that look of despair on her face! All this mess of Philippe's has just come too soon after her trauma in Texas....or maybe there's more to it. I should have—what? What should I have done? What could I have done? The story had to be broken. It wasn't just a political decision; it was a legal one. We couldn't sit on information like that; we would have all ended up in prison!

When Mark finally mounted the steps of the old mansion, Lovey met him at the door and urged him inside. "I gotta talk to you, Mr. Mark. Miz Rachel was gone all afternoon, and when she come home, she looked real bad. Then she went off to bed without eating a bite of food. I couldn't even get her to drink a cup of tea!"

"Not good." Mark winced as he spoke. "Not good at all. Give me some more details. Think back, and tell me exactly what happened when Rachel got home after Philippe's announcement."

"She didn't come home—not for hours, and when she finally did, she was all muddy and I could tell she'd been crying."

Lovey wrung her hands. "She was real upset and saying things like 'they's no use in trying to make things better 'cause ain't nothing ever gonna work out anyway.' She just decided to give up."

"That doesn't sound like Rachel."

"It sound just like the Rachel that first showed up over here right after her husband got killed. She was good and broken then, and she's not far from broken now. I tell you, I's worried to death about her."

"She's exhausted from those weeks in Texas. Anybody would be. And even though she came home with some answers about her mother's behavior, she's still trying to make her peace with the way her family handled everything."

"They didn't handle nothing! That's the problem. They just let that little girl shoulder all the meanness that was around that house."

"I know, but I think she just needs time now. Time to rest and to sort everything through."

"How she gonna do that with this Sassy problem popping up?"

"What Sassy problem?"

"That girl done run away with Jamal."

"Does Rachel know?" Mark asked.

"'Course she knows. Alice come tell me right after you left here yesterday. I had to tell Miz Rachel so she could call the sheriff."

"Did she call him?" Mark demanded anxiously. "She didn't go off on her own looking for Sassy, did she?"

"No, she called him. Then she just went up to bed."

"This happened last night?"

"Yes, sir. Right after you left. She just dragged herself up to bed. Wouldn't eat nothing at all. This morning she didn't come downstairs till she's ready to leave for the campaign headquarters."

"What did she say this morning?"

"Not much of anything. I made her eat some toast, but she didn't do no talking."

"This is all beginning to make sense. No wonder she was so distraught this morning. She's feeling like a failure because of Sassy, and the trouble with Philippe isn't helping a bit. Not to mention all the bullying she endured in Texas just two weeks ago."

Lovey nodded. "Then that Mr. Louis had to go and call her.

And he ain't happy at all 'cause he's heard all about Mr. Philippe's trouble and that Lisette lady—"

"She's no lady, Lovey," Mark said sarcastically, "far from it, but never mind that now. You say Louis called? Did he blame Rachel for any of this?"

"Oh, no! He just want to come here soon as he can get here to take care of Miz Rachel. He gonna save her! As if I can't take care of my girl! I been taking care of her all this time, ain't I?"

"Of course. When's he coming?"

"Who knows? Miz Rachel tell him not to come 'till late tomorrow afternoon, but I don't trust him. Not one little bit!"

"Lovey, calm down now." Mark patted the old woman's shaking shoulder.

Lovey's lips quivered as she choked out, "I's just afraid she gonna leave. That man ain't gonna make her happy. I just know it."

"This is not settled by a long shot, Lovey. I am not giving up!" Mark insisted. "Rachel's emotionally and physically exhausted; she has a right to be."

"But what we gonna do to help her?"

Mark massaged his temples as he thought. Finally he answered, "I'm going to talk to her before Louis gets here, and I'm going to make her see that she is in no condition to make decisions about her future. That's what I'm going to do."

"I's gonna go see if she's awake." Lovey headed toward the stairs and began to climb. "And I's gonna pray harder than I ever prayed. God gonna get good and tired of old Lovey 'fore this is over."

Mark sank down on the bottom step to wait, but quickly found that in spite of his exhaustion, he couldn't sit still. He jumped up and paced the length of the hall as he tossed fragments of prayer up to God.

Moments later Lovey leaned over the upstairs railing and quietly called down, "Miz Rachel be sound asleep. You want me to wake her up?"

Sorely tempted, Mark hesitated. "No," he finally said. "Let her sleep. There's always tomorrow."

"It got to be before noon," Lovey insisted as she descended the staircase. "I tell you that Mr. Louis ain't gonna do what Miz Rachel say. He gonna come when he want to."

"I'll be here in the morning. I promise you that. Good night, Lovey." Mark hugged her gently and headed toward the front door. "Get some rest," he called back.

When he heard no response, he stopped at the door and looked back. Lovey was standing in the hall with her fists on her hips. She was so focused on a higher power she had forgotten him entirely. "Lord, we's gotta have a talk in the kitchen!" he heard her proclaim, and for the first time in his life he felt sorry for God.

Mark slid into his car seat, but he couldn't make himself start the car. He just sat there looking up at Rachel's bedroom window and mentally arguing with himself. Let her sleep; go home; tomorrow is soon enough, he thought. No, I can't leave her. This all feels too familiar. I'm inches away from losing her, and I know it. But this time I'm not thousands of miles away, toting a gun in a jungle. Louis is smart; he knows that this is the time to make his move. He'll be here long before noon, long before anyone expects him. I've got to talk to her before he comes!

Suddenly Mark started the car, "I better get what I've got to do done now," he muttered as he turned the car around and drove down the drive.

As he approached Philippe's house a few minutes later, he was greeted by a stand of media people who poked cameras at his car window and yelled questions at him. Finally he edged the car through the mob and stopped to identify himself with the police who were keeping the press at bay.

The house was dark inside when Mark entered except for one light in the library. Mark was in no mood for a discussion about the investigation, but Philippe called out to him as he passed in the hall.

"Quite a circus out there, isn't it?"

"Yeah. About what I would expect."

"Party leaders just called and demanded a meeting tonight, but I'm in no hurry to confer with them. They can just wait and sweat a while as far as I'm concerned. Where were they all afternoon while I was being crucified by the press?"

"Crucified?" Mark's voice was laced with sarcasm. "Did you say 'crucified'? Interesting choice of words, Uncle!"

"Well, maybe I'm overstating it a bit," Philippe tossed back, "but you have to admit that Lisette has done a bang-up job of making me look bad on all the talk shows, and the public is eating it up."

"So what's new about that?"

"Nothing." Philippe conceded as he scrutinized Mark's face. "Well, anyway, we've got to work out some kind of strategy with the party this weekend while people are focusing on Easter, so you and I are going to meet them tomorrow—"

"No." Mark cut his Uncle off. "Leave me out of this for now. I'll be giving all my attention to Rachel."

"What's wrong with Rachel?"

"She's just wiped out by her weeks in Texas. There was a lot more going on than just Jack's heart attack. A lot of family ugliness. She's really depressed."

Philippe peered at him for a long moment. "So depressed you can't attend a meeting tomorrow? That seems a bit odd."

Philippe waited for a response, but when none came, he added, "There is more to it, isn't there?"

"That student of hers, Sassy, has run off with her drug-dealing boyfriend, and Rachel blames herself because Gunner attacked the girl last spring and she can't seem to straighten her out."

"She's not responsible for what Garth Gunner did to that girl or anybody else!"

"I know that; you know that. But Rachel is holding herself responsible, and I plan to be there for her. She's my first priority from this point on."

Philippe sighed and clapped Mark on the shoulder. "As she should be," he said slowly, nodding his head. "As she should be. You're investing wisely, my boy. I wish to heaven I'd made a good marriage my priority."

Mark nodded curtly and turned to leave the room. "Don't underestimate Louis," Philippe called after him. "He's more than rich. He's smart. He can give Rachel a clean slate and a life of luxury."

"But he doesn't love her the way I do," Mark replied as he reached the hall. "How could he? He doesn't even know the real Rachel!"

"Good luck, son!"

Mark called back over his shoulder. "Philippe, if I win this one, there will be no luck involved. God is going to have to do it for me."

Mark showered and sat down to try to read himself to sleep. His body was bone tired, but his anxiety kept the adrenalin pumping through him and forced him to jump up every few minutes to stare out the window in the direction of Belle St. Marie. Every time he peered into the pines, he was confronted by a steady, sad stream of rain. At midnight he finally gave up the fight, pulled on his clothes, and slipped out of the house. Aware of the vigilant press waiting at the gate to Philippe's house, he picked his way through the dripping woods, down the dark path toward Belle St. Marie, toward Rachel.

When he reached the expansive lawn around the plantation house, the rain had turned into a drizzle, and a heavy fog blurred his view of the large, white mansion. Uncertain what he was going to do next, he stood and stared up at Rachel's room as the cold drizzle formed drops which hung to the edge of his hood before dripping onto his eyelashes. Blinking irritably, he scolded himself, "Make a decision. Wake her up or don't wake her up, but don't stand here staring at her window like a love-sick kid!"

Abruptly he turned away from the house, his decision made, and headed toward the path down to the pond. Minute by minute slowly clicked by as Mark trudged through the wet woods, and mentally checking each second off, he urgently wished for the light of dawn. "She needs sleep," he kept reminding himself, "first and foremost, she needs sleep. And I need....what? Rachel, of course! I need some time face to face with her. Not now, not now! Got to wait. So here I am again on this path from my boyhood, only this time I'm not sitting in some foreign country just imagining this walk, this pilgrimage in search of supernatural help. I'm actually walking it. Dear God, don't let me lose her again!"

Mark reached the pond. Dull, dark water. Too dulled by the mist to reflect even its overhanging trees. "No golden swan tonight," he whispered. "That's okay, God. I can do without it, but you've got to send some kind of light to Rachel. Please...." He broke off his words as he sank down on a wet log and looked across the coal black water. "Miss Elinore, I sure hope you're praying for your granddaughter. I'm trying, but your words were always so much better.

Rachel's legs twitched under the covers as her breathing quickened and became raspy. "Daddy!" she mumbled as she thrashed from side to side of the bed. Her eyelids fluttered over sleep-veiled eyes as she dreamed that she was stumbling down the hall of an intensive care unit, frantic with fear. Desperation fueled her as she struggled into one bed-filled cubicle after another. Heart monitors beeped louder and louder, and yards of plastic tubing began to ensnare her ankles and hobble her efforts. "Where's my father?" she demanded of the ghostly nurses who floated around her. No answers. Just ephemeral figures in white, who shook their heads slowly and clutched at Rachel, retarding her search. She forced her way through the clinging hands and struggled into yet another cubicle. Fear scalded her stomach and rose into her throat as she focused on the perfectly still body, the sheet pulled over its face. "No," she moaned as she approached the inert figure. "No, Daddy, no."

Slowly she pulled the sheet back and discovered the face of her mother. Rachel gasped. "I hope you's happy!" a loud voice shouted from a supernaturally tall, dark figure, which suddenly materialized on the other side of the hospital bed. "You's made your mother sick again, you devil chile!" The figure extended its arm and pointed an elongated finger at Rachel. "You ain't never been nothing but trouble since the day you's borned!"

"Where's Daddy?" Rachel's voice quivered with fear. "I want Daddy!"

Slowly her mother began to sit up. Rachel shrank back and watched in terror as her mother's face mechanically turned toward her, its eyes opening and piercing into Rachel's. "Why couldn't you wait like other girls waited?" she demanded. "Stanton Berry was the finest young man in the state, but you....you betrayed him!"

"No! I didn't do that!" Rachel exclaimed. "I wasn't even born! Where's Daddy?"

Patsy disintegrated into dust right before Rachel's horrified eyes, but her whining voice bounced off the walls, "What will people say? Oh, Mammy Cassie, we're ruined!"

Rachel tried to scream, but she could make no sound. Grasping at the knot of entangling tubes around her ankles, she finally fought her way free and lunged toward the hall. A cold, gray rain blew across her face as she broke out of the cubicle. The ICU hall had become dark, and Rachel was forced to inch forward, waving her frantic hands in front of her to feel her way down the corridor. "Daddy!" she called out into the rainy hall. "Where are you?" Her foot slammed into something soft, but unmoving, and Rachel froze as the thought of a human body raced through her mind. "Daddy," she moaned, "no!" She flung herself on her knees and lifted the heavy form toward her face. She fought to see through the rain, her heart pounding wildly, the words "No! no, no!" repeating staccato fashion from her lips.

Finally, with the body just inches from her face, she saw its features. The bloody, cut, swollen face swam before her eyes. "Sassy!" she exclaimed. "Oh, dear God! What's happened?"

Sassy moaned as Rachel cradled her in her arms. "You'll be all right...I promise...you'll be all right...I'll take care of you."

"I's gonna break you in half, lady!" a furious voice boomed

overhead as Rachel watched a giant foot swing into Sassy's body and shake it. Rachel jerked her head up, and stared all the way up to the ceiling where she finally found the end of Jamal's towering body and his vicious face. "I's gonna break you—"

"Rachel!" a totally different voice commanded from behind. Startled by its volume, she swung her head around. "Rachel, remember who you are! These disreputable people are not your responsibility." Louis walked out of the darkness and stood next to her. "Come!" he insisted as he leaned toward her and held out his hand. "I won't have you involved in such tawdry affairs."

Sassy moaned in Rachel's arms as Jamal's giant foot once again slammed into her body. "But what about Sassy?" Rachel asked. "Who will help her?"

"You were not made for such things, Rachel," Louis pronounced. "You were made for beauty." He swept his hand to the right, and Rachel watched in amazement as a shimmering light appeared and revealed a glowing azalea bush. Mesmerized by its rosy-red flowers, Rachel loosened her hold on Sassy and began to crawl toward it. Her spirits lifted to magical heights, and feeling as if she could fly, she stood, ran toward the flowers and threw her arms around the bush. Tears of joy streamed down her face. She lifted her hands to wipe them away, but her hands were covered in mud. Confused, she watched in dismay as mud began to coat the arching branches of the azalea, hiding the flowers from her. "No!" she cried. "No, please!" Urgently she shook the branches, flinging mud all over herself, but the filth continued to spread on the bush, covering and suffocating the last of the flowers.

Rachel screamed, "No!" so loudly she woke herself.

Gasping for air, she jerked herself up straight in bed and struggled to understand where she was. She darted her eyes around the room until she felt sure she was safe in her bedroom at Belle St. Marie. "Oh God!" she exclaimed. "How could You let me dream such a horrible thing?" She flung aside the twisted, damp sheets and slid her feet down to the cold, wooden floor. As soon as she knew she could stand, she stumbled toward the French doors, flung them open and walked out on the verandah. Dark drizzle greeted her, but it was real and cold and sharpened her mind. "Just a dream. Daddy is safe," she breathed. "Thank you, God. Thank you! But what about Sassy? I don't know. I don't know!"

She slumped into a wicker chair and held her head in her hands. "I can't do it, God," she whispered. "Don't you remember? I told you in Texas. I can't fix all these people."

The steady drizzle drummed very gently on the roof of the verandah, just as it had done for centuries, and Rachel began to focus on the sound. So many years of humans living under this roof, she thought. So many births and deaths. Celebrations and griefs. Morning, afternoon, evening, night and morning again. One foot in front of the other, walking through their days here. Struggling through their lives here.

She stood and walked to the railing. "Lovey says you can see the dawn in the darkest part of the night." She stared out into the wet darkness. "I can't! Oh how I wish I could! Oh Grandmere, if only I could believe like you did, like Lovey does. If only I could live in the peace of faith." She leaned over the railing and tried to pierce the darkness with her physical eyes.

"What's wrong with me, God?" she whispered. "I'm so worthless! Why can't I cope with life? Other people do, but I can't seem to get it right no matter how hard I try. Why can't I reach some place of peace?"

Too exhausted for an existential battle with herself, she stumbled back to her bed and slept.

When Louis and Andre drove up to the mansion at dawn, they found Mark rousing himself from a chair on the lower verandah.

"Camping out, are you?" Louis asked sarcastically as he mounted the stairs. "Isn't it a bit late for such theatrics?"

"I'm here now."

"A lot of good it's done Rachel," Louis sneered contemptuously. "You've allowed a climate of sordidness to swirl around her."

"Rachel has been dealing with family issues you don't begin to understand."

"Her father is past danger."

"There's more to it than Jack's heart attack."

"Whatever. The point is, Rachel needs to leave all this behind her and go live the life she was born to live. You can't give her that; I can. If you love her, you'll let her go."

"What Rachel needs is to let go of her family's definition of her as worthless unless she performs miracles and keeps them all happy! She needs to learn that her circumstances—good or bad—are not the basis of her worth. If you love her, you will let her grow."

"There is no need for what you call 'bad circumstances' in Rachel's life. Everything that surrounds her should be beautiful."

"Rachel is not an ornament for your life, Louis! She's a real, thinking, feeling human being. Furthermore, no one's life is always beautiful. Life is hard; as long as Rachel is on earth she will have to struggle with—"

"Not if she has a strong man to protect her!"

"You're not strong enough, Louis! Neither am I. Only God can protect Rachel!"

Louis laughed harshly. "When is He going to show up for work?"

"He's here."

"Spoken like the loser you are. You're a fool, Mark. I would have thought that all your years out in the world would have taught you something about reality."

Mark's face flushed with anger, and he took a step toward Louis.

"You two can argue until Gabriel blows his horn!" Andre stepped between the younger men. "I'm going inside to care of Rachel." He stormed toward the door but turned back to issue a warning. "There will be no ungentlemanly behavior in Rachel's presence. Do I make myself perfectly clear? I'm ready and willing to throttle either one or both of you if necessary." Andre raised his cane and shook it at them.

The front door opened suddenly, and Lovey exclaimed, "Mr. Andre! You's already here."

"I should have come yesterday by myself! It's the least I could have done for Elinore. What must she be thinking of us all? Letting Rachel be exposed to such things. It's unthinkable!" He turned and shook his cane at the younger men again. "You two remember what I said!"

Lovey looked mystified by his words but quickly said, "Come on in, Mr. Andre. Miz Rachel still be sleeping, but you just settle in the parlor, and I'll get your bags."

"No, indeed, you will not, Lovey. Let one of these two ruffians do the carrying. They ought to be good for something."

"Yes, sir," Lovey answered as she held the door open wide and Andre entered.

The two rivals stared at each other until Louis, his face a portrait of contempt, turned and entered the house, closing the door behind him. Mark walked to the edge of the verandah and slammed his open hand against one of the huge white pillars. "Just let me hit him once!" he pleaded as he looked heavenward. When no heavenly permission came, Mark took a deep breath, prayed for self-control, and entered the house.

He found Louis roughly questioning Lovey. "How long has Rachel been asleep?"

"Since about 6:00 last night, Mr. Louis."

"When is the last time she ate?"

"I don't know, Mr. Louis. She wouldn't eat anything when she come home—"

"Are you actually standing there telling me that you haven't fed your mistress any food for 24 hours? What are you thinking, woman?"

"Back off, Louis!" Mark commanded as he grabbed Louis' arm. "Lovey would die for Rachel, and you're not going to talk to her that way!"

"You back off, Mark!" Louis countered as he flung his arm free. "If you people were taking care of Rachel—"

"That's enough!" Rachel commanded from the staircase and startled them all into silence. "How dare you two disgrace this house with such behavior? Both of you may leave this minute!" She turned back to climb the stairs.

"Rachel," Louis called after her. "You are not thinking clearly. I will handle this--"

"On the contrary, Louis," Rachel interrupted him, her voice icy with anger. With great dignity she turned around. "My understanding is sharpening by the second. I am the mistress of this house and the controller of my own future. You may leave now! Both of you."

"Thank you, Jesus!" Lovey clapped her hands together as she watched Rachel continue her climb up the stairs. "She gonna be alright now."

"Absolutely unacceptable!" Andre shook his cane at Mark and Louis. "Entirely reprehensible behavior. Both of you, get out of here this instant!"

Neither man moved, both obviously unwilling to give up the battlefield.

"Mr. Mark," Lovey said quietly, "if you love Miz Rachel—"

Mark nodded and turned to leave.

"I expect no less honor from my son," Andre warned Louis.

Louis turned and followed Mark out the door.

"Now." Andre turned to Lovey. "There are no adequate words of apology for my son's behavior toward you, Lovey."

"Ain't no need, Mr. Andre. I don't care about nothing but Miz Rachel right now. Did you hear her? Just like Miz Elinore."

"Indeed,," Andre agreed. "She is the image of my beloved Elinore." He straightened and tapped his cane lightly on the floor. "We must attend to her needs. If I may be so bold as to make a suggestion, Lovey, I do think a bit of tea and toast is in order now that she's awake."

"I's thinking exactly the same thing," Lovey agreed as she turned toward the kitchen. "And I'll fix you some breakfast, too."

"There's no need—"

"This be Belle St. Marie, Mr. Andre! We ain't never failed to serve our guests, and we ain't gonna start now."

"No, of course not. Just put Rachel first, please. It's the least I can do for my beloved Elinore."

"What you can do for Miz Elinore is keep those two men away from Miz Rachel. She need rest, and they needs civilizing!"

"Consider it done." Andre tapped his cane sharply on the floor as Lovey hurried toward the kitchen. "I shall stand guard right here all day if necessary."

Under Andre's control, Belle St. Marie remained quiet the remainder of the day. The sheriff came by, Philippe tried to visit Rachel, and Jack called from Texas. Andre permitted no one to interrupt Rachel's rest—not even Louis, who finally abandoned the house in a fit of frustration and checked into a hotel. Lovey busied herself encouraging Rachel to eat and sleep. When she wasn't upstairs, she was in the kitchen with Alice cooking the Easter Dinner she was determined to prepare. Alice tried to slow her down, but her every attempt was met with the same response, "This be Belle St. Marie. Miz Elinore wouldn't never lower the standards, and we ain't either! Besides, Miz Rachel gonna be just fine by tomorrow. You mark my words, she gonna be all dressed up and down at the church for Easter Sunday."

Around 4:00 as Lovey was loading up a tray for Rachel, Mark knocked lightly on the kitchen door and walked in. Lovey opened her mouth to protest, but Mark held out branches of rosy azaleas in full bloom. "Why they shine just like rubies!" Lovey exclaimed. "Where'd you find them?"

"Down by the pond. I can't seem to stay away from the house unless I stay down there. Anyway, I was just sitting there praying, and I spotted these in a shaft of sunlight."

"But there ain't been no sunlight. Just ugly old gray clouds."

"I know. I think these may be one of God's glimpses of splendor."

Lovey cocked her head. "I don't understand…."

"Would you just give them to Rachel? I think they're meant for her."

Lovey took the branches of vibrant color. "They's beautiful

and couldn't do her nothing but good. I's gonna put them in a special crystal vase." She turned back toward the cabinets and busied herself arranging the flowers. "I don't suppose there's any message you wants to go with them, is there?" She turned back and winked at Mark as she added the vase to the silver tray.

"Well, as a matter of fact." Mark held out a piece of ragged paper he had obviously torn out of a pocket-sized spiral notepad.

Lovey stuck it under the napkin. "I'll see she gets it. Now you get on outta here. Mr. Louis is staying away; you gotta do the same. Ain't neither one of you gonna see her till tomorrow. I's decided."

"Just tell me how she is, and then I'll go."

"She's looking a lot better and calmed down considerable. She's been eating some. She gonna be at church tomorrow, and you can see her there."

"I'll go, then." Mark turned back toward the door.

"But don't you quit praying, you hear?"

Mark nodded. "You can count on that! I feel like my whole life is out of my control."

Lovey smiled up at him. "It always has been, Mr. Mark."

Rachel opened her sleep-dimmed eyes when she heard Lovey enter her room.

"I's brought you some early supper 'cause you ain't had no real meal today," Lovey announced as she set the tray on a marble-topped bedside table and turned the lamp on. "You best sit up."

The rosy-red flowers on the silver tray sparkled in the golden light, and Rachel exclaimed, "How beautiful! Where did you find them?"

Lovey vigorously plumped the pillows, "Mr. Mark brought them to you. Here now, you sit back and eat some of this supper."

Unable to take her eyes off the flowers, Rachel automatically dragged herself back to the headboard. "Look how they glow! Why, they're as bright as the rose candle."

"I don't know about no candle. Now, I's gonna put this tray in your lap."

"No." Rachel waved her away and reached for the vase. "Where on earth did Mark find these azaleas, Lovey? They were all beaten down in the mud yesterday." She turned the vase in her hands, admiring the pristine color. "Look! You can even see the markings inside the blossoms. Oh, Lovey, they're not the least bit muddy! Did you wash them?"

"No, honey. They's just like that when Mr. Mark brought them into the kitchen."

"I wonder where he found them. The ones at the gate were smashed by the hail and covered in mud."

"He said he found them down at the pond. Said they's all lit up by a shaft of sunlight."

"But it's rainy outside, isn't it?

"Still drizzling. It's been a dark day, and he was good and wet when he come in, but don't you worry about any of that. Tomorrow's gonna be a perfect Easter Sunday. Now you gotta eat." Lovey took the vase from Rachel's hands and placed it back under the lamp. "Here," she said and put the tray on Rachel's lap. "I don't want to find one bite of this food left when I come back."

"Yes ma'am," Rachel answered absentmindedly. "Look how the rosy color reflects off the marble. Just like the candle in church."

"I's gonna take those azaleas outta here if you don't eat."

"Yes ma'am." Rachel dragged her attention to the food.

"Eat every bite," Lovey repeated as she left the room.

Rachel reached for the napkin and opened it. Mark's note fluttered out, and all thought of food vanished from her head. She scanned the writing, then slowly read it aloud.

"Azaleas glowing like rubies for you, beloved Rachel. Another glimpse of splendor, perhaps. I think that's what Miss Elinore would have called them. I know she would say to you, 'Remember, Rachel, you are God's worthy child. Do not be swayed away from that truth by current circumstances. Wait for God to lead you.' Can you hear her, Rachel? I can."

Rachel dropped the paper and set the tray aside on the bed. She reached for the azaleas and turned them in the lamplight. "Oh, look at them, Grandmere! Just like the rose candle that promised that Lent would end. And Lent has ended, hasn't it? What's next, I wonder? Dear God, I haven't forgotten that I promised to let You choose the direction of my future. But I hope You remember that I asked you to make it totally obvious to me what I should do. I never thought I'd ask for this, but I need drama, Father!"

Chapter 24

When Rachel stepped outside the church door after Easter services, she was filled with the joy of a young child who has just discovered the first bright yellow daffodil of spring. The sun had broken through the clouds and was finally shining after two days of incessant rain. The world looked reborn, freshly washed and ready to start a whole new existence. She sighed happily and turned her face up to the skies to catch the gentle yellow rays waiting to caress her face.

"This is good," Mark announced as he arrived at her side. "One more day of water, and I would have started growing fins."

"This is great," Rachel agreed. "And you would have looked awful with fins." Suddenly changing the subject, she added, "Sunday dinner will be so much more pleasant; we can open the French doors. You're coming, aren't you?"

"Wouldn't miss it. Here come the others, so I better get my bid in immediately. Will you ride back with me?"

"Sure."

"Well, here we are!" Andre announced as he escorted Lovey toward Rachel. "All ready to feast ourselves into oblivion. Now, where on earth is Louis? Oh, there he is!" Andre chuckled, "He's been captured by your Cousin Emilie, Mark, and by Marge, the indomitable schoolteacher. You better go rescue him, Rachel."

"Not a chance," Rachel said. "I wouldn't take on those formidable ladies under any circumstances."

"Absolutely," Mark agreed. "If they want Louis, they can have him."

"Mark!" Rachel called him down.

"Sorry." Mark grinned at her. "Tell you what I'll do, just to show my good will. I'll go help old Louis get the cousins into his Mercedes. Come on, Andre, let's get Lovey settled in the car, too."

"But what about Rachel?" Andre demanded. "Surely she's riding with us."

"There won't be room," Rachel hastily responded. When Andre looked disappointed, she added, "We'll all be together at the house in just a few minutes."

"Very well, My Dear." He looked at Mark darkly. "But be careful."

Mark ignored Andre's look and reached for Lovey. "Come on, Lovey, let's settle you in Louis' fancy car."

"No need for that," Andre insisted. "I'm sure I can—"

The sound of a roaring engine drowned out his words as everyone on the parking lot turned to stare at a speeding car that tore across the asphalt.

"Who on earth is that?" Mark shouted. "Is he crazy driving through a group of people like a bat out of—

"Mark! That's Jamal." Rachel shouted back. "And he's got Sassy with him! We've got to stop him. He's obviously drunk."

"More likely, drugged."

"Whatever. Mark, we've got to stop him and get Sassy out of that car!"

"You take care of the ladies, Andre!" Mark ordered as he raced around to the driver side of his car.

"I'm going with you!" Rachel jumped into the car.

"Then buckle up. He's spotted us; he's speeding up."

"Mark, stop him!"

"All we can do is follow them, Rachel." He sped up. "But if we get too close, he'll just drive faster. We better hang back and just pray they make it to wherever they're going."

"They must be going to Sassy's or somewhere on the plantation. This road doesn't go anywhere else."

"When he stops, we'll get Sassy away from him and call the Sheriff."

Rachel peered ahead and held her breath as Mark continued to keep back where they could just barely see Jamal's car.

A few moments later they rounded a curve, and Jamal's car had vanished.

"Where are they?" Rachel demanded.

Much to Rachel's amazement, Mark stomped on the accelerator. When she looked up at his face, she saw that he had turned white.

"What is it? What's wrong?"

Mark said nothing; he just kept his eyes on the road.

"Mark! What is it?"

Suddenly he braked the car, stopping it on the shoulder, and the truth hit her so hard it knocked the wind out of her. "Oh no!" she cried. "The river! Oh please, God, no!"

Before she could say another word, Mark was out of the car, running toward the wooden bridge that spanned the normally shallow river. As she jerked open the car door, all the obvious conclusions flew through her mind. Days and days of rain. A swollen, rushing river. A slippery, wooden bridge. No sight of Jamal's car.

Rachel ran after Mark, and when she reached the bridge, she saw the broken guard rail, the tire marks gouged into the muddy hillside and finally Jamal's car nose down in the foarming current. The car itself created a temporary dam for the rushing flood, forming a pool that continuously filled and then crashed on over the car.

Horrified, she watched as Mark scrambled down the hillside and dove into the water. He swam toward the pool, but as he reached it, the sheer power of the water slammed him into the car. He grabbed the frame of the open window but in seconds the violent waters claimed him. He was sucked under by the power of the currents.

"No!" Rachel screamed as she staggered back from the edge of the embankment and stared at the spot where Mark had disappeared. The furious waters seemed like a malignant spirit, taunting Rachel with their cruel powers. Rachel froze, powerless, sickened, until one word flew through her mind: "Pray!" In a flash she remembered Grandmere on her knees.

"Grandmere!" she cried, and that one word led her home. "God! Jesus! Help us!"

Immediately Rachel's body regained its power, and she ran down the muddy embankment, fell backwards violently and slid to the bottom. Stunned, she lay in the mud, then roused herself, staggered up, and mud sucking at her feet she scanned the water looking for bodies.

There was no sight of Mark.

The raging water had swallowed him up. He was out there somewhere drowning with Sassy and Jamal. The enormity of the loss striped Rachel of her pride in her own powers. Frantically she tried to think, but no answers came to her. Once again she tried to exert her physical strength, but she could not move.

For the first time in her life Rachel was totally helpless, and she knew it. She was finally in a position to understand the

Truth—and she did.

"Jesus!" she cried. "Help me! I can't do it. I can't save them."

The river rushed by, lapping only a few yards from Rachel's feet. The sun sparkled playfully on the water's surface. Rachel stood, her own life suspended in time, while the natural world moved on all around her. "Jesus." She merely breathed the word this time. "Jesus."

Suddenly she saw Mark's head pop out of the water, and strength surged into her. Mark was swimming back to shore, and he was towing someone. Rachel forced her feet free of the mud, lunged down to the water's edge and waded into the pool behind the car.

"Rachel!" someone shouted from above her. "No, Rachel! Stop!"

She jerked her head around and searched the top of the bank. Louis was standing there. "Stop, Rachel!" he commanded as he began to descend the hill.

"Help us!" she screamed as she waded further into the water.

Mark swam to within ten feet of her, then pushed the body he was towing toward her. "Here!" he shouted. "Get back on the bank."

Rachel plunged forward, staggering in the swirling, muddy water and grabbed the limp arm of the person he had shoved at her. She dragged the person back toward the bank as she screamed at Mark. "Stop! No! Don't go back!"

But he ignored her, and she watched him disappear into the foaming waves again.

"Rachel!" Louis shouted as his strong arms grabbed her from behind. "Let go, Rachel. Turn loose! You must save yourself."

Rachel tightened her grip on the limp arm and strained harder to pull the body with her as Louis dragged her uphill.

When they were safely out of the rushing water, Rachel fell to her knees in the mud and tried to turn the body over. "Help me, Louis. We've got to use CPR."

"Don't be a fool, Rachel! It's obviously hopeless!"

Rachel threw her whole weight against the limp body and turned it over. Staring up at her was Sassy's face. "It's Sassy!" she cried. "Oh, thank God! Louis, help me. We've got to revive her!"

Louis jerked Rachel up and away from Sassy as he shouted, "I won't allow you to do this. She is beneath your consideration.

You're coming with me!"

"Beneath my consideration!" Rachel exploded. "She's a human being!"

"She's a fool, and she's made her choices."

"Then go help Mark!" Rachel shouted at him as she flung herself on her knees at Sassy's side.

"Mark is a fool too." Louis responded coldly.

Rachel snapped her head back and gave Louis one look of utter contempt before she turned her attention back to Sassy.

In less than a minute Sassy was breathing again and coughing up water. Rachel stood and frantically searched the water's surface for Mark.

When she finally spotted him in the middle of the river struggling with another body, she staggered toward the edge of the river again, the mud sucking at her feet. Louis grabbed her. "Stay here!" he commanded as he reached down and pulled off his shoes. "You've completely lost your senses. I'll go, if it's the only way to save you." He waded slowly into the river while Rachel watched and prayed and listened to Sassy who had begun to sob.

It took both Mark and Louis to drag Jamal's body up onto the slippery embankment. In spite of his own exhaustion Mark immediately began CPR on Jamal while Louis stood, his arms crossed on his chest, and watched.

Rachel collapsed next to the sobbing Sassy and held her as they watched Mark try over and over again to revive the young man.

Sassy's sobs mutated into wails that combined with the distant sound of sirens. The whole scene became so unreal to Rachel that she could not measure the passage of time.

When the sheriff and EMS attendants came sliding down the embankment, Mark was still working on Jamal. They had to pull him away, to force him to give up.

Louis came over and lifted Rachel to her feet as the EMS took over the care of Sassy. Still dazed, she allowed Louis to pull her half way up the hill before she came to her senses. Then she stopped, shook herself loose from his grip and turned back for Mark. He was still at the bottom, so she held out her hand to him, determined to wait for him.

"Go ahead, Rachel," Mark called. "I'm coming."

Rachel shook her head firmly.

"Yes," he insisted. "Go on up. I'm coming." It was only then that she allowed Louis to help her climb the rest of the way.

When they reached the top, Lovey grabbed the mud-covered Rachel as she repeatedly exclaimed, "Oh, thank you, Jesus! Thank you!" Andre wrapped his raincoat around her, and the other women babbled incoherent words of gratitude and consolation.

Louis stepped forward, took Rachel from Lovey, and commanded, "Get in the car, Rachel. I'm taking you home; you don't belong in the midst of a scene like this."

"We's gotta get you home," Lovey agreed, "and get you dry and clean and see if you's all right, Honey."

"Absolutely right!" Andre chimed in.

"I can't just leave! What about Sassy? And Jamal?"

"They are not your responsibility, Rachel!" Louis insisted. "Remember who you are!"

"Who....am....I?" Rachel spat the words at Louis.

"Rachel D'Evereau! The heir to a great name, a grand tradition—"

"No, Louis! No! I'm just a child of God. No different from Sassy. I'm just as flawed as she is, and I'm just as equally loved by God because he made us both."

"Rachel." Louis regained his tone of reason. "You are understandably confused. This has been an ordeal you should have never encountered. I'm going to take you home. I am going to keep you safe, and Lovey is going to take care of you. Now that's settled."

"No, I'm going to the hospital with Sassy! I won't abandon her." Rachel turned back toward the hillside where she saw Mark climbing toward them.

"No, Honey!" Lovey caught hold of her. "You gotta take care of yourself. I can get Alice to go stay with Sassy."

"Lovey is right!" Louis insisted. "If you won't listen to me, listen to her."

"I'm going to the hospital, Louis! Take everyone else home."

"You're going home where you belong!" Louis grabbed her arm. "You've been involved in enough irresponsible, life-threatening behavior for one day."

"Irresponsible? I had to help Sassy! I had to help Mark!"

"Sassy is not worth risking your life for, Rachel. And as for Mark, only a fool would jump into a swollen river like that."

"Mark is not a fool!" Rachel shouted.

"Is that a fact? What else would you call a man who jumps into a raging river to rescue two worthless people who've chosen their own fate?"

"I would call him a hero!" Rachel jerked her arm free and glared up at Louis. "And only a coward or a heartless man would stand by and watch!"

"Now, now." Andre jumped in to soothe the situation. "We're all quite unnerved and with good cause—"

"Andre's right," Mark said as he approached. "There are more important things to deal with now—"

Shivering, Rachel turned to Lovey and the other women. "Come on, all of you; get into Mark's car. I'll drive. We're not far from the house. I'll shower quickly and come back here and pick up Mark and—"

"No, Rachel," Mark interrupted, "You're soaked and freezing. Get into Louis' car. He'll take you ladies home. You wait for me at Belle St. Marie."

"But what about Sassy?"

"Sassy is in shock; there's nothing you can do. They're bringing her up the hill to the ambulance, and they'll take care of her."

"And Jamal?"

"No one can help him now."

"Oh, no!"

"Go home, Rachel." Mark put his arm around her and turned her toward the car. "You must get warm, or you'll be sick. I'll be there soon."

"I won't leave Sassy!"

"Rachel! You've done all you can do right now," Mark insisted as he pushed her further up the hill. "I want you to go home with Lovey and the other women."

"Please, Miz Rachel," Lovey pleaded, and Rachel relented and moved toward the car.

The elderly Andre Simone looked beaten as he stared at the roaring river, at Jamal's body on the shore, and the men struggling to bring Sassy to an ambulance. "What a pity!" he muttered. "And to think we could have lost Rachel, too. What would Elinore say if she were here?"

"Don't worry, Papa," Louis said. "In the end, the better man will win."

Andre turned to look his son in the face. "The better man has won, son.This is the end."

Chapter 25

Rachel was shivering uncontrollably by the time she reached the steps of the front verandah, but all she could think of was Sassy regaining consciousness in the ambulance or the emergency room. "I've got to get to the hospital!" she insisted as Louis helped her up the steps. "Sassy will be scared to death, and she's probably—"

"Absolutely not!" Louis answered. "I won't allow you to—"

"That will do, Louis!" Andre silenced his son as he stepped between him and Rachel. "What Rachel needs first is warmth. Go upstairs and fill the bathtub."

"You want me to run Rachel's bath?"

"I can run Miz Rachel's bath," Lovey declared as she struggled out of the car. "It ain't fitting—"

"We can't stand on ceremony, Lovey. Speed is of the essence." Andre put his arm around Rachel's back and almost carried her up the steps. "Fill the tub, Louis! Make yourself useful. What must my beloved Elinore be thinking? God rest her soul!"

"Dire circumstances require dire actions," Rachel answered as her teeth chattered. "That's what Grandmere always said."

"Exactly!" Andre agreed. "Now let's get you upstairs. Louis, go fill that tub! Lovey, you make some hot tea."

An hour later Rachel was hurrying down the staircase, with Lovey hustling to keep up with her, when the phone rang.

"I'll get that," Andre said, but Louis reached the phone first.

After a curt "hello," he listened, scowled, and handed the receiver to Rachel. "It's Mark calling from the emergency room."

Her conversation was brief; she put the receiver down and locked eyes with Louis. "Sassy is still unconscious. I'm going to be there when she wakes up. There's no point in arguing with me.”

He shook his head in disgust. ”Absolutely pointless to do this to yourself. Don’t you see that this kind of people will just keep making stupid choices?”

”It’s called being human, Louis, and we all do it. We all make stupid choices.”

“And you’re making one now. That girl will never learn to choose wisely.”

“You may be right, Louis, but she’s alive. Because we intervened, Sassy is still alive to make her next choice, and maybe, just maybe this time she’ll choose better for herself.”

“But most likely she won’t, Rachel, and you’ll be throwing your life away.”

“No, Louis, I will be gaining my life.”

“She can do nothing for you but harm you!”

“You’re wrong. She’s a godsend to me. Every time I recognize her God-given worth, I am forced to recognize my own.”

“Even if you fail to help her? As you most surely will.”

“You’re missing the point, just as I’ve missed it all my life. My worth is not based on my success. It’s a gift, and the best way for me to focus on that fact is to see the God-given worth in other people, especially people the world scorns.”

“You are confused, Rachel. Just look at those the world admires. They, or their families before them, earned that admiration.”

“I have looked at them, Louis. I’ve even been one of them. And underneath all their successful performances, at the heart of their beings, they are insecure, anxious and depressed.”

“Just as you will be, Rachel, and sooner than you think. Oh, I know you think you’ve saved Sassy again, but mark my word, you can’t fix these people!”

“I know that now. God has to do the fixing; I just do the small things. I’m just His hands and feet for a few people.”

“What a waste!”

“What a joy!”

Andre walked to Rachel, took her hand in his and kissed it. “So like your Grandmere. So like my beloved Elinore. How many times have I heard her say, ‘God doesn’t make any trash.’”

”Utter nonsense!” Louis protested.

”Utter truth, son.”

“It’s time for all of you to get in touch with reality! Come on, Papa. We are going upstairs, pack, and return to the real world."

"I'll leave the 'real world' to you, son. With Rachel's permission, I'd like to take her to the hospital. I doubt I'll be of the slightest help, but I'll be there doing what I can for Elinore's beloved granddaughter."

"I give up!" Louis bolted for the staircase. "When you come to your senses, Rachel, call me!"

It was Mark who drove Rachel back toward Belle St. Marie several hours later. She had been by Sassy's bedside when she regained consciousness, and the doctor had assured her that Sassy would make a full recovery.

"Can you believe it?" she now asked Mark. "How could so much happen so quickly? Oh, thank God she's safe! Thank you for saving her."

Mark took her hand, but said nothing until they came to the last bend in the driveway. He stopped the car and turned to her. "Are you too tired to walk down to the pond? If you are, just say so...."

"No, I'm okay, but what about you? You're the one who's been diving into rivers rescuing people. How is your back?"

"I'm okay."

"Some fresh air does sound good after the emergency room, and I could use the serenity of the pond."

He helped her out of the car, and taking her hand in his, he walked slightly ahead of her down the narrow path. Neither spoke as they circled the old magnolia and continued to the woodsy water line. Rachel took in a deep, audible breath of the fresh air, spotted a fallen log bathed in a ray of sunshine, and gratefully sank down on it. "This is bliss," she said. "I've had enough drama." The moment she spoke the word "drama," her face lit up with the joy of understanding.

"What is it?" Mark asked.

"That's exactly what I asked God for."

"For drama?"

"Yes, for drama," she murmured, but said no more as she slipped into her own private thoughts. She was so absorbed in contemplating how God had answered her prayers that she hardly noticed Mark until he walked to a bush and broke a piece off of it.

"What are you doing?" she asked.

He returned to her side and handed her the branch of ruby azaleas.

"Oh!" She drew her breath in sharply. "I can't tell you what these meant to me when Lovey brought them to my room. She told me you had found them in a shaft of sunlight, but the weather was so dark. Another 'glimpse of spendor.' Just as you said in your note. Like the golden swan."

"That's exactly what they were." He slowly knelt down on one knee. "Rachel, will you marry me?"

She looked deep into his eyes. "I thought I had lost you when I saw you disappear under the waves in that swirling river. I thought you were dead, and I did not want to live in a world without you."

"Is that a 'yes'?"

"Yes! Yes, I'll marry you!"

Mark stripped a blossom from the azalea and placed it on her finger. "This is the only ring I happen to have with me at the moment. Will it do?"

"A 'glimpse of splendor' will more than do!"

He stood and pulled her into his arms. "What a journey," he murmured into her hair. "Thank you, God. Thank you."

Recommend *Glimpse of Splendor* to your book club

Kay Moser is available for free half-hour chats with your reading friends. Contact her at mailto:kay@kaymoser.com or on FaceBook.

Discussion questions
to aid your book club discussion are available at
www.kaymoser.com/reading_groups.cfm

Connect with Kay Moser on FaceBook at
"Kay Moser's Reader-Friends"

Enjoy another captivating story from Kay Moser!

Counterfeit Legacy
Book One of the Charleston Legacy Series

Caroline Bradford Randolph is a Dallas socialite who has discovered that neither her wealth nor the legacy of her famous Charleston, South Carolina ancestors can satisfy her deepest longings. When a freakish storm gives Caroline the chance to hold the most cherished Bradford heirloom in her hands for the first time, she discovers that it contains a secret that may well destroy the prestigious legacy of the Bradfords. Since she has based her life on this legacy, hard choices loom ahead for her.

Should Caroline cover up her discovery in order to protect her marriage to wealthy industrialist David Randolph? Or should she investigate the truth of her proud ancestry in hopes of finding the fulfillment she so desperately needs?

Will Caroline discover the true Bradford legacy in time?
Come to Charleston with Caroline.
Enter the world of the Bradfords.

Counterfeit Legacy

Chapter 1

Caroline Randolph did not notice the ominous, gray-green clouds swirling over her house as, her hand trembling, she lowered the telephone receiver. "It's done," she whispered. A violent shudder shook her as she contemplated the medical procedure she had just scheduled. "I've got to go through with it."

As tears flooded her eyes, she reached for a calendar to record the appointment, but before she began writing, the angry, impatient storm unleashed its power. Crack! Boom! The ear-splitting sounds of lightning and thunder startled her so much she jumped from her chair and whirled around to stare out the French doors. Amazed, she watched garden statuary topple over and quickly understood that this was no typical spring thunderstorm assaulting her 19th century home in Dallas, Texas. This storm intended to spare no one's house—not even the home of Caroline's wealthy, powerful husband, David Morgan Randolph, the owner of Randolph Industries International.

A second flash of lightning crackled across the late afternoon sky, and seconds later a boom of thunder shook the house as a ferocious gust of wind slammed into it. Caroline instinctively ducked and fled to the main hall as the mansion shook to its foundations. Crouched under a heavy walnut table next to the stately staircase, her heart beat wildly as she hid from the howling wind, jagged lightning and booming thunder. Tornado! The word flew through Caroline's mind. I need to—

There was no time to think further; a ferocious gust of wind blew the heavy front door open, and Caroline felt the sting of hail on her face. She screamed and covered her head as the front door banged wildly and the hail tore at her skin. A deafening crash in the drawing room shook the floor under her.

Suddenly the violence was over.

Confused by the abrupt change, Caroline struggled to understand that the front door was no longer banging against the wall, that although the hall was littered with hail, the sharp pieces of ice were no longer attacking her skin. The thunder now sounded more distant, and the flashes of lightning were no longer so close they were blinding. All that was left of the storm was a torrential rain streaming straight down to the ground—and whatever damage the storm had left in the drawing room.

Trembling, Caroline crawled out from under the walnut table and struggled to stand on her shaking legs. Finally able to stumble to the front door and close it, she looked in dismay at the hail that covered the center hallway of the elegant old house which she had so carefully restored. Strength began to surge back through her legs as she realized that she had escaped the violence unharmed. But my house! That horrendous crash in the drawing room!

Nauseating fear rose in her. Hurrying to the double doors of the drawing room, she placed her hands on the elegant brass handles, but stopped short of pushing them open. "You have to face this eventually. Whatever has happened is only becoming worse as you stand here quivering," she tried to scold herself into acting. "Open the doors, Caroline!" She threw her weight against the doors, and they flew open.

She swept her eyes down the length of the room, spotting the valuable, precious things she had placed there, checking them as if they were her children. A remarkable number of things were in place. The two ends of the long rectangular room were essentially untouched, but the middle of the room was tangled in a mass of wet tree limbs. Immediately she understood what had happened; this tree was the venerable oak that had grown across the street in her neighbor's yard. It had been the pride of the block, but now it had fallen, and the very top of the tree had crashed through the large central window of her magnificent drawing room.

The uppermost branches had scraped down the wall directly across from the window, leaving great scars on the plaster as they stripped it free of all decorations. Despair rose in her at the sight of smashed chairs, a crumpled love seat, and crushed mahogany tables; this room had been her masterpiece of restoration.

Suddenly Caroline's mind flew to the single, most treasured item she owned, a family heirloom that had survived over 125 years. It was preserved in a shadowbox frame that had hung on the now-damaged wall. "Oh no!" she cried as she sprang into action. "I must find it. Oh, it just can't be destroyed. It just can't!"

She scrambled to the tree and picked her way through small branches, peering down carefully at the items that were smashed beneath her feet. Finally she saw the back of a large, framed item. "It's ruined!" she cried, but as tears filled her eyes, she pushed aside several more wet branches and pulled the shadowbox from the debris. Broken glass flew around her, and she felt the sting of a cut on her left hand, but she ignored it in her anguish to discover if the heirloom could be saved. Struggling back out of the soaking branches of the tree, she examined the shadowbox. The glass that had protected it for decades was gone, but her great-great-grandfather's silk vest, her most prized possession, seemed to be undamaged.

Aware now that her left hand was bleeding, her most pressing fear was that she would get blood on this precious vest. She wrapped the hem of her skirt around her bleeding hand before carefully pulling the vest from its frame with her right hand. Hurrying out of the damaged room and into her sitting room across the hall, she laid the vest on her desk and continued on to the downstairs bathroom to bandage her hand.

A shocking glimpse of herself in the mirror revealed a frightened, battered woman staring back at her. Her long, auburn hair was tangled and plastered to her head. Her grayish-blue eyes were bloodshot and surrounded by swollen lids; a mixture of her tears and the rain had left her face dripping. How could this happen to me? To me!

Her left hand began to throb and reminded her that she had come to bandage the cut, so she flipped the light switch on. "No electricity!" she exclaimed, then sighed, "Of course." Reaching for a fresh white towel, she cradled her bleeding hand in it, and as she examined the cut, an unbidden, unwelcome question forced itself to the front of her mind. Will I ever be able to look at either of my hands again and not see blood on them—if I do this thing?

She swiftly covered her bleeding hand with the towel as she scolded herself. "What absurd nonsense! This is just a bleeding cut on your hand. That's all it is, Caroline. It has nothing to do with—with—with that! Don't let your fertile imagination run away with you."

She uncovered her left hand to rinse it. Once again unnerved by the sight of the blood, she jerked her head up and stared angrily at herself in the mirror.

"I tell you this has nothing to do with—with—nothing to do with anything in the past or in the future!" She spoke the words forcibly, determined that they would become her truth, but her eyes betrayed her. They obviously did not believe her.

She jerked the cold water faucet on and stuck her bleeding hand under the water. "You should be more concerned about whether you need stitches in this hand. You've made your decision about the other matter."

Another voice, deep inside her disagreed. No, you haven't. You're not at all sure you can do it, Caroline.

Hoping to leave that unwanted voice behind, Caroline snatched gauze from the vanity and fled the bathroom. As she returned to the main hall, she forced herself to consider her physical dilemma. What on earth am I going to do about a tree in my drawing room and no electricity? I wonder how badly damaged the neighborhood is. How long will it be before someone comes to help? Panic began to rise in her, but she fought it down. "I'm not hurt, not really," she reassured herself aloud, "but how many people around me are hurt? And what about my family? Mother and Grandmother?" Every question she asked herself increased her anxiety until she finally snapped at herself, "Stop it, Caroline! No doubt the officials have control of the situation. You must be sensible. Think about the neighbors. Can you see anything from the front porch?"

She pulled open the front door, stepped out onto the porch and gasped. The street was littered with uprooted trees and downed power lines were crackling and sparking in spite of the driving rain. Her neighbors' houses were all standing, but they showed various degrees of damage.

"Is anyone in your house injured?" a man wearing a bright yellow rain coat and helmet shouted from the street.

"No, I'm okay," she yelled back, "but my neighbors—"

"Go back inside!" he commanded. "The streets are too dangerous. We're checking every house for injured people."

"But what do I do?"

"Just stay put!" he called back as he continued down the block.

She went back inside, closed the heavy door, and felt terrifyingly alone, as if the last person on earth had abandoned her. "Oh, I wish David were here," she cried, "or that Hannah hadn't already left." A quiver of fear ran through her. "No, it's stupid to wish such things. If they had been here, they might have been hurt. I've got to take hold of myself; I can't just stand here shaking," she reproached herself. "I'd better check on the family." She went to her study and snatched up the phone. "Dead! Of course!"

Anxiety threatened to enshroud her again. "You simply have to wait," she told herself. "Do something to get your mind off the storm." She began to cheerlead herself as she walked around her sitting room. "Everything looks fine in here. The main hall was not disturbed except for the hail that blew in. The damage in the drawing room seems to be contained in a single area right in the middle. The wind's not blowing, the rain's coming straight down, so the water damage isn't getting too much worse. The tree, of course, is lying in my drawing room, but there's nothing I can do about that. I should mop up the water off the wooden floor in the hall. Yes, that's what I'll do."

After mopping up the melted hail, she found herself alone again in the battered house as evening approached. Impatiently she went back into her sitting room, grabbed the TV remote and started clicking buttons. Nothing happened. "What am I doing?" she demanded. "There's no electricity!" She paced around the room, then startled herself by shouting, "I just want to get out of here!"

She went to the French doors and stared out. The rain was still pouring, the clouds were low and dark, but there was no wind. She saw several bright flashlights and could vaguely see the people holding them. There was nothing to do but wait in the dark for the city employees to come clear the streets.

"I've got to have some light," she told herself firmly, "and I must concentrate on something. Otherwise this waiting will drive me crazy." She lit the five candles in a candelabrum on a side table and placed it on the mahogany table next to her favorite chair. Then she thought of the flashlight in the downstairs bathroom, but as she started for the door, she remembered the bloody towel she had left on the vanity. "I can't face all that again," she whispered. "I don't want to think beyond right now."

She settled in her favorite chair, pulled the candelabrum closer, picked up the vest, and carefully removed the remaining glass fragments. "I've never even seen this vest up close," she intentionally began a chat with herself. "As long as I can remember, it's been behind glass in its frame. I remember staring up at it on the wall in Grandmother's drawing room. How important it seemed to be as Grandmother told me all those marvelous stories about her wealthy, powerful grandfather. By the time I was twelve, I would shiver with excitement when she promised me that the vest would be mine some day. I never thought she would give it up while she lived, but she did. Of all the wedding presents David and I received, this vest was the one

I treasured most. Oh, thank goodness it's safe!"

She began to examine the ivory-colored, silk vest. Even though it was a man's vest, it was covered with intricate embroidery, crafted in tiny stitches of silk thread. The major motif of the design was a delicate vine which trailed across the vest with a leaf or tiny flower growing here and there from the vine. "Such a design would be considered feminine now," Caroline murmured, "but men of wealth wore embroidered vests for centuries. What beautiful needlework this is!"

"To think that James Bradford, my great-great-grandfather wore this! This vest is my connection to the great Bradford legacy I've always treasured. Oh! If it had been destroyed, I would have had to tell Grandmother it was gone. I believe it would have killed her. How lucky she was to have actually known James Bradford! I have always wished I could have. Well, if there's anything good about this storm, it's the opportunity it has given me to actually touch James Bradford's vest, to feel a little closer to him."

She began to trace the intricate tendrils and tiny leaves of the vine and to place an appreciative finger on the little flowers that someone had embroidered so many years ago. There were several stains. She considered their possible sources, as if she were handling the vest to prepare it for a museum presentation.

"This is undoubtedly a tea stain. This one is darker. Perhaps it is coffee." She ran her finger over the stain. "And this one," she came to the third, gasped, and quickly drew her finger back. "This one looks like— No! It's not—it is red wine," she insisted to herself. "A very dark red wine, a burgundy, no doubt."

Hastily she moved her attention to the hand-crafted button holes and the beautiful buttons. She examined the pockets of the vest and contemplated the type of gold watch that had undoubtedly been housed there. She stuck her fingers into the left-side pocket and felt a strange, rough stitching at the bottom of the pocket. "That's odd," she murmured. She pulled out the lining of the pocket and realized that the heavy watch her great-great-grandfather had tucked there had worn through the lining. Someone had meticulously hand-sewn the bottom of the lining back together. Caroline studied the darning stitches used for the repair and then stuffed the lining back into the pocket.

She turned the vest inside out and admired the careful, even stitches that connected the lining of the vest to the ornately decorated outer shell. Slowly, methodically she ran her finger along the edge of the neck of the vest, admiring each tiny stitch some unknown seamstress had made over 125 years earlier.

Unexpectedly her fingers hit a crisp place in an otherwise pliable fabric, and at the same time she heard the slightest crackle. "How odd! There's something stuck between the vest lining and the outer shell," she exclaimed to the empty room. "Something is sewn into the vest. What is it and who would do such a thing?"

Once again she ran her fingers over the area and listened. She heard the same crackling noise and felt something stiff under the fabric. She bent the area between her fingers and heard the crackling noise again. "It's definitely a piece of paper," her excitement rose, "not a very large piece of paper, perhaps two or three inches square. What on earth is it? Why is it here?"

Slowly she began to work the paper down from the neck area of the vest across the chest, back toward the pocket. As she diligently worked at her task, the candlelight flickered in the darkness, casting a circle of light around her chair.

"There!" she exclaimed when she had achieved her goal. "If I want to, I can open the stitches where the pocket lining has been repaired and read what is on this piece of paper." Unable to resist the temptation, she hurried to her desk drawer and came back with tiny needlepoint scissors. Leaning over the vest, she pulled out the pocket lining and carefully snipped just a few stitches, just enough to open the lining two inches. Then she put the scissors down on the table and looked at the opening.

The five candles cast strange, dancing shadows across the silk she had unstitched. All thoughts of the storm and the tree that had crashed into her drawing room were erased from Caroline's mind. "If I want to, I can reach into the past by reaching through that opening and pulling out that piece of paper. I can reach back into the 19th century and know something. But what? Will I be disappointed? Will it be a perfectly commonplace piece of paper, some meaningless list, some scrap of a business document?"

She made no movement to retrieve the paper. She was mysteriously drawn to it, but she was afraid it would disappoint her. "What do I want to find? What do I seek, sitting here now, facing the most important decision of my life?" She peered into the hole.

"What do I want to find?" she asked herself again. And instantly she knew the answer. "I want to find the solution to my present dilemma. I want to find a way out of this horrible thing I must do."

No storm, no damaged heirloom vest had been able to divert her mind completely from her problem. No matter how many times she had told herself, "I won't think about that now"—a piece of her mind was always thinking about it. For some insane reason, she now believed the answer she sought was on this piece of paper and had been there for more than 125 years.

"Well," she said with more bravado than she felt, "whatever it is, I must know."

Gently she thrust two fingers into the opening she had made and clasped the piece of paper and pulled it forth. It had ragged edges and was folded in half. Obviously someone had hastily torn it off of a larger sheet of paper, folded it, and given it to her great-great-grandfather. She stared at it unopened, petrified that it would not bring her what she needed.

Finally she took a deep breath and opened it. In faded brown ink a spidery, feminine handwriting spelled out, "He knows nothing. Meet me at midnight." There was no signature.

Caroline was so startled by what she read she could not absorb the words. She blinked her eyes, held the paper closer to the candlelight, and read it again. It was not addressed to anyone, but it was obviously meant for her great-great-grandfather because it had been put into his pocket. "He knows nothing. Meet me at midnight."

She was disappointed. This piece of paper did nothing for her life. It did not move her one-inch closer to a solution of her problem. Anger rose in her, and she was tempted to crush the paper in her hand, but she could not release the notion that there was a reason she had found it. "My great-great-grandfather must have put a note in his pocket, a note which went through the hole in the bottom of his pocket. Someone repaired the hole without knowing the paper was there. But why didn't the seamstress who repaired the pocket notice the floating piece of paper? Apparently no one has noticed it, or no one has been interested enough—or desperate enough—to retrieve it. It is here for me. I know it is! But what does it mean?"

She read it again. "He knows nothing. Meet me at midnight." Her imagination leapt into action. "A woman wrote it, apparently handed it to my great-great-grandfather, but she refers to some 'he.' Whoever this 'he' was, it was important that he didn't know something. It was important enough to her to cause her to write this note and give it to my great-great-grandfather. But what woman would he be meeting at midnight?

What difference does it make to me? What possible difference can it make over 125 years later to anyone, much less to me?"

The spell-binding sequel to *Counterfeit Legacy*

David's Grit
Book Two of the Charleston Legacy Series

David Randolph, owner of an international corporation, is one of Dallas' most admired men. His enormous wealth and power give him control over thousands of lives, including that of his beautiful wife, Caroline. From Texas to London to Tokyo, David wields his power ruthlessly just as his father taught him to.

However, behind his facade of bravado, David is crumbling, tormented by nightmares and fast losing control of himself. Initially Caroline blames herself for his coldness toward her and for his erratic behavior, but as he increases the number of his sudden, unexplained business trips, she becomes suspicious. She travels to Charleston, South Carolina to consult with her mentor, Great Aunt Kathleen.

What is disturbing David so drastically? Why is he secretly suffering from anxiety, self-doubts, and a shattered self-image?

Only David knows the truth about his first marriage and the death of his first wife, Danielle. Can he continue to hide the truth about his past deeds from Caroline? If he does, will he miss out on the greatest gift of his life?

Can anyone or anything teach David that happiness grows from one's center to one's surface and that joy comes only when one gives oneself away?

Made in the USA
Lexington, KY
24 November 2018